A PERFECT WIFE AND MOTHER

"A BRILLIANT FIRST NOVEL with a fresh plot, snappy dialogue, and truly intriguing characters. Alexandra Frye captures the angst of upper-middle-class suburban and corporate life, then introduces a few of our worst nightmares. A well-wrought, sinister, and plausible tale told with wit and insight."
—Nelson DeMille

Praise for

A PERFECT WIFE AND MOTHER
by Alexandra Frye

"THRILLING . . . TIGHTLY SPUN . . . Layers of plot build a compelling, at times chilling, novel filled with convincing dialogue and vivid characters . . . the prose is brisk, fluid, and entrancing."
—*Publishers Weekly*

"ONE OF THE BEST SUSPENSE NOVELS I'VE READ IN YEARS—as smooth and sleek as a high-caliber bullet. The machine-tooled precision of plotting and the ominous, steadily increasing suspense made me think of Ira Levin. This is the kind of book for which weekends were invented."
—Stephen King

"SPELLBINDING. I was hooked from the beginning. I loved the characters—real people living every parent's nightmare—and their story kept me on edge from the start." —Mario Puzo

Please turn the page for more extraordinary acclaim. . . .

A Perfect Wife and Mother

Alexandra Frye

Island BOOKS

ISLAND BOOKS
Published by
Dell Publishing
a division of
Bantam Doubleday Dell Publishing Group, Inc.
1540 Broadway
New York, New York 10036

This is a work of fiction. Names, characters, places, and incidents either are the product of the author's imagination or are used fictitiously, and any resemblance to actual persons, living or dead, events, or locales is entirely coincidental.

ISBN: 0-440-21736-9

Reprinted by arrangement with Viking Penguin

Printed in the United States of America

Published simultaneously in Canada

June 1994

10 9 8 7 6 5 4 3 2 1

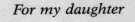
For my daughter

10 September

"Jesus Christ, I've been locked up with them in that suite—what time is it? almost nine!—eleven fucking hours—and we're not through."

"Where are you now?"

"I'm in the hotel lobby, where else? It's my suite and I'm at a fucking pay phone in the lobby! I had to get the hell out of there. They smoke those heavy Limey cigarettes, you get cancer just walking in the door."

"Where do we stand?"

"I'm sweating like a pig. Can you imagine? I'm standing in an air-conditioned hotel lobby and I'm sweating like a fucking pig."

"Where do we stand?"

"I'm coming to that. The good news is they want us real bad. Wall Street presence, they gotta have it, don't ask me why. They say they're not letting me leave here tonight without a deal. It took eleven goddamn hours, but now there's an offer on the table."

"How much?"

"You sitting down?"

"Yes, I'm sitting down."

"It's rich."

"What are the numbers?"

"A meager twelve times earnings, averaged from 1981 through this fiscal . . . Well? For Christ's sake, friend, that's nine figures! For each of us! You and I can buy fucking Switzerland!"

"Payable in dollars?"

"No, escudos. For Christ's sake, of course it's dollars! Eighty percent at the closing, twenty holdback."

"How long a holdback?"

"Ten for a year, ten for two."

"Arguable. But I'm not understanding something. We'd have taken a ten multiple. How did they come up with twelve?"

"Because I never gave them our number."

"But their attorney had it, didn't he?"

"The bigger the deal, the more he stands to make on it."

"I see."

"Is that all you have to say, for Christ's sake? With the payday we've been waiting for? Why you bought in in the first place?"

"No, that's not all I have to say. As far as I'm concerned, I'm ready to approve a letter of intent immediately."

"Yeah, well, there's the bad news."

"What bad news?"

"No letter of intent. They don't want it. Counsel says there'll be nothing in writing till after they've finished their due diligence, and then we'll go straight to contract."

"I thought he was on our side."

"He is, but they're his clients and that's how they want to do business."

"Why?"

"They're bugs on secrecy."

"So are we."

"Yeah, but they don't want anybody else jumping in and starting a bidding war. They say that's why they're ready to commit to a premium now."

"In other words, offering twelve when they knew we'd take ten?"

"Maybe."

"With nothing in writing, what are they committing?"

"Their word."

"Their word?"

"Hey, I'm tired, why don't you go sit in the room with the bastards? You listen to all that phony stuttering and stammering for eleven goddamn hours, and they act like we're still the fucking colonies."

"How do you feel about no letter of intent? You're the chairman of the board."

"Okay, more or less. Reasonably okay. They're a big outfit, and they don't want to be embarrassed. Plus they're ready to move fast."

"How fast is fast?"

"A month, maybe two."

"So there's a window of two months in which they could change their minds?"

"Yeah. But what are they going to find that'd make them change their minds?"

"You're better placed to answer that than I am."

"Come on, don't give me that shit. We both know where the bodies are buried. But the numbers are the numbers. Everything I've given them so far is substantiated in the numbers."

"Are you sure?"

"*Damn right I'm sure.*"

"*What about personnel?*"

"*What about personnel?*"

"*They're going to want to talk to some of your people.*"

"*Yeah. In confidence and under my control. They also want me to clean house before they take over. Let me be the bad guy. They'll knock any extraordinary expenses incurred off the income statement . . . Hey, I gotta get back up there. Well, partner, what's your pleasure, do we have a deal?*"

"*No.*"

"*WHA-A-T? You're kidding, aren't you? With nine figures on the table? Who else is gonna offer us a twelve multiple of shit in today's market? And you're ready to walk away?*"

"*I didn't say that.*"

"*Oh? I must be hard of hearing, what did you say?*"

"*If they don't want a letter of intent, tell them you want a good-faith payment into an escrow account.*"

"*A good-faith payment?*"

"*That's right.*"

"*How much of a good-faith payment?*"

"*I leave that to you. Enough so that they'll feel it if they walk away.*"

"*But God Almighty, this isn't the rag trade, this is the fucking British Empire! Question of pride, they'll never stand still for it.*"

"*Yes they will. If they're as serious as you say, they certainly will.*"

"*Yeah, and who's been haggling with them all day long? Now we're gonna be up the whole night!*"

"*Talk to their attorney about it, he'll understand.*"

"You *talk* to him about it."

"You know that's impossible."

"I don't believe it. I don't fucking believe it. You own twenty-nine percent of the company, and you stand to make a fortune, and now you're nitpicking! You're actually nitpicking!"

"I'm sorry, you and I have agreed to agree, and I—"

"Yeah, yeah, I can't act without you, do you think I've forgotten? For Christ's sake. Look, I gotta get back up there, as far as they know it's all my call. How serious are you on this?"

"I'm very serious."

"To the point of a deal-breaker?"

"Yes. But I'm counting on your powers of persuasion."

"Jesus Christ Almighty."

Part
One

Georgia
Levy
Coffey

21 September

I can't resist calling Larry at work.

"Guess what, darling? I've found her! I mean, I've actually *found* her!"

"Found who?"

"The baby-sitter! She just walked out the door. I felt like chaining her to the pillars. She's starting eight-thirty, Monday morning."

"Great," says Lawrence Elgin Coffey, with all the affect of a leftover noodle.

Okay, he's always hated me calling him at the office, and once upon a time, I could even understand it, sort of—when he was still a salesman, elbow to elbow, the way he described it, in the "Aquarium" on the fortieth floor, with everybody on the horn and the computers crunching numbers. But now?

"Her name's Harriet," I go on. "Harriet Major. She's almost twenty-two, from the Midwest—Minnesota—a dropout from the university. Apparently there was some kind of love affair that went wrong. But now she wants to go back to school, and she has to earn the money."

"If she's from Minnesota, what's she doing in New Jersey?"

"Her stepfather. Her stepfather lives in East Springdale."

"Oh? Who's her stepfather?"

"How should I know? I've got the name written down, but what difference does that make?"

"Did Justie meet her?"

"Yes."

"And?"

"Well, you know our son. He was his usual timid self, hardly said a word. But he'll be fine. The minute she left, he started nagging me about when she was coming back to play with him."

"How much you paying her?"

I've been waiting for him to ask this. What else do married couples have to argue about?

"Ten," I say without hesitation.

"Ten dollars an hour?"

"That's right."

At last, affect. He whistles into the phone, and I don't have to be there to see him twiddling his hair with his fingers.

"Christ Almighty, Georgie!" he bitches. "That's over four hundred a week, over twenty grand a year! Hey, is the job still open?"

"Get off my case, Coffey," I retort. "I've been dying on the vine out here, you know that. And I'm almost seven months pregnant, what do you want from me?" I force myself to soften my voice. "Oh God," I say, "you don't know what a weight's been taken off. No pun intended, darling. But I feel as though I can breathe for the first time in months."

Call it manipulation, but it also happens to be

true. It's been the summer of the Great Dearth, when the baby-sitter became an endangered species. I advertised in the St. George *Times* for sixteen consecutive weeks, and all I got were Creole-speaking grandmas from the Islands, whose idea of child care, I know from watching, is to kaffeeklatsch on park benches while our children strangle each other in the sandbox.

Not for me. I've heard too many horror stories. Instead, *faute de mieux*, and stuck, and in my second trimester of pregnancy, I became, at thirty-two, a full-time suburban mommy.

It's been a long, an excruciating summer.

"Are you telling me we can't afford it?" I ask Larry over the phone.

"Of *course* we can afford it! That's not the point."

"Then indulge me. You know what I've been going through. Or, if you can't indulge me, at least indulge your son."

"Oh shit, Georgie," he groans, but that's the sum and total of it, for now.

Noogies.

Besides, he hasn't met Harriet Major. I have.

In fact, I all but hired her over the phone. I think I knew it the minute I heard her voice. For God's sake, she can speak the English language! She is also direct, self-assured. We chatted on the phone— that is, *I* chatted, chattered—nerves, I guess—and then, that same magical morning, she was standing on the threshold to my living room, poised, her mouth half-open.

"I think it's the most beautiful room I've ever seen," she said. "It's . . . perfect."

And it is, or almost.

And so is Harriet Major.

We talked. She sat on my curlicued Victorian couch, a total stranger, hands in her lap, her straight blond hair dappled by sunlight, the strong features of her face in shadow. We even talked about restoring wood, of all things. (She asked.) The couch on which she sat was my first serious piece. I'd bought it for ninety dollars, a relic at a St. George estate sale, figuring that if I wrecked it, it was only ninety dollars. I learned to strip with a toothbrush, with a Q-tip where the toothbrush won't fit, with a matchstick for the tiniest crevices. When I was finished, the reupholstery, in striped silk, cost me eight hundred dollars—Larry thought I was nuts —but I've since been offered four thousand for the piece. Then I started on the room itself that, when we moved in, had been stained a dark and morbid mahogany like the rest of the house. I wanted the original natural oak. I got it too, removing the decorative molding around the fireplace rosette by rosette, gluing them back when I was done staining and oiling, and I'd just begun on the central staircase when I discovered I was pregnant with Justin.

End of project. I called in the professionals for the rest of the house.

"God, what a marvelous talent," Harriet said. "Bringing things back to life like that."

"It's not a talent," I corrected. "Just hard work and time. Mountains of time."

"Would you ever be willing to teach me?"

"I'd be glad to one day, but not while I'm pregnant."

"No, of course not. But I'd have thought—"

"It's the fumes," I explained. "Zip Strip, absolutely lethal stuff. Even normally you have to do it with the windows wide open and fans blowing. God knows what it would do to a tummy baby."

The words came out without my thinking, and I burst out laughing. I explained. Justin, at three and a half, and with my bulge finally visible, has discovered tummy babies, also egg babies, and that he himself was a tummy baby. He can't get over it, not only that he was my tummy baby, but that I was once his grandma's, that his grandma had been his great-grandma's, and . . .

"It blows his mind," I said, thinking: What am I babbling about, to this stunning young creature who, to judge, is a long way away from the grandeur and misery of motherhood? "Probably the first thing he'll ask you," I said to her, "is if you were one too."

"Well, I was," she answered gravely, "except that my mother is dead now."

"Oh God, I'm sorry. I—"

"No, no, it's nothing," smoothing her hair away from her eyes. "I was just wondering what he knows, or doesn't know, about death. People dying. Some parents have very particular ideas."

I don't, but I appreciated her sensitivity. Strangely, though, my passing praise—or what I meant as praise—seemed to disconcert her. She tossed her head briefly, as though in denial, and quickly changed the subject.

It was hard not to gape. She is simply ravishing. She's about my height, but something—perhaps it was the strong sculptured features, the erect posture—gave the impression of stature. Gray-blue eyes, prominent cheekbones, upturned lips, strong chin, the whole framed in straight and glinting blond, shoulder-length. (Time was—at Dalton, Barnard—I'd have killed for hair like that!) Long fingers, well-tended nails. No makeup that I could detect. Watching her move that morning, I could only think, with a groan, of the trainer I'm going to have to have in again, once the baby comes.

At her age, maybe her face still lacks a certain character. That's what my mother would say. But then there are the eyes, the look. That steady, long-lashed, gray-blue gaze.

She seemed totally oblivious to it.

Women like that—beautiful women who pretend not to notice it—have often irritated me.

"I think you'd better tell me," I said finally. "What's a lovely and well-spoken young woman of twenty-one doing applying for a baby-sitting job?"

It seemed to unnerve her a little. She simply stared at me for a moment, until I realized that she wasn't focusing on me but on something behind me. Then she averted her eyes, gazed down at her hands.

"I've been through a pretty rough time recently," she said, looking back at me. "I guess I'm not used to talking about it."

"Well," I said, "you don't *have* to. I didn't mean—"

"No. I don't mind. You've every right to know."

It turned out that the first real love of her life—some campus romance, I gathered—had ended last spring when the young man in question took up with someone else. Johnny was his name—Johnny One-Note, she said with a wry smile, explaining that he was a buff of old pop tunes. Apparently she'd taken the loss hard.

"I guess I pretty much went under, Mrs. Coffey," she said. "I didn't take my exams. I couldn't talk to people, much less bring myself to go outside. Most of my time I spent calling him in my mind, but I never once picked up the phone. I don't remember even eating anything other than candy bars. And all the time, I hated myself—I knew I had to get out of there and regroup—but I could hardly get out of bed. Feeling too sorry for myself, I guess. And *ashamed!* Can you imagine that, Mrs. Coffey? He was the one who left me, but *I* was the one who felt ashamed?"

I nodded, smiling in sympathy. It had been a long time—a very long time, it seemed—since I'd felt that kind of oh-so-emotional hopelessness. I burbled something to the effect that her Johnny One-Note would scarcely be the last man in her life. "I think, though," I added, "that if we're going to end up working together, you ought to start calling me Georgia."

She thanked me for that. She seemed vastly relieved, now that she'd gotten the story out.

"Anyway, it's over," she said. "It really is. I got myself out here, to my stepfather's, and now, finally," with a half, sort of sly, smile, "I'm regrouping. I mean, in addition to needing the money, I want to get back into the world, do something, be useful to somebody."

"How far did you get in school?" I asked.

"Oh, I would have—was supposed to have—finished my junior year."

"With just one year to go?"

"That's right."

"Well, it'd be nice to help you get back there, wouldn't it?"

"I'd like that very much."

"And are you okay here? With your stepfather, I mean?"

"Oh yes, that's fine. I can stay as long as I want. Most of the time, I'm free to come and go. Luckily I have my own car."

"What does your stepfather do?"

"He has his own business, in New York. You can call him if you want to. I put him on the list—Robert A. Smith?—not as a reference really, but just to have someone local. The rest, I'm afraid, are all in Minnesota."

I glanced down at the list she'd given me, handwritten in a neat and girlish script. Names, phone numbers, dates of employment.

We passed easily to the details of the job. I told her about Group, the little toddlers' school Justin goes to two mornings a week. Then I said, "You really should tell me, Harriet. How much do you need to earn?"

"I think you should pay me whatever you think is fair," she replied.

Two things, in fact, crossed my mind. One was that I'd found the answer to my troubles and that there was no way I was going to let anyone else steal her, least of all because of a few dollars. The going rate, in St. George, is six dollars an hour, seven tops. And the second thing—this is what I said, aloud—was that the person to whom I entrusted my most valued possession, it seemed to me, ought to make at least as much as the person who cleans my house.

"That means ten dollars an hour," I said. "That's what I suggest. Does that sound fair?"

"I think it's generous," she answered, smiling. "Too generous, actually."

"Well, then that's that. Unless you've something else, I think all that's left is for you to meet the 'valued possession' in question."

"Yes," she said, laughing with me. "I'd like that very much."

Justin knew what I was doing, whom I was talking to and why, but when I called him down and introduced him to Harriet, he ducked away, clutching some toy he wouldn't reveal. And stayed there, wordless, listening without seeming to.

We talked around him for a few moments. I told him Harriet was going to come play with him, starting Monday morning, would he like that?

No answer.

"A little R-E-G-R-E-S-S-I-O-N this morning," I apologized. "He isn't usually like this."

And a small Pinocchio nose for Georgia, I thought —you should hear his father on the subject—but Harriet smiled back at me, at Justin next to me.

"It's okay," she said. "Sometimes boys are a little like puppies. They need to sniff you out first."

Normally an idea like that would have tickled Justin, but he didn't react. Wouldn't. I took this as a signal to end the conversation. Not that it mattered because I'd already made up my mind and he could scream his head off, but I stood, smiling, saying, "Well, it seems as though we've made a deal, Harriet. I'm awfully glad, and I hope you'll be very happy here.''

"I know I will be," she said.

I extended my hand, but then she did the most extraordinary thing.

Instead of responding to me, she slipped forward onto her knees, on the carpet, and, her arms outstretched gently toward Justin, she said very calmly, "I think you heard my name before. I'm Harriet. Harriet Major. I think I'd like to be friends with you. What did you say your name was?"

Surprised, I almost answered for him, but in the same breath I felt him straighten next to me and move hesitantly toward her. His right hand came forward too, taking hers, and then I heard his small voice:

" 'ustin. 'ustin Cawpey."

22 September

It's Saturday night. We're at the Penzils', their end-of-summer party. I almost didn't come. When Larry came home from his sacred tennis this afternoon— he and Joe Penzil against Mark Spain and somebody else—he started working me over about how much I'm paying Harriet. At first I thought it was because they'd lost, but he wouldn't let it go, even while we were dressing. How could I piss money away like that? If I really wanted to piss money away, there are homeless people lying all over the streets of New York; I'd do better handing out dollar bills on the corner.

I took a little of it, defending myself. Then I said,

"What are you really worried about? Are you afraid I'm going to tell people tonight? And that they'll make you the laughingstock?"

"Well," he said, "what you're doing certainly is inflationary."

"Inflationary? What's not inflationary? Isn't your salary inflationary?"

"What do you mean by that?"

I didn't know exactly what I meant.

"Never mind," I said. "If you want to be perfectly safe, then I won't go. I don't feel like it anyway. I've got a splitting headache."

"Aw, Georgie, for Christ's sake. You pull this every year. We've got to go. Jesus Christ, they're our *friends!* And you look beautiful! Look, honey, I'm sorry. You're right. It doesn't matter. Pay her whatever you damn want to."

Maybe I do pull it every year, or threaten to. It's at times like this that I most miss our friends in the city—my friends really, as the people at the Penzils' are Larry's. The net-worth set, Wall Street mostly, the women mostly housewives and mothers. And whatever he says, I look like shit—a tub no matter what I do, in the billowing black chiffon and my tear-drop, baroque-pearl earrings—and then there are the insufferable compliments of the women:

"Why, Georgia, you look positively *blooming!*"

But it isn't that either—the people, or what I look like. And I *do* have a headache.

It's Harriet. Harriet and my paranoia.

Earlier, I tried the first number on her references list: 612 area code. A snooty, upper-register voice answered: "You have reached the Colwell residence. Neither Dr. Colwell nor I is available to talk to you.

If you wish, you may leave a message after the tone."

Instead, I hung up.

Because what if she doesn't show? Suppose she's had other interviews? Suppose someone else has offered her twelve? Fifteen? It sounds crazy, but don't people do crazy things when they're desperate? And aren't there a lot of desperate mommies in St. George?

Suppose she's decided: Georgia Levy Coffey is too spoiled, too whiny, too neurotic overall? (All true.)

Suppose she's been hit by a truck?

What would I do?

I'd slit my wrists, is what I'd do.

I've thought of calling her at her stepfather's, but to say what? (Are you still there? Is everything all right?)

And no Nuprin during pregnancy. No aspirin. Not even a Tylenol.

No Dr. Craig till next Thursday.

Only Helen Penzil's catered dinner, set up on round tables that overflow out of the dining room. Helen's idea of sophisticated is to separate the couples, and I find myself, with her, at Mark Spain's table, where the conversation has turned to Anxiety, The Age of, and, inevitably, Michael Milken. Dear old Michael Milken, for the umpteenth time. To this crowd, the king of junk bonds is still magic, like the Mahareeshi, or whatever his name was, and no matter that he pleaded guilty, "I mean, he made in the *ten* figures! Say what you will, that's pretty fucking awesome!" A lot of speculation about his sentencing, what kind of secret deals he must have cut, what he's done with all the money.

I drift, worrying about Harriet.

I almost miss the question. That is, I do miss it—something about sex. Then I realize abruptly that Mark Spain is eyeing me across the table, lidded hawk's eyes over a hawkish nose, wide nostrils, sardonic smile, and that people are laughing . . .

At me?

I flash, feel myself flush.

"I'm sorry," I say, not understanding, "did I miss something?"

"I think you did," the lawyer answers. "I suppose you were lost in prenatal communion. The question put to you was: Would you like to have sex with Michael?"

"What? With whom?"

Generalized laughter.

"Forget that your husband is in the room, Georgia," Spain says, "or that in your current state sex with a man may be about the furthest thing from your mind. Imagine yourself in other circumstances, a free woman. You've just been introduced to Michael Milken. Does it cross your mind: A man who made that much money, I wonder what he's like in bed?"

"What Mark's getting at, Georgia," Helen Penzil cuts in, "is if money, enough money, gives a man irresistible sex appeal."

"That's not my point at all," Spain says, his eyes on me. (Poor Helen. In her defense, she is Joe's wife, and Joe is Mark Spain's protégé at their law firm.) "Go on, Georgia. Does it cross your mind?"

I want to say the game's dumb. Or that you, Mark Spain, make my skin crawl. Or that the Milkens, from what little I've read, are a pair of nobodies who got in way over their heads. But all of them are watching me expectantly.

"No," I manage to say, "not at all."

This arouses groans, comments—of disapproval? disbelief?—but Spain waves them off.

"Why not?" he persists.

"I've never so much as met the man."

"Yes, but you'd have to have been in Timbuktu not to be aware of him. What is it about him that turns you off?"

"Nothing," I answer. "I guess I just don't see what's so sexy about money."

Spain's eyes crinkle, his nostrils flare. I feel as though he's about to make me the butt of some joke. Instead he says, "At last, the voice of common sense. And from an expectant mother, no less. But money can still buy things, can't it, Georgia? Even people?"

"Are you asking me if I'd *sell* myself to Michael Milken?"

"At some price you would, wouldn't you? Or to me? Or anyone?" A sardonic smile. "Doesn't every one of us around this table, man or woman, have a price? At some figure?"

"You're not serious, are you?" I ask.

"Very serious."

"I'm sorry," I retort angrily, "but I find the question offensive."

"And well you should," he replies. "But shocking as it may seem, my dear, we live in an age when men and women do buy and sell each other, all the time. Michael's genius was that he understood that literally everyone is for sale. What he never understood, though, is that the only true leverage is power, not money. Power interested him only in passing, and he was always quick to pass it on. He lacked the true predator's instinct. At the end, when he too was sold out, by his friends and business partners, all that was left was a poor little rich boy sitting at his computer with his pants down.

"And that, dear Georgia," the hawk's eyes lidded again, "is why you wouldn't think about going to bed with him."

So much, I think, for Michael Milken.

And Georgia Coffey? I'm still flushed by the exchange, his supercilious tone. I feel somehow like a piece of goods picked up in a store, fingered, put down again. How *dare* he? Somebody asks Spain if he's jealous or just bragging—guffaws all around—and the conversation now revolves around him.

I excuse myself, slip away unnoticed. Upstairs, in the master bedroom, I call home. Clotie says they're fine, just fine. She's my cleaning woman. As a special dispensation, she agreed to sit with Justin. (Ten dollars an hour.) They've been watching TV. I want Justin to go to bed, ask her to put him on. When am I coming home, he wants to know. Soon, I say, very soon. And when is Harriet—" 'arrit''—coming to play with him? I take a deep breath. Monday, I say. Monday morning. But not unless he gets plenty of sleep first. He's going to need high energy for Harriet, I tell him.

I dread going back downstairs. Is it Spain? I only know the man through the Penzils, and before tonight he's never paid me the slightest attention. Thank God for small favors. According to Larry, he put together some of the biggest deals of the eighties. A competitor, Larry says, "one hell of a." He's

also, by reputation, something of a philanderer, in
his fifties, mind you, late forties anyway, and—I
know this from Helen—he and Gloria fight like cats
and dogs.

Finally I descend, holding on to the banister. Dinner is over; the guests have moved into the living
room. My headache is gone, replaced not by nausea
exactly but intimations of nausea. Heavy, achy feeling in my legs, and I have to stop every few steps to
catch my breath. Up until now, I've had a trouble-
free pregnancy, but it's as though some warm and
sickly wind, the last wind of summer, has gusted
through me, leaving a residual coating. I hardly ate,
yet I'm sticky from sweat, and now there's the re-
newed throbbing at my temples.

I want to go home.

The party has divided into male and female, except that, instead of "retiring," the men have simply
gathered around their self-appointed guru, Mr.
Spain. Joe Penzil's in their midst. I rather like Joe.
More than Helen, really. He's Larry's closest friend,
an ex-Marine turned Wall Street lawyer in his thirties, and it invariably amuses me to see Larry and
Joe together: Penzil with his sawed-off crew cut,
small but dark and intense, and the laid-back Coffey
—Big Bear, as he's known to his friends—still hand-
some, still boyish despite the bald spot.

And smart too, my husband.

You don't get to be magna cum at Dartmouth, or
do the Shaw Cross training program, which people
say is tougher than any MBA, or become a managing director, or earn in the high six figures (over a
million, the year he turned thirty) on a moron's IQ.

And there's the rub.

Because Larry is standing closest to Spain, and Spain apparently has been working him over. I can see Spain's eyes flash, long index finger skewering, and Larry has his head ducked forward, down, and he's listening. Then, abruptly, a great burst and roar of laughter from the entourage. Spain apparently has struck home. For a second, Larry simply stares, mouth agape in his moon face. But then, head back, he too starts to guffaw, and even though I can't hear the words, I can see his great paw on Spain's lapel and shoulder, and now he's nodding, talking earnestly—*schmoozing*, he'd say, even though he's not Jewish—"Hell, honey," he'd say, "what do you think I do for a living?"—and I think, he can't *like* Spain, he . . .

Or have I got it all wrong? Is this really male bonding I'm witnessing?

While Spain's eyes, now circling the room, have just lit on mine?

The Penzils understand my apology. It's the fatigue, the headache, I don't even have to explain. I have to take care of myself, my baby.

But Larry doesn't get it.

"Great party," he says in the car.

Okay, so he's pissed.

"I'm sorry," I say. "I'm just not feeling too well."

"Not to worry."

"What did Spain say to you?" I ask a moment later.

"When?"

"Just now. What was it, some kind of joke?"

"Look, you may not like him," tightly, "but he's one of the savviest guys on the Street. Maybe *the*."

And one hell of a competitor, I add for him in my

mind. But the conversation is over. We're home, in silence, inside of five minutes. Clotie leaves, Larry heads toward the den—something about a nightcap —and upstairs I check Justin. He's breathing lightly in his bed with an arm flung over his head and Meowie, his cat, curled between his legs.

I feign sleep later, but when Larry gets into bed behind me, his bulk behind mine, and I feel his insistent pressure beneath my buttocks, I relent. Gingerly, I bring him inside me. (An act of atonement?) The position hurts, though. I can't even think of coming.

But later still, drowsy yet tense, listening to his rhythmic snore in the darkness and shifting clumsily back and forth in search of a position I can relax in, I feel the queasiness all over again. The twist in my stomach. It's Harriet, I think again, not the party or even Mark Spain. I've been thinking about Harriet. Clearly Harriet's too good to be true. She's not going to show. She's . . .

And then what? Then, assuming I don't slit my wrists after all, I guess I'll run my ad again. And again . . .

Bad vibrations. Something malevolent.

Malvolio. Who was Malvolio?

Shakespeare.

Wanted: one bright, young, sane woman, English-speaking, to save Barnard alum from terminal atrophy of the brain.

God.

My father intervenes. *Why do you always anticipate the worst, Georgie? Why bring everything down on your head? Or try to?*

Or Craig, my shrink of the moment: *Does the fate*

of humanity truly hang on whether she comes to work for you or doesn't?

Actually, I realize, that's not Craig. That's me asking the question.

I'm wide awake now. I get up, prowl. Check Justin again. Downstairs, turn on all the lights. Drink water. Malvolio. Can't find the Shakespeare. Eat.

There's always eating.

28 September

The magic holds all week.

The luxury of it! Sheer, unadulterated, positively sinful!

Monday morning, eight-thirty, the bell rings and there she is, smiling at Justin and me, in Minnesota sweats with the letters running down one pants leg, so fresh and young and scrubbed I can't help thinking: a good thing Larry catches the 7:12. Justin takes her away immediately, to show her the ropes, and that afternoon we tour St. George. Seeing it through Harriet's eyes, I realize, yes, how impressive it really is, from the stately mansions with their views of the New York skyline to the quirkier Victorians (including mine) dating from the end of the century, and the great spreading trees, oak and beech and hemlock, and even the ersatz "Elizabethan village" from which the town center grew. Tuesday, I take them both to Group, which is held in the basement of the Unitarian Church. Since it's a co-op, I'm relinquishing my Class Mommy duties to Harriet.

Wednesday, I turn off the intercom that's plugged

into Justin's room. I know they've been building castles out of MegaBlocks and the Lincoln Logs I thought he was too young to manipulate. I've heard them working on his consonant sounds—his *S*'s and *F*'s, *V*'s too, have been so slow in coming that I've thought about taking him to a therapist. I've also overheard laughter—peals of it. Then Thursday—yesterday—while Justin napped (unprecedented event), Harriet gave me my first back rub.

Talk about sinful pleasures!

When I ask him how he likes her, he says, "*Grr-eat!*"

Today is Friday. Right after lunch, I send them off to the park in the Volvo. Harriet drives well, I've discovered (what doesn't she do well?), and the Volvo has the car seat. I take the keys to her old Civic just in case, but then, finding myself with (deliciously) nothing to do, I lie down on my bed. I'm lulled by the canopy lace stirring gently overhead in an afternoon breeze and the distant whirr of Clotie's vacuum cleaner.

I awake—afternoon—with a jolt of anxiety. Did the baby just kick me?

The digital clock says 4:18 in red numerals.

It's too quiet. Where's Justin?

I sit upright, holding my breath. And then let it go. Why, with Harriet. Of course!

Still, shouldn't they be back by now? 4:18?

But why? It's another gorgeous day, seasonably warm, and if something's gone wrong, wouldn't they have called?

But are there phones in the St. George parks? Suddenly I can't remember. I don't think I ever noticed. Suppose they couldn't find a phone? Or the phones are broken?

But this isn't New York. This is definitely *not* New York City.

Besides, what could have happened to them in broad daylight? In St. George, New Jersey?

And how do I even know they're not back? My house has twelve rooms, on three floors.

I get up, search. Upstairs, down. Nobody. Even Clotie has already left for the day.

Once planted, the idea won't go away. Haven't I myself noticed strangers in the parks, men without children? And what about the milk cartons, the ones with the photos of missing children on the front and back panels?

I can't help myself. Maybe it's hormonal, but goddamn, why *hasn't* she brought him home?

They've been gone over three hours!

Hyperventilating—not hard to do in your seventh month—I grab my purse, grab her keys from the butcher-block counter in the kitchen.

I can barely wedge myself into her Civic, even with the seat all the way back. It's been years since I last tried a stick shift, and I never really learned. I start up, lurch, stall. *Damn!* I start again, stall again. What if I've flooded it? Tears of frustration welling. With a terrific grinding sound I get it going one more time, manage the driveway, find another gear, and lurch onto our road. And then—new thought—how do I even know which park they went to? We covered them all, Monday, including the closest one on our side of the town center and the big one he likes best because it has the best swings. God Almighty, why, in such a well-heeled town, where every house has a backyard and most a swimming pool, do there have to be so many parks?

I do the parks. They're repaving Main Street again, which means detours and traffic lights that make no sense, and by the time I find them—in the big park with swans on the lake and broad fields for soccer and kite-flying—I'm flushed and dripping sweat. I've just spotted the Volvo. I manage to tuck in near it, stalling one last time, and stumble across the uneven ground, under the trees, toward the playground.

The sandbox is full of kids. Not mine.

The swings?

No.

Past the last row of stone benches, beyond the sandbox . . . I see them!

My impulse is to shout, run forward, but an inner warning holds me back: *For God's sake, Georgie, don't lay all your fears on him.*

He and Harriet are halfway up the high slide.

All summer, I've refused to let him go up it. "You're too small," I told him, "and it's too dangerous. Look, only the big kids are doing it."

This wasn't entirely true. We'd both seen kids smaller than he shoot down it like missiles. About halfway down, the shining metal buckles out, then back in, and I've always expected to see one of them go soaring off the buckle and break his neck.

Maybe it's never happened, but does that mean it can't?

There must be fifteen steps or more, from bottom to top. Enormously high and Justin—they're close to the top—looks so tiny. But Harriet is right behind him and, I guess, means to ride down with him in her lap—something I'd never do, pregnant or not.

They've reached the top. I watch him swing his legs forward into position. He hunkers down. I can see his little hands gripping the side rails while, from behind, Harriet talks intently to him.

But then—suddenly—she's climbing down, alone, backtracking the way they came.

No, I think, goddammit, *no!!* I may have shouted it aloud. I can see his hesitation, the doubt on his little face—he *is* too small!—and suddenly I imagine what it looks like to him: the ground swaying, so far below him, the giant gleaming sweep of metal.

Harriet's just spotted me. She's already at the bottom of the slide, beckoning to him. She waves. I can see her lips moving: "Hi, Georgia!"

And Justin sees me too.

And lets go.

I watch him plummet. I hold my breath. His body hits the buckle, swoops over it and . . . back in. Then, with a whoosh, he slides through Harriet's outstretched hands and hard into the dirt.

The landing has to have hurt him, but he's running toward me like a dirty Indian.

"Me *did* it, Mommy! Me did it all by my 'elp!"

He still says "my 'elp," two separate words, for *myself*.

I have to sit down. I slump onto the nearest bench, stone with wood slats painted green. Too much, too fast. I close my eyes to purple dots and bursts on a black field, nausea in my stomach and the baby kicking up a storm.

Justin's tugging at me. Then I feel hands on my shoulders.

Harriet's.

"Are you all right, Georgia?" I hear her ask.

I nod, fighting off tears.

"It's really okay," she says softly. "Don't worry, I'd never let him do anything he can't do."

I shake my head.

"Shouldn't have done it," I manage. "He could have hurt himself terribly."

"I didn't think there was a chance of that. He wanted to do it."

I open my eyes. Through a blur of tears I see her head. It blots out the sky. I want to let the tears go—sheer relief—but then I see Justin's flushed little face, and I take slow deep breaths instead until the baby quiets inside.

I pay her for the week, cash in a white envelope. We stand on the front porch between two of the graceful Victorian columns, while Justin, already bathed by Harriet, runs around us in the Giants sweats outfit his father insisted I buy him, and slippers with Mickey Mouse faces.

It's late, twilight. Past six, and up till now she's always left at six on the dot.

"I'm very sorry about today," she says, holding the envelope in her hand. "This afternoon. Really I am. I'm sorry I upset you."

"It wasn't your fault," I reply. "You were right anyway. Probably I'm much too overprotective."

"I shouldn't have let him do it."

Saying, I think fleetingly, just what Mommy wants to hear?

"Anyway," I say, "it's over."

Except it isn't. It was in me, in the park, to fire her

on the spot. Selfish, to be sure, but isn't she here to make things easier for me? And if, right or wrong, every time I can't see them, hear them, I'm going to have to worry about where they are, what they're doing, then what's the point?

What holds me back, of course, is Justin. Already, after just one week with her, I don't know that I could do that to him.

What would I say to him?

I expect her to leave. Instead she lingers, in the Friday twilight. It's as though she's gearing up to say something. Suddenly it occurs to me: Suppose I have it reversed? Suppose *she* wants to quit? How do I know, maybe she can't stand criticism, maybe she can't stand . . .

"Please don't," she says quietly. Her eyes hold mine.

"Don't what?"

"You were thinking of firing me," she says.

Startled, I reach out, touch the white balustrade. "Well . . ."

"I want the job. I can't explain, but I really need it." Her voice is so earnest. "It's very important to me. I know I'll do better next week. I promise I will. I'll check everything with you first. I'll—"

"But Harriet," I interrupt. "It's fine, really. Let's forget about this afternoon. It's done, over. And I don't *want* you checking with me all the time, I really don't."

I can't get over it, though. It must have been her outward poise that had me fooled, her air of confidence, but underneath, apparently, is just another scared and sensitive little girl—well, young woman —who is in addition, I think, a thousand miles from home, and living with a stepfather she doesn't like talking about. (Is he remarried? I can't remember exactly what she said.) And knowing no one else, it seems, no friends, and taking care of someone else's kid, in a strange house, with a strange employer who's over six months pregnant and given to jumping at shadows?

Could I have done it, at twenty-one?

All she wants, I realize suddenly, is a little reassurance. (Is that such a crime?) While all I've done, for God's sake, is think about *firing* her!

I feel a rush of sympathy for her, remorse too. I tell her the truth—that I think she's done wonderfully well with Justin, that, from the minute she arrived, he's never looked back and already I can see the changes in him. Good changes. I tell her that I won't stand on ceremony with her, and she shouldn't with me either, if anything is wrong. We need to trust each other. Or even if she's just lonely, wants to talk, whatever . . .

"The truth is, Harriet," I say, "it feels as though you've been here much longer than a week. Already," smiling, "I can't imagine how we'd cope without you."

She smiles back at me.

"Thank you," she says. "You're a very kind person, Georgia. I also think—probably I shouldn't say this, but I think you're the most beautiful woman, pregnant, I've ever met. I really do. I mean, you, your home . . . it's all so perfect . . ."

It's in me to touch her, embrace her despite my bulge. I reach, but she seems to duck, calling out, "And then there's this young camper!" She swoops Justin off his feet and into her arms, grinning at him, and watching them, hearing his laughter, I think again: *Those gray-blue eyes. Devastating, even to a very young man.*

"Take a chill, Phil!" she exclaims to him. "I'll see you Monday morning!"

"Relax, Max!" he answers back, delighted.

She hands me my son. I hold him, and together we watch her drive off in the white Civic, both of us waving, and I think to myself, on that particularly mellow, end-of-September evening: *You silly goose, she's going to save your life.*

14 October

"I've been waiting to hear from you."

"Yeah, well, they just walked out the door. Another day in the suite. It's driving me nuts."

"How did it go?"

"Slow. They're taking their fucking time."

"I was afraid of that."

"Yeah. But so far so good. We've given them everything they've asked for."

"What about personnel?"

"They still want me to clean house. I'm about to oblige them."

"That's not what I had in mind."

"Oh? Yeah, well, we're still arguing who they get to talk to. It's sensitive. They understand I can't let them get down to the cleaning women. I'm trying to keep it to people who know nothing, or know too much, if you catch my drift. On the other hand—"

"Logically they're going to want to talk to him, aren't they?"

"Who?"

"You know whom I'm talking about."

"Yeah, right. Well, look, as far as that's concerned,

we've got three choices. One, we leave him alone, hope they never find him. Too risky, I say. Two, we try burying him in a corner. It's a little late for that, though. Three, we let him go."

"What have you decided?"

"I say: Let him go. It's the cleanest, the least risk."

"Are you sure?"

"Remember, he won't be the only one who gets canned. It's gonna be lean-and-mean time around here."

"He'll be bitter."

"So? Everybody's bitter about something."

"And vindictive."

"You mean he could talk? Sure, he could talk, but who'll listen? He doesn't know enough. Shit, who's going to waste their time with a bunch of wild-sounding allegations?"

"They might."

"He knows nothing about them."

"Not now. But we live in a very small world."

"Well, anything's possible, but on a scale of one to ten, I'd say that's pretty remote."

"Your job is to minimize the risks. What does their attorney think?"

"Their attorney? For Christ's sake, what makes you think I talked to him about it?"

"Because you talk to him about everything."

"Jesus. Either you're pretty fucking clairvoyant or—"

"What does he think?"

"Well, I didn't go into all the details, naturally. He said someone like that, who could be obstructive, I should get him off the premises. Said I should string him out till it's over, do a little tap dance with him."

"Can you do that?"

"Shit, I can tap dance with the best of them."

"Good."

"I take it that means I'm outvoted?"

"No. As far as I'm concerned, it's your decision. You're the chairman."

"Okay. I'll deal with it then."

"When? I want to know exactly."

"I'll do it this week. Wednesday. That's when I'm doing the others."

"That's fine."

"He may come crying to you."

"I expect him to."

Lawrence
Elgin
Coffey

16 October

The other phone rings, the private line. It's 8:15.

"Larry Coffey here," I say automatically, picking up with my right hand, "would you please—?"

"Larry, tomorrow morning. Nine-thirty, thirty-ninth floor Conference. Any reason you can't make it?"

It's the Great White Himself. (On the private line?)

"No. What's up, Leon? Anything you want me to bring? Hello?"

But he's hung up already.

"Shit," I say aloud. Then, into the other phone, "Sorry, babe, I got interrupted. You were saying?"

I've got south Jersey on the other line, Gerry Mulcahy, my early-morning schmooze. That's how I start my days, with coffee on the pull-out of the desk and my Gerry Mulcahys on the horn. I punch the board while we talk, give him some of the overnight numbers—which he could as well get from the Aquarium, but there's nothing like Big Bear first thing in the morning, is there? When you've just stepped out of your shower?

They keep bankers' hours in south Jersey. *Not at The Cross,* I like to tell my trainees. *We start at eight, sharp. If you think you can't make it, go sell shoes on Fifth Avenue.*

"Sorry, babe," I say into the phone, "I've got to cut you off now. Something's come up. Corporate shit, you know how it is. I'll catch you later, at your desk, or you call me. How much? Yeah, we can do something with that. I know, the market sucks, what can I tell you? We've been there before, babe. Later."

I hang up on Mulcahy. My console is lit up, as usual. All incoming too, like Flight Control at JFK, and I could tell you who each and every one is. 8:18? We're into the Central Time Zone already. Denver and Texas come later, California too, though not by much. Money men get up earlier in California. They've got to make the opening.

All of them pissing and moaning too, looking to recoup. Recoup? Hell, looking for a fucking miracle. Looking for Big Bear to produce a fucking miracle, one that'll keep the regulators off their case.

At least Mulcahy has cash. Mulcahy always has cash. I scribble a note to Howie about Mulcahy's 180 grand, tell my secretary to deliver it to the Aquarium, tell her to tell all the others I'll call them back later, and head down the interior staircase to the thirty-ninth floor.

A different atmosphere. Carpeting, hunting prints on the walls. Private johns. You knock first on the thirty-ninth, and nobody's in his shirtsleeves.

"He's not in," Annabelle Morgan says, glancing

up at me from her CRT in the outer office of the Great White's suite.

"I already know that, honey," I answer. "I just talked to him." If he'd called from inside the office, he'd never have used my private line and he'd have had Annabelle set the appointment. "But what's going down? What's it all about?"

"What's what all about?" she says.

She's one beauteous piece of work, Ms. Morgan, and just as well-spoken, just as snooty. Keeper of the Great White's lair and secrets. The Aquarium pundits like to bitch that she earns more than they do, but hey, this is an "Equal Opportunity Company," guys, doesn't it say so under the corporate logo? It also happens to be ninety-nine percent male and lily-white, at least in the jobs that count, which makes Ms. Morgan a double treasure.

The idea that the Great White has done something —anything—without telling her must be tickling the hackles on her long and lovely neck.

"He wants to see me tomorrow morning, nine-thirty," I say. "How come you don't know about it?"

"Well, I don't." Coolly. "All he told me was to clear his calendar."

"For the whole day?"

"Morning till night. Do you want me to find out for you when he calls in?"

The message is clear enough: Do I want the Great White to know that, five minutes after he called me, I was nervous enough to snoop?

I tell her not to bother. She turns back to her PC, but when I head out, though still not looking up, she adds a parting barb: "You should know, sugar, you're not the first one who's been in here to ask."

I duck into Schwartzenberg's office—he'll know
—but he's not there either.

Upstairs, I finish my duty calls and, out of habit,
patrol the Aquarium. It takes up most of the fortieth
floor, sellers and traders elbow to elbow. Normally,
even in a slow market, it's bedlam city, where the
filtered air takes on its sweet, faintly aquatic smell.
Nobody, including building engineers, has ever
been able to determine why, but it's distinctive to
The Cross and the fortieth floor. Someone once said
it's what making money smells like. More likely it's
what you get when you put sweat and nerves together with electronic machines and windows that
don't open and the remnants of crullers, sandwiches, mustard, coffee.

Sellers and traders. My old stomping grounds.

In '87, when the Great White decided I was making too much money and made me a shark, complete with title, private office (cum windows and
secretary), and a bonus in lieu of commissions, I
was expected, automatically, to move downstairs.
Instead, I opted to stay put on the fortieth. It was
the smell, I told people. How could I run other people, teach them the tricks of my trade, without that
secret elixir that takes a bunch of harmless guppies
—Ivy League for the most part—and turns them
into ravenous carnivores of the financial depths?

The Great White, at the time, applauded the decision—the Great White is very hands-on, too, or likes
to think he is—but who knows, maybe it was a mistake. Hey, if I'd been on the thirty-ninth all along,
maybe I wouldn't have to deduce what's coming
down, secondhand, from Annabelle Morgan and
hints dropped by others, and the great glum, doom-

filled quiet that prevails in the Aquarium this Tuesday morning in October.

It's like a morgue, a deep-sea catacomb. It's like the middle of the night or a weekend except the phones are blinking, the CRT's humming, and people are at their desks. But not talking. Human bodies, living, breathing—but barely. I can feel the pall, the droop. Eye contact at a minimum.

Hey, what the fuck's going on? For Christ's sake, aren't I their honcho, their cheerleader, their wet nurse all rolled into one?

Not today. Today I'm Them. I'm a shark.

I get it out of Howie. Another kid from Dartmouth, tall and gangly—they don't make shirtsleeves long enough for MacFarlane's arms. I culled him from the surviving trainees last year. I thought he had the makings of a seller. He did. I check him on Mulcahy—yes, he's already done Mulcahy—then pull him off the line.

"What the fuck's going on?" I ask him in my office.

"You don't know?" he challenges back.

"I don't know squat," I say. "You tell me."

He stares at me a minute. I can see the Adam's apple bobble in his throat.

"Either you don't," he says finally, "or you're a bigger son of a bitch than I thought."

"I've been called worse, babe," I say. "Let's have it."

"It," at least according to MacFarlane, is going to be a bloodbath. The Aquarium is already calling it Bloody Wednesday. According to MacFarlane, there's going to be a deep slice right through the whole company, every department, from the mailroom up to and including managing directors. According to MacFarlane, they're cutting checks in New Jersey even as we speak—New Jersey's our backroom—and Schwartzenberg is out there, personally overseeing the operation.

I grill him. What does he know firsthand? It turns out he knows shit firsthand. But it's all around, he protests. So-and-so has heard this, so-and-so that. There's a hit list, he says. Someone he knows—an anonymous source—claims to have seen it.

I chalk it up to the Aquarium, at least for his benefit. In that frenzied, sealed-in atmosphere, rumors sprout, and die, like fungi. Maybe one or two people *are* getting canned, maybe more, but by the time the Aquarium is done with it, it's Bloody Wednesday.

I chalk it up to the Street. It's been going on all year—ten percent cuts, twenty in one or two places —and you hear the kids getting off on severance packages and personal bankruptcy instead of BMW's and Rolexes. Probably people MacFarlane went to school with are lining up for unemployment.

Sure it's enough to make you jump at shadows. Who wouldn't jump?

But aren't we insulated? Mr. Average Joe Investor, who got blown out of the market in '87, has never been our customer. What does The Cross give a shit if he's still on the sidelines? We still have our S&L's (those that haven't gone under), and the commercials, the insurance guys, the pension funds, the credit unions, assorted other heavy hitters.

MacFarlane just said something that didn't register. Maybe it didn't register because I'm thinking: *Aren't we insulated in other ways too?* But that's for me to know and Howie to guess at. The way I guessed at it, once upon a time.

"I'm sorry," I say, "run that by me again?"

"I said: 'For God's sake, Bear, you don't have to recruit me.'"

I stare at him a second. Then burst out laughing. He has me there. What I've just laid on him is a version of my recruiting speech, the same one I used earlier in the year. (Yeah, they put me on the committee, what the hell are you going to do?) And Howie should know, shouldn't he? Didn't I make him work on the sucker?

"I'm sorry, babe," I say. "I get carried away. But it's true, you know? And do you think any of *my* guys would get canned without my knowing about it? Look, I still say it's bullcock, but I'll make some calls. If there's anything there, I'll let you know. Meanwhile, the meter's running, and if all we can do is sit here, schmoozing each other, aren't we stealing our fucking salaries?"

He leaves, shaking his head—either I'm the asshole, or he is. Fair enough. If he's right, then the only thing I can figure out is that, tomorrow morning at nine-thirty, the Great White is going to give me a quota: This many stay, Bear, this many go, you do your own dirty laundry.

But that makes no sense either. Look at the record, Leon, I tell him in my mind. There's not a swinging dick among them who hasn't made us a bundle, by any measurement. If you're really talking about contribution to the bottom line, then my guys are fucking untouchable.

Besides, that's not the Great White's style. Leon Gamble is strictly management-by-intimidation. The more I think about it, the more I think that, if there's going to be a bloodbath, he'll want it known, inside The Cross and out, that he's looked every sacrifice in the eyeballs. Even if it takes him from sunrise to sunset.

With Schwartzenberg at his elbow in case someone brings up a legal question?

I make some inside calls. It's one of those mornings, though. Is half the thirty-ninth floor already out to lunch, at ten-thirty?

Out of a few stray spores does paranoia grow.

I make some outside calls.

I call Penzil.

As well as being my tennis partner and train buddy, he's as plugged in as anybody I know on the Street. Maybe he's got to be. A sawed-off runt, ex-Marine, Fordham Law—that's love-forty, game, set, and match, in Skull & Bones country. Plus he's older than most associates. But Joe's going to make partner at Lambert Laughin Spain or bust his gut trying.

"What's up, Bear?" he says. "You guys already made your nut for the day?"

Old gag.

"You hearing anything about us? The Cross, I mean? Like the great shakeout coming?"

"How would I hear something like that and you not?"

"There're rumors flying all over the place. Something about a hit list. And Gamble wants to see me tomorrow morning."

"Oh, c'mon, Bear. You? Either it's a slow day over there, or somebody's put something in your coffee."

I agree with him. Still.

He's heard nothing, he says, but he promises to make a call or two—discreet ones, he says—and let me know if he finds out anything.

He calls back within the hour.

"I think you'd better talk to your rabbi," he says.

I stand up in my chair.

"Why?" I say. "You mean something *is* happening?"

"Just what I said."

"Come on, Joe! For Christ's sake, you're my best friend! What do you hear, who'd you hear it from?"

"I can't, Bear."

Then the full import of it hits home.

"You mean it's me too?" I say, unbelieving.

"Just do what I say. We'll talk later."

And he's gone. Joseph E. Penzil, Esq.

My rabbi.

That's what Penzil's always called him. Not even Penzil knows his identity.

I spend the afternoon in a state of shock, trying to raise him. I call at one—out to lunch; at two—not back yet; at three—yes, he's back, but tied up in a meeting.

Do I really not want to leave a number where he can reach me?

No, it's okay, I'll call back later.

"I'm sorry, Mr. Elgin, I've given him your message. Are you sure there's nothing I can help you with?"

Elgin's my code name, for when I had to call him at work.

"No. Just tell him it's pretty urgent. I'll call back."

I try to raise Penzil again—maybe I can squeeze

something more out of him—but he's out of the office, gone for the day. So is everybody else, it seems.
Except me. And my rabbi.

He's the one who insisted on the code names, all
the hush-hush stuff. The way he once put it, Wall
Street is networks within networks—that's how it
operates—and the most effective ones are those the
fewest people know about. Georgie calls him my
CIA crony. Once I asked him if he himself had ever
done a turn at the Company. He only laughed, shaking his head, said, "But I knew a number of people
who did. Probably I could have, too. In my day, they
used to recruit the campuses quite openly, alongside
Procter & Gamble, Merrill Lynch, other Fortune
Fives."

Francis Hale Holbrook, Dartmouth '56.

When you get down to it, how much else do I
know about him?

It doesn't matter. What matters is that, twice during my career at The Cross, at crunch time, I went
to him and lightning came out of the bottle.

Finally, near five, I raise him. No, he's heard
nothing about imminent events at Shaw Cross. If I
want—but is it really that urgent?—he can arrange
to meet me later. He'll have to do some juggling.

It's really that urgent, I tell him.

Half an hour later, I call him back. Yes, he'll meet
me for dinner, but not until eight-thirty.

I go uptown to the club, run into a few people I
know and back onto the street. They're all letting it
hang out a little, after a day in the trenches, and for
once, I'm not up to it. Hey, they're all *employed!* For
all I know, at nine-thirty tomorrow morning, Big
Bear will be *kaputski.* The more I think about it, the

more it makes no sense. The more it makes no sense, the more I need a drink.

I head for a friendly Third Avenue saloon.

The thing is, there *are* no jobs on Wall Street. The traffic is all one way.

By the time I remember to call Georgie, from Third Avenue, probably I've had one or two too many.

"How can you do this to me?" in her most plaintive voice, when I tell her I'm still in the city. "I'm seven months pregnant, and all by myself, and stuck with a kid who won't go to sleep, and you know how I hate the house alone at night."

We've only lived there six years. We've got the whole place wired by a system that cost a sweet ten grand. If a mouse so much as farts in the house when the system's on, the St. George cops'll be at the front door inside of five minutes.

But Georgie is Georgie.

I suggest she ask the sitter to stay on.

"Harriet?" she says. "Do you have any idea what time it is?" It's almost seven. "She's out of here like a shot at six. Her damned stepfather. You *know* she won't work at night!"

Do I? Maybe I do. I've never even met the girl. I'm gone when she shows up in the morning; she's gone by the time I get home.

"Look, Georgie," I say, "I can't help myself. Something's come up."

"Something *always* comes up. Do you realize how many nights you've been home on time this month?"

I don't. She reminds me. I remind her that a big part of my job is schmoozing the customers. When they come to New York, they don't want their Aquarium man, they want Big Bear—and dinner, a Broadway show, the watering holes afterward.

But this is different.

"I've got to see Holbrook," I say.

"Holbrook! For God's sake, why can't you talk to him on the phone?"

I decide, on the spur, not to get into it. As far as Georgie's concerned, the money's my problem, always has been. As long as the bills get paid—and that includes her gardener, her pool man, her trainer, her housekeeper, her baby-sitter, and all her other assorted cooks and bottle-washers—she doesn't care where it comes from.

I want it that way too, she'd tell you.

"It's okay, honey," I said. "It's just dinner, and I don't have the car. Not to worry, I'll make the eleven-thirty at the outside. I'll call you when I know."

"Okay," she says, her voice small and tight, "you do that."

She hangs up first.

Later, I walk east—way east, almost to the edge of Sutton Place. I have to get my act together—for the restaurant as well as Holbrook. He doesn't like disarray. As for the restaurant, it's the kind of joint almost guaranteed to put guys like me ill at ease— with the menu all in French, and the stuff on trolleys you don't recognize, and maître d's and assistant maître d's hovering, talking rapid-fire French to each other over your head.

When I get there, Holbrook's already at the table and deep in consultation with the chef, a blue-eyed young Frog in a white hat and apron. They're organizing our meal together—I've never known Holbrook to order off the menu, although he always reads it—and after introductions and handshakes, the chef wiping his hand on his apron first, I sit, order a Scotch from the hovering maître d', and wait for them to finish.

Francis Hale Holbrook, Dartmouth '56.

Beyond that, there's a wife I've never met, two children in college (only the younger one—a girl—is up at Hanover), a house in Pound Ridge, another on the Vineyard, a third in Palm Beach.

He likes to sail. Obviously, he's something of an epicure. He's also a—what's the word?

Oenophile.

Physically, he's hardly changed. When I first met him—it was the winter of '77, when he tried to recruit me for his company—he reminded me of a diplomat more than a Wall Street buccaneer. He still does. It's not just the elegance—never a hair out of place, the foulard tie impeccably knotted, the handkerchief in his lapel pocket—but the set of his head, the way he talks. He has one of those narrow, fine-featured, New England faces that never seem to grow old and this clipped, sometimes ironic manner of speaking. On the Street, although his name's familiar, and his firm's certainly is—small, specialized, immensely profitable—what you get is, "Holbrook? Oh yeah, they say he's one smart son of a bitch," or, closer to the point, "Even the guys who work there don't know him very well."

My rabbi.

Although I turned him down in '77, we stayed in touch. I see him maybe a couple of times a year, phone calls in between. Old school tie aside, I've sometimes wondered what's in it for him, but all he's ever said is that he needs to keep tabs on the young Turks in the business.

Dinner is served. I eat because it's there. I lay it out for him, trying to keep the paranoia out of my voice. I have a few more Scotches. He sips claret, carves his meat.

He's heard something too. Without the specifics, the word is around that Shaw Cross is cutting back.

"In fact," he says, "if you hadn't called this afternoon, I was going to call you."

From Shaw Cross's point of view, he's not surprised. The nature of the beast, he says. The beast, meaning Wall Street, grew fat during the seventies and eighties, not just in the form of salaries, but in office space, information systems and so on. The bloated giants of the industry, he says, were the worst offenders—prodigious waste—and now they've panicked. But even comparatively well-run firms like Shaw Cross face it too: a tired economy, a depleted customer base, and cutthroat competition for the remaining investment dollar.

At some point, I say, "All this may be true, Frank, and I'm not disagreeing, but where does it leave me? As far as I know, at nine-thirty tomorrow morning, Leon Gamble's going to bite my legs off at the knees!"

"Are you sure?" he asks, unperturbed.

"Reasonably sure."

"How can you be, if you haven't talked to him yet?"

"I have my sources."

"Good ones?"

"I think so. I hear there's a list, a long one, and I'm on it."

He thinks about it a moment.

"Putting aside the question of whether or not that would make sense from Shaw Cross's point of view, can they do that?"

"What, fire me? Sure they can."

"Really? I thought you had an employment agreement."

"I do. It terminates in January."

"So that at the very least, they've got to pay you from now till then?"

"That's right. Ninety days, give or take." With taxes coming up, I think, and a house that's worth less now than its mortgage, and a wad of bills to choke a fucking horse.

"What's the renewal clause in your agreement? I assume it has one."

"Yeah. Ninety days. Their option to renew. They've got to let me know ninety days before termination."

"I see. And they've said nothing to you before now?"

"Not in so many words," I answer. "The truth is, I never thought about it." And for Christ's sake, why should I have? I'm a fucking fixture, like the furniture. There's something else on the tip of my tongue too: that if it ever comes to hardball, I can give them a very hairy time. But Holbrook is Holbrook; down and dirty's not his style. Instead I say, "You're right, Frank. I won't know anything for sure till nine-thirty tomorrow morning. But haven't you always told me: *anticipate?* Try to see what's coming and be ready for it?"

He nods, smiles his tight New England smile.

"Touché," he says. Then: "And so? What do you see coming?"

He's waiting for me, fork raised, still smiling faintly. Maybe it's been too long a day, but I'm missing his point.

"I think I'm about to be fired," I blurt out. "Tomorrow morning. That's about as far as I can see right now."

His eyebrows go up, the fork lowers.

"I was thinking a little longer term," he says. "Let me phrase it differently. What do you see Larry Coffey doing with the rest of his life? Is he going to stay a hired hand, if a highly paid one? At Shaw Cross? Elsewhere?"

For just a second, I think he's about to offer me a job.

No. On the contrary, he says that, as far as he's concerned, he'd jump at early retirement, if he could only find someone to offer it to him. I take this as a joke—isn't he CEO of Holbrook & Company?—but he means it too. For antediluvians like himself, he says, the game is about played out anyway. But for me?

"All I'm suggesting, Larry, is that you raise your sights a little. Nobody can say what the investment business of tomorrow is going to look like, but for young people with brains, experience, connections, times of crisis are also times of incredible opportunity. Maybe in your current state of mind, all you can see—understandably enough—is your head on the block and the sword in the air and a bunch of bills to be paid. By the way, when's your new baby due?"

"December," I say.

"And all's well? With your wife?"

"Yes, thank you."

"Good. Then as far as tomorrow's concerned, I think you should go with an open mind. Gamble, from what I know of him, is no fool. Maybe the panic has touched him too, I couldn't say. But what's interesting in your situation isn't Gamble. Gamble's going to do what he's going to do, and from what you say, you have no control over it." He pauses, as though giving me room to disagree. Then: "The interesting thing is you. You've been in the business how long? A decade?" I correct him. "God, is it that long already? Thirteen years. Thirteen years, in any case, of superb experience, and the rest of your working life in front of you? All I'm suggesting is that maybe the best thing that could happen to you right now is for Shaw Cross to cut the umbilical."

It's the wrong message, for tonight anyway. I'm a doer, for Christ's sake, not a crystal-ball gazer.

Hey, I can't *afford* to be!

The thing is, though, I've been there before with Holbrook—twice. The same kind of airy conversation—what did I want? what were my objectives?—but both times, although he denied he'd had anything to do with it, lightning struck, in the form of job offers from Salomon, the second time from Merrill Lynch. The first got me a full commission out of The Cross—unprecedented—even though the sharks kicked and screamed. Then, after Gamble became Great White and pulled the plug on commissions—this was '87, just when the bottom fell out of the market—I had Merrill Lynch in the wings and, from Shaw Cross, the managing directorship, the employment contract, the guaranteed minimum bonus.

Somehow, though, it's different this time. Hey, I'm thirty-five now! That's *old* for a high-roller on the Street! All I really want to say is: *I'm sorry, Frank, but I can't see past the end of my nose tonight, I'm too goddamn shook. I need a bailout, a comfort zone.*

But that would be very wrong.

Tough night.

It gets worse.

We finish up. I realize it's almost eleven, that I'm going to have to fly to make the last train. Plus I haven't called Georgie.

He signs the check on the back. Then we have to shake hands with the chef, exchange comments. Great dinner, I say. Holbrook goes into more detail. Something, I gather from my prep-school French, about the sauce on the *gigot*. Finally, we're outside, under the awning, where they have his Jag already parked and ready to go.

No chauffeur tonight, I notice.

"Are you okay?" he says. One of the maître d's is holding the driver's door open for him. "I wish I could drop you off, but we go in different directions, don't we?"

Yeah, St. George and Pound Ridge. Apples and oranges.

"I'm fine," I said. "I've just got to run."

"Of course." But still he holds me back. "I want you to think seriously about what we've said. Keep your eyes and ears open. Look for the opportunities. And, of course, keep me informed."

"I will, Frank. And thanks."

But again: "Call me in the afternoon. I'll be at my desk."

"Fine, Frank."

I find a taxi. I tell him Thirty-second and Sixth—the PATH station. Then I realize I'll never make it that way. I ask what he'll charge to drive me to St. George. That way I'll even beat the train, be home at eleven forty-five at the outside.

St. George, where's that? New Jersey, I say. He's some Israeli or Arab, I can't tell which. No New Jersey, he says.

I bitch, plead with the bastard. Lots of luck. Finally we settle on the Hoboken station—just through the tunnel and back. I agree to double his meter.

We rocket downtown, through the Holland Tunnel, across the dark back streets of Jersey City, Hoboken, to the terminal. I throw money at the driver and sprint for it. I miss the fucking train by inches, seconds. I can see the last car pulling out past the platform.

Son of a gun. There's another guy like me, suit and briefcase, no tie. We grin at each other in commiseration across the station. Better call Georgie, I think. I hesitate. Better see if there's a taxi first.

By the time I get back outside, there's one lone taxi—some scavenger, waiting for a poor bastard like me—and the other guy who missed the train has beaten me to it. He's just climbing in.

"Hey, wait a minute!" I shout after him. "Where you going?"

"The Fells," he says.

Not too bad. We make a deal—it's fine with him,

as long as we take him home first—and another deal with the driver. Those are the only deals I've made all day.

It's long after midnight when I get home. First I have to go to the St. George station to pick up my car. I'm sober as a judge. There'll be hell to pay with Georgie, but when was I supposed to have called?

I turn into our driveway. The house above me is lit up like a beacon, all three floors. From the outside, it looks like a ship at night on the crest of a wave.

Georgie, I think. Scaring off the bogeymen.

But then—what the fuck? The colored lights, slowly twirling?

There are two cop cars under the portico. And shadow figures moving around on the porch, also inside the house. For Christ's sake, the front door's wide open!

I get out of the car, almost fall, run. My heart fucking pounding.

Up the front steps. A uniformed cop is just coming out through the front door, sticking his gun back in its holster.

Georgie is in the angle of the front porch, only her nightgown over her belly. Bare feet, face white as a ghost, mouth ajar. Clutching Justie in her arms, and Justie is squawling his head off.

I damn near lose it when I see them.

"The house is secure," the cop announces, the one in the doorway.

It turns out to be nothing. Something, maybe an animal, set the alarm off, and that brought the cops. Even so, I spend one horrendous night dealing with my wife, fielding her accusations. The next morning, in the kitchen, I'm hanging on to the coffee mug with both hands when there's Harriet at the front door, Justie's baby-sitter, introducing herself to me —holy shit!—but then Georgie's coming downstairs, ready to bite my head off all over again.

It's Bloody Wednesday.

The sharks in a frenzy. The Aquarium roils, goes red.

And it's my turn.

17 October

"Yeah, I'm still in my office. You know what they're calling it around here? Bloody Wednesday."

"How's it going?"

"What the fuck, do you think I like to see grown men cry? Days like today, I wish I was pumping gas in Iowa."

"That's not what you're paid for."

"I know, but I can always dream, can't I?"

"How did it go with him?"

"Well, I made him an offer."

"And?"

"Hard to tell. Of course I made it sound better than it really is, though he doesn't know that. Well, he didn't exactly jump at it, but he didn't jump out the window either. Said he wants to think about it. I suggested he run some numbers. Has he called you about it?"

"Yes. I'd say he's intrigued."

"Jesus Christ. I hope to hell I haven't let you talk me into one humongous mistake."

"Nobody has talked you into anything. It was your decision."

"Sure it was. I was for biting the bullet, you know that. Thanks to you and our friend, the attorney, now I'm gonna to have to tap-dance him for as long as it takes."

"I repeat: It was your decision."

"Sure. Well, maybe we'll get lucky, maybe he'll find another job."

"Maybe he will."

"Let us pray."

Georgia Levy Coffey

16 November

Some say it's hormone swings, some say the third trimester blues.

I have a feminist friend, Lynne Snyder, who tracks my horoscope and is worried about Pluto. (She also believes we've entered a Dark Age and won't come out of it until Gaia worship is reestablished on the planet.)

My mother says it's Larry.

Craig, who's paid to say it, says: "Why are you so convinced something's wrong with you?"

Because it is, Doctor. Believe me.

But Dubin, my ob-gyn, upon hearing my litany—the constant lethargy after sleepless nights, the shortness of breath, the achy joints (Could it be arthritis? But aren't I too young for arthritis?), the nauseating waves of a nameless but almost chemical anxiety that brings the taste of metal to my palate—nonetheless pronounces the baby fine; me too.

Dubin tells me to relax, drink my milk, and listen to Mozart.

But I never had this with Justin, did I? At least I don't remember it.

Someone said that's what keeps the race going: that you forget how awful it was the last time.

Sleepless nights, punctuated by sudden, inexplicable stabbers in my uterus. I become convinced they're not Braxton-Hicks but something else. Then, when I'm on the verge of getting Dubin out of bed, they stop. Beached whale, bathed in sweat, listening to the sound of my own pulse pounding in my ears.

I date it from the night the alarm went off, over a month ago, when Larry didn't come home. The next morning, after he'd left, I had the alarm people in, and they checked the system top to bottom. Everything, they insisted, was in good working order. They thought it must have been one of the casement windows in the living room, the one with the loose lock. When the wind blew hard, the lock gave and the window sprung open, triggering the siren.

The St. George police thought the same thing.

Fine.

But they weren't here, the night before, when I heard the noises downstairs. I was alone in the house, and Justin was asleep. Eleven-thirty had come and gone—the last train—and still no word from Larry. How did I know where he was? I was upstairs in the bedroom, on my chaise longue, my diary open on my lap, and Ted Koppel was signing off on "Nightline." I remember clicking off the TV. Midnight, and wide awake, listening.

I've never gotten used to the night sounds. At least in the city they're human: sirens, trucks, screaming arguments, even gunshots. But sometimes, out here, there are little thuds overhead (squirrels? raccoons? a burglar on tiptoe?), and some nights it's the wind.

Even when there's no wind, Victorians creak.

In summer, it's the din of crickets.

This was none of the above. This was a dull and intermittent banging, not nearby.

Maybe a loose shutter, I thought?

I got up, moving heavily from one bedroom window to another. I could make out the swaying tops of our trees. Earlier, I'd turned on the outside floods —I feel safer that way—but suddenly, peering out over the overhang that covers the front porch, I realized that, to anyone hiding in the shadows, I was totally exposed.

Suppose they'd counted cars in the driveway and knew Larry wasn't there?

I remember the sudden urge to brush my teeth because of the sickish metallic taste. Instead, I forced myself to go downstairs, in the dark. The banging continued, but even in the front hall I couldn't locate where it was coming from.

I'd just gone into the living room, in darkness, when suddenly—all around me—the alarm siren literally exploded in my ears.

Probably I was shrieking too. I grabbed for a telephone, but the line was dead. How could that be? My second impulse—it's still vivid, and I'm still ashamed of it—was to tear out the front door and run for my life. Instead, somehow, I got myself upstairs. I grabbed Justin, covers included, out of his bed, clambered down the back stairs (which I'd never used, pregnant, because they're dangerously steep) to the kitchen. And out the back door, flying past the pool, tripping into the driveway, the dark road.

I stood in the middle of the road, heaving, clutching my son in my arms, until the police came.

Fine.

The police came, Larry came. It was only the window in the living room.

As for the phone, it has to go momentarily dead when the alarm goes off, because the emergency signal is being transmitted to the security service.

I had people in to repair the loose lock that same day, also the shutter moorings outside. For good measure, I ordered another arc of floods to be embedded in the ground beyond the porte-cochère.

But I also had a long talk with Harriet.

I asked her to move in, at least until the baby came. I'd always been against live-ins, I admitted— a question of privacy—but now I needed her. I didn't see how I could make it through without her. Obviously I couldn't count on Larry, and I knew I couldn't stay in the house alone another night.

"I know it's only been a few weeks," I said, "but I've come to look on you practically as a member of the family. I think you're wonderful. And I need you now—for me. I really do."

Of course, I added, there would be more money for her, too. And no expenses. She could save practically everything she earned.

To my disappointment she hesitated, even when I took her up to the third floor to show her the living arrangements I had in mind. There are three lovely, sun-filled rooms up under the eaves, one with a skylight, plus a separate bath, and views all around including, on one side, a panorama of the New York skyline. I'd decorated them originally with myself in mind. More recently, I'd had the idea that, once the children were older, it would be for them. But now, I said, it would all be hers. If she wanted, but *only* if —for we both knew what he'd say—we could move Justin upstairs too.

It was lovely, she agreed. But, hesitant, she'd have to see.

Finally I wormed what it was out of her. The step-father. She didn't know if he would approve. Well, would it help if I talked to him? Oh no, that wouldn't be necessary, not at all. He might not disapprove either, necessarily, she'd just have to see.

By the next day, though, it was all fine. She moved in that same night, and we celebrated, Justin and I, by taking her out to a sumptuous lunch.

Strange young woman, nevertheless.

When I ask her about her past, she closes up like a bivalve. She says, "Georgia, please, let's not. It's pretty boring stuff, really. Besides, now is what counts, now that I've started over."

Of course I more than make up for her reticence. I tell her everything. When Justin's not there—at Group, or asleep, or playing by himself—or sometimes even when he is, I confide in her, spelling out the words I don't want him to hear, letting her attentive gaze, her soft, reassuring comments, wash over me. I've also used her shamelessly since she moved in—for driving me places (with Justin in the backseat); for back rubs; for standing by when I shower, lest I slip, and blow-drying my hair afterwards; for bringing me warmed milk on a tray, with honey, sometimes a plate of oatmeal cookies the two of them have just baked.

(She even *irons!* Larry's handkerchiefs. Says it relaxes her.)

In some ways, she may be the younger sibling I never had. Yet try her on a Monday morning when she shows up from her weekend, all puffy-eyed and surly, then closets herself all day with Justin. No, "surly" isn't fair, but moody, absolutely uncommunicative. Once she said she needs Mondays to "decompress." (Decompress from what? The stepfather? Some boyfriend she hasn't told me about?) I asked her, well in advance, about Thanksgiving, thinking she might want to go home to Minnesota where I think she still has some family, and that we'd offer to pay for her ticket. Oh no, she said, startled, she'd much rather stay east, with us. If that was all right? Fine, I said. But when I suggested inviting the stepfather to Thanksgiving dinner, Oh no (visibly disconcerted), he'd have other plans.

Soit, as they say in French. So be it.

Occasionally, when I catch her unawares, I find her gazing out a window, a far-off stare. Her legs are apart, and she's rolled forward onto the balls of her feet, almost to tiptoe, fists propped on the windowsill, and on her face is such a grim and tight-lipped expression. Jaws set, chin jutting. Very un-Harriet. Although I invariably back away, it's occurred to me that she's thinking about *him* then, Johnny, the broken love affair she told me about. But I've never, since that first day, gotten her to talk about it.

Only once, an idle remark: "I've always had trouble with men."

I think of this as her *French Lieutenant's Woman* look.

It's even occurred to me she might be gay.

Larry, though, can't keep his eyes off her.

Neither can my son.

As far as Justin Coffey's concerned, I think he'd lay down his life for her, I really do.

All fixed: alarm, shutters, Harriet.

And then there's Larry.

Some fifty people were fired from Shaw Cross on "Bloody Wednesday" last month, but thank God, Lawrence Elgin Coffey wasn't one of them. Apparently he thought he was going to be. At least that's how he explained all the hush-hush with Holbrook the night before. Instead they made him an offer— "right off the dorsal fin, honey, totally unexpected" —and when I cornered him that night, in the den, he was still "running the numbers," still trying to see if it would "fly."

I made us shrimp wok, took it in to him on one of our lacquered trays with a Bass Ale and chilled glass mug and a little vase of mums from the garden. He was sitting in the Stickley I gave him one Father's Day, talking on the phone. One of its little desk arms was piled high with papers; the other held the phone, a tumbler of Scotch, a yellow legal pad with pages folded back, and his calculator with the printer.

He was in his stocking feet, his shoes across the room under the desk. At this point, I knew nothing of what had happened, but I was all geared up. The minute he got off the phone, I announced that I couldn't go on living as before, not seven months pregnant.

Distractedly, he said he understood.

"Not to worry, honey," he said, still focusing on the calculator tape. "Everything's going to change now."

Then I told him I'd invited Harriet to move in. I expected a monumental row, but all I got out of him was, "Dynamite move, Georgie. You just do whatever you have to do."

"Well, maybe," I said, exasperated, "you could stop whatever you're doing for just two minutes, and tell me what the hell is going on. And where you really were last night?"

He looked up at me, his moon face now in a big grin, then stood, stretched, and then, picking up his bowl in one hand and his chopsticks in the other, he told me about Lawrence E. Coffey and Company.

We now refer to it around here as "The Deal."

Most days we're going to make a fortune; every so often, there's trouble, everything stops, and we're on the phone endlessly—with Holbrook, Joe Penzil, other people. ("We," of course, is Larry.) Essentially The Deal, as he explained it, is that he's becoming—I guess has already become—a kind of independent agent, selling Shaw Cross "products" on commission. And working from home until he gets his act together—a mixed blessing—although he still goes into the office most mornings and his salary, under his old "deal," doesn't run out till January.

"The beauty of it, Georgie," he declaimed that night in the den, "is that it fits Reality like a glove. When you stop to think about it, what am I if not a great seller? If the whole industry is going back to fundamentals, and that, for me, means selling— Kee-rist, when it comes to selling, I'm a fucking genius!" Grinning broadly, his glass mug raised in some kind of a toast. "The old Bear still has a few secrets up his sleeve. Believe me, baby."

For what it's worth, I do believe him. Maybe other people don't—I'm constantly asked how he is, a kind of once-removed pulse-taking—but if Larry Coffey believes, I do, too. For one thing, I've been there before with him. The time they took his commissions away at Shaw Cross, we had the same crisis atmosphere, the near-total self-absorption, the interminable telephone huddles with Holbrook et al. But Larry came out on top then and, to judge from what's been happening this time, he's going to make a success of Lawrence E. Coffey and Company too.

Craig thinks I'm jealous.

Maybe I am, a little. I used to think my husband makes a truly *astounding* amount of money. (I still do, actually.) But now that I've seen a little of him in action, his indefatigable enthusiasm when he's on the "horn"—"shoring up my customer base," he calls it—I can't but think that's what God, in his wisdom, made him to do.

As for me, I quit the work force seven years ago. All it took, at the time, was Larry's running the numbers for me and the (gruesome) discovery that what I made in a year on the magazine, after deductions, was what he pulled down in a good week.

Exit Career Girl.

Enter, seven years later, your classic, and very pregnant, Suburban Mommy.

Is that why God made me?

It's as though I'm having the post-partum first. I wake up this morning from bad dreams I can't remember. Drenched in sweat. And the baby kicking, the terrible taste in my mouth, the dragging, aching limbs, and, transcending the physical, a weird sense of foreboding so powerful I feel as though I have to get out of here or go mad. Out of my body would be best, but I'll settle for out of my room, the house, St. George.

But to go where?

Yesterday was my last session with Craig till after the baby. I can't take the back and forth to the city any longer, even with someone else driving. Just getting in and out of the car, I could use a derrick. I'm a hippo. I've gained over thirty pounds, which Dubin keeps saying is fine. I can't even see the scale anymore below my bulge, I have to call Harriet, and it could be my scale is off, but Dubin's doesn't lie.

Craig did wish me luck. But then, with his habitual and insufferable banality, he opined that my troubles lately may simply have been that I haven't had enough to do!

(What did he mean by that? That if I don't have things to do, I revert to my natural state, which is one of pure hysteria?)

It's true, I've never been so pampered. I have Clotie five days a week now, and she and Harriet have taken over most of the cooking from me. I hardly see Justin anymore, he's so devoted to his precious " 'arrit." A few weeks ago, I let him move upstairs to the room next to hers (their idea, not mine) and had the workmen in to redo his old room into a nursery. I had them paint it a neutral yellow just in case (although I'm *sure* it's going to be a girl this time), but now it's done, they're gone, the new furniture has been ordered (because Justin's old stuff, in the basement, turned out to be mildewed), and what am I supposed to do with myself other than focus on a body that doesn't feel as though it's mine anymore?

If Dubin tells me to listen to Mozart one more time, I think I'll scream!

On an impulse—a weird one, admittedly—I've just gotten my mother on the phone. I find myself asking if I can come over.

"In the city?" she says, a little surprised.

"Yes." (Where else?)

"Well, of course you can, when do you want to come? And how will you get here?"

"Today, actually. This afternoon. I thought I'd stay for dinner, maybe spend the night in my old room, stay tomorrow, maybe even Sunday."

"But what's wrong?" my mother says. "Is something wrong?"

"No, of course not," I answer, knowing how her mind works. What I'm really thinking, I suddenly realize, is: Friday night dinner. Throughout my childhood, my father, who is Jewish—my mother isn't—but who never set foot in a synagogue (at least he hasn't in my lifetime), nevertheless insisted on saying the blessing over the Friday night bread. (In Hebrew, no less.) "I'm just feeling a little antsy, is all. The pregnancy blues. I guess it's the endless waiting." I add, "I'd like to see you too."

"You mean you'd like to see your father," she says tartly.

"I mean I'd like to see *both* of you," I correct.

"But if you're here, who's going to be taking care of Justin and Larry?"

"Well, Harriet's here for Justin. And—"

"Oh, is she? Since when is she working weekends too?"

And—of course—she isn't. Well, I decide, she'll have to this once. If necessary, I'll pay her double whatever it works out to be. Just this once, she can just do it. Do it for me.

But she won't.

After I hang up from my mother, I call her in, and she says, "Georgia! I know I've committed to staying all the time once you go into the hospital, but that's not for a couple of weeks. And you know I'm always gone weekends. Whatever could you have been thinking?"

"I wasn't thinking," I admit. "But it's important to me. Damned important. If I don't get out of this house, I'm going to go absolutely nuts."

But, to my amazement, I can't budge her, not even to staying over tonight if I come home tomorrow.

"I'm sorry, Georgia," she says quietly, "I just can't. I've other plans."

"Other plans? What other plans?" Then suddenly —I can't help it—I fly off the handle. "How can you do this to me—I thought we were *friends?* Don't you realize how important it is to me?"

And how (to my simultaneous shame) she is, without a doubt, the best paid nanny I've ever heard of? And what about all the little gifts I've bought her— the sweaters, the silver earrings with her birthstone, the framed Redoutés for her room?—yet have I ever asked her to do *anything* outside the confines of her job before now? And how (worst of all), if she's ever going to amount to anything in this world, doesn't she think she'd better learn to accommodate herself a little to other people's needs?

I stop, shocked by everything I've just said. It's *horrible!* For God's sake, this is *Harriet!*

I burst into tears.

"Oh, God . . . ," I stammer, unable to look at her. And, lamely, something about the pregnancy, hormones, claustrophobia. I can't bear to look up.

Finally I do. She's smiling at me.

"Let me see what I can do," she says calmly.

Now, no matter what I say, I can't dissuade her. She leaves. She's gone a good fifteen minutes. While she's gone—other horrible confession—I pick up the receiver to see if she's talking to him (her stepfather, I mean), but I get the dial tone instead. I must have missed them. She comes back shortly afterwards, her face uncommonly pale but her chin jutting with resolve. What she's going to do, she says, is stay through Justin's supper, then go home, have dinner with her stepfather, then come back and spend the night here. She'll stay as long as I need her tomorrow during the day, but she'll have to be gone tomorrow night. Will that help?

"Oh, Harriet," I say, "it's all so *stupid,* so unnecessary. For God's sake, why can't Larry and Justin fend for themselves for just one night and one day? Or I won't go. What's gotten into me? What do I think's going to happen to them, that they'll *starve?*"

But she won't hear it, won't hear my apologies either, and when I mention money again, she cuts me off. She has to leave to pick Justin up from Group, but after lunch, the two of them drive me all the way in to Riverside Drive, and when I emerge from the car, I can't help thinking: *Why on earth am I doing this?*

Maybe to be with my father?

He isn't imposing physically—he's rather short in fact, and slightly built, and bald-pated though with a long and silver-gray fringe—and, unlike most psychoanalysts I've met, he's quiet socially. Self-contained. Maybe that accounts for his appeal to women, that and his eyes. They're dark, piercing, impenetrable at the same time. Even when he's simply listening, observing, they seem to shine.

But he doesn't get home till almost eight.

My mother, meanwhile, works me over about my weight gain—how will I ever get my figure back? how could I have let it happen?—and then starts grilling me about Larry. What exactly is he doing now? Forming his own business, I explain. But isn't that something of a comedown for him? Wasn't he an officer of the company, and a very prestigious company? And for most people who go out on their own, it takes a long time, do we have enough money put aside?

"Well," my mother says, "at least now he won't have any excuses, nights."

"What do you mean by that?"

She looks at me, surprised. Haven't I, myself, complained about how often he comes home late? And what about the night the alarm system went off?

I end up defending Larry, how a big part of what he does involves wining and dining his customers and that's unlikely to change.

"Well, Georgia," she goes on, "I don't see how

you stand it. I've told you for a long time that you'd better put your foot down. What right does he have to leave you all alone, particularly when you're pregnant? And how do you know where he is, all those nights?"

"Are you accusing him of having affairs on the side?"

"I'm not accusing him of anything. That's your business, not mine. You've got to live with it. All I'm saying is that if I'd put my foot down years ago with your father, maybe things would be different now."

And there we are. I realize, too late, that I've let myself be sucked in. I'll be damned if I'll ask her how things are between them, but once launched, she needs no help. He treats her like garbage, she says. He's always hiding behind his precious patients, or trying to, and her whole life is nothing but a misery of well-founded suspicions and his ducking. The saddest part, I think as I listen, isn't that there's no basis for her rancor—my father, I'm aware, has been less than faithful over the years—but that she feels compelled to involve me in it.

I manage to escape finally by pleading fatigue. In my old room, I lie down on the bed. Not to sleep, however. The few old familiars—the bed, the dresser, my old desk with the flip-down front, the same rose-patterned wallpaper—no longer say *me*, and the room has taken on a strangely anonymous character. Occupant gone, destination unknown. A little later, I steal down the back hall and into my father's study.

It was always, for me, the magical center of our apartment. A small room, then as now. Its one window gives out on a shaft, and the only furniture, apart from the bookshelves that line the walls, is his writing desk and chair, an electric typewriter on its own rolling table, and his old easy chair with the overhanging floor lamp. When I was little, the shelves contained a virtual library of psychoanalysis. Since then, I realize with amusement, it has become a library, mainly, of Herbert Alan Levy. His own published works are there, in all their editions and translations, the relevant manuscripts in neatly labeled boxes, and row upon row of his "casebooks." These are cloth-bound blank books, ordered through his publisher. Each of his patients gets one or more volumes, a kind of diary of his or her treatment, and they constitute the source, or raw material, of his published writings.

Virtually every important conversation I've ever had with him has taken place in this room. I can almost hear the echo of the little girl who sat in his lap or, later, the teenager who straddled the desk chair back to front, her arms draped. I can (do) mark the crises of my young life in terms of my visits to that room.

But that was then, now is now.

I leave, wait, help my mother with dinner, call home.

He comes at last.

All during the meal, I find myself wondering: How can I get him alone? No answer. But over coffee in the living room, he says, "Georgie, is everything all right with you? Aside from the fact that, any day now, you're going to have a baby?"

"I'm okay, more or less."

"Really?" he says. "You look troubled to me somehow."

"I've been telling her that all day," my mother interjects.

"Is there anything you want to talk about? Just to me?" His eyes still focused on me.

He asks it a little cruelly, as though she's not there. I glance at her—reflex of guilt?—but she stands, saying in an ironic tone, "You don't have to ask my permission," and abruptly we're alone.

"I'd like that very much," I say.

"I thought so. Well, come along. Let's go in the back. It'll be quieter there. I'll give you an hour on the house."

Old joke between us.

In his study, he puts me in the easy chair and sits at his desk backward, straddling the chair as I used to. His chin resting on his fists.

"You really don't look so hot, Georgie," he says. "*Is* there something wrong?"

I'm tempted to answer: *Nothing and everything.* Now that I'm alone with him, I'm tempted to say a lot of things, my whole Daddy's Little Girl megillah. Instead I burble something about it having been a difficult pregnancy, the last couple of months.

But he doesn't let it go.

"What does your gynecologist say?" he asks.

"Dubin?" I shrug. "Dubin calls me the very model of a baby factory. Says we're both fine, mother and baby, all the vital signs. My cervix is holding nicely; the baby is growing; etc., etc. Says I should relax, let people wait on me, drink my milk, and listen to Mozart."

"Is that so terrible?" he asks, smiling.

No, of course it isn't. And as for the symptoms I've suffered this past month—the sharp contractions that convince me I'm about to deliver early, the shortness of breath and the queasiness, assorted aches and pains, even this morning's rampant rebellion—what will he make of them if Dubin makes nothing? Or the sensation that my body has been taken over for another purpose, when in fact it has?

The pregnant woman's syndrome, I think. But this is my second time around, not my first, and I don't remember any of it with Justin. (Was I too excited with Justin? Too enthralled by the grandeur of motherhood?)

My father asks about Justin. Wittily, I think, I describe how his grandson has fallen in love, at three and a half, and how I've lost him not only to Harriet but to the Age of Chivalry—knights, castles, and the Holy Grail. He asks about Larry (never having been a fan), and I find myself defending my husband all over again, The Deal and Lawrence E. Coffey and Company. He asks about my therapist. I tell him I think Craig is something of a dunce. He laughs, says there's no law he knows of that says an analyst has to be a genius in order to be effective—but is it my imagination or is he secretly pleased that I find Craig lacking what, face it, only Daddy can provide?

"Then what is it, Georgie?" he asks in a sympathetic tone. "What's really bothering you? It can't just be the pregnancy. You've done that before."

Sympathetic or not, the question irritates me momentarily. Who was it who said that if men had to bear babies, the race would long since have been extinct?

But he's right, of course. He almost always is.

And then, just as I'm thinking that, I suddenly, unaccountably, start to cry! Second time today. Oh

God, I'm so *ashamed!* But I can't stop, and knowing I can't only makes it worse. I'm aware, sniveling and sobbing, that he's on his feet and next to me, one hand on my hair, and offering a white handkerchief. I take it.

"Oh God," I manage. "Talk about hormone swings!"

But I can't stop. It's like a storm that has to run its course. Or some weird chemical rush inside my body. I sob, and get the hiccups, and blow hard into the handkerchief, but the honking, snorting sound—hippos, elephants, whales—sets me off again. I hate it, hate myself for blubbering like a two-year-old. And in front of him!

But if I can't cry in front of my own father, who then?

"And you're *right*, Daddy," I protest tearfully, "this isn't my first time, it's my *second!* But you don't know what it's like in here!"

I try to describe it, but I can't. I gather myself while he watches sympathetically. I start over again with today, how I woke up feeling trapped inside my own skin, and the dreams I couldn't remember but that set off the panic in me, the overwhelming urge to get out, the baby kicking as though it too had to get out, and then the awful scene with Harriet.

"What it is," I say finally, "is that I'm frightened in here almost all the time. It's been going on for a month, more. Nameless fears, jumping at shadows. Maybe it *is* just the pregnancy—I feel like shit, physically—but I wake up convinced something bad is about to happen, or maybe already has but I don't know about it, and I know that sounds stupid if I don't know what it is, but that doesn't mean it's not there, does it?"

"What does Craig say?"

I flare at this.

"Do you know what he says? He says I'm not keeping *busy* enough!"

My father smiles.

"I'm not understanding, though, Georgie," he says. "Is it that you're afraid something bad's going to happen to your baby?"

"Maybe. Or already has. Or to me, or both of us."

But that's not it either. Sometimes I think I'm going to drop the baby any second, sometimes I think she'll never come out, but I guess that's normal. What I feel is more free-floating, unfocused, I can't explain. It's like a character in some Stephen King novel, when the bad's right there but nobody knows it. Except I doubt my father has ever read a Stephen King novel.

He's closed his eyes, rubs at the corners. The gesture calms me somehow. I used to tease him about it. He does it, he's always joked, because it gives him a precious few seconds to think of something — anything—when he's supposed to produce an insight for a patient. Only tonight there is no special insight. All he says is that I only have a few more weeks to get through and then, whatever I'm afraid of, it will be over. Meanwhile, I just have to grit my teeth. Getting through, gritting my teeth. He reminds me that I've never been very good in situations over which I've no control. He reminisces: about when I was little and just learning to talk, God help them if he or my mother didn't understand what I was trying to say. I've heard this before. I remind him too that, if he's right about me and my need to control situations, then it must be a straight gene pass-through, father to daughter.

We laugh familiarly together.

At the same time, there's something missing. Didn't I cry, confess? So where's my catharsis? Instead, he looks at me, I look at him, and I realize suddenly that I'm looking at an old face, tired, distracted even. Maybe his mind is elsewhere? Well, but he *is* old, I think, sixty-six this year, even though he still keeps a full slate of patients. What right do I have to inflict myself on him?

I want to reach out, smooth the wrinkles on his face, check, as I once did, for places he may have missed, shaving. In the end, though, we're just gazing at each other. A little sadly, I think. At least I feel the sadness in me.

I stand. Half-cuddling his head, I kiss him on the forehead. He stands too, and we hug awkwardly because of my girth. I feel his hand briefly in my hair, and then he's patting me gently on the back.

Old gestures.

"I'm glad you came," he murmurs. Then, smiling at me, "It's a great life if you don't weaken."

Old line.

17 November

I sleep better than I have in months. Well, longer at least, for when I wake up, a little before ten, the taste is in my mouth again and I'm assaulted by new waves of anxiety. What am I doing here, separated from my family? Suppose something's happened to them? That they need me? Am I so selfish—so self-absorbed, anyway—that I could just *abandon* them like that?

My father has already "made his escape," on a Saturday, and my mother is fuming. According to her, he had a call early this morning. One of his patients had a crisis during the night. He left immediately, not knowing when he'd be back.

I'm just about to call home when the first stab hits me. I all but double over, but I can't double over. The grabbing pain makes me gasp for air. I sit down. Oh, God.

It passes. I realize I've broken into a sweat. I try to remember the breathing exercises from Justin. I didn't take the course this time because I didn't think I needed to. Failing to remember, I take deep slow breaths.

I wait. Three, four minutes. My mother is somewhere else in the apartment. I'm not feeling the baby. Then—the same suddenness, no warning—it hits again.

I fight the panic, the tears that well involuntarily from the biting pain.

When it passes this time, I call home. I talk to Harriet, Justin, Larry. All of them seem strangely distant. I tell Harriet what's happening. Justin asks, "Why are you calling, Mommy?" Struggling for calm, I tell him it's because I miss him. Apparently this doesn't make much of an impression—he and " 'arrit" are watching Saturday morning cartoons.

I end up hollering at Larry. When I ask him to come get me, now, he hesitates. Something about some calls he has to make. The Deal. (On a Saturday?) He says he thought I was staying over till to-

morrow anyway. I tell him, for Christ's sake, I'm
cramping, I think I'm going into labor! He reminds
me that I'm not due for another three weeks, probably it's a false alarm, and then my mother—she
must have come in without my hearing—is shouting
at me, "Just tell him to meet you at the hospital!"

The next attack is some ten minutes later, then
longer, then quick, quick, three- or four-minute in-
tervals. My mother has made me lie down. She
wants to make me tea, but all I can take is water.
After an hour of it, I call Dubin's office, get the answering service, and then, a few minutes later, Dr.
Orloff calls me back. He's a partner in the practice.
I don't know him, except that he has a black mus-
tache and an oily voice and somebody said his ex-
aminations hurt more than Dubin's. He too
mentions the hospital. He's headed there himself,
wants me to meet him there. Clearly it's a matter of
his convenience. I say back—maybe I'm shrieking—
that I don't want the hospital, and for that matter, I
don't want him, I want my own doctor. He says
that's impossible, he's covering for all the office's
patients. Now I *am* shrieking—the idea of a stranger
delivering my baby!—and I've got Dubin's home
number, and he's always told me not to worry, any
time, morning, noon or night . . .

I guess Orloff's happy as not to get rid of me. Half
an hour later, Dubin calls me back. Apparently he's
on a golf course somewhere in Westchester, even in
November, but no matter. He listens to me, tells me
to take it easy. He says what I'm describing doesn't
sound like the beginning of labor to him, but that
doesn't matter either. He'll meet me at the office at
one.

A little over an hour.

I lie down again. I hear my mother mobilizing Harriet, Larry. She tells them what Larry should bring. My last contraction is in the taxi heading downtown (fingernails digging into the upholstery), and then there's Dubin, in his white coat over a V-neck sweater, rubber gloves on his hands, bending over me and saying, "Okay, Georgie, let's check the two of you out."

Irritable uterus.

It's nighttime now. I'm home again; the house is quiet. Harriet has gone off, Justin's asleep, Larry's watching some football game downstairs. I'm on my chaise longue, writing in my diary.

Dubin gave me two choices. Either I can go into the hospital now, and stay there until the baby comes, or I can go home, but to bed. No activity and, yes, rest and relaxation.

"But what's wrong with me?" I asked him.

"Nothing at all," he answered. "In fact, everything looks fine. Your cervix is holding nicely and it hasn't begun to soften. The baby's in good position, the heartbeat regular. No fibroids. I see no reason why you shouldn't carry to term."

"Then why is this happening? And why do I have to go to bed?"

"Because we want to keep the uterus quiet, and I don't want to give you anything for it, this late in the day. Too much activity has been known to stimulate early labor, and even though the baby's already viable, we don't want to encourage the process. Besides, what's so bad about a couple of weeks in bed?"

Nothing. Nothing really.

My father just called. He sounds depressed. One of his patients, a reformed drug addict, tried to commit suicide last night, and right now my father can't dispel the idea that he'd have been better off succeeding.

Unusual, I think in passing, for him to admit something like that.

I tell him about me—paltry stuff by comparison. I ask him to thank my mother again. I thank him, too, for last night. He says what's to thank him for. For listening, I say. It did me good. We wish each other good night, and I hang up, and there we are, me and my baby, and my irritable uterus.

Still, there's a question none of them has answered. Not Dubin, or Craig, or my father.

Why do I lie awake, so many nights, anticipating the worst?

15 December

"What do you mean precisely, that he's out of control?"

"Call it what you want, I can't string him out any longer."

"Don't say can't. I think you've handled him magnificently so far, and you're almost there, aren't you?"

"Almost there? We'd be done if it weren't for them! Now they're taking off for the holidays. The bombs could be falling, and they've still got to have their fucking hols."

"Well, that's how they do things in the more civilized countries. Why can't you go on vacation too?"

"I've already been on vacation as far as he's concerned. I've been in Europe, Japan, you name it. I've been to the fucking moon. I've ducked, I've been out sick, I've practically gotten under my desk. Don't forget, he still comes in almost every day."

"So what are you telling me? That you're the problem?"

"Come on. He's been talking to the wrong people, for one thing."

"What people?"

"You know who I'm talking about. Some of my oldest friends, yours too, originally. He's been telling them that from now on they'll be doing business with him and him alone. He's even tried to get some of them to sign a piece of paper. No way I can let that go on."

"Why not? Aren't you planning on deep-sixing some of them?"

"Not all of them, for Christ's sake. Do you want me to put us out of business? How would that look? And how would it look if the guy I've told them they don't have to bother about because he's out of the fucking business ends up with a hundred percent of our customers?"

"A slight exaggeration."

"Even so. I've had to ask people to stop talking to him. It's fucking awkward. By now he's gotten that message, and I understand he's more than irate . . . well, isn't he?"

"Yes."

"Hell, he's not that dumb. Plus his wife's about to have a baby."

"What on earth does that have to do with it?"

"It makes him jumpy, volatile. I hear it's been a difficult pregnancy. Jesus Christ, I wish to hell I'd pulled the plug a couple of months ago."

"But you didn't."

"Yeah. Well, it's easy for you to say, you're not in the fucking trenches. I tell you, I've had it. I'm not kidding. Finished. I can't do it anymore. I say it's time to bite the bullet."

"With everything that's at stake?"

"With everything that's at stake."

"All right, let's look at that a minute. Assuming you do it, when would that be?"

"I don't know. I thought I'd let him pick up the final paperwork tomorrow. Maybe he won't read it right away if his wife drops her baby. The minute he does though, it's going to get ugly."

"What do you think he'll do?"

"I think he'll start screaming his head off in every direction. Unless we stop him."

"Do you think he'll find anyone to listen, the week before Christmas?"

"I don't know. He might."

"So you're agreed there's a risk, but you're ready to run it?"

"What about you, partner?"

"What do you mean?"

"What about the insurance?"

"I don't know what you're talking about."

"Come on. I understand there's some kind of insurance policy. Maybe the time's come to cash it in, whatever it is."

"Where did you hear that?"

"Never mind. I—"

"I repeat: Where did you hear that? I want to know, and I want to know now."

"Hell, don't get your balls in an uproar. A little birdie told me."

"Who?"

"Okay, okay. Our friendly neighborhood counselor."

"You mean their attorney?"

"None other."

"Have you told him I'm involved?"

"Of course not!"

"Are you sure?"

"Of course I'm sure, what do you—?"

"And what precisely did he say?"

"Nothing. He just said that, if push came to shove, there was insurance. He said it showed admirable foresight on all our parts. I didn't know what the fuck he was talking about."

"Is that all he said?"

"That's all he said."

"I see."

"Well? . . . Is that all you're going to say? I see? What's the insurance?"

"It's nothing. You don't know anything about it."

"Oh, no? Hey, that's great! I love being left in the dark! What the—"

"You listen to me now. Listen carefully. I'm going to take care of it. Unless you hear otherwise from me, you go ahead and do whatever you have to do."

"But—"

"I said: I'll take care of it."

"Wait a minute, if you think . . . Hello? Hello? . . . Goddamn son of a bitch!"

Lawrence Elgin Coffey

17 December

When it all comes down, it all comes down.

I'm a father again. That's what I have to keep telling myself. There I am, in the hospital this morning, holding the little bundle in my hands. A fucking miracle. Dubin has already sewed Georgie up and left, and Georgie is out like a light, but I'm holding my baby daughter, little Miss 7 lbs. 4 oz., and the tears are running down my cheeks.

Look, the whole thing's been a little hairy. Everybody was totally convinced Georgie was going to drop the baby ahead of time. Then suddenly she's more than a week overdue, and trying to wait it out but no sign of labor, and then Dr. Dubin starts talking C-section. This was last Friday. The next thing I know, it's today, Monday morning, early, and I'm driving her in to the hospital.

Dubin said on Friday that the only alternative was induced labor, with a real possibility we'd end up with a C-section anyway, but in extremis. "Let's do it now," he recommended. "There's nothing to be gained by waiting. I've got a slot open Monday morning. That way we'll get you out before Christmas. Nobody wants to be stuck in a hospital over Christmas.''

"Including doctors?" I said.

He laughed at that, but Christmas aside, I know what it's all about. It's the malpractice insurance. They don't take chances anymore. The slightest complication and it's C-section time, and Dubin had a slot open, and he doesn't want to be stuck over Christmas either.

"I don't really care," Georgie said bravely. "I've already had the so-called birth experience anyway, and it's not all it's cracked up to be."

Jesus, I thought, that's major surgery and, as experienced as they are at it, it's . . . well, it's still major surgery.

"I just want it over," Georgie said.

But the spinal doesn't take with her. She's sitting on a hospital table, naked except for one of those half-smocks, and these two mechanics are poking and probing at her back. She's shivering like a leaf. It hurts, she says, plus they've taken all her jewelry away, even her wedding band. But the spinal doesn't take, they end up giving her full anesthesia anyway, and she's crying because it means she'll miss the birth altogether. That's how come I'm the first of our family to meet our daughter, Miss 7 lbs. 4 oz., with a hospital identification bracelet on her tiny wrist. She's fine, they tell me. Then they take the bundle away. They tell me Georgie's fine too but that she won't really be coming out of it for another hour and a half.

I call downtown. According to Annabelle Morgan, my deal is ready—finally, the bastards—and I can pick it up any time. It takes all my powers of persuasion to get her to messenger the papers to the hospital. I meet the messenger at the information desk, and I'm back upstairs by the time Georgie comes out of the anesthesia.

That's where I am now, in a state of shock.

Georgie looks like hell, her skin all gray, but she's trying to smile.

"It's a little girl, honey," I tell her, bending over her. "We've got ourselves a baby daughter."

"I know," she answers faintly.

"How do you know that?" She made such a big deal, during all the ultrasounds, of not wanting to know.

"It doesn't matter," she says, trying to smile some more. "I've always *known*. Inside. I know her name too."

"What's her name?" I say, but even as I say it, her eyes are closed, she's dropped off.

Her parents show up, but I'm in no shape to talk to anybody. The room is crammed with flowers, including—you want irony?—an arrangement from good old Shaw Cross. Georgie wakes up again. They want to give her Demerol. She doesn't want Demerol, she wants her baby.

Somebody—her mother?—says to me, "Isn't she a gorgeous baby?"

"Yeah," I mumble. "Awfully proud too."

I guess I am, or would be if I wasn't in such a daze.

I've already read my deal.

Read it? I already know it by heart, the cocksuckers!

The operative clause anyway.

The bastards have clobbered me. They strung me out for two months—two whole months!—and now, at the end of the day, they've bitten me off at the knees!

For Christ's sake, I'm out of business before I even get started!

I can't leave the hospital, though. How can I leave?

I have to outwait everybody.

Jesus.

Finally they're gone. I lean over Georgie, her hair dark against the pillows.

"Her name is Zoe," she says softly, looking up at me.

I almost ask, *Whose name is Zoe?*

"Zoe," she repeats. "Zoe Coffey. Your new daughter. Zoe Elizabeth Coffey. What's wrong? Don't you like it?"

"No, fine. It's a fine name. Zoe Coffey. It even rhymes."

"I love it," she says.

"Look, honey, it's been a horrendous day. They've put you through the mill. You need to get some rest now. I guess I'm a little tired too, and I still have to go home, check on Harriet and the kid."

"Do you think I should take the Demerol? I'm hurting awfully."

"Of course you should." I bend over, kiss her. "You do whatever you want to do. And I'll be back, first thing in the morning."

I read it to Penzil over the phone, the minute I get home. It—the operative clause in the agreement—says:

Coffey will be free to develop his own accounts ("The New Accounts"), which will henceforth be considered his in exclusivity, *provided, however, that Coffey agrees not to trespass on any of the Company's pre-existing accounts or relationships.*

"Is that new language," Penzil asks after I've repeated it, "or a new concept?"

"New? It's out of fucking left field! Totally!"

"What exactly does it mean to you?"

"What do you mean, what does it mean? It means what it says: 'Coffey agrees not to trespass on any of the Company's pre-existing accounts or relationships.' For Christ's sake, the stuff I sell? Big Bears? It's pretty sophisticated, Joe, high-ticket. It's not for your average pigeon. Do you know how many customers there are, worldwide? Shit, if I can't 'trespass on pre-existing accounts,' which means anybody The Cross did business with before, which means anybody *I* did business with before, then who the fuck am I supposed to sell to? Georgie's cousin Millie in Houston?"

"Now calm down, Bear. Are you telling me you had no inkling this was coming?"

"Joe! They've been diddling me for two whole months, you know that! It's been like pulling teeth, getting the paperwork out of them, and there was this detail to negotiate, that to decide, and Gamble was away, or Gamble's been too tied up, or—"

"But this is substantive, Bear. This isn't just a detail."

"No shit, Sherlock! Joe, I had everybody lined up, all my old customers! They knew that. They knew I was talking to them right along! What they're doing now is putting me out of business!''

Even as I say it, I hear Holbrook in my ears. *Expand your customer base.* He's been saying it for weeks, that I can't rely solely on my Shaw Cross contacts. And God knows I've been trying.

"Maybe it's just a negotiating tactic," Penzil is saying.

"*Negotiating* tactic?"

"Maybe somebody—Gamble, I don't know—woke up at the last minute and realized they were giving you the store for no good reason. Maybe somebody said, 'Why the hell are we paying Coffey a full commission on house accounts? It's going to cost us a fortune.' Maybe they figured the only way they could back off was to hit you with a worst case and negotiate their way out of it when you blew your cork. Maybe—"

But it's *not* a negotiating tactic. Suddenly I get it, the whole picture. They've just dropped the other shoe.

For the last week or so, my phone has gone progressively dead. Mulcahy, first. No, Mr. Mulcahy isn't in the office, he's away on vacation. Where? On some island in the Caribbean. But can't I call him there? I'm sorry, Mr. Coffey, the phone service down there is practically nonexistent. But Mr. Mulcahy will be calling in once a day, do I want to leave a message?

I leave a message. He doesn't call. Maybe I'd have thought it unusual—time was Gerry Mulcahy wouldn't go to the john without calling me first— and left it at that, but then it happened again. This one out sick, that one also on vacation.

In early December?

Of course I noticed it! But I didn't have time to focus. Once Georgie's due date arrived, and the baby still hadn't dropped, she hit this deep depression. She'd been flat on her back mostly—Dubin's orders—and now, I could tell, she was scared shitless. I'd hear her calling for Harriet, and when I went upstairs to see how she was doing, Harriet would be leaning over her, over the bed, and she—Georgie—would say something like, "I'm hanging in there, Larry," in her small voice, "I'll be okay," and I couldn't tell her *anything* about what was going on. I couldn't concentrate. I just couldn't *focus!*

And now this! This isn't the beginning of a negotiation. This is the *end* of one!

Penzil is saying something about legal remedies. Penzil thinks that, provided everything I say is true and documented, I have the basis of legal action, with damages. Penzil is asking me about my paper trail.

"I don't give a flying fuck about my paper trail!" I yell at him. "I want Gamble by the short hairs!"

"Now calm down, Bear." That's what he keeps saying, over and over, that I should calm down. Keep cool. Nothing rash. It's late, I should sleep on it. We'll talk about it in the morning. Am I taking the 7:12? He'll meet me on the platform. Above all, I should calm down.

I calm down enough to know that, for once, I don't want Joe talking me out of anything.

Even back in November, well before my phone went dead, I may have smelled a rat. This was when the Great White had Schwartzenberg running inter-

ference for him, and I had a draft of an agreement
(without the no-trespassing clause), but every time I
tried to pin Schwartzenberg down, I got stuff like,
"You know him as well as I do, Larry. He's got to be
hands-on," or, "Leon says just go ahead and set it
up, we'll pick up on the details later."

So that's what I did. I set it up. For two fucking
months.

But I also stirred up the ashes a little.

The Aquarium had been damn near decimated on
Bloody Wednesday. The Great White cut a wide
swath through the ranks generally, but Big Bear's
troops tasted the sword almost to a man. It made no
sense. Even Howie MacFarlane, for Christ's sake. If
anyone didn't deserve it, it was MacFarlane. Do you
know what the poor bastard's doing now? He's driving a taxi, while his résumé sits in a pile on a hundred or so desks. I've told him, "I hope to hell you
don't find anything. Just sit tight till I get my act
together."

Everybody I talked to, when I was still going in,
mornings, said, "Yeah, it's tough, but you know the
score, Bear. It's the times. We're all bleeding."
Meanwhile, I was told to give over my accounts
temporarily to some four-eyed young nerd who'd
been parachuted in off the trading desk, and I said
to my customers, who thought The Cross was playing some kind of joke on them, "Just hold on to your
money, guys, the Bear'll be up and running come
January."

After a while, though, I stopped going in. It was
too much of a downer. One day a hero, the next a
bum, because not only did the survivors treat me

like some kind of leper, so did people I ran into who'd been put out on the street.

"It stands to reason, Bear," MacFarlane explained. "In their eyes, you came out smelling like a rose. For all they know, you sold them down the river."

"But that's a crock!" I protested.

"You and I may know that, but . . ."

"*Do* you? Do you know that?"

"Yeah," he said, but with about as much conviction as a caterpillar trying to cross Fifth Avenue in rush hour.

Still, it was MacFarlane I turned to in mid-November.

"Come on, babe, I need your help," I told him on the horn. "You're still pretty plugged in at The Cross, aren't you? I want to find out what the fuck's going on." I alluded to the runaround I'd been getting from Schwartzenberg, but beyond that, the sentiment on the Street was that The Cross had overreacted on Bloody Wednesday and no one knew why, not even Holbrook. Sure, as Holbrook pointed out, in a privately held company only a handful of people know the real numbers, but even in a quiet market, which was the understatement of the year, was there any way The Cross could actually be losing money? Only making less, maybe. And even then . . . ?

"You're right about one thing, Bear," MacFarlane reported back—this was late in the month. "Something definitely is going down, only nobody at my level knows what. As far as what you said, it's true, the Great White's been out of the office a lot, and when he's there, he's mostly closeted with a handful of people." He named them. All the inner circle, plus Harvey Cross, who was the last of the Shaws and Crosses and something of a joke inside the company. "Also," MacFarlane went on, "people I talked to say he's really been chewing ass. Even more than usual. Up one side and down the other. They say it's Armageddon time, like he's trying to milk every last nickel from the operation before the roof caves in."

"But why?"

"Who knows? Do you suppose it could it be some kind of investigation?"

"What kind of investigation?"

"Beats me. Who would it be? The IRS? SEC?"

"Did anybody say that?"

"No. But the people I talked to said Gamble's become a bug on documentation. Everything's changed. The way it is now, they say they're up to their armpits in paperwork."

I wondered, at the time, if MacFarlane was playing cat-and-mouse with me but decided he was just a smart kid guessing, the way I used to guess when I was in the Aquarium. I'd always been careful to protect him from certain things I either knew or suspected. If he was guessing right, I thought, maybe it explained a lot of things. But not, I also thought, why they were jerking me around. *If* they were jerking me around?

And then my phone went dead, early December.

And now Penzil's talking about paper trails and telling me to keep calm. Sleep on it.

Yeah, Runt, and if pigs had wings . . .

18 December

I'm calm enough to get myself up in time to catch the 6:48, where I don't know a soul. I call Georgie from the World Trade, tell her I'll be late getting to the hospital. Something's come up and I have to stop by the office first. Then I ride up to the thirty-ninth floor. I'm determined to beat Gamble to his desk.

I even beat Annabelle Morgan. I walk into the Great White's inner lair, shut the door behind me, sit in his fucking chair. I'm still sitting there, a little after eight, when he walks in.

Black briefcase in hand. Elegant son of a bitch, except for the white socks. Why the white socks, everybody wants to know? The Aquarium wits have always had a field day with the white socks, but as far as I know, nobody's ever dared ask him, at least and lived to tell about it.

He stops cold when he sees me there. His mouth goes open a little and his shaggy eyebrows up. Then down. It just isn't something you do at The Cross: occupy the Great White's throne.

"Well, Larry," he says, noncommittally, "what are you doing here this early? What's up?"

"Don't let me get in your way, Leon." I stand. "Come on. Sit down."

I have the agreement out on his otherwise polished desk top. It's open to the relevant paragraph.

"Sit down, Leon," I repeat, ushering him. I stand next to him, pointing at the agreement. "Have you read this?"

"What's this? Oh yeah, our deal with you. Of course I've read it."

I didn't notice Annabelle Morgan come in behind him, but here she is, tall and chic and surprised as hell to see me.

"Hi, Larry," she says. "How—"

"No calls for the minute, Annabelle," the Great White interrupts. "Just leave the door open, thank you. Now Larry, I—"

"Have you read this part?" I say, pointing again. " 'Coffey agrees not to trespass on any of the Company's pre-existing accounts or relationships'?"

It can't be news to him. He reads it anyway, and then I can see the wheels turning, like he's choosing a reaction off some inner menu. He picks "Grunt" first, a short sound. Then his head comes up, his hand combing the mane of white hair, and he studies me. The beginnings of a smile at the corners of his mouth. Then, no smile.

"You know, Larry," he says, "you think you run the most efficient organization in the world, bar none, and then something happens and you realize it's a crock. I told Vic, 'Coffey's going to shit a brick when he sees this, you'd better talk to him first.' Hard to believe, but I take it from the expression on your face that he didn't? That he just gave it to you, without explanation? Is that correct?"

"That's correct."

Vic is none other than Victor Schwartzenberg, Chief House Counsel of The Cross.

The Great White is shaking his head.

"What a fucking comedy of errors," he says, disgusted. Then he booms out: "Annabelle?" Then thinks better of it, tells her to forget it when she appears in the doorway. And back to me: "You want to know what really happened, Bear? I didn't read this myself until last week. Of course, I spotted the omission right away. I said to Vic, 'For Christ's sake, the way you've drafted this thing, you're giving away the store. We can close the fucking doors, Coffey's going to own us.' Obviously, that was never our intention, much as we want the deal with you. It was just bad drafting. I told Vic to talk to you about it, but come on, Bear, admit it, we go back too far together. You didn't really expect us to let you cherry-pick our customer list, did you?''

I stare down at him for a minute. I said: "Dynamite try, Leon.''

His eyebrows go up again.

"What do you mean by that?'' he asked.

"I mean that two months ago almost to the day, you made me an offer. You, not Schwartzenberg. You were putting me in business for myself, you said, your Number-One Seller. The next day, I started talking to these same customers you're now telling me are off-limits.'' I name names, ticking them off on my fingers. "I've been talking to them ever since, Leon, and you know it. You've known it all along. Some of them are your best customers. You talk to them all the time. You could have stopped me any time you wanted to.''

I've just called him a liar, pretty much, and I expect him to react in kind. He doesn't, though.

"You've got it wrong, Larry,'' he says evenly. And nothing more.

"You knew it all along,'' I repeat. "For Christ's sake, you've been stringing me for two whole months, using Schwartzenberg as your front man. First it was this, then it was that. He had to talk to you, you weren't here, you were out sick, you were

in Timbuktu. I've been busting down the fucking
doors to get the final deal out of you. So finally,
yesterday, I got it. Right up the ass. And let me tell
you, Leon, this is no oversight. What kind of jerk do
you take me for? You—"

"Let's stop wasting our time," he interrupts.
"There's only one way we're going to resolve this."
He half-stands. "Annabelle!" he shouts at the open
door. "Get me Schwartzenberg. I don't care where
he is, what he's doing, I want him in here."

We wait a minute or so. He starts pulling papers
out of his briefcase, a signal, I suppose, that I'm in
his way, but I don't budge. Then Annabelle Morgan
sticks her head in the door. Surprise, surprise: no
Schwartzenberg. As far as anyone knows, he's en
route to the office.

"Then get him on his car phone," the Great White
tells her.

"I don't think he drives. He takes the train."

"Son of a bitch." Then, to me, "Well, if you want
to stick around, Larry, we'll talk when he gets here.
There's no point going any further without him."

"I can't stick around," I say. "I just—"

"Oh, that's right, I almost forgot!" Brightening,
big smile, standing. "Congratulations, Bear! It's a
girl, isn't it? Everybody okay?"

He holds out his hand. I don't take it.

"Let me ask you something," I say. "Who told
them to stop talking to me?"

"Who told who to stop talking to you?"

I list the names for him. "For the last two weeks, I
haven't been able to get through to a single one of
them. They won't take my calls, they're gone,

they're in Timbuktu, too. It's no coincidence, Leon. It's a fucking stone wall."

"I don't know what you're talking about," he says.

"Oh, come on, this is Larry Coffey you're talking to, remember me? The Big Bear? Somebody told them to stop talking to me, and don't tell me it was Schwartzenberg, for Christ's sake, I wasn't born yesterday. It was you, Leon. You're the only one they'd have taken it from."

For just a second, I've got him. I can see his lips working, spreading his cheeks, the jaw muscles clench. It's the big boil inside, the Great White on a rampage, and I'm supposed to back off and crawl under my rock.

But I don't back off, and once again, I can see the wheels turning as he controls himself.

"Let me talk to you as a friend for a minute," he says. "We all get a little paranoid sometimes, say things we don't mean. You're going through a rough time, Bear, don't think I don't understand it. Big changes in your life, and your wife just had a baby, that's enough to drive any man crazy. I'll tell you what I'm willing to do. If you can't hang around today, let me talk to Vic, see if there isn't something we can do to ease the pain. We'll work something out. You call him whenever you can. I'll tell him he's got to see you right away."

"If that clause stands the way it's written," I say, pointing at the agreement, "then there's nothing to work out. Tell me straight, Leon. Does it stand?"

"Of course it stands. It has to."

Just like that. I guess it's his cool that unnerves me. I feel as though somehow I've blown the situation. Or maybe, though it's taken me two months to wise up, it's that he's fucking me, and there's not a goddamned thing I can do about it.

"Tell me one thing, Leon. Why didn't you just fire me in October? Wouldn't it have been easier? Or were you just trying to save another severance package?"

"I told you at the time. You're far too valuable to this company."

"Only now you're putting me out of business?"

"I think you're grossly underestimating your own capabilities."

"Thanks, Leon," I say bitterly. "So what are my choices? Just tell me what my choices are."

"Choices? The sensible one I already gave you: Wait for Vic. A point here, a point there, it could make a big difference to you in the long run. But if you want to, you can always sign it the way it is, right now. I'll sign it too, and we can get on with it."

He says it offhandedly, as though he really doesn't give a shit one way or the other.

"But the clause stands?"

"The clause has got to stand."

"What I feel like doing," I say, "is wiping your ass with it."

This time he's quick to react. Eyes small, jaws tight. Voice full of Great White menace.

"That's enough now. You're way out of line, Larry. You do what you want to do. You can also walk out the door, that's your decision. But this conversation is over."

He's standing too. A little shorter than me but heavier. Also a good twenty years older.

"It's not over, Leon," I say, unblinking. "Let me

tell you something. You can send me down the tubes if you want to, but I'm taking you with me. You, The Cross, the whole goddamn company. Let's not fuck around with each other anymore. I can do it too. I know enough, where the bodies are buried, and you know I know it."

He doesn't blink either.

"That sounds like a threat to me," he says.

"That's exactly what it is."

"Do you want to repeat that in front of a witness?"

"I'd be glad to." Christ Almighty, does he think I'm *bluffing*?

"Are you sure? Do you really want to start something you could regret for the rest of your life?"

The son of a bitch is staring me down. I feel myself break out in little sweaty prickles all over.

"Annabelle?" he calls out, his eyes not leaving mine. "Please come in here a minute." Then, when she does, "Shut the door behind you, please."

She shuts the door. The three of us are standing, in the Great White's office, Annabelle Morgan looking questioningly at her boss.

"Mr. Coffey has just said something to me that I'd like him to repeat. All you have to do is listen." And to me: "Go ahead, Larry."

It's Rubicon time. All of a sudden I've the dryness in my throat. God Almighty. Thirteen years down the tubes and maybe a whole lot more. My whole fucking career. Well, go ahead, Julius, cross the fucker.

I repeat it.

* * *

Into the downtown canyons, and all the way to the hospital, I'm shaking like a wino. Two parts anger, one part fear, mix and stir well.

Georgie is in the midst of breast-feeding the baby. She always said she'd never do it, and she didn't with Justie. Not for her, she always said. But in the middle of the night, last night, and after all she's gone through having this baby, she decided she had to try it. You never know, Zoe could be our last. Except now she's anxious over whether Zoe's getting enough milk. Do I think she's latching properly? Also she—Georgie—slept badly. And hurts like a son of a bitch. This much I can tell later when I help her to the john. Something about her wound being held together with staples—can I imagine?— right across her belly. Metal staples. It's positively medieval.

"But Larry, why are you so distracted? So jumpy? You've hardly sat still since the minute you got here."

"Jumpy?" I say. "I wasn't aware of it. I guess I hate to see you hurting like this."

"I know," with a tired smile, "but look what we've got in exchange."

"Yeah. Little Zoe."

"Zoe Elizabeth Coffey. I haven't told anybody the name yet."

"How come?"

"I want us to live with it first, make sure we like it. Well? What's wrong? Don't you like it?"

"Sure, it's fine. It's a fine name."

"But do you *love* it? . . . *Larry*, can't you *focus* for a minute? You seem a million miles away! We both ought to love it. We're all going to have to live with it a long time."

Christ, what am I supposed to say? That, much as I love my new daughter, I don't know how I'm going to pay for the roof over her head, come the new year, so what difference does it make if her name is Zoe or Christabelle or Marie Antoinette?

"I love it," I say. "Zoe Elizabeth Coffey."

"Well, let's live with it another couple of days, till we're sure. I want us to be sure."

I stay until I'm too pent up to stay any longer. Then I kiss both of them good-bye, saying I'll be back later, and head over to the club. They haven't even opened the bar yet for lunch, but I sit there and, taking a deep breath, start making my calls. No Penzil, no Holbrook, nobody who's going to tell me not to do anything rash. Instead I start with Mac-Farlane, knowing I won't get him, but I leave a message on his machine—I want his ear to the ground again—and then I get onto some other people I know, who were close to the Drexel situation. The way I put it is that a customer of mine—no names, but I owe him—has come to me for advice. For reasons of his own, he's ready to blow the whistle on one of our competitors, but he's scared, understandably, about what could happen to him along the way. So who can he talk to discreetly in the regulatory agencies? I need a name, somebody who'd be willing to protect him, at least at the very beginning.

Sign of the times. To a man, their first reaction is that I have to talk him out of it. I say I've already been that route and failed. My guy's mad as a hornet, there's no way I can stop him. I don't know all of what he has—I don't want to know—but I'm pretty sure he's going to spill it no matter what I say, and the best I can do, under the circumstances, is make sure he doesn't spill it to the *Journal* or the *New York Times*.

It's midafternoon by the time I get what I want. Some can't help, or won't, but finally I come up with a name—the same name—from two different sources. A Department of Justice lawyer called Joe Richter, who's attached to the U.S. Attorney's office.

By then I've had a few rounds at the bar. The lunch crowd has long since vanished. I'm wondering if this Richter might already be looking at The Cross. I'm wondering if there was anything in what MacFarlane said, back in November.

Hey, Joe Richter, it's Big Bear on the horn, how'd you like a nice money-laundering scandal laid right in your lap?

Hey, says the Great White, baring his white fangs, do you really want to start something you'll regret for the rest of your life?

Rubicon city.

I make the call.

I can't tell whether he knows who I am or not. I suggest an exploratory meeting, strictly off the record.

Done. For tomorrow. In an uptown watering hole I know, not that far from Georgie's hospital.

When I hang up, though, I realize I'm shaky again, inside, and it's not from booze. The fucking enormity of it, Jesus Christ, have I gone stark raving? *Don't do something you'll regret for the rest of your life.*

But the son of a bitch *gored* me!

There's not a soul in the world I can tell right

now. That's getting to me already. Even before I've met with Richter, I'm the loneliest guy in town.

Talk about things you'll regret. I call Georgie. I'm at the club, I say, but something's come up. Mulcahy's in town (sotto voce), and I'm sorry as hell about it but there's no way I'm going to make it back to the hospital.

"Are you all right?" she wants to know in her small voice.

"I'm fine," I lie.

I can hear people noises in the background. She's telling me who's there—she says she doesn't know where to put all the flowers—and I'm trying to tell myself that's why I'm not going back to the hospital, because I can't face any of them right now.

Georgie says she misses me. So, she says, does my daughter. Well, I say, I'll call when I get home if it's not too late. Else I'll be there in the morning, first thing.

And there goes another lie.

Easy, honey, once you get the hang of it.

It gets worse.

Sweet Jesus.

I'm home after dark. Justie has finished dinner and Harriet has him in the tub. There are phone messages from any number of people, but they can wait, and so can I, sipping Scotch in the den, until she brings him down.

We talk awhile. Last night, by the time I got home, they were both asleep. That is, all the lights were out on the third floor.

I tell Justie about his baby sister. The kid yawns.

Harriet's done wonders with him, according to Georgie, but he still looks awfully puny to me.

Georgie's genes, I guess.

She doesn't stop looking at you. She has this way of looking you over, up and down, as though her eyes are coming right in through your pants. It started when she moved in—the eye contact, the off-hand remarks, the accidental brushes and touches —only one time, the night Georgie stayed over at her folks, it wasn't accidental.

She said . . . well, she said a lot of things that night. I did too. We were in the den, and she was perched on my desk, legs dangling, and she kept telling me she shouldn't be there, that it was awful, laughing her soft, throaty laugh meanwhile, until I wanted her so badly I could taste it. We kissed finally, one of those long, exploratory, wraparound jobs, and I couldn't believe it, she was so young, fresh. Smelled like a meadow in summer.

She pushed me off. She tried to pass it off as a great misunderstanding, and when that didn't work, she pleaded with me to lay off her, and when that didn't work, she started to cry, even though—and this I will swear to, Georgie, on a stack of Bibles— she'd started it.

She said she couldn't do it to you, not as long as you were pregnant.

Whatever that meant.

Hey, I may be no Boy Scout but I'm not exactly a rapist, either.

Ever since then, though, it's been sheer torture, just having her under the same roof. Maybe I should have said something to you—shit, I know I should have, but like what? "Honey, we've got to get rid of

Harriet?"—but you were upstairs in bed, and I
didn't, and sometimes just the sight of her, like tonight, like when her eyes are working me over and
she's brushing her hair back, laughing a little, asking me how it feels to be a daddy again, running her
fingers slowly along one temple to behind the
ear . . .

If I ever needed R&R, it's tonight. And you're not
pregnant anymore.

Good God Almighty.

She's taken him upstairs, his head nodding off in
her arms, and I'm waiting for her to come back
down.

She doesn't.

I'm standing the whole time in my doorway.
Glass in hand. Sometimes I'm aware that I'm holding my breath, sometimes that I'm taking these deep
draughts. I can hear my own pulse pounding.

Finally, I go up after her.

The lights are all out on the third floor.

I mean, what the hell are you supposed to do
when the pressure boils over?

I guess some guys beat the daylights out of their
wives and kids. Some tie one on. Some get laid.

Or all three.

Upstairs, in the darkness.

"For God's sake, Larry!" she hisses at me through
her closed door. "Not with him in the next room!"

"Then come downstairs with me," I tell her.

We spar back and forth through the closed door.
She's not saying no either, but there's Justie, and I
tell her Justie would sleep through an earthquake,
but if it's Justie she's worried about, there's the

whole house, pick a room, the whole outdoors, even in December, I promise her, she won't be cold.

I hear her laugh at that. What does she want from me? I can taste her!

Then I try the door. She's locked it. Goddamn, in my house people don't lock the doors!

I rear back. I ram the fucker in.

Pitch dark.

"You're *crazy*, Larry! Be reasonable, your wife just had a baby! Cut it out now! I won't, not this way! For God's sake! *Stop* it, for God's sake!"

Something like that. Because I don't give a damn, I'm going to have her this time whether she wants it or not. I'm heaving and banging into stuff with her in the dark, struggling and dripping sweat, the two of us.

Then, loud and clear: *"Get the hell out of here!"*

Sweet Jesus Christ.

I must have let go of her, because somehow, suddenly, she's switched on a light, and now, in the light, she's all cowering, and I see her face screwed up, and her body's shaking even before a sound comes out. She's got on one of those knee-length T-shirts, white with a big yellow Tweety Bird on it.

She looks wild, but not sexy wild. Now she's laughing her head off, but it's one of those mean, rictus-y laughs, the not-funny kind. In between she's babbling stuff I don't get, except that, poor bastard, I don't have a clue, and somehow, tonight, that seems to be the laugh riot of the century.

Well, I guess I don't—don't have a clue—at least as far as this little prick teaser's concerned. But she's shut my systems down, and when she tells me to get out again, I get.

I'll tell you, honey, she may be great with Justie, but underneath she's one screwed-up piece of work.

Okay, so it's not my finest hour. Look, Georgie, I'm sorry as hell, that's all I want to say to you. That, and that, at the end of the day, I still love you.

Justie slept through the whole damn thing.

19 December

"Yes? Who's this?"

"He's talking."

"I'm sorry, it's the middle of the night, I—"

"I said: 'He's talking,' for Christ's sake! . . . Hello? Are you there?"

"How did you find out?"

"That's my business. Goddamn it, man, I thought you were going to keep this from happening."

"Are you sure of your information?"

"Very sure."

"Who's he talking to?"

"A federal shyster, name of Richter."

"No names, please."

"Okay, a goddamn nameless federal shyster."

"Do you know what they said?"

"What the fuck difference does that make?"

"You've always assured me he doesn't know enough."

"And you assured me you had it under control! You let me go ahead and stick it to him! For Christ's sake, as long as he's talking, the wrong people can end up hearing about it. It's a goddamn good thing they're out of the country. He says if they . . ."

"Who says? Who else knows about this?"

"What do you mean, who else knows about it?"

"Just what I said. Whom have you been talking to?"

"Nobody! Do you think I'm crazy?"

"At least one person."

"What do you mean, one person?"

"The person who told you. I want to know who it is."

"Sorry, I—"

"It's their attorney, isn't it."

"Listen, I—"

"You don't have to say anything."

"I don't see what the fuck you're so afraid of. He's in it with us, isn't he?"

"So you keep telling me."

"Because it's true, and you know it! But what are we going to do? I gotta know, so does he! We've got a goddamn time bomb that's going off, and if we don't—"

"You're going to do nothing. You did what you had to do, now you're going to stay perfectly calm and do nothing."

"But—?"

"We're going to control the damage."

"Oh? Just like that?"

"Yes, since you ask. Just like that."

Georgia
Levy
Coffey

19 December

It's Wednesday morning. Zoe Elizabeth Coffey is two days old.

I just got off the phone with Harriet. I had Justin first. He has a cold—I could hear it—and then there was something, teary-voiced, about a Christmas party they're having at Group, and he's supposed to go as a knight with a cardboard sword and helmet, but Harriet says he can't go. Then she came on.

She's giving him Triaminic for the cold. I agreed that he shouldn't go to the Group party. Everything else, she said, was okay on the home front, more or less.

There was something funny, though, about her voice. Funny? No, but she sounded subdued, quiet.

"Are you all right?" I asked.

"Me? Oh yes, I'm fine."

Then I asked to speak to Larry.

"Oh?" She sounded surprised. "But he's not here. I'd have thought he was with you by now."

"Well, he hasn't shown up yet. You saw him this morning, didn't you?"

"No. I mean, he was already gone by the time we got up. Is there something you want me to tell him, in case he calls in?"

"No, that's all right. When did you see him last?"

"Do you mean actually saw?"

"Whatever."

"I mean, he must have gotten home pretty late last night. We were already asleep, Justin and me. But why, Georgia? Is something wrong?"

"No, nothing. Nothing at all."

Only, I thought, something *was*. Could she be covering for him somehow? He'd said he was with the Mulcahys, the day before, those awful people. But had he been?

But why would he have lied?

Then, brightening, she said, "But aren't you going to tell me something about the baby? Is she wonderful? I think it's such a beautiful name, Zoe. And I'm so glad you decided to breast-feed! It makes me very proud, Georgia. I mean, proud of *you*."

And it didn't even register!

It only niggled. Something. We chatted on.

But it registers now! Oh yes it does, you presumptuous bitch!

I'm lying in my bed in a state of shock. Zoe's asleep in her bassinet. Thank God nobody's here.

She's lying to me! They're *both* lying to me!

Because how does she know the name? How, if she didn't talk to Larry last night or this morning, does she know what Zoe's name is?

Moreover, how does she know I'm *breast-feeding*?

Conceivably he could have told them the night before last, Monday. What was it he said? That when he got home that night, he was on the phone with

Penzil? Something about The Deal? And that he only had time to tell Justin he had a baby sister and that Mommy was fine?

Well, he could have let the name slip. Zoe. Even though he wasn't supposed to.

But he didn't know I was breast-feeding till Tuesday!

Why?

Because it only happened the night after Zoe was born, when I was alone with my pain, and they have a rule in the hospital, if you're not nursing, that you only get to see your baby every now and then. It seemed so damned unfair to me. After all I'd been through, at least I wanted my daughter, wanted her bonding. I called the night nurse, demanded my child. She refused. I cried, I screamed at her like a banshee. She said, well, why didn't I try it? (They all seem to think that if you don't breast-feed, you're a bad Mommy a priori.) Finally, very early in the morning, I capitulated. She brought me Zoe, helped with the first latching. I was so damned clumsy. Panicky too, I guess, and hurting, with a whole network of plastic tubes running out of my wound.

But there we are.

But Larry knew nothing about it till yesterday!

And if he didn't know about it till yesterday, and if Harriet didn't see him last night or this morning, then how does she know I'm breast-feeding?

She must have seen him after all.

But why would she lie about a thing like that?

I can think of only two reasons.

Either he didn't come home at all and she is covering for him—but in that case how *does* she know? —or . . .

With Justin in the next room!

Every time I think about it, I flood. Heat just under my skin, little bubbles of sweat, in the overheated atmosphere. I'm on overload. Little things, little details, gestures. Right under my nose, the whole time! It all comes back to me. Stray glances between them. Her sometimes sullenness, his uncommunicativeness.

With him, of course, that was The Deal. Always the Deal. He was so-o-o wrapped up in The Deal.

God Almighty, not only did I bring her into the house, but I actually coaxed her into moving in! I *coaxed* her!

But how did they manage it, all this time? I hardly left the house! Did he wait till I was asleep at night, then sneak upstairs?

With Justin in the next room?

That weekend before Thanksgiving, Friday, when I went off to my parents. She couldn't stay, absolutely adamant, and then, all of a sudden—a miracle—yes, she was staying. (Who did she call, that morning? Larry?) And the next day, when he finally met me at Dubin's office, so distracted, something about The Deal, always The Deal . . .

But it was *never* The Deal!

It was *Harriet!*

And I keep seeing Justin in the next room!

He calls. Full of apologies, he's going to be late, won't show up till late this afternoon.

I want to tell him not to bother, don't.

They serve lunch. I push the tray away, uneaten. The nurse's aide argues with me. I have to eat because of Zoe. I take a few bites, like chewing chalk.

Instead, I swallow my rage. I call my mother. I

imagine her saying I told you so, and I can't face it. I invent some explanation, tell her not to come. I don't want to see anyone except my father. I think: I could get my father to drive to New Jersey, fire Harriet on the spot, retrieve my son.

But how could I do that to Justin? How would he react if his grandfather suddenly appeared and put him in a car and drove him back to Riverside Drive?

I clutch my daughter for dear life. She stares at me, silent, beautiful blue eyes now open in a look of perpetual amazement.

I explain to her: "We're stuck, my darling. Your daddy's been bad, very bad, but we're stuck in this horrible hospital, and I hurt, I've got these damned pieces of metal in the place where you came out, and there's nothing we can do about it. We have to wait till we get out. Then Momma will fix everything. It'll be all right, you'll see. But right now we have to be strong. And wait. We have to be very strong together."

The person I really want to fire, of course, is my husband.

It is late when he shows up. He has on his big winter coat, the bulky one with the alpaca lining, and his most sheepdog expression. His left hand is jammed in his coat pocket, as though he's clutching something inside the coat.

I can see it in his eyes. For just a second, I think he's about to confess. *Oh, Georgie, I don't know what got into me*, etc., etc. That's how he'd start, all contrite and serious.

Instead, he shuts the door carefully behind him

and, unbuttoning his coat, produces a bottle of champagne.

"I thought we could drink a little toast to our daughter," he says jovially, "with the good old Dom." He waves the bottle in the air.

The idea revolts me. I want to tell him: Why don't you take it home and drink it with your slut? But I've made up my mind. I'm doing nothing, saying nothing, till I get home.

He's saying something about doing something crazy. Something about crossing the Rubicon, his personal Rubicon. (I'll say.) About how he wants us to be proud of him, me, Justin, Zoe too.

He says he's a changed man.

"I look at you with the baby," he says, and he shakes his head, swallows, "and all I can say is . . . Well, it moves me. Moves me incredibly." For God's sake, is he about to *cry?* "The craziest thing about it, honey, is that I feel totally liberated."

Great.

"I'd like you to go now," I say. "I'm too tired to talk."

"It's okay, honey, you don't have to say a word. Just listen to—"

"Please," I interrupt. "I mean it, Larry. I want you to leave now."

He stares at me, uncomprehending, like some big bewildered animal.

"Georgie, I—"

"Just leave me alone. That's what I want."

"But why?"

"I don't want to discuss it now. Just go."

"But Georgie, I can—"

"Just go. I don't want any explanations. I want you to go. Now."

I put all the scorn I can muster into my voice, and all the humiliation, the hurt, the tears I've shed today with only Zoe for my witness. And if there's any lingering doubt in my mind—could I have it wrong? have misinterpreted?—the guilty expression on his moon face wipes it out.

"Georgie, what did you hear? For Christ's sake, it's not what you think! I—"

But his voice trails off.

You cheating, son-of-a-bitch bastard! Why don't you go get sympathy from her?

Eye contact gone. Confused, he retreats, turns, turns back, stumbles, opens the door.

One last plea—"Georgie!"—but it fails to move me.

He's gone now. The champagne bottle still in his fist.

Immediately I think: Why *didn't* I challenge him? Then and there, in the damned hospital bed, with my daughter in my arms and the staples still in my belly? And if I'd never hired her, if I'd never married him, if and if and if. Oh God, I've been through it all a hundred times already!

Because I've *always* given him the benefit of the doubt. All the late nights, the Holbrooks, the Mulcahys. And all along it's been going on right under my nose!

How long is "all along"? How do I know? How do I know *anything* about him?

And her? She of the soulful glances, the tender, sisterly words?

22 December

Saturday morning, Larry's already here.

I was up most of the night, stewing. It's not that I'm flinching from it, I know exactly what I'm going to say. But there's Justin. How explain to him? And, once she's gone, how am I going to cope with him?

I must have dozed off for a little while, until Zoe woke me up, fretting.

"It's okay, darling," I murmured to her sleepily, offering my nipple. "We're going home today."

We both dozed off again.

Everybody except Larry is late.

Dubin, to examine and release me. And the staff pediatrician, who has to sign off on Zoe. Then there's some complicated business with the hospital administration. Why didn't somebody warn me about it before? The floor nurse insists she needs a cashier's receipt before we can leave.

Larry's gone off to deal with it. Dressed and packed, I wait with Zoe for what seems like hours.

I feed Zoe again. Larry comes back. Done. But then the floor nurse stops us again. They have a "fail-safe" procedure for making sure I go off with the right baby.

"But why couldn't you have told me this before?" I shout at her across the counter at the nurse's station.

"I'm sorry, Georgia, we've—"

"And what gives you the right to call me by my first name? You don't know—"

"I'm sorry, Mrs. Coffey."

I yell at her—this is my baby, does she think I don't know my own baby?

A year ago, she explains (with professional patience), a woman walked in off the street and out of the hospital, with a baby she had no claim to. That, I say, is really reassuring. That, the nurse says, is why they have the procedure.

Finally, Larry leaves to get the Volvo, which he parked in a garage, and a black security guard, after checking Zoe's plastic bracelet against his roster, escorts us down the elevator and out to the main entrance, where he waits with us until Larry drives up.

It is almost eleven and freezing outside.

The city is dirty, bleak, and the crosstown traffic horrendous. I sit in the backseat with Zoe. I tried wedging her into Justin's tiny old car seat, but she sagged and drooped no matter how I tried to prop her. Finally, danger or no danger, I unstrapped her, and I hold her cradled in my arms.

We hardly talk. I ask Larry if the baby nurse arrived before he left. No, he says, but he called the agency yesterday. They assured him she would be there. Clotie and Harriet can let her in.

Great, I think.

Then, for no reason, I remember the tree. It almost makes me cry. Christmas is only a few days off —some Christmas—but for Justin's sake, what are we going to do about a tree?

I must have said it aloud, something.

"Not to worry," Larry says over his shoulder, from the driver's seat, "it's all been taken care of."

"What's been taken care of? You mean you bought a tree?"

"Not only bought but it's already up and decorated."

Sign of the times. Always in the past, we bought the tree together, and I did the decorating, adding several new ornaments to the collection each year.

"Harriet and Justie helped me," he says.

Oh great. Just great.

He tries to use the tree as an opening. We have to talk, he says. It's crazy, going on the way we're going. For his part, he can explain everything. It's not what I think, he says. He says it's been a crazy time for him.

I don't bother to answer. I look out the window at the bleak city, the bleak tunnel, the bleak route west across the Meadowlands. I have it all planned. The minute we get home, I will hand Zoe over to the nurse. Then I'll take Harriet Major aside and tell her exactly what I think of her. She'll have till nightfall to pack her stuff and get out. (I can't remember if I have enough cash in my *secrétaire*. Well, if I don't, she'll have to take a check.) Then I'll take Justin and tell him she's leaving and hope for the best. After that, Lawrence Elgin Coffey can do all the explaining he wants to.

Heavy traffic, I notice. The Saturday before Christmas.

Giants Stadium.

The Giants are having a super season, Larry remarks. There's a chance they'll go all the way.

Good for the Giants.

It seems to be taking forever. Maybe that's because I feel as though I've been away forever. Five days, and everything's changed. Five days in a hospital bed, I think, and my whole life's been turned on its ear.

The thought makes me queasy, that and the back of my husband's head.

"We're going home, my darling," I whisper silently to Zoe. "In a few minutes, you're going to meet your brother. And it'll be okay, I promise you. Momma's going to fix everything."

The streets of St. George, at long last. The north end near the highway, where the houses, as though they belong to some other town, are aligned in tight rows on gridiron streets—"starter homes" in real estate jargon, but you get the St. George School District in the bargain. Red lights, trees, bare branches forming gaunt alleys under a glassy sky. Christmas decorations. Somebody has a big plastic Santa on the front lawn, pulled by reindeer, with a bigger cartoon bubble coming out of his mouth. "Ho Ho Ho," the bubble says.

The cemetery sloping above us, then the Victorian pile of the St. George Inn, where the food is terrible and no one I know has ever stayed.

We turn past the inn, under the stone arches of the railroad, and snake west toward the ridge line. Here the lots are larger, the cars in the driveways more expensive, the plantings elegant. Turn-of-the-century Victorians, center-hall Colonials, now and then a massive gloomy Tudor. Wreaths on the doors, glimpses of lit trees in the interiors. Then, a last blinking red light, and we're across, winding into our neighborhood through the giant oaks and banks of rhododendrons, and finally, finally, home.

It's lunchtime.

Clotie and the baby nurse are waiting for us. Justin and Harriet aren't.

Clotie says she got to work at eight. Mr. Coffey

had already left. The baby nurse arrived about ten. Sometime between the two, apparently, Justin and Harriet went off in Harriet's car.

Clotie saw them; the baby nurse didn't.

"But didn't she tell you where they were going?" I ask Clotie.

"No, ma'am. I just saw them go, that's all. She had Justie all bundled up in his snowsuit, account of the cold."

"But didn't you ask them?"

"Ask them what?"

"Where they were going? I mean, they *knew* I was coming home!"

"No, I didn't, ma'am. I was just doing my work, was all."

"But what time was that?"

"I disremember."

"Maybe they went Christmas shopping," Larry says.

We're all still standing in the front hall, in our overcoats, and I'm still holding Zoe.

"*Christmas* shopping?" I retort. "On the day I was coming home? When they knew I was coming home and bringing Zoe?"

He shrugs. "Maybe they're stuck in traffic. It's fierce out there, probably the stores are jammed too. I don't know, maybe they went out for lunch. There's no need to get so worked up about it."

"But she should have told someone. She *knew* we were coming home. It's . . . well, it's goddamned *irresponsible!*"

It is also, I think, the last straw. Whatever shred of sympathy I might have harbored for Harriet Major has just gone out the window.

The damned phone keeps ringing. Each time I grab at it, primed to explode, but it's always somebody else calling to welcome me back.

I cut people short. I punch the stepfather's number. I let it ring eight times the first time, ten times the second. But what happened to the answering machine? Why would she have turned off the answering machine?

I ask the operator for help. The line's in good working order, she says. But no one is picking up.

They're not back at two, three. She always said her stepfather had a business in New York. I look up Smith in the Manhattan phone book. There are three Robert A.'s, one a doctor. I think the middle initial is A. And there are tons of Robert Smiths and as many R. Smiths, and how do I know the business is under his own name, and what would it be doing, open on a Saturday?

I punch a few numbers. They lead me nowhere. Nobody knows what I'm talking about.

They're still not back at four.

Larry suggests he drive off to search for them. That, I tell him, would be the absolute height of stupidity. Where is he going to look? Which direction would he go in?

Finally I confront him. I don't care anymore, I'm too crazed.

"What do *you* know about this?"

"Georgie, for Christ's sake—"

"I want the truth now! Do you think I don't know what's been going on between the two of you? How *dumb* do you think I am?"

"Oh, Georgie, I—"

His abject tone infuriates me.

"Don't you 'Oh Georgie' me! I want to know where they are, what you know about it."

"But I don't know *anything* about it!"

"Are you sure? Absolutely sure? Where they were going, what they were going to do?"

"Yes, I'm sure. I didn't even see them this morning. When I left the house, they were still asleep."

"How do you know that? Were you up there on the third floor?"

"No, I wasn't. For God's sake, Georgie! You've got it all wrong, I—"

"Just answer my question! How did you know they were still asleep?"

"I just assumed they were."

"But her car was still here when you left, wasn't it?"

"I don't know. I guess I didn't notice."

"Didn't notice? How could you *not* notice?"

"Georgie, for Christ's sake, it was still dark outside! I had to leave to get you! But what difference does that make anyway? Clotie saw them later. She saw them go off in the car!"

"You *bastard!*" I shriek at him. "Don't you *dare* raise your voice to me! They've been gone over six hours! Something bad's happened to our son, and *you're* responsible for it!"

"But, Georgie, you don't know that! That's cra—"

"You're damned right it's crazy! *I'm* crazy, the whole world's crazy!"

But I can't stand it anymore, can't stand the sight of him, the sound of his voice. I push past him, make my way painfully upstairs. The whole world *is* crazy. And something *has* happened to my son, something bad. Good God, my little boy!

I realize I'm sobbing. *BECAUSE I'VE KNOWN IT ALL ALONG!* All my premonitions, my crazy forebodings, I thought it was about Zoe—no, I thought it was about *me!* My whining, puling, neurotic, hormonal, goddamn stupid-bitch princess self! But it *wasn't!* It was real the whole time, and I knew it was going to happen, and it was going on right under my nose! Justin, my son, my little boy, oh God, and somehow I let it. I let it happen *right under my nose!*

But he's so . . . he's so . . .

Oh my *God!*

Makes me wild. Feel this gaping, this huge hole opened up. I'm having trouble breathing, catching my breath. Can't think, see. Because he's gone, into the hole, and he's so . . . so *helpless!* I'm lying on my face, and I can feel the wet, and there's an ache so great, this enormous welling in my throat . . .

Jesus God, my little *boy!*

Sometime later, Larry comes into the bedroom. He talks at me from behind. I stay on my side, my back to him.

"I just talked to the police," he says. "The St. George cops. They say they've had no report of any accident. Nothing involving a Civic, or a young woman and a small boy. I gave them their names and a physical description. The guy I talked to said he'd call around to the nearby towns, the county cops, the state troopers. I'm supposed to call him back later. Is there anything else you want me to do?"

I don't answer, can't.

A little later, when I'm sure he's gone, I glance at

the digital clock. It's after five. Outside, it's already pitch dark.

25 December

They weren't back at six, at seven, eight.

They never came back that day, or the next.

The police can't find a trace of them.

Gone.

Every time I see the Christmas tree downstairs, I start to cry all over again. After the first day, when they made me check to see what, if anything, of Justin's and Harriet's was missing, I've never gone near the third floor again. But I can't avoid the tree. It stands like some accusation in the living room, all my ornaments hanging on it, and the blue and silver balls, the colored lights.

It's Christmas Day. I'm still waiting and there's still no news. I've just demanded that Larry take the tree down.

The numbness has set in. And my breasts have dried up.

Part Two

Rebecca Anne Dalton

22 December

It's 5:00 A.M.

I haven't slept.

He said, "You're to bring him here." All week I've been making up excuses. He knew they were excuses. He likes that usually, but not this time. Finally I said, "You know I'm going to." "When?" he said. "Tomorrow morning if not before. The minute Larry leaves." He said, "You know what will happen to you if you don't." I said, "Yes, of course I do."

I tiptoe around, grabbing stuff, my room, his. I've got these two canvas Gap bags of Georgia's, one for him, one for me. When they're almost full, I lug them downstairs in the darkness. I'm such a wreck I almost start singing. In the kitchen I fill the remaining space with food, whatever comes to hand: Dino cookies, apples, pretzels, a couple of his three-pack juices.

I tap my code into the alarm panel, carry the bags out to the car, my shoulder purse. Pitch-black. My God, I'm going to have to deal with the car first thing. Meanwhile the cold chatters my teeth. I'll have to dress him for it. Unstrap, restrap his car seat, just to make sure. Then back inside, upstairs, to get him.

"Shhh," I tell him softly when he comes half-awake. "It's questing day, sweets. It all starts today. But we have to be very quiet."

He nods, drowses off again. Heavy noodle in my arms. I hold him while he pees, then while I dress him, stuff him into his snowpants, snow jacket. I carry him downstairs, my hand poised to clap over his mouth. Afraid he'll wake up Larry. Not a big risk but right now everything is a big risk.

I almost fall with him, going down the front steps. Hang in there, Becca. I get the passenger seat forward, load him into the back. My hands are shaking as I snap his harness shut. He's awake now, his eyes open like saucers, but not a peep. I keep telling him it's questing day, that it's okay but we have to get away very quietly, nobody knowing.

Maybe he's scared too. Disoriented anyway.

It's Saturday morning. As far as the Coffeys go, I figure we've two hours at worst, and there's a chance Larry won't even notice. He has to leave early, get Georgia and the baby. Probably he'll think we're still asleep.

Unless he sees that my car's gone?

But I always park on the other side, away from where they park theirs. There'd be no reason for him to check.

Clotie next. She usually shows up around eight. Probably she will notice—we're usually in the kitchen by then—but, with Larry gone, will she do anything about it?

A baby nurse is coming too.

Chances are it'll be when they get home from the hospital. That can't be any sooner than nine-thirty. Maybe ten, maybe later.

Four hours to get rid of the car.

Unless he's watching me now?

But I can't think about that. I'm not going to think about that.

I drive west, out of St. George, to the interstate. Pitch dark, surreal. Still, I drive with my neck on a swivel, and once, when a pair of headlights roars up behind us, I almost lose it.

I sing. I sing Madonna, Whitney Houston, Elton John. Cole Porter. The speedometer at sixty. I don't dare go any faster because of the cops, even though the cops wouldn't know anything about us yet. In between songs I feed him Dino cookies and fruit juice in a box over the backrest. And tell him our plan. Beginning with our quest names.

He already knows most of it, our names included. He knows all about knights and ladies, witches, warlocks, quests and dragons and the Holy Grail. It started almost the day I met him. I'd say, "You don't have to sleep, but if you just lie down for a little while, I'll tell you the next part." And he would, and I did, with a little help from Tolkien, *The Wizard of Oz*, *The Once and Future King*.

It always freaked Georgia, that I could get him to nap.

"This isn't the quest," he says from the backseat.

"Why not?"

" 'Cause it's winter."

I say, "That doesn't make any difference. It's still a quest. It's our quest."

"But you said quests aren't for winter. 'Cause of snow."

"Did I?" Damn. I know I did, and why.

"Uh-huh. Not in winter."

"But is there any snow? Look out the window, do you see any snow?"

"No. But it's winter. You said—"

"I know what I said, and it's true, most quests aren't in winter. In the old days, it was too cold. People stayed in their castles, otherwise they'd have frozen into ice. But now we have heaters. Even cars have heaters. Do you feel cold right now?"

"No."

"Well, can you think of any reason why people shouldn't go on quests in winter?"

But he's not convinced, I can tell. Just once, one time, I mentioned to him that someday maybe we'd go on a quest, he and I, and he's never stopped asking since. When? When will we go?

"Look, Danny," I say, "do you want to know the truth? The whole truth? I had a dream last night. It's what woke me up so early. I was scared. I know you'll say: it was just a dream, but sometimes I think dreams are more than just dreams. This one, anyway. In it, the warlocks were coming to get us. I think I actually saw one of them, through the trees. He looked terrible. I thought: how can they be coming to get us, it's winter, aren't they supposed to be asleep? But they weren't asleep, not this one anyway."

"How many was there?"

"I couldn't tell, sweets. But it only takes one, really. You know that. One bad warlock, and if you're not ready, you end up in the dungeon. And then there's no quest, nothing. It's over before it's started." I glance in the rearview, but the angle is wrong, I can't see him. "Anyway, that's what woke me up, and I realized: If we're ever going to do it, it's got to be now, right now. Before the warlocks get here. And that's why we're on our way."

He doesn't say anything for a minute. Then: "Are any oarlocks behind us? Chasing us?"

"Warlocks," I correct automatically. "I wouldn't be surprised."

"And 'itches?"

"Witches. Wherever there are warlocks, there are bound to be witches. At least one."

"Why?"

"You know that. Because warlocks work for witches. Anyway, that's why we've got to change cars. That's why we have our new quest names. What's my name again?"

"Us really going to change cars?"

"Yes, of course we are."

"When?"

"Soon."

"Oh. Can us get a rocket car?"

"I don't know about that. We'll probably have to take whatever they give us."

"Why?"

"Because that's the way it works."

"Oh please, can't us get a rocket car?"

"We can try, but I doubt it. But I just asked you a question. You haven't answered it yet."

He falls silent again.

"Becca," he says finally.

"Good!" I say. "And what's it stand for?" He

can't get it. "Ruh-becca," I say. "Try it." He does. "And what's our last name?"

"Dalting," he manages.

"Not bad. But it's Dal-*ton*, not Dal-*ting*. Try it."

"Dal-*ton*."

"That's good. Now say it together, quickly. Dal-ton."

"Dalton," he says.

"Perfect! And what did you say your name was?"

"Danny."

"Danny who?"

"Danny Dalton."

"Oh that's *terrific! Sir* Danny Dalton, if you like. And who am I? I mean, how are we related?"

"Big 'ister."

"*Great!* Well, Danny Dalton, why don't you just sit back and chill out and let's get it *rolling!*"

The sun has risen behind us. We cross the Delaware River and on into Pennsylvania. It's still too early, the first town we come to. We drive on. Danny Dalton, I must say, is a trouper. He's hungry, but I don't want to stop yet. I feed him cookies and juice till he doesn't want any more. Then I bite the skin off an apple and feed him the inside. He's hanging in there. Finally, we get to another good-sized town, where I drive around until I spot a car rental sign on a side street, part of a local garage. It's open. I circle the block, stop on the next street, and try to figure out what to do next.

Because I can't take him with me. On the other hand, how can I leave him alone in the car, on a strange street in a strange town? And, if it all works, what am I going to do with the Civic?

I take a deep breath, turn around in the driver's seat, face him.

"Here we go, Danny. This is it, our first big test. Switching cars. It's part of our disguises. I'm going to go get us the new car, and it's something I've got to do by myself. If the warlocks see me alone, I don't think they'll pay any attention. That means I've got to leave you all by yourself for a little while. I'm going to take you out of the car seat and lock the doors. I'll leave the windows open a little for air. You're not to talk to anybody while I'm gone, no matter what. Don't worry, I'll be back soon with the new car and then we'll do the switch. Meanwhile, Danny, you've got to be very brave. That's a big part of quests, remember?"

He nods. He has that squeezed, serious look he always gets when he's concentrating hard, or trying not to be afraid. I drive us back near the car-rental place and park, catty-cornered across, as close as I dare. Then I undo his harness, tell him to hunker down on the backseat. I hand him an open bag of pretzels. I kiss my palm and blow it to him. He catches it on his cheek, the way he always does.

Our first big test.

I walk across the street and into the garage. It's a local place, a working garage from the look of it, which rents cars on the side. That's what I want. Some of the places like Hertz won't rent to people under twenty-five. Plus that's where they'll look first, the national renters.

The man in the garage takes my MasterCard and driver's license, eyes me suspiciously. I expect that. He looks from me to my driver's license and back again.

"What's a pretty girl like you doing renting a car way out here?" he says, studying me.

I'm ready for that too. I tell him my story. It's about the man I'm in love with, or have been in love with, maybe still am—actually he's a professor at the college—and how we were supposed to go to Florida for the holidays. But last night we had this tremendous fight, and he's just brought me into town and dumped me. And how I've taken the week off from my job to go to Florida with him, and I'm still determined to go, all the reservations have been made and paid for, and I'll be damned if I'm going to wreck my life because of him.

Sad story. I tell it straight, and he takes it in. On the other hand, he's still suspicious.

"You driving to Florida all by yourself?"

"That's right."

"That's a long haul."

"Actually, I've driven it before. I have family down there—near Jacksonville?—and it's not too bad. Plus I'll need a car, once I'm there."

I could kick myself for not having said Washington, D.C. Don't people go to Washington, D.C., for the holidays? But I said Florida.

He asks me if I don't have a car of my own, at home. A lot of questions, I think, but I explain, calmly enough, that from where I live in New Jersey, my job—I work in New York City—is a bus commute, and though I can use my stepfather's car sometimes—I live with my stepfather—I certainly couldn't take it for all that time.

He nods. "How do I know you'll bring the car back, Rebecca?"

"Well," I say, smiling at him, "I guess you never

do know, do you? In your business? But you'll have my MasterCard number. And to be honest with you, I've got enough hassles in my life right now without another one.''

I keep my eyes on him the whole time, a steady, level gaze.

He buys it, I think. Finally, he goes inside a little office with a window looking out into the garage. From where I stand, I can see him at the telephone. As casually as I can, I walk the few steps to the entrance, the street, where I can see the Civic across the way but no Danny. There's no one else around. And back inside, where, through the window, the man is holding my driver's license and MasterCard up near his face and talking into the phone.

I hold my breath. I haven't used the card in ages. The expiration date is still a few months away, but there's a chance the Witch has canceled it. Now the man is either waiting or listening. Either way, I think, it's taking a long time. I clutch the keys to the Civic in my pocket. If he does anything funny, I'm going to run for it.

He puts down the phone. No expression on his face. Now he's rummaging through his desk, at the same time beckoning to me through the window.

Well, Becca, here goes nothing.

I go in.

He's bending over the desk, filling out the paperwork. There's the car rental form and two Master-Card forms, one for a deposit, he explains, which he'll give me back when I bring the car in, one for the rental itself. A deposit? I say. That's right, a deposit, take it or leave it. Then he goes over the insurance options.

I take everything, sign everything.

The car he gives me is a small blue Chevy. Automatic shift, which I hate, and over 30,000 miles on the odometer, but he says it's the last one he's got.

Once free, I drive quickly around the neighborhood until I find a semi-abandoned street. Vacant lots on either side, a warehouse building, a couple of dilapidated houses. Few cars. I park the Chevy. Then I half-run, half-walk, back to the Civic, trying to keep out of sight. Danny is right where I left him, only the top of his head visible, though he sits straight up as soon as he sees me. He's still holding the bag of pretzels.

"We did it!" I tell him excitedly. "Now back in the car seat, dude, we're on our way!"

I drive us back to the block where I left the Chevy. I glance back and forth—not a soul. Then I transfer Danny and the car seat, and clean out the Civic. I've had it in mind to take the license plates too, but decide against it. Maybe they'll find the car sooner or later, but it will be sooner, I guess, if I leave it without plates.

So long, Honda. Hello, Chevrolet.

So long, Justin, so long, Harriet.

24 December

That first night, at our first motel, I do my own disguise. I bought all the stuff I need in a drugstore, complete with curling iron and Dark Auburn coloring, but it comes out a total mess. When I take the turbaned towel off my head, I look like I'm wearing a magenta mop. Finally I venture out of the bathroom, and Danny laughs his head off. He thinks it's a joke-joke, an absolute hoot.

Ah well, too bad.

I've gotten better at it since. Now, I guess, I just look like some cheapo tootsie who snaps her gum at high school dances, and that's not bad.

Danny is both harder and easier. There's not much you can do to change a three-and-a-half-year-old knight. Don't tell anybody, but he's the one in the Pittsburgh Steelers outfit, with the padded jacket and the cap and the high-tops with the orange-and-black laces.

I think he looks awfully cute.

Georgia would have a fit, I imagine, over what he eats. It's only been two days, but already I'm having trouble with quest food. Bologna, American cheese (white, please, not yellow), peanut butter, Pepperidge Farm white (he likes the crusts trimmed off). I force him to drink milk, with some success. Juice. Fruit's no good, except for a few bites of bananas.

Oreos.

Sir Oreo, in his underpants and a Pittsburgh Steelers cap.

But what am I supposed to do, Georgia? You can't cook in motels, it's too dangerous to eat out on a quest, and still we've got to eat.

And TV. I know you'd say he's watching too much TV—I've always been careful about that—but he's the guardian of the lair when I have to go out scouting for food, and guardians of lairs always have TV to help them pass the time.

Cartoons.

Look, if there weren't cartoons on TV, we'd be in major trouble. Turtles, Looney Tunes, Heathcliff, with the clicker in his hand. Wiley Coyote. He cracks up every time Wiley Coyote falls off a cliff.

God, what am I doing, apologizing to Georgia for *television?*

Just feeling a little crazy, that's all.

We hit this great motel yesterday, great in terms of TV anyway. It has channels I've never even heard of. I've just had my first real night's sleep in . . . well, my first real night's sleep, and now it's morning, I'm awake, and he's curled up in the next bed, all cozy, and finally I can say to myself, Well, you've done it, Rebecca Dalton, it looks like you've really *done* it! It gives me gooseflesh all over. I think back over every detail, and I think, even if he's on our trail, which I imagine he is, how is he going to find us? Even if he's already found the garage, and the man has told him Florida, and he thinks that was just something I said to fool him, and he's bought maps, poring over them (with his reading glasses on), thinking Minnesota probably, and how far could she go in a day? Four hundred miles, five hundred miles?

I picture him in his usual chair, the living room, book open on his lap, reading glasses down his nose. Or playing solitaire, long fingers snapping the cards. Waiting for me to do something. Waiting for me to grab the cards, or his glasses, dump the table over, any damn thing. Waiting for me to go to the bar, why don't you go pour yourself a drink, my nude and lovely bitch, watching me go, the big 1.75-liter Dewar's, filling the damn tumbler while his eyes follow me, spilling a little, mopping the spill, sipping, shuddering from the raw bite, he likes—

"Hi, Becca."

From the next bed.

I jump sky-high.

"Well, good morning, Sir Danny. How'd you sleep?"

"Great."

Rubbing his eyes with his fists.

He'd have given anything to see me jump like that.

I was never allowed to wear clothes in the house, that was a rule.

Well. But isn't that the past?

Good morning, Danny Dalton.

We go in little steps, Danny and I. That's the thing about quests. When there's danger, you slip away in easy stages. Fifty miles a day, no more than a hundred.

I'm going to have to leave him this morning to find a supermarket. He's awfully small to be left alone, but you do what you have to do. I'm determined that we be seen together in public as little as possible.

"You're going to have to be a big kid, Danny," I tell him later. "A grown-up practically. I'll be back as fast as I can, but while I'm gone, you can do your coloring, watch TV, whatever you want, but you're not to open the door to anybody, understand?"

He nods seriously.

"No matter what?"

Nods again.

I make sure he's plugged into cartoons, lock the door on my way, drive off.

I top off the gas tank en route. What I have in mind is: We're safe for the minute, maybe, just

maybe, we can stay in the great motel another day.
And tomorrow is Christmas. I've been wŏrried
about Christmas, even though he hasn't mentioned
it. I still think my best bet is to try to skip it. On the
other hand, I'd better have a present for him just in
case. And one for him to give me.

I find the supermarket. It's jammed. I pick out a
giant canned ham, pasta and potato salad and cole
slaw from the deli, hard rolls, canned cranberry
sauce, a mammoth apple pie for dessert—enough,
anyway, for two days of feasting. I scavenge the col-
oring-book rack for Danny and splurge on the sixty-
four Crayola set and a box of fat, nontoxic Magic
Markers. For him to give me, I choose a card of
brightly colored barrettes and a selection of velvet
hair ribbons. And then I look for the end of a check-
out line.

It's totally surreal. All the lines snake back from
the cash registers into the narrow aisles, and every
cart in front of me is filled to the top. Obviously—
why didn't I think of it?—people are shopping for
two days. I've been telling myself—told him—that
I'll be gone no more than an hour, and it's already
been forty-five minutes. But if I abandon the cart
and leave, what will we eat?

The line inches forward. Finally, I'm up level with
the magazine rack. I reach for *People*, anything to
take my mind off my watch, and glancing down at a
pile of newspapers underneath, I see . . . his picture.

I clap my hand to my mouth, I can't help myself. I
don't think anybody's noticed. Newspapers are
stacked on the floor, under the magazines. Pretend-

ing that I'm just passing the time, I stoop, pick one up as casually as I can.

Yikes!

They're calling it the "Christmas Kidnapping." But it isn't even Christmas yet! And there's his *picture*, "Justin Coffey" underneath, and in the short article a description of both of us. Police in six states on special alert.

Which six states?

It doesn't say.

Nothing much about me. I'm just Harriet Major, the baby-sitter.

I fold the paper and put it back, picture-side down, reach instead for *People*. I thumb through it without seeing anything. When someone taps me on the shoulder, I freak, but it's only the woman behind me in the line, telling me to move forward because there's room now on the moving belt.

I pay cash, flustered lest someone see how much cash I'm carrying in my purse. By now I'm convinced everyone is staring at me. I flee into the parking lot, throw my bags into the car, fight my way through traffic onto the unfamiliar road.

By the time I get back to the motel, I've been gone almost two hours. The door to our room is wide open. I can see it from behind the wheel.

I leave all the stuff in the car and run for it.

A woman has him clutched in her arms. I've never seen her before. She has a kerchief tied around her head, and she's scolding him in some language—Spanish?—and he's kicking, flailing, pointing, and his little face is all splotchy.

The TV is blasting.

"Let him go, goddamn you!" I scream at her.

Then I grab him away from her, feel him clutch me hard, and shove at her with my free arm while she shrills at me in whatever the language is.

A cleaning woman. I slam the door in her face.

I understand what happened even before he gets it all out. He *didn't* open the door for her, she had a key. And he had to go, and he couldn't get his pants down, and he was afraid of the big potty in the bathroom, and finally (all contorted) he thought I wasn't coming back.

"Look, Danny," I say. I put him down, kneel, hold onto his shoulders. "Whatever else happens, I'll *always* come back for you. You have to understand that. Becca will *always* come back."

He nods, but even after we've cleaned him up, he's still clutchy, and he starts to wail again every time I put him down. I end up yelling at him—the wrong thing. And then I hear the door open behind me, and I all but jump out of my skin.

I jerk around, still holding Danny. A youngish man is standing in the open doorway, in a tweed jacket, with a sweater underneath. He says he's the assistant manager.

"Is everything all right, Miss?" he asks.

The cleaning woman must have reported us.

"Oh yes," I get out. I'm trying to rid myself of Danny—to get him down and behind me—but he won't let go. "I'm just having a little trouble with my kid brother, that's all."

"You sure?" he asks. "Nothing I can do for you?"

"Oh no, we're fine really. Please. We'll be leaving in a little while."

Still he lingers in the doorway, looking us over.

He acts as though he expects us to skip out on the bill, but didn't I pay in advance—cash—when we got there?

"Don't forget to leave your key in the room when you go," he says.

"I won't," I answer. "And thank you. Thanks a lot."

Finally this seemed to satisfy him. He leaves. But the minute the door shuts behind him, I put Danny down and start stuffing our belongings into the Gap bags. For God's sake, I'm shouting in my mind, his *picture* is in the papers! Don't motels sell newspapers? Doesn't this mean we're going to have to change cars again?

I grab Danny, grab the Gap bags, out the door, into the Chevy. Off. But even as we drive out past the motel office, I can see the assistant manager watching us from the doorway.

A little later, from the backseat, his small voice: "Don't be scared, Becca. It's okay."

"Don't be scared about what?" In fact I'm so jittery, or scared, or whatever I am, that I realize I've just missed the turnoff to the interstate.

"Them won't find us."

"*They* won't find us. But who's they?"

"Back there."

"Back where? At the motel?"

I force myself to concentrate on my U-turn, then head back in the direction we came from.

"Her wasn't a 'itch."

"She wasn't a witch. Who, the woman at the motel?"

"Uh-huh."

"Well, you're probably right. How could you tell?"

"Her 'air."

"Oh? What about her hair?"

"Not blond."

In spite of my nerves, I laugh aloud. I remember telling him that some witches have dyed blond hair. Certainly the meanest one I ever met did. And speak in deep-down voices like this. I also remember telling him that you can never be a hundred percent positive, because some witches wear disguises.

He never forgets a thing.

I swing us onto the interstate ramp, heading west.

From the backseat: "Was he a oarlock?"

"Who? Oh, you mean the man at the motel?"

"Uh-huh."

"Well, I guess he might have been. I'm not sure, it really didn't occur to me. Do you think he was a warlock?"

"Uh-huh."

"How could you tell?"

" 'neakers."

He *was* wearing sneakers, I noticed it too. But have I ever said warlocks don't wear sneakers? I don't know, maybe I have.

"Don't be scared, Becca. Them won't find us."

I want to stop the car, hug him.

Instead I say: "Relax, Max."

And from the backseat: "Take a chill, Phil."

25 December

He knows what day it is from TV. At one of the breaks between his morning shows, the announcer wishes everyone a very merry Christmas.

I half-hear it. I'm lying in bed, awake, wishing I had a cup of coffee and gearing up for some more explaining, but the next thing I know, he's kneeling on my bed.

"Is it Chris, Becca?" he says.

For once, I don't correct him.

"Yes, it is."

He's gazing down at me gravely. Maybe, for all I know, he's thinking about his mommy and daddy and the tree in the living room. Presents under the tree. He hasn't mentioned them once, though, since we left—not once. Damn, I think, here it comes.

Instead:

"It's okay, Becca. Quests. No time for Chris."

Out of the blue, I feel myself close to crying. I don't want him to see that. I turn my head away, get up, retrieve our presents from one of the supermarket bags.

I hold out his to him, keep mine.

"You're absolutely right," I say. "But that doesn't mean we can't wish each other Merry Christmas, does it? Merry Christmas, Danny."

"Merry Chris'mas, Becca," pulling at the crayon box.

But it's time to get rolling again.

24 December
Police Bulletin (Mock-up)

MISSING

Suspected Abduction

(photo Subject tk)

JUSTIN ELGIN COFFEY

Date of Birth: 6/21/87
Height: 37″ Weight: 31 lbs.
Hair: Brown Eyes: Brown

Last-seen date: 12/21/90 in vicinity of
St. George, NJ

NOTE: **Subject probably accompanied by Harriet Major, age 21, white female, height: 5′4″, weight: 110 lbs., hair: blond, eyes: blue.**

CONTACT POLICE DEPARTMENT,
ST. GEORGE, NEW JERSEY
TELEPHONE: 1-800-tk

Georgia Levy Coffey

27 December

The aerial shot looks almost as though the Goodyear blimp took it. I've seen it over and over. It shows the twin chimneys of my roof sitting over their steep gables, bare trees, the pool covered for winter and Justin's swings and sandbox set, the Robinsons' tennis court, then, lower down, cars and television vans parked on our road, the front lawn and my trellised rose arbor, the porte-cochère, the white columns of my front porch.

Probably some news helicopter took it. Every time I see it, I think the same thought: *If only they could lift the roof off, then they'd have me, a fish in the fishbowl.*

I've become addicted to my own story.

I've done whatever's been asked of me. I've met several times with Capriello, "Detective Lieutenant Robert Capriello of the St. George police." He belongs to the deli family. Everybody in St. George shops at Capriello's, and there are branches now in several neighboring towns. I've always heard it said that the sons who don't work behind the counters

are mafiosi, but this Capriello reminds me more of
an aging small-town accountant, with ruddy cheeks
and small, rheumy eyes and shirt collars too tight
for his neck. He said: "I don't think we need get
carried away, Mrs. Coffey. Ninety percent of these
cases are resolved in a couple of days. Either the
kids'll come back by themselves, or we'll find them
safe and sound."

This was the first morning, Sunday. I wasn't reas-
sured. In front of Larry, I told Capriello my version
of what happened. Essentially, that the Great Seducer I'm married to drove Harriet away, and she
took my son out of spite or revenge.

This brought on our last shouting match, while
Capriello stared at the floor. Larry swore that he
never slept with Harriet. He admitted to trying but
claimed Harriet had turned him down.

"If that's true," I hurled at him, "then she's got
goddamned better taste than I do!"

I've hardly spoken to him since.

There was more, though. He admitted to breaking
down the door on the third floor, trying to get at
her. (This, oh, yes, was on a night when his wife was
in the hospital, having just had her baby. *And with
my son in the next room!*) He told it with his head in
his hands, red-faced, claiming he'd been crazed by
other stuff going down in his life.

Some seducer.

He swore he'd exchanged no more than two
words with her after that. And that had been Tuesday. They'd disappeared on Saturday.

Even if what he said was true, though—and I
have my doubts—it still fits my version. He couldn't

keep his paws off her. In the end, he drove her
away.

My *husband*, for God's sake!

But guess what? Not even a hint of it, so far, has
gotten into the media. No "Second Love Nest Un-
covered in Christmas Kidnapping," although it
would be a juicy follow-up to the one in East
Springdale, where Harriet lived with her "stepfather." This has got to be Larry and Capriello in col-
lusion, protecting the Bereaved Daddy as well as the
sacred honor and reputation of St. George.

Instead, to the extent that there's a villain of the
piece, it's me. That's right. I'm the one in seclusion,
The Negligent Mommy.

I've also met, once, with a Special Agent Karnishak of the FBI. He's attached to some kind of missing children information center in Washington.
Apparently it's the law now that any missing child
has to be reported to the FBI. I guess the reason I
liked Karnishak better than Capriello is that he
didn't set out to reassure me.

But I can't stop watching the so-called news.
Even when they trash me. My friends call it morbid
fascination. So does my father, who's genuinely
worried about what's happening to me. I've let everything else drop, except for Zoe. My parents
moved in last Sunday, and my father canceled all
his appointments for the next day, which was
Christmas Eve. My mother has taken over the
household—she was the one who hired Clotie's re-
placement when it turned out Clotie had lied to me
(to hide the fact that she didn't show up at the house
till almost ten last Saturday, by which time they
were long since gone)—and my father has taken

over dealings with Larry. Together they do the police, "media control" (for one thing, nobody's allowed on our property), and they've hired some local lawyer, another Italian name, who argues with the police about things like the wiretap they want to put on our phone.

Conforti—that's his name—says they can do it with a warrant, whether we like it or not. Well, I say, let them get a warrant. I don't want them listening in when I'm talking. And I certainly don't want them around when Harriet calls.

She will. I know it. But I think I'm the only one who does.

One of the first things they wanted was pictures, photographs of Justin and Harriet for some police flyer. I know I took a roll, or part of one, last October, but the only shot I could find, after turning the house upside down, showed Harriet kneeling behind Justin on the front lawn, her face in shadow. I had plenty of Justin for them. They tried a police composite for Harriet, but the more I corrected the artist's sketch, the less it looked like anybody I recognized. I think they've finally sent out the flyer with a picture of Justin only.

The same thing happened with the phone numbers. The day I first met Harriet, she gave me a list of references—people I think she said she'd sat for in Minnesota. I know I made one call, got an answering machine, but then she was already here, and I forgot about it. For a while—a few days anyway—I'd had her list stuck to the refrigerator door by magnet. Maybe it got thrown out. But once the subject came up, I pulled the kitchen apart obsessively, drawer by drawer, cupboard by cupboard,

and the sideboard in the dining room where I sometimes stick things, and my *secrétaire*, my dresser,
and no, goddamn it, I couldn't remember the name
of the people I did call, either.

Then someone suggested the phone bill. The
phone bill? I found that—the bill for September—
and there it was, September 22, 612 area code. Colwell was the name—that was it!—but the Colwells
turned out to be a middle-aged couple, no kids. He
was some kind of surgeon. They spent a month every fall on a European trip. They'd never heard of
Harriet Major.

Another nail in my coffin.

The police found the house in East Springdale the
first day. I had no address for them, but they traced
it through the telephone number. Ever since then,
day by day, the details have come out. The house
was rented to a New York company, with a midtown
address, and the lease had been signed by Robert A.
Smith, President. The rent was paid each month by
a check drawn on a New York bank. The bank account was also in the name of the company, and the
same Robert A. Smith signed the rent checks, also
checks to utilities like New Jersey Bell and PSE&G.

But—surprise, surprise, the company turns out to
be a fiction. So is Robert A. Smith, at least in name.

The house, once the police got into it, bore no
traces of either Harriet or Robert A. Smith. Or,
needless to say, of Justin Coffey. The telephone was
still working. There was an answering machine too,
but no tape.

I've seen some of the neighbors interviewed on
television. They said Harriet had lived there since
last spring and that she'd been there all the time

during the summer, but only weekends since. The man who visited her there several times a week usually arrived at night, and his car would be gone in the morning. Some said he drove a fancy foreign car—possibly a Jaguar. Others said an American car. But if Robert A. Smith, or whatever his real name is, is Harriet's stepfather, then, as one of the neighbors put it on camera, he must have a lot of stepdaughters. Because Harriet, they all agree, isn't the first young woman who's lived there.

The media are having a wonderful time with this —"Harriet's Love Nest"—although one TV reporter, who managed to get inside, called it "about as sexy as a Holiday Inn."

The State of New Jersey has no record of a white Honda Civic registered to a Harriet Major, a Robert A. Smith, or Robert Smith Enterprises, the fictional New York company.

The police out in the Twin Cities can't come up with any trace of a Harriet Major, nor does the University of Minnesota have any record of her ever having been a student there.

More important, the "police in six states" who've been put on "special alert" (I keep hearing this. It drives me nuts. Why six states? Why not fifty?) can't find any trace of her either. Or of Justin. Or even of the white Civic.

The longer it goes on, the less anyone knows. And the less anyone knows, the more they turn on me.

I'm the one who knew Harriet best (Why don't they try my husband?), but I won't talk to anyone. I'm "in seclusion." Doctor's orders. But how—here it comes—could I have hired her in the first place? How could I have played it so fast and loose? Complete with "sidewalk interviews" on the streets of St. George, people who claim to know me and who say things like, "Well, you know, people like her, all that money, they think they can buy everything. They don't really care." Or (this was a St. George mother): "I imagine she feels pretty awful, and I do feel terrible for her, but it's sort of her own fault. I mean, some people take terrible chances with their children."

I've become a subject for *Oprah*.

Nobody knows what it's like, not even the people closest to me.

Christmas Day I did try. My mother prepared the dinner, and I dressed, gave Zoe over to the nurse, went downstairs. But the minute I walked into the living room and saw the tree, I lost it—I mean, literally, in the downstairs john.

Since then, I've retreated upstairs. I can't eat. Dutifully, my mother brings me trays, but I don't touch a thing. "At least this way," I tell her, "the weight problem will take care of itself." And since I can't even nourish my daughter anymore, what does it matter what I put in my stomach?

Nobody knows what the waiting is like, or how the dread *brrring* of the telephone jolts me, and I grab for it over Zoe, only to hear the threatening voices, the well-wishing voices, the women pretending to be Harriet, the "journalists" pretending to be anybody, the demands for money, the offers of money.

Yesterday, the day after Christmas, somebody—I think it was the *New York Post*—reported we'd already had a ransom demand. Since then, the phone hasn't stopped.

At the very least, my parents say, I should let someone else answer for me.

I continue, automatically, to pick up myself.

Every time with a knot in my stomach.

I'm convinced something could happen to Zoe next—if I let someone else handle her, if I let her out of my sight for more than two minutes. My mother says I've got to get up, dressed, out of my room, do something. Instead, I small myself into my chaise longue, the portable phone and the remote clicker on the end table next to me. And I wait, Zoe's tiny swaddled body tucked into mine. And I watch my story unfold on television.

She is my only consolation. I talk to her constantly. I marvel at every little detail of her: the sounds she makes, her gluttony at bottle time (she's made the switch to formula without looking back), the deep blue wonder of her inquiring gaze, her tiny hands. I won't let anyone else feed her, change her. I say to her: "If I somehow failed with your brother, if he is puny because of me, or has trouble with his consonants, or if he's been carried off because of my negligence, no, it will never happen to you, my darling.

"Because Momma won't let it," I promise her, the tears streaming down my cheeks.

Nobody knows what it's like when your milk dries up and the doctors say there's nothing to do, nothing whatsoever, it's over.

Helga Harris.

I never could stand her on the network news. Too

pushy and brassy-blond, I always thought, and according to Selma Brodkey, who works in TV advertising, she slept her way onto prime-time. But then there was some scandal involving her and the anchorman, and now she's back on "Five-to-Six," which is local, and, leave it to Harris, she's found a different angle.

"This is Thursday, December 27. I'm Helga Harris."

I'm only half-listening as she begins. Something about the anxious times we live in, the threat of war in the Gulf, the economy, blah-blah-blah, how we seem to thrive only on other people's misery. But then . . .

". . . the Christmas Kidnapping," she just said. "The disappearance last weekend from St. George, New Jersey, of little Justin Coffey and his baby-sitter, the mysterious Harriet Major. And the terrible plight of his parents, Lawrence and Georgia Coffey."

She goes on: "Why has the case so fascinated the public and the media? First, there is the mystery woman, Harriet, the baby-sitter, young and apparently beautiful, and in the absence of details about her life, we've been free to invent her for ourselves. And then there's St. George, that posh and insulated suburb. Aren't we New Yorkers a little jealous of people who live in safe places like St. George? A little resentful, too, because they've somehow finked out on us? Finally there are the Coffeys themselves, Lawrence and Georgia, your quintessential yuppie couple, he a Wall Street executive, she the daughter of a prominent psychoanalyst."

The familiar aerial sequence has come on as she

talks. Followed by images of Justin. Then a wedding picture of "the quintessential yuppie couple." Where she got that picture I've no idea.

"Lawrence and Georgia Coffey," Harris says, "as any parent will understand, are living a nightmare. They are the victims. Yet we of the media have treated them like the villains of the story. Thanks to us, they live today in a virtual state of siege."

By now I'm sitting forward in my chaise. Helga Harris, of all people.

"I've heard it asked: How could an intelligent, college-educated woman like Georgia Coffey have been so careless? How could she have entrusted her child to a woman she knew so little about? When Georgia hired her, Harriet Major said she came from Minnesota. Apparently she didn't. She gave Georgia references. Georgia has admitted to the police that she never checked them. Major said she lived with her stepfather in East Springdale, New Jersey. We now know that she did live in East Springdale, but that the man in question apparently wasn't her stepfather.

"But why didn't Georgia check? Why didn't she ask questions, call? How could she take it all on faith?"

Because I just did. Because I'm a trusting person.

"Why *wasn't* she perfect? Isn't that what we're supposed to be: perfect wives and mothers?"

Harris pauses, as though expecting an answer, but there's none.

"I have this to say on the subject," she goes on, now full face on my screen. "I happen to be a working wife and mother. I, too, entrust my children to strangers. Yes, they come with references, and I interview them and call the people who've recommended them, but they are still strangers. Like other mothers, I do what I do because I have to do it, and out of good faith, hope, and with my fingers crossed.

"But I, too, live with the constant fear that what has happened to Georgia Coffey could one day happen to me.

"Georgia Coffey, we've never met, but if you're listening, my heart goes out to you."

"I'm listening, Helga," I murmur aloud. "And I thank you."

"Meanwhile, the police investigation in the Christmas Kidnapping continues. This is Helga Harris."

Later, same day. I'm watching the "Ten O'Clock News" on another local channel. The anchor has just announced a possible new development in the Christmas Kidnapping case—what possible new development?—and suddenly there are aerial images of the heavily wooded ridge line that runs above our house and above much of St. George. It's actually a wildlife preserve belonging to the state, with a reservoir on the far side, some hundreds of acres, all in all, at the junction of three towns. Raccoons live there, and skunks, deer, some say even bears, and on weekends there are picnickers, joggers, lovers who carve their initials into the trees.

But this isn't a weekend. This is the middle of winter. What I see, from the news helicopter, is a line of uniforms advancing out of the woods onto a grassy area, and two of the men in the middle are being pulled forward by German shepherds on leashes.

". . . special team from the New Jersey State Police," the reporter is saying. "Today they combed some two-thirds of the area in question, looking for the missing Justin Coffey and his baby-sitter, Harriet Major. Darkness ended the search, but the searchers will be out again at daybreak."

I'm standing up in a state of shock, clutching Zoe in my arms. I can't believe nobody told me. Dogs! Police dogs! Now Capriello is on TV, our one-man police force, something about not being surprised that they found nothing but that they have to follow up every lead.

I put Zoe in her portable crib and head downstairs. Larry looks up, startled, when I burst in on him. He's on the phone.

"Georgie! What—"

"How *dare* they!" I rage at him.

"Wait a minute." Then, into the phone, "Howie, I'll have to call you back." He hangs up. "How dare they what, honey?"

"This is our *son*, for God's sake! He's not just some piece of meat!"

"Georgie, what the hell are you talking about?"

"I'm talking about Justin! I just saw it on television. They're looking for him with *dogs!*"

I tell him what I've just seen. Of course it doesn't surprise him in the slightest. He knows all about it. The police got an anonymous tip about the wildlife reservation. Like everything else, they have to check it out.

"But he's not dead!" I blurt out. "Justin's not dead!"

"Of course he's not. You and I may know that, Georgie, but—"

"You're damned right we know it! And so they waste all that time and manpower . . . ? But how come *you* know so much about it?"

"Capriello told me."

"Oh, did he? And nobody saw fit to tell me?"

"Georgie. Georgie, honey. It was only an anonymous tip. And you haven't exactly been willing to talk to people lately, you know?"

It's true enough, I realize suddenly, but that doesn't stop me.

"I want to see him in the morning," I say peremptorily.

"Who?"

"Capriello."

He looks surprised. For a second, I think I can read his mind—*What does she want to get in the way for?*—but he doesn't say it. Instead: "Sure, honey. Whatever you want. I think I can arrange that."

"Please do," I say.

28 December

"Do you think Justin's dead?" I ask Capriello point-blank.

We're alone, downstairs. It's morning. He's short and white-haired, always in a business suit, and his ruddy cheeks always look as if he's just come from a barber shave.

"I think that's one eventuality we have to look at, Mrs. Coffey," he answers. "Among others."

"But why? What possible evidence is there that he's dead?"

"Only negative evidence so far."

"What's negative evidence?"

"That Harriet hasn't contacted you. Mostly these cases don't last very long. If it's money, there's usually contact in the first day or two. But that hasn't happened, and that leads us to consider other eventualities."

"So that's your negative evidence? That she hasn't called?"

"No, not just that."

"Then what else?"

"That we haven't been able to find them. Not a single trace of them. Even with all the publicity, and this case has had a ton, no one's come forward."

"But how hard have you looked?"

"How hard? Look, Mrs. Coffey, considering that it's Christmas and—"

"What on earth does Christmas have to do with it?"

"A lot of the men take time off. We're always shorthanded over the holidays. But—"

I feel about to explode.

"Christmas! Are you telling me you don't have enough manpower?"

"We never have enough manpower, Mrs. Coffey."

"But you still have enough to go out with the dogs on a wild goose chase?"

"You mean yesterday's sweep?" he asks, unperturbed. "Those were the state boys. We'd gotten a tip. I didn't think there was anything in it, but we have to follow up. But I don't want you to think we're not getting the job done, Mrs. Coffey. If you take into account all the jurisdictions that are involved, not only in New Jersey, plus the FBI is coming on board, hundreds—probably thousands—of man-hours have already been spent on your son's case."

I'm not impressed. I ask him about Robert A. Smith, the possibility that he, whoever he really is, kidnapped both Justin and Harriet. Have the police thought of that? Of course they have, he claims, it's an angle they're pursuing actively. Then why haven't they found him? Don't they have a physical description? The physical descriptions are conflicting, he says. But don't they have fingerprints from the house in East Springdale? Aren't those traceable? They've had all the expert help they could ask for, he says. So far they haven't been able to trace anything, but they're still working on it.

"Whoever he is, Mrs. Coffey, he's a very clever customer. But we haven't given up on him, far from it."

I don't believe the Smith theory anyway. I still believe that the Great Seducer drove Harriet into acting on her own.

I say as much.

"Larry has been very cooperative," Capriello says. "Whatever went on between him and this young woman is a great embarrassment to him. But what bothers me—maybe you can help me here—is, if you're right, why would she have taken Justin with her? I can understand her taking off herself, but why would she have taken Justin?"

It doesn't escape me, in passing, that Larry is "Larry" while I'm "Mrs. Coffey." But I can't answer him. I don't know. Only Harriet knows. And until we hear from Harriet, the rest is chickens running around with their heads cut off.

Capriello mentions their flyer. He says Larry thought I wouldn't want to see it, but he has one with him.

I have to hold it in both hands. It makes me think of milk cartons and those little advertising postcards that come in the mail with pictures of missing children on one side. His picture. "Suspected Abduction."

"But you do think he's dead, don't you?" I say, handing him back the flyer.

"I didn't say that. We just have to consider that eventuality."

"But it's only been a week," I protest. "Not even." Then, when he says nothing: "But what do *you* think?"

"I just said, we—"

"I don't mean *we, the police*. I mean *you*. You personally. Do you think he's dead?"

The question seems to fluster him—his hand goes up involuntarily, touches the knot of his tie—but all I can get out of him is that they're pursuing every avenue.

Of course, I think wildly. He doesn't have to say anything, doesn't even have to have an opinion. *It's not his kid!* What's Justin Coffey to him other than an open case on his blotter, or whatever they call it, or a picture on his damned flyer?

And what am I to him, other than another hysterical suburban mother?

"Well, let me tell you something, Lieutenant Capriello. Justin's *not* dead. If he were, I'd know it. I don't know how, but I'd know it. And let me tell you something else. I'm not going to let this case end up like the Patz boy, the one in Soho, where a decade goes by and the police tell everybody they're still looking for him. This is *my* son. If you can't find him, I will, even if it means I have to stand on street corners handing out your stupid flyers!''

I mean it too, and I'll be damned if I'll let him see me cry. I tell him that, from now on, I want to know everything the police are doing, and I don't want to hear it from my husband and certainly not from the television news. I hardly hear his placating response —something about believe me, Mrs. Coffey, and our cooperation, and how it's just as important to the St. George police to solve the case as it is to me. I'm thinking something else. I'm thinking that if I want Justin back, I'm going to have to fight for him. I'm thinking that if, for example, the case has become a media free-for-all, then I, poor downtrodden Georgia Coffey, am damn well going to have to learn to use the media myself.

After Capriello leaves, I call Selma Brodkey.

I guess we were too competitive in college to be friends, really—always after the same grades and, once or twice, the same young men. I always thought I was prettier, Selma smarter. Or maybe quicker, sharper. She went into advertising, I into magazines. She climbed the ladder; I dropped out. (She's still single.) But we've stayed in touch, and I think of her as a friend, though of the second tier.

I haven't talked to her since well before I went into the hospital for Zoe. Of course she knows my story. She says she's been meaning to call, but she was too appalled, too upset for me. We commiser-

ate, we chat. Then I outline for her what I have in
mind, with the main proviso that, if it does happen
and once the segment is aired locally, it be made
available to any station, nationwide, that wants to
use it.

Selma sounds doubtful. Yes, she knows some of
the people over there, though mostly on the business side. Usually, she says, the producers pick their
own subjects for interviews and go after them themselves. But maybe, she thinks—just maybe—she can
pull in a favor or two.

"But I'm not asking for *favors!*" I remonstrate.
"I'm the fish in the fishbowl, don't you get it? You
should hear the phone calls. I'm the Bad Mommy
who's been in seclusion and wants to talk!"

"Of course I get it!" Selma snaps back. "Let me
see what I can do."

"Selma, I'm sorry, but for God's sake—"

"I know how important it is, Georgia. Let me get
off now. I'll talk to you later."

We hang up. The waiting starts. I begin to think
it's crazy, counting on Selma Brodkey. How do I
know she isn't calling around, telling people about
this idiot woman she knows who thinks she ought to
be on TV just because her kid's been kidnapped?

Shouldn't I be trying other people? How come I
don't know anybody who works directly in television?

Or should *I* call the station? Cold, like that?

I can't bring myself to do it.

I'm thinking of Andy Warhol and his fifteen minutes of celebrity.

It's already afternoon. Probably Selma's gone by
now anyway. Try getting anyone in advertising or

publishing on the phone Friday afternoons. That means I've blown it. I, Georgia Coffey, awoke from stupefaction long enough to make one lousy phone call on behalf of my son, and I even blew that. Timid little mouse. That's what my first nanny called me, I guess because I was always small: "Miss Mouse." It's almost dusk. The early winter dark is somehow worse in your own house than in the city, more palpable, more claustrophobic. It closes in, shuts out the world. You're stuck, prisoner in your own small environment, and you might as well be living on the moon.

What am I going to do? My God, he *could* be dead! I read somewhere that of the twenty percent, or ten percent, whatever it is, of cases of missing children that *aren't* resolved within the first week, some huge percentage are *never* resolved. That is, the children are never found, alive or dead. Like the Patzes. They're still waiting, after how many years? How can they go on living?

The phone's ringing. Oh, my God. It's already after six.

It's Selma.

"Did you think I'd forgotten about you?" Her voice is cloying, sets me on edge.

"No, of course not."

"Well, Helga has jumped at the idea. They accept your conditions. They want to shoot it Monday morning, in your house, for their Monday afternoon show."

I'm so overwhelmed, I can't speak, think. Monday? But Monday seems forever. By Monday, if there's no news in between, Justin will have been gone nine days.

"Why not tomorrow?" I ask. "Or even Sunday?"

"Because she's not on the air weekends."

"But what difference does that make? They still do news, weekends. Couldn't they put it on the 'Sunday Night News'?"

"Because she wants you for *her* show, dear heart, not somebody else's. That's how it works."

Selma tells me to stop being difficult. She's right, of course, it doesn't matter, I can wait. Helga Harris's producer, she says, will be calling me to make the arrangements.

"Oh God, Selma," I say. "Thank you so damn much. I'll never be able to repay you."

She says I owe her nothing. She wishes me luck.

Later.

I can't sleep, too keyed up.

I know exactly what I'm going to say. I have it all here, locked inside.

I'm not going to tell anyone about it either until the last minute. I know they'll try to talk me out of it.

Zoe's the only one.

"We're going to be on TV together, darling," I tell her. "You and Momma. We're going to talk to Harriet. We're going to have our chance."

31 December

"Have you found them?"

"What? Oh, hi, Mr. Smith. Happy New Year."

"Well?"

"No, not yet, but we're close."

"You've been close before."

"I know. She's some smart kid. At least we know the car she's driving now."

"You knew that a week ago."

"Yeah, but she's changed again. Whenever we get close, she switches cars. Look, it's a big country out there."

"In other words, you're nowhere."

"I wouldn't say that. It's a matter of time. We'll find them for you."

"I'm giving you twenty-four more hours."

"And then what?"

"Then I'm going to have to fire you."

"Hey, wait a minute, Mister. You want to play hardball? Listen, I can . . ."

"You can what?"

"Never mind. Look, I'm sorry I said anything. We'll give it our best shot. But you've got no idea how tough it is out here."

"How tough what is?"

"Getting people to work New Year's, for one thing. For most people, it's supposed to be a holiday."

"That's your problem, isn't it."

"Yeah, I guess it's my problem."

"Are you saying you need more money?"

"No, I'm not saying that. I just want to get the job done for you."

"Good. Now what about the other matter?"

"What other matter? Oh, the calls? Yeah. When is it you want us to start?"

"You have the schedule, don't you."

"Yeah, I've got the schedule. It says—"

"Just follow it, please."

Rebecca Anne Dalton

31 December

I awake in pools of sweat, heart pounding. The thin pillow is crushed in my arms. I'm on the edge of coming.

Disoriented by darkness, metallic smell, lights flickering somewhere above my head.

Oh God, will I *never* be able to get away from him?

Faint breathing near me. Danny. He's asleep next to me, same bed. The television is still on.

I must have dozed off.

I was watching an old movie, actors I didn't recognize. And feeling sorry for myself because it was New Year's Eve, and on New Year's Eve I was stuck in a motel room, somewhere in Ohio, with a three-and-a-half-year-old boy.

"It's not your fault," I remember telling Danny quietly, leaning over him in his sleep, touching his hair. "Nowadays I don't know any boys older than you or younger than whatever he is."

He told me forty-seven. I never believed him.

Then I must have dozed off. Dreamt of him.

"Put your drink down," he used to say. "Put it down. Why don't you come over here now?"

The signal in the words, his voice. Long fingers. Faint smile, intense eyes following me. The clutch in my stomach, no matter how many times I lived it.

I did what he said. Off came his reading glasses. He put them aside. Also the book he was reading. His eyes watching mine.

"Now take your position and calm down. Why don't you tell me about your day?"

There was never much to tell, until I started working for the Coffeys. Then there was Larry—had I met the father yet? and, later, had I touched his cock yet?—stuff that I knew turned him on. But I would stand in front of him as he'd instructed, my hands propped on the arms of his chair, legs apart, rolling forward onto the balls of my feet, onto his waiting palm, telling him about my day, telling him stories about Larry.

"You're so eager tonight," he might say, stroking me, "so compliant. What happened to your defiance?"

"Just eager," I would reply, reading his mood.

"Really? Or is it that you want it over with?"

"No, no. But please, I'm very eager."

"Well, what would you like? Do you want me just to stroke you while you talk? Or would you prefer something else?"

By then, his hand, dry and firm against my muff, would have begun to probe, and even though I'd long since learned what to expect, I still rose up in reaction against it, which he liked, my vagina squinching involuntarily as though to escape, and up onto tiptoes, leaning forward over him, the weight of my body making my arms start to tremble.

"You really don't want it then?"

"Oh no, please."

"Would you prefer something else?"

"No."

"Would you like to spit in my face?"

"Oh please, no."

"Why not?"

"Because . . . because . . ."

By then his fingers would be inside me, and I would be helpless against the wet of me, my own uncontrollable response which I had long since stopped trying to control, and my ass would have just started to rotate slowly, in compliance, defiance, whatever he wanted.

"Say it," he'd say.

"Because . . . because I love you," I'd manage.

"Yes?"

"And . . . adore you. Oh yes, I adore you."

"Open your eyes then," because my eyes would be jammed shut. "Open them."

And I would be looking at him, just inches away, his gaze full on me, calculating my mood. And, often, feel his hand slip away from me, his fingers, leaving me at the brink.

"You're always too quick," he would say. "First lick my fingers clean."

Invariably I would shrink back. But his free hand, by then, would have seized me by the nape, and I would take his sticky fingers into my mouth, taste the sour taste of me on his flesh, lick, "open your eyes, please," because I would have squinched again, "just pretend it's my cock. Imagine you have my cock in your mouth instead, you'd like that, wouldn't you?'' and I would nod, unable to speak, suck vigorously, or shake my head, depending, "If you really want it, I may let you have it later," and I would nod again, or shake my head, trying to say "Oh please let me," or "No, I don't want it," depending, except the words wouldn't come, only the expression in my eyes, imploring him to give it to me, imploring him not to.

Only then, if I was lucky—I would always know by the slight huskiness that came into his voice, the hardness of his eyes, whereas if I'd somehow failed to gauge his mood, there would be more first, sometimes he would have to punish me—but if I was lucky and had played my role "honestly," then it would be time for me to open his trousers, pull it free, which was the only test of whether I had succeeded or failed, and seize it, please God, in its throbbing erection, fit it hastily with its condom, guide it into me, spreading the wet lips of my vagina, impale myself upon it, while my ass rotated to hold me off it and my breasts smothered his face, and my arms, now gripping the back of the chair behind his head, trembled to the point of yielding, and talking to him, shouting—he always made me— I felt his growth, felt his hands grab the cheeks of my ass and spread them violently, and, inside me, the shuddering, rolling, involuntary twitching of my own coming, I want, don't want, oh please, can't stand it, do me, don't, please give me your come, please God don't come in me.

The truth? The honest to God truth is that I wanted it. I *always* wanted it.

So help me, I still want it.

*   *   *

I get up, achy, go into the bathroom, brush my teeth. Study my weirdo face in the mirror.

Great hair, Becca!

He used to grab me by the hair when he was teaching me, hard handfuls. He bent my head, and the tears gushed from their ducts, and I begged him, "Please! I'll try again! Please let me try again!"

Back to the room. It's only a little after ten. Crack one of Danny's juice boxes. Cellophane-packed Oreos. TV, on a high platform up in the corner.

Thank God for TV.

I flip channels with the remote control, find a news show. I only watch news while Danny sleeps. It is some kind of special about Times Square. Mounted cops with blue helmets. I can't concentrate. Nerdy as it is, I always secretly wanted to go to Times Square on New Year's Eve, in nothing but a fur coat, and watch the ball drop.

Exactly a year ago, I thought these same thoughts at Looney Tunes. Me and Johnny One-Note and the fur coat on Times Square.

The Witch was into fur, and fuck endangered species. I could have stolen one from the Witch.

I thought that thought too, a year ago.

I never even got to spend New Year's Eve with him. He dumped me first.

A reporter is interviewing people behind the barricades. They've been there for hours, and the reporter, shaking his head, says there's still over an hour and a half to go.

Commercials. My mind wanders off.

Twelve buried roses.

Regular news.

The motel air, musty, metallic, reminds me of Looney Tunes too. I ought to get up, open a window, even if it's freezing outside.

A year ago, the windows didn't open.

Something about the Christmas Kidnapping.

Something: ". . . recorded earlier today, in her own home . . ."

But—suddenly—I focus—it's Georgia, on TV! That's the living room, that's the pretty couch with the curlicued back.

They must have brought television cameras right into the house.

God, what if Danny saw?

He's still breathing evenly, eyes closed. Next to me.

I get up, click down the volume, stand in front of the bed to block his view. I'm glued, my fist tight on the remote control.

It's Georgia all right. Her face looks so small. Very tired too, pinched. God, she's holding the baby in her arms. Zoe? Must be Zoe. All wrapped up in a bundle.

It's not an interview. I recognize the other woman from TV, can't think of her name, but all she's done is introduce Georgia and now the camera's on Georgia, straight on her, and she's talking.

"Harriet," she says, "Harriet Major." My hand goes to my mouth. "I have asked to be on television in order to talk to you, woman to woman. I have no idea where you are. I have no idea either why you ran away, unless someone took the two of you, or why you took Justin with you. I just know that if you are all right, so is Justin. You have already taken such good care of him."

Her voice sounds funny. Maybe it's the TV, her nervousness. It sounds cracky, unsteady. Normally she has a very clear voice.

"I want Justin to come home now, Harriet. He is too young to be away from home so long, and my life is a wreck without him. I need him. He needs his mother. Surely you can understand that. You are too sensitive a person not to."

I realize that she must be holding notes in her lap because she stops talking, glances down. Then up again, and her eyes find . . . me.

It's as though she's talking only to me, right in the same room.

"If you're listening, Harriet—please listen. Give me back my child. If you can't bring him back yourself, call me from wherever you are and I will come immediately.

"And know this, Harriet. If you give me Justin, I promise you—I swear it—nothing bad will happen to you. We will bring no charges against you. I swear I will see to it that you'll be free to go about your own life.

"What is it you want, Harriet? You have to tell me. Is it money? If it's money, then you have to tell me.

"Harriet, I thought we were friends. I have *always* looked on you as my friend. I haven't stopped. The only thing I hold against you is that you never told me what was wrong, but it doesn't matter. Whatever happened, whatever made you do what you did, you are still my friend. I appeal to you now: Give me back my child. You are too young a woman. You have your whole life in front of you. Please don't ruin it, I beg you. It isn't too late. I am trying to help you. Whatever you're afraid of, we can deal with it together. Please call me."

She looks away again, not at her notes. Bites her lower lip. When she looks back at the camera, I see that her eyes have filled with tears.

"Please call me," she says quietly. "Please. I miss Justin. I'm very frightened. But the truth . . . real truth . . . I miss you too."

Is she finished? She's stopped talking. Now it's the TV woman talking again, but I can't watch it anymore. I'm sitting down on the edge of the bed. I'm shaking all over, like crying except the tears aren't coming, the ducts are all dry and burny. I must have clicked off the TV. The screen is uniformly dark. I realize I'm still clutching the clicker in my sweaty hand.

You never told me what was wrong. I keep hearing that, over and over. It's a horrible accusation.
You never told me what was wrong.
It's true.
But how could I have told her? Would she have believed me? Suppose I'd said: I've been living with a man I've only known six months, but he saved me from a mental institution where I was stuck ever since my mother decided I was an evil promiscuous bitch and that sticking me there would keep me from doing her any more harm?
And if she'd believed me, would she have hired me? I *had* to have the job.
The thing about Georgia Coffey, I used to think, is that she's never been miserable. The first time I met her, she struck me as one of those people who al-

ways make you feel as though nothing's ever really gone wrong in their lives.

Georgia Coffey would have said: "You mean you actually went off with a man you'd never seen before? How on earth could you do a thing like that?"

The idea makes me laugh. But now I've brought her misery too. I could see it in her small, tight face.

The Witch said, "You can get men with your twat, but you'll never have a real woman friend."

Who knows, maybe she was right?

One hot day last summer, I drove out to Bernardsville. It took less than an hour. I don't know what I had in mind, it was just an idea. Something to do. Maybe I thought I'd catch her in bed with someone new. Just to see the look on her face when she saw me.

I'd say, "Who's the evil promiscuous bitch now?"

Or I'd just lock her in the closet maybe.

I parked on the road and walked up the lane barefoot between the hedges, in shorts and a halter top. As soon as I saw the house, I started to lose my nerve. I mean, I was free, wasn't I, sort of? What was I doing, for God's sake, tempting fate? When I hadn't see her in almost two years? When I'd sworn I never wanted to see her again, as long as I lived?

Tough shit, I was there. Go stick it to her, Becca.

Three or four cars, including a new-looking Mercedes, but I didn't see a soul, although, once inside, there were noises from the kitchen. A TV, I thought. When I was little, I liked to watch the soaps down there with the cook.

I sneaked upstairs, and down the long hall where she used to march me. I tiptoed down to her bedroom. It was all frilly, pink and white and pillowy, scented just the way I remembered it, as though she could hide how stinking she was with expensive eau de cologne. Her bed was empty, though—too bad. So was my room, naturally. Everything there was pretty much the same—what did I expect?—except neater. She must have gone through the drawers, throwing my stuff out. I got as far as my bathroom, the far mirrored door, but when I opened that just enough to see the old furniture in the next room, chairs piled on chairs, and whiffed the same awful musty smell, I chickened out. For a second I imagined the closet, I didn't have to see it. Then I re-treated the way I'd come, past all the closed-off rooms nobody ever used, and back down the great main staircase, half-expecting to bump into one of the Spanish maids—"So, La Señorita, you coming down for lunch today?"—and it wasn't until I stole through the library that I spotted her.

She was lying by the pool, alone, on her back, her chaise in the flat position. I could see the top of her head, dyed hair glinting in the sun. Burn, baby, burn, but her flesh would be oily with sunscreen. I remembered standing one time almost in the same place, with Uncle Mark, watching her. That other, hallucinating summer. His arms around me. We'd just been fucking upstairs on her bed, and I was still half-stoned, and I remember him chuckling in my ear. "Do you think we should tell her?"

The memory almost made me giggle.

I watched her from the library windows, and I didn't feel a thing. She didn't move. Either she was dead or asleep. It was very hot outside. A blinding sun sent little waves and shimmers all across the concrete to the bath house.

But then, while I watched, one arm moved off the chaise. It came out sideways, groping for her drink. She didn't even look, just groped, found the glass, pulled it to her mouth.

Gin.

I could all but smell her breath.

Fumes of gin.

Then I realized I was shaking. Standing still, but shaking. Too afraid to move, too full of rage, something. And my brain immediately kicked into overdrive—what was I doing there? suppose Robert had been calling me? suppose he was coming early and I wasn't home?—and I remember thinking somehow there is always somebody worse than the last one, and I ran, back out the side way I'd come in, down the lane as fast as I could, back to the Civic, gunned the Civic.

Nobody saw me.

Home in time, no messages.

Lucky me. I never told him about it.

Look, I needed the job. I worked on him all summer about it.

"Who do you think would hire you?" he said. "To do what?" And, "What do you want a job for? Is it the money? Is there anything you need that I haven't gotten you?"

"No," I answered. "But I've got to have something to do. Come on, Robert, I'll beg you if you want me to. When you don't need me, I feel like I'm turning into, I don't know, some kind of vegetable."

"Some vegetable," he said. He taunted me about it. I should take up gardening, he said, or maybe quilting. Develop new talents. But it must have given him an idea, because one day in September—

I'd taken to buying the local papers, circling possibilities in the want ads—he said, "Why don't you try this one?"

I couldn't believe it. I thought he was joking. Then I was so excited, I hugged him. It was a miracle from heaven. I actually hugged him.

The ad, though, called for references, and of course there wasn't anybody in my past who knew me as Harriet Major. The name was his, as was the reference list he gave me, which I copied over in my own writing before I went for the interview. I shouldn't worry, he said with a sardonic smile. It was his small contribution to my joining the work force.

He questioned me about the Coffeys, right from the start. When he let me move in with them, did I really think that was out of the goodness of his heart? But it was only when the business with Larry began that I knew that the job he'd approved— Georgia Coffey's ad—was no accident, and by then it was too late.

Come come, my bitch, since when are you so prudish?

I tried—I mean, I didn't mind flirting with Larry —but I couldn't really bring myself to do it. Instead, I embroidered the story for him. What I did to Larry; what Larry did to me. When I told him I wasn't coming with Larry, he made suggestions. It turned him on, the whole problem of getting me to enjoy it with Larry, and some of the time I even thought that was it, the turn-on of it, because otherwise what did he want with a Wall Street guy who was starting his own business?

Until the last weekend.

Georgia was hysterical. She was overdue, and she'd just learned, that day, that she was going to have to have a C-section. Everything was a rush, the operation was scheduled for Monday morning, and how could I walk out on her like that? How did I expect her to take care of Justin in addition to everything else?

In fact I pleaded with him, over the phone. It did no good. I got him to let me stay over Friday night, but Saturday I had to go. Georgia screamed at me. I swore to her that I'd be back as early on Sunday as I could, but I went.

I was a wreck by the time I got to the house. He was waiting for me. He told me to take my clothes off the minute I walked in the door, no shower, nothing. I did, but suddenly I felt inside that I couldn't go on. I guess it had been building up. I felt like a fly in the spider web, all tangled in my own lies.

He wouldn't even give me time to pour myself a drink.

"I want to talk about our friend, Mr. Coffey," he said.

"What about him?"

"As much as you may have enjoyed it, there's another reason why you've been sleeping with him."

"What reason? What are you talking about?"

There must have been more to the conversation than that, but not a lot. Still, something I said, or the way I said it, or, God knows, the look in my eyes, made him turn suspicious, and he broke off what he was saying.

Instead he started questioning me about Larry. When was the last time I'd slept with him, where

was Georgia, what did Larry say, and so on. I didn't
last very long. In the end, I admitted that I'd never
once slept with him, that I'd been lying about it the
whole time.

"Oh?" he said. "You've been lying to me? Now,
why would you have done a thing like that?"

"Because I couldn't," I answered.

"Couldn't what?"

I started to stammer. "Couldn't. Couldn't do it,
Robert," I got out. "Don't you understand? Couldn't
do it to Justin. To Georgia. Couldn't do it to myself."

"Couldn't do what?"

"Couldn't wreck everything."

He kept his eyes on me for a long minute.

"You've never listened to me," I went on. "How
much it's changed me. They treat me like a normal
person."

He said nothing, no expression. I was used to
that. Then he smiled. Then laughed dryly.

"A consummate performance, Becca," he said.
"Highly resourceful. Leave it to my bitch to find a
new way to tease me."

"It's not a joke," I said. Somehow, this time, I
wasn't going to back down. "It's the truth." Then,
when he still didn't react, I stumbled on. "Anyway,
it's over between us. I'm going to leave you now."

I didn't plan to say that. It even shocked me to
hear it come out. But I thought: however he pun-
ishes me now, whatever happens, it's going to be
over.

He was very calm at first. Extreme, icy calm.

"Since you've disobeyed me," he said, "of course
you're going to have to be punished. Why don't you
go get ready?"

I poured myself a drink first. Then I went into the bedroom and lay down on my back and waited. Soon enough, I thought, he'd follow me in. I spread-eagled myself to save him the trouble and waited for him to tie me down. If anything I felt tired—tired of him, I guess. Very tired. I couldn't even think about what was about to happen. I don't think I much cared.

It seemed a long time. Then he came in. I expected him to go to the closet for his equipment. Instead, he sat on the edge of the bed, near me.

"Tell me, dear Becca," he said, taking the glass out of my hand and putting it on the night table, "what do you think is the worst thing I could do to you?"

I laughed a little. I felt beyond his mind games. I think I told him I'd rather leave that up to him.

"Really?" he said, his eyebrows raised.

"You're better at it than I am," I said.

He seemed to be considering that for a moment. Then:

"In addition to having disobeyed me, you're telling me now that it's over? That you're leaving me?"

"Yes."

"Does that mean you feel nothing for me? After all this time? No love? No hate?"

"I didn't say that."

"Well, what *do* you feel?"

For once, I wasn't going to let myself be baited.

"I'm just very tired," I said.

"Oh, yes. Poor Becca. But what are you going to do after I've finished with you? Go back to the Coffeys?"

"I don't know. Why don't you just do whatever it is you're going to do?"

"Yes," he said. "Good idea."

At this he leaned forward—toward me, I thought. I flinched a little, in spite of myself. But no, he reached instead for the telephone on the night table.

Somehow I got scared.

"Who are you calling?" I asked.

"I thought I'd better call your mother," he said blandly, the receiver in his hand. "I thought I'd better tell her to come get you."

I guess I went a little crazy. I remember lunging at him, struggling, trying to grab the phone out of his hand, and him holding it away, shaking his head. "No, no," he said. "I'm sorry, but you really leave me no choice. After all, I'm the one who's now responsible for you, I took you away from that place, and if it's over between us, somebody's going to have to take charge of you. You can't function on your own, you know that. And who else is there?" I clawed at the phone, clawed at him. I was shouting, crazed. He wouldn't, he couldn't, I kept shouting at him, and, in my mind: *Once she's finished with me, she'll only send me back! I'm not going back there!* I guess I shrieked that at him too, because I remember him saying, "You're right, that's what she would do. But wouldn't that be better than me?" And how it was too bad but I really couldn't be left on my own, anyone would see that, didn't I agree, so that he had to call her, who else was there now that I'd rejected him, and how since everything in the house was really his, he'd of course have to take my belongings with him, I'd greet her naked at the door when she came for me, her own twenty-one-year-old daughter, depraved as ever, but what she could or would do with me could hardly be worse than all the things he'd done, could it, and having already survived once at the institute, what made me think I couldn't again?

On and on, the phone raised in his hand, but whatever he said, my own imagination jumped past. *Evil promiscuous fat little pig bitch,* slamming me with whatever she could put her hands on, trembling with the pleasure of revenge, back into the closet with me, oh God, and before I knew it I'd wake up in nirvana city where the drugs knocked my brain cockeyed while the shrinks whispered in my ear about taking responsibility for my own acts and the seriously weirdo sickies, men and women with their mouths ajar, harmless it turned out, but looking like they wanted to tear me to shreds . . .

Guess what? I begged. On my knees, I clutched at his pants in my panic. He couldn't. Please, anything, but he couldn't. Anything else. I offered to suck him, lick out his anus clean, any of the special things I did for him, anything he wanted, everything. I begged him to kill me first, anything, but not that, please, oh God . . .

He slapped me just once, very hard, across the cheek. I was on my knees on the bedroom carpet, clutching at him, and he had the phone raised high, and with his other hand he slapped me.

I deserved it. I was very hysterical.

"Look at me, Becca," he commanded.

I looked up at him, through my tears, and he seized me under the chin, forcing my head back.

"You will never, ever, do anything like this again."

"I promise. I . . . I won't."

"Swear it."

"I swear it."

"You will do exactly what you are told to do."

"Yes."

"You know now what's in store for you if you ever lie to me again."

"Yes. I swear it."

He put the phone down.

But his pale complexion had turned swarthy, and his own hands, I realized, were now shaking. He tore at his clothes—he'd never stripped in front of me before—and then he took me. No condom. I didn't care. He grew huge in me. He kept telling me he loved me, how much he loved me, loved me, loved me. I didn't care. I was too done in to respond. I had no response.

On Sunday, he let me go.

Then, sometime the next week—if I'd had any doubts it was Larry he was after—he started in on Justin.

Someday, when I write the story of my life, I'm going to tell what it's really like to feel afraid all the time.

I've become an expert.

That, and running away.

But something funny happened to me that next week. Maybe it was that I was back in the house, the safety of the house, with Justin. On the one hand, I kept reassuring Robert over the phone that I had every intention of delivering Justin to him, and I kept telling myself the same thing. He'd won. He owned me now as he never had before, and yes, I would bring Justin to him before Georgia got home, and I'd stay there with Justin until Robert was finished with him, and then he could do whatever he wanted with me.

I'd learned my lesson; I understood; he didn't have to worry about me.

I believed it too. At the same time, though, I stalled, invented excuses. Every time I had the opportunity—and we were alone a lot that week—I'd look at Justin and I'd say: I'm going to do it, yes, but not today.

Then there was the mess with Larry. Trouble, too, with Georgia. Larry must have told her something, I could hear it in her voice. Everything was coming to an end.

And then suddenly it was Saturday. Friday, he said, "Today's the day, dear Becca." He knew Georgia was due home the next morning, that Larry was going to get her at the hospital first thing. "I can't wait anymore. If he's not here by tonight, I'll have to come get him myself. Please don't make me do that. You know what the consequences will be for you."

That night, after Larry came home, I thought I saw his Jaguar parked on the road outside.

The warlock in winter.

I lay awake that whole night, too afraid to fall asleep. I guess I knew by then that I wasn't going through with it.

Welcome to the real world, Danny Dalton.

Alone in the motel on New Year's Eve, hugging my knees, I'm crooning softly.

Blues, torch songs, one of Johnny's songs. Hoagy

Carmichael, I think. I don't remember who Hoagy Carmichael was exactly, but Johnny was hooked on songs of the thirties and forties, films too. He taught me the songs. He played the piano, I sang. We made love to the songs. He thought I could make a career, singing, once we got out of college. I had black in my voice, he said, black soul, even though I was as white as snow.

Oh God.

I was going to transfer to the university my sophomore year. We were going to live together off-campus, the top floor of a house.

But the Witch had other ideas.

So, I guess, did Johnny One-Note.

And there were other complications, including Uncle Mark.

Look, after all that happened, I probably deserved to be committed. But so did she.

Danny just stirred.

I bend over him, in semidarkness. He's still asleep, his eyes closed, but his body is restless, fidgety. I know the signs.

He's talking in his sleep, sounds more than words. Then the sounds give way to a kind of anxious, stammering whimper.

I lean close to him, try to shush him.

Then: "Mom-mee? Mom-mee?"

The cry knifes through me. His night cry. No matter how long he and I are together, no matter what, the one he'll cry for in his sleep will still be Georgia.

I cuddle him in the darkness, try to quiet him.

It doesn't work. He wails, now he's sobbing, pointing crazily.

"What do you want, Danny?" I ask him anxiously,

clasping him to me. "Oh God, sweetie, it's just me, Becca. What do you want?"

His eyes are open, inches from mine.

"Jutesy," he manages, hiccuping.

I find him a box of juice without turning the lights on, spill some of it puncturing the hole with a straw, then hold him propped up while he drinks. He takes only a few sips before falling back onto the bed. He reaches for me. I pull him into me, his head into my breasts, and his little hand reaches up for my hair.

My hair is his magic, even dyed. He tugs it, breathes it in, relaxes into sleep. Maybe it doesn't matter what happens to me, but at the end of the day there's the kid.

"Happy New Year, Daniel Boone," I whisper to him.

I hold him a long time that way. His fingers stay entwined in my hair long after he drifts off. I'm still holding him. If I let him go, I'm afraid he'll wake up again and call for Georgia.

What would she do if she picked up the phone and heard: "Hi, it's me, I just wanted to wish you a Happy New Year?"

Could I say, "He was in danger, that's why I took him away, but he's okay?" And have the courage to hang up before she started asking questions? Before the police could trace the call?

Because if the police could trace the call, so could he.

Could I say, "I didn't plan it this way, Georgia, please believe me?"

Keep singing, Becca. Eventually you'll croon the whole world to sleep, and then, when you wake up, it'll be a brand-new year, and then . . .

1 January

"Hullo? Hullo?"

"Is this Mr. Lawrence Coffey?"

"Yeah. Who the fuck is this?"

"Never mind. I'm calling to ask if you want your kid back."

"What? Who is this, goddamn it? For Christ's sake, it's three o'clock in the fucking morning! You've got—"

"Just answer the question, Mr. Coffey. Do you want your kid back?"

"You're damn right I want my kid back! What's more, I'm going to get him back. Now—"

"Then just keep your mouth shut, Mr. Coffey. That's all you got to do. You don't talk to anybody about anything, that's all there is to it. Not a soul. You just keep your mouth shut a little while, and everything will take care of itself."

Click.

"Who's this calling? Who is this?"

"Georgie, is that you?"

"Yes, I'm here."

"I think he just hung up."
"But who was it?"
"I don't have the foggiest. Did you hear?"
"Yes. I'm coming down."

Georgia
Levy
Coffey

1 January

The den is totally dark. I click on the overhead lights. Larry is standing next to his Stickley in his socks, no shoes, staring at nothing. I guess he must have fallen asleep there.

He turns to me, blinking at the sudden light.

"Do you know who that was?" I ask him.

He starts to shake his head, then his hand clutches at his temples.

"Oh Jesus, my head."

"I'm sorry," I say, "but right now I don't care about your head. I hurt too. Do you know who that was?"

He's staring at me now, bleary eyes in a moon face.

"No," he says. Then, with a half-laugh, "Probably some crank. Everybody wants to shut me up these days."

"What does that mean? Shut you up about what?"

"Never mind, Georgie. I think I'm about to throw up. Why don't you go back to bed?"

He rubs at his eyes with the heels of his palms, but

I don't care what he feels like. I'm wide awake, and my own insides are churning.

"Larry, was that a crank or wasn't it? And *what* are you supposed to keep your mouth shut about? Do you know something you haven't told me? For God's sake, this is our son's *life!*"

My voice is shrill. I can't help myself. Somehow this caller sounded real to me.

Larry stares at me some more, his mouth a little open. Thinking, not answering. Now he's shaking his head slowly from side to side.

"I'm having trouble believing it, is all," he says finally. "I'm . . . I mean, Wall Street may be down and dirty, but they're still not into kidnapping."

"What are you having trouble believing?"

Once again, the distracted look. It makes me want to scream.

"Oh shit, Georgie," he begins, and now I can hear the anxiety in his voice. His fist is cupped at his mouth. But he catches himself, sighs deeply. "Okay," he says, "you want to hear the dirt, I guess you're going to hear it. I still can't fucking believe it." Sighs again. "But I think you'd better make us some coffee. It's going to be a long conversation."

I tell him to put the water on, that I'm going upstairs for Zoe. That's what I'm doing, but I'm so rattled I don't know what I'm doing.

Three in the morning, the sudden jarring ring of the phone, but we must have had dozens by now, almost always when we're asleep. Most have been women, including one who keeps calling to vilify Harriet. Mean, awful people. Malicious kids too, who give themselves away by giggling.

But this one was . . . different.

Older, a male voice. Flat, matter-of-fact, working class. *Just keep your mouth shut, Mr. Coffey, that's all you got to do.*

Maybe it was that—the flatness.

But I didn't expect Larry to *agree* with me!

For God's sake, I feel as though I don't even know him anymore! And just a few hours ago—New Year's Eve—the most dismal of all the dismal New Year's Eves—we had a rapprochement of sorts. I'd been upstairs with Zoe, waiting for the phone to ring, jumping every time it did because I thought it might be Harriet. Instead, only people calling to wish us well, Joe and Helen, even Holbrook (for Larry), friends from the city. And then I heard his tread coming up the stairs, heavy, unsteady, and there he was, leaning against the door jamb in a billowing rugby shirt, a bottle of Rémy Martin in one hand, two of my Baccarat snifters in the other, and I had to laugh in spite of myself, because he was trying hard to look like Cary Grant.

He wanted to toast the new year. I declined. But he came in, praising me for the Helga Harris interview—"I've got to hand it to you, Georgie"—and teetered over Zoe's crib, and then he perched on the edge of the bed, drinking, and it all came pouring out of him. His own anguish, his own frustration with the police, his own fear that Justie might be dead, mingled with bitterness over something the Great White had done to him, and how he felt it all coming down on him at once, and for the first time in his life he didn't think he could handle it, just couldn't hack it.

I hadn't, I confess, given that much thought to

what he'd been going through, and it shook me to
see him that way.

"And there's us too!" he carried on wildly. "We
can't just stop living, Georgie! Separate bedrooms,
for Christ's sake, that's one hell of a marriage." He's
been sleeping in one of the guest rooms, at my insis-
tence. "And now it's New Year's and look at us,
we're in fucking *mourning!* Whatever's happened, it
can't go on the way it is between the two of us. All
that matters is that I love you! No matter what. For
Christ's sake, Georgie, I *love* you!"

And he'd started to cry, and in spite of everything,
I opened my arms to him. I hugged him, patted him
the way I would Justin, and the idea crossed my
mind, bittersweet, that that's exactly what he was, a
great big boozy needy bear of a child.

And somehow, at least for that minute, that was
okay.

But three hours later the phone rang, jerking me
out of sleep, the flat voice that wasn't a crank, and
now Larry is going to tell me the "dirt," and from
the sound of it, it's as though, after seven years of
marriage, he's got a whole hidden life I know nothing about.

My hands are shaking as I pick Zoe up. It's a miracle she doesn't awake. It won't last, I know. I'll
have to warm up a bottle downstairs.

We've been talking for a good hour, longer. Larry
mostly. I've made two pots of coffee and, for him,
scrambled eggs, Canadian bacon, English muffins.
We've had Zoe awake and starving, and eating, and
now she's asleep again, wrapped up in her Kanga-
rocka-roo on the butcher-block counter.

It all started, he says, in 1985, the year he made a million bucks, which was also the year he started selling "Big Bears." A Big Bear, he explained, was a kind of sandwich, a slice of this, a slice of that— "tranches," he called them, but then he lost me in a barrage of initials: CMO's, IO strips, PO strips, something called "Remics," it didn't matter, he said. Because money started coming out of the woodwork, brand-new S&L's, state-chartered banks, credit unions, accounts nobody ever heard of but all with money to burn and all of them, so it seemed at the time, coming to the Big Bear at Shaw Cross. One new customer leading to another, and none of them too particular about where the money got placed, as long as it got placed.

"You take a guy like Mulcahy. You met him, didn't you? Came out of real estate. The little Irishman with the hand-painted ties? Sure, I had to work for it. I schmoozed the hell out of him. I talked to him five days a week, fifty-two weeks a year—still do—or did—and when he sneezed, who do you think blew his nose for him? But whenever he got stung—and it happened—you know what he said? He said, 'Not to worry, Bear, there's more coming.' "

I don't see what Gerry Mulcahy has to do with the anonymous call, but he waves me off, says he'll come back to it. Then comes a long digression on Shaw Cross, all about how, after he became a shark himself, he stayed on top of these "gray accounts," even though he doled out their day-to-day to his guys in the Aquarium. And when the Great White put The Deal to him last October, he thought they were his customer base, that he would continue to sell them Shaw Cross products just as he always

had, and make money too, and in fact he'd had
them all lined up, ducks in his pond. Until the Great
White pulled the plug on him.

"I've been such a sap, Georgie. Look, it's been a
crazy time for me, all fall. You were about to drop
Zoe, and, well, a lot of shit was going down all at
once. I missed the signs. What can I tell you? I
missed the fucking signs."

It all has to do, apparently, with some clause in
The Deal that he didn't get to see until the week I
was in the hospital. It prohibits him, he says, from
doing business with any of his old customers. Effec-
tively, he says, it puts him out of business before
he's even started. Once he saw it, he stormed the
barricades, but it did no good.

"Do you know what the son of a bitch has done
now?" he says bitterly. "The Great White called me
last week, Leon Gamble himself. Says in view of the
awful business with Justie, they're keeping my old
contract in force indefinitely. Till it's all over, and
then we'll talk again. Says that'll be one less thing
for me to worry about. But do you know what that
means, honey? It means that as long as we *don't*
find Justie, I can still put food on the table! The
lousy son of a bitch. How do I know *he* didn't pay
the guy to call us tonight? How do I know *he* doesn't
have Justie?"

He's pacing now in his socks, and twiddling at his
hair the way he always does when he's agitated, but
I still didn't see the connection between his business
problems and Justin.

"The big question is why, isn't it? Why did they do
it to me? I mean, look, Georgie, I know I'm no genius, you could even say I've been lucky, but I'm

also pretty damned good at what I do, and I've made The Cross a potful over the years. I put it to Gamble that morning, while you were in the hospital. 'Leon,' I said, 'why are you doing this to me?' He gave me some bullshit that The Cross couldn't afford just to give me those accounts. But the real reason—the only one that makes sense—is that they want me out of the loop."

"The loop?" I say. "What loop?"

"The circuit. The information circuit. The dirty-money circuit."

"The what?" I say.

"That's right. Dirty money, funny money, that's what this is all about." He half-smiles at me. "I guess I've been like a fence, honey. Like a receiver of stolen goods. Hell, I know it. I think I've always known it."

I stare at him, uncomprehending.

"It's got to be, Georgie," he goes on. "Look at it this way. Do you have any idea how many S&L's have gone belly up the last couple of years? It'll be in the thousands by the time we're done. Look, we were selling them all sorts of paper, stuff they could book as assets while they spread their losses over umpteen years. The regulators knew it too. It's been a political hot potato for a decade, more. Only sooner or later, it caught up with them. They ran out of cash. Bad management, fraud, shitty investments, worse investments to cover up the shitty ones, then boom, another one bites the dust.

"But my guys? Not a one, honey. And not because they're smarter than the next guy either. If there was any logic, Gerry Mulcahy would have been first in line at bankruptcy court.

"So why wasn't he? Why is he still on his feet? Because the cash kept rolling in. I never asked where it came from, he never told me, but he was dumb enough—this was a few years ago—to let on that they kept double sets of books, and once—maybe he'd had too much to drink or maybe, for all I know, he wanted me in on it in case was ever trouble—I got a glimpse of their income statement and balance sheet. I mean, the real ones. They showed their losses all right—and they were reserved up the giggy—but their assets were growing so fast, all he had really had to worry about was placing the money. He was a fucking conduit, that's all."

"You're saying it was dirty money?" I ask.

"Look, it was complicated shit. It'd take me a week to explain, and I don't know the whole of it. He did the same dumb stuff they all did, but underneath it there was always cash. Some of his investments with me came in from the Caymans, Panama, once or twice Switzerland, but a lot of it direct too. I just followed his instructions. I was too busy selling. I mean, we're talking millions, Georgie. And Gerry Mulcahy was only one of my guys."

His voice trails off. He's sitting again, perched on a kitchen stool and draped over the butcher-block counter, tracing a groove in the polished wood with his forefinger.

"I've been some asshole, honey," he says. "All along, I thought I was this hot-shit seller, and all I was was your A-Number-One patsy. I think I was set up from the beginning. I think they needed somebody who was too busy raking in the chips to look too close. Or if he looked, would keep his mouth shut."

"But even if you're right," I ask, "why would they want to shut you up about it now? It makes no sense. You say you've known about it a long time. Why now?"

He doesn't answer. He's simply shaking his head slowly from side to side, his eyes on the counter.

"But you didn't do anything illegal, did you?"

He's still shaking his head. He says he doesn't know, that he'd have to ask a lawyer if he did anything illegal, and it surprises me, in passing, that he hasn't already asked a lawyer. Isn't Joe Penzil his best friend? And what about Holbrook? He never makes a move without consulting Holbrook. But he's clearly thinking of something else too—the phone call?—and not telling me, and that unnerves me.

"Are you telling me Justin was kidnapped because of what you know?" I manage to ask. "Is that what you think?"

It sounds crazy, even as I say it.

No answer at first. Then: "They're being investigated, honey. The Cross. It has to be. I bet it's already started."

"Investigated by whom?"

He shrugs.

"The U.S. Attorney's office," he says, staring at the counter.

"How do you know that?"

"I've got my grapevine," he says. "The place is locked up tighter than a drum. Gamble's suddenly gone apeshit over security, and Schwartzenberg's got lawyers, auditors from outside, crawling all over the place. They must have known it was coming last October. They must have decided to shut down my whole side of the operation, get rid of the bodies. Why else did everybody stop talking to me? I think the Great White's scared shitless about how much I know."

"To the point of *kidnapping?*"

Again he doesn't answer. His eyes seem riveted on a groove in the butcher block, and now, crazily, I'm starting to believe it—he clearly does—and I'm panicking.

"But what are we going to do about it?" I cry out. "The man on the phone said you've got to keep your mouth shut and we'll get Justin back, but what does that mean? How long are you supposed to keep your mouth shut? Larry, look at me! For God's sake, what are we going to do?"

He looks up at last, white-faced. His moon eyes stare at me, surrounded now by dark circling shadows, like halos in reverse.

"Shit, Georgie," he begins. But then he breaks off, a helpless gaze.

"For God's sake, what are we going to *do?*" I repeat. "Are we supposed to sit still and do nothing?"

"I guess it's too late for doing nothing," he says. Then something like: "Don't get me wrong, honey, not in a million years . . . Jesus Christ, had I known what was going to happen . . . while you were in the hospital . . . just exploratory, a fishing expedition . . ."

I stare back at him in disbelief.

"What in God's name are you talking about?" I explode at him.

"I'm trying to tell you, Georgie! I've already

talked to somebody, but it was *before* Justie!" His hands are up, palms up, as though in self-defense. "Christ Almighty, I had no way of knowing."

"No way of knowing what? What are you saying?"

What he is saying, or trying to say, and my hands are shaking, listening to him, is that the week before Justin was kidnapped, while I was in the hospital with Zoe and after his confrontation with Leon Gamble, he already had a conversation about Shaw Cross—preliminary and confidential, he keeps saying—with a lawyer from the Justice Department. Somebody by the name of Joe Richter.

3 January

By the time we went to bed, the first light of 1991 had come up weakly through the bare trees outside. I stood by my kitchen windows, staring at the blue tarpaulin that covers the pool in winter, dirty with sodden leaves and water that ought to have been cleared away.

Happy New Year.

Maybe Larry slept. I didn't.

A "fishing expedition."

He keeps saying that. He's said it to me, he's said it to Karnishak since and Capriello, everybody. His conversation with Richter (he keeps saying) was very general. He depicted himself as an innocent bystander, a conduit, like somebody who might have witnessed a crime without even knowing it was a crime. He was looking for some kind of guarantee from Richter before he went any further—not just confidentiality but, if it came to that, immunity from prosecution too.

Richter turned him down.

And that was all there was to it, Larry told me, has told everybody since. The way they left it, he was to call Richter if he decided to go forward. And if he didn't? Then—according to Larry—they both agreed that their conversation would never have taken place.

"Have you talked to him since?" I asked him, that same New Year's morning.

"Yeah, I have. But nothing substantive. He called a couple of times last week, wanted to know if I'd made up my mind. He sounded pretty eager. I got the feeling—not in so many words, but that they were already looking at The Cross. But I said I couldn't do anything, not till this thing with Justie is resolved."

"This *thing* with Justin? Is that what you call it, this *thing*?"

No answer.

According to Larry, he told nobody about Richter, not even Joe Penzil. Not even me. He claims he tried telling me while I was in the hospital, the night I sent him away because of Harriet. Maybe he did, but all I remember is that guilty, sheepdog expression on his face. As far as Joe Penzil went, Joe did know he was under the gun, that The Cross was fucking him, but so did a lot of other people.

"And what did Joe say?" I asked him.

Joe's advice had been not to do anything rash.

"But you went ahead anyway?"

"Georgie, how many times do I have to tell you? It was just a fishing expedition."

"And the next thing we know, Justin is missing, and now we get a phone call telling you to shut up?"

"Jesus Christ, we don't even know if the phone call's connected. Maybe it's our own paranoia. For all we know, it was another crank."

"But you think it's connected yourself, don't you?" I looked at him. "Well, don't you?"

No answer.

But if it was paranoia then, it certainly wasn't when the second call came, and the third. The telephone, which was my hope—I was absolutely convinced, Monday, that Harriet was going to call—has now become my enemy. I dread its ringing. Once I picked up on him myself. I was sure it was he, even though he hung up as soon as he heard my voice, and sure enough, within minutes, the phone rang again. This time Larry got it, and it was the same message, the same flat voice.

They've sent the tapes off to some lab for voice analysis. I've only just found out about it, but apparently, for the last week or so, our phone *has* been tapped. It seems my dear husband authorized it, via Conforti, the local attorney, and "somehow" they neglected to tell me. Maybe it's a good thing, although I don't know what they expect to find from voice analysis that I can't tell them—that the speaker was (is) white, American, male, working-class, somewhere between thirty and fifty.

Small world.

It's Thursday now, two and a half weeks since Zoe was born, and I ought to be well on my way to recovering. Instead, I'm an emotional wreck. I'm going to see Craig. I called him yesterday, asked if he could fit me into my old Thursday time slot. Yes, he said. Only after I hung up did I wonder if he knows what's happened to me.

He must know. If he doesn't, he must be the last person in the world not to.

I asked Helen Penzil if she'd come sit with Zoe and the baby nurse while I'm gone. Crazy, I guess—why have a baby nurse in the first place?—but I haven't been away from Zoe since she was born, and I wouldn't leave her otherwise.

So Helen is there, and I'm driving. Everybody was against it—Larry wanted to drive me in, my father offered to come out and get me, my mother insisted I take a taxi—but I don't care. It's my first time behind the wheel, my first outing of any kind, and even though I still hurt in my belly, the simple automatic gestures of driving are a kind of liberation. I'm going somewhere, actually *doing* something, and I guess it's a measure of how the police can keep developments in a case under wraps when they want to that, when I emerge between the banks of rhododendrons that border our driveway, there's no longer any gauntlet to run.

It's been ten days, ten whole days since the Christmas Kidnapping. That must make it old news.

Strange, but when I finish telling Craig the story, I find myself tongue-tied. I have no opinions. What's happened has happened. It just is. My son is missing, thanks in large part to his father, and that's just the way it is.

End of subject?

We stare at each other.

"I wonder," Craig says finally, "if you're not also a little relieved."

"Relieved?"

He nods. "You mentioned how guilty you felt at first. You said you felt responsible in the beginning. It was your fault for having hired Harriet in the first place."

"Oh sure!" I exclaim. "To find out that my son was really taken by the Mafia or some Colombian drug cartel instead of a twenty-one-year-old woman? That comes as a great relief."

Maybe I'm exaggerating a little—as always, Craig's obtuseness irritates me beyond belief—but am I really? Yesterday morning, I heard Karnishak, the FBI man, say it right in Larry's face: "If what you're telling us now is true, Larry, then the list of possible perpetrators might be as long as your Rolodex." Larry had been alluding to dirty money, but when Karnishak tried prodding him on details, Larry kept breaking it off to huddle with Conforti, the local attorney who's supposedly representing us, and, once, for a phone conversation with Joe Penzil. I stood it as long as I could. Then, in front of everybody, I shouted at him, "How dare you? Isn't it a little late to worry about incriminating yourself, or slandering somebody, or whatever it is you're so worried about? Our son's *life* is at stake!"

I know he's since talked to Richter, the Department of Justice lawyer, and that some kind of investigation is in progress. But so far it's given nothing.

Oh yes, great relief.

But Craig only gazes at me, with all the affect of a Wrigley's chewing gum ad.

He actually does chew gum, on occasion.

A reformed smoker? Who knows?

"I feel like such a fool," I say.

"Why is that?"

"I'll tell you why." I realize I'm gritting my teeth. "Do you know what my husband is saying now? That he's taking 'full responsibility.' Oh yes. He admits that he brought it down on us—unintentionally, he says—and the only way he can live with that is by doing whatever he has to to get Justin released, whether that means keeping his mouth shut or pointing some fingers."

"But why should that make you feel foolish?"

"Because they've taken over my house! The downstairs anyway. You should see them. They've turned the den into Mission Control, and *he's* the one in charge. They're all in there, he and the police, the FBI, the lawyer, all huddled together as though it's first and ten at the Super Bowl—" I see him as I say it, head lowered, damned fingers twiddling at his hair—"except *he's* the quarterback, and they're all explaining the plays to him, his options."

"That sounds more like resentment to me," Craig says mildly.

"*Resentment?* Of *course* I resent it! I'm *furious!* I now think he did something crooked, whatever he says, and now we're all paying for it. But there he is, Mr. Take-Charge, taking 'full responsibility.'"

Craig says nothing. I glare at him. I've already had this conversation with my father. He said, "There's no law that says a psychoanalyst has to be a genius, Georgie," and I said, "But there's no law he has to be a schmuck either." And a pretty one besides. Because he *is* pretty, in a very Wasp-y way. Not much older than I am, if at all. Sandy hair, blue eyes, the rugged, denim-shirted, tweed-jacketed type. Could be a model—for Wrigley's.

I had my father check him out at the beginning. He came out of Payne-Whitney, impeccable credentials.

"I'll tell you this much," I snap at him. "If it weren't for my son, Lawrence Elgin Coffey and I wouldn't be living together right now."

The words bang off the walls. Did they penetrate? Or just carom off his head?

He nods.

"And how does that make you feel?" he says. "Resentful, angry, anything else?"

I explode. "Is that all you can say? I mean, goddamn it, I've just made a fairly major revelation, and is that the best you can do: how does it make me *feel*? No, don't tell me, you're going to ask me what I would have you say, aren't you?" Another nod, and this time the trace of a smile. "For God's sake, is that why I'm paying you a hundred and twenty-five bucks an hour?"

Even though Larry's insurance covers it.

Or used to.

But suddenly, before he can say it—Why *are* you paying me a hundred and twenty-five bucks an hour?—I feel the tears welling. Welling? *Gushing!* I hate it, losing control, and in front of him, but I'm powerless to stop them. They flood out of me like a tapped well. It's not him, it's not Larry. It's . . . it's everything. Suddenly, oh God, I'm completely done in.

I reach for the box of tissues on the end table next to me, blow hard, wad them in my fist because I know there's no place to throw them, but this only helps momentarily. Then I'm off again, sobbing uncontrollably.

"I'm sorry," I blubber, lips quivering. "I can't help it. It's just that I feel . . . I feel so damn . . . so goddamn . . . *helpless.*"

Eureka, Georgia! Out with it, girl!

Because this—my own helplessness . . . well, it has to be my oldest theme. Certainly it predates Craig. Greenberg used to say, "Of course you feel helpless, you're a woman." (Greenberg, needless to say, was a woman too.) In the past, though, it's always tied into Daddy, all the fallen hero stuff, and how, lest the helplessness overwhelm me, I've always felt compelled to prop him up in my mind no matter what. But this time, it's . . . it's everything. It's the feeling of having to try to hold everything together, all by myself. It's me waiting by the phone, and Larry "taking charge," and somewhere my son, Justin Coffey, my helpless little boy with the dark mournful eyes. And, oh God, how helpless I am now to help him!

I see Craig glance surreptitiously at his watch. If he says it—"Well, that's all we'll have time for today"—I think it's in me to wring his neck, but of course he doesn't. He just nods at me one last time and scrapes back his chair. I cry my way out of his office instead, and still when I'm driving, fighting the rush-hour mob through the Lincoln Tunnel and west. When I get home, it's already dark, I struggle up the front steps, in the door and up the stairs, gasping for breath, to where an astonished Helen Penzil is standing up in the nursery, and the baby nurse stands too, their mouths ajar. "Georgia, what's wrong?" "Nothing," I manage, and I snatch my Zoe into my arms, warm bundle, and clutch her, hug her, and I guess I'm still crying. Or all over again.

Oh please, God, let it end. Please, please, dear God, let it just end.

3 January

"Hey there, Mr. Chairman! Happy New Year and good evening. You all set for next week?"

"Jesus Christ."

"What's wrong? My clients are hot to trot. They'll be here Monday or Tuesday. You're going to be a very rich man."

"I may not make it till Monday or Tuesday, the way things are going."

"Oh, come on, what are you talking about?"

"I'm not in the mood for your humor, Counselor."

"Humor? I don't get it."

"Don't tell me you don't know what's going on. The shit's hit the fan, that's what."

"Have you forgotten something? I've been away on vacation. Even hard-working lawyers are entitled to a few days off."

"You'd have had to be in Timbuktu not to have heard."

"Heard what?"

"The Coffey kid?"

"Oh yeah, seems to me I did hear something about that. The Christmas Kidnapping. I thought that was

a little extreme on your part. Ingenious, but a lit-tle—"

"On my part? What the fuck are you talking about? I told you, I'm not in the mood."

"I'm not joking, Leon. It stands to reason. The last time we spoke, it was because Mr. Coffey was shooting his mouth off to the wrong people. If I'm not mistaken, I was the one who found out, and I was the one, out of the goodness of my heart, who told you about it. The next thing that happens, the boy has been taken. If it wasn't you, it was one hell of a coincidence."

"It wasn't me."

"Are you saying—?"

"I could even prove it if I had to."

"Oh? How's that?"

"Because we're in deep shit, all of us. It's all about to blow up in our face."

"What do you mean?"

"I just had a visitor, that's all. Let's say it was the ghost of J. Edgar. Seems our friend—Coffey—has been shooting his mouth off again, only this time he's named names. Seems the son of a bitch got some threatening phone calls, somebody telling him to keep his mouth shut, and now there's a fucking list out, and guess who's on top of the list?"

"You?"

"Me."

"Jesus Christ. I mean, I'm very sorry to hear that, Leon. What did you tell your visitor?"

"Him? Fuck him. I told him the man's paranoid, that there's no substance to his allegations. I told him I run a reputable company, that we deal with reputable people."

"Good. Did you see the list?"

"Sure I saw it. Everybody on it's been alerted."

"Good."

"For the time being. But if I had the kid, what do you think I'd be doing, playing fucking gin rummy with him? Do you think any of this would have happened?"

"No. But who do you think has him then, Leon? If you don't."

"How should I know? The papers are talking about this girl, the baby-sitter."

"I saw the papers too, Leon. But I'm asking you. Who do you think has him?"

"Beats me."

"You disappoint me. I'm terribly disappointed. All this time, I thought we were pretty close friends."

"Friends? What are you talking about?"

"Who's your silent partner, Leon?"

"My si—? You know I can't tell you that."

"I know that's what you've always said. But this is a new ballgame."

"I can't tell you. I made a deal."

"That's okay. I just wanted to see where your loyalties are today, now that you're the one who's under the gun. It doesn't matter anyway. I know who he is, Leon."

"You WHAT? For Christ's sake, don't fuck with me, I—"

"Holbrook, Leon. Francis Hale Holbrook. We're all friends, Leon. I've known him for years."

"Son of a bitch. How'd you find out? Did he tell you?"

"Nobody told me. It's the kind of thing I make it my business to find out. I've known all along."

"For Christ's sake."

"Think back, Leon. Nine, ten years ago, your illustrious company was moribund. The competition was killing you. Everything the Crosses tried turned to shit. We talked at the time, you and I. We kicked around a number of solutions. I even encouraged you to buy in yourself. A year or two goes by, and suddenly you're the rising star, on your way to chairman in a company which has always had a Shaw or a Cross at the top. And suddenly you've got money to burn, you're rolling in cash, and everybody's saying, good as Leon is, The Cross must be doing it with mirrors. I said to myself: good as Leon is, he must have gotten backing. Maybe my nose was out of joint that you'd never come back to me. But I made it a point of honor to find out."

"A point of honor? Jesus Christ, I thought we were friends! Why didn't you ever tell me?"

"That's not how you wanted it. But now I find myself in a curious position. I can kill this deal if I want to, which I don't. Or maybe, just maybe, I can save it. Tell me, when's the last time you talked to him?"

"Talked to who?"

"Your partner."

"The fuck. I can't even raise him on the phone. I've left messages everywhere I can think of."

"I see. And he's left you holding the bag, hasn't he?"

"You're damn right."

"With a kidnapping investigation on top of everything else? Well, I've got my own theory as to what's happened. I—"

"What's your theory?"

"Never mind. But let's put our cards on the table, Mr. Chairman. What's in it for me?"

"What do you mean, what's in it for you? If the deal goes through, you're going to collect a fat fee from your clients."

"Leon, let's not waste our time! If you win, you and Holbrook are in the nine figures. If you lose, God knows where it'll end up. You could even go to jail, my friend."

"Jail! Come on, let's not exaggerate, I didn't—"

"Listen to me now. I think I can stop it. I can see a way to make us all whole. The deal, the Coffey kid, everything."

"You can? If you really can, then what the fuck are you wasting time talking to me for?"

"Because it's going to cost me. Because I want to be compensated for my efforts."

"What? Oh, sure. We'll take care of you. If you make it happen, we'll take care of you."

"Ten points, Leon."

"Ten points? What ten points?"

"Ten percent of yours. Yours and his. That's what I want."

"You're kidding! You've got to be kidding! Jesus Christ, you'd blackmail your own mother!"

"I'd prefer for services rendered, Leon. And I'd say I'm being very conservative. Think about it. What's to prevent me from asking fifty percent? Wouldn't you rather have half a loaf than nothing?"

"Jesus. I've gotta talk to Frank."

"I thought you just said you couldn't reach him. You're not conning me, are you?"

"No, no. No, for Christ's sake! I just can't speak for him."

"*Yes you can. As far as my clients are concerned, they'll be paying you. You and the minority family interests. Whatever you do with your share after is your business. If the deal goes through, I want ten percent off the top. Ten percent of what they pay you.*"

"*I've gotta talk to Frank.*"

"*There's no time, Leon. If it's all about to blow up in your face, I've got to get started. Have you got a fax there?*"

"*Where? Here at home?*"

"*You do, don't you?*"

"*Yeah.*"

"*I'll have a document for you in half an hour. I'll make it very simple. All you do is sign and return it.*"

"*But wait a minute! How do I know what you're going to do?*"

"*You don't, Leon. Believe me, you're better off not knowing.*"

"*But ten points is still fucking millions! How do I know you're not conning me? Suppose you do shit and it all works out?*"

"*Would you rather I told my clients not to come next week? After all, that's almost my obligation, wouldn't you say?*"

"*You son of a bitch.*"

"*We're friends, Leon. Come on. Let's keep it that way. Everyone has got his price. Just give me your fax number.*"

"*This is Robert Smith Enterprises. There's no one in the office right now. Please leave a message at the tone.*"

"*Hello, Mr. Smith, and Happy New Year. By the way, I enjoyed your message—'no one in the office* right now.' I've just got off the phone with a mutual friend of ours, who's very distraught. He thinks you've abandoned him, and as an attorney, I must say I think he's right. It appears to me that things have gotten a little out of hand for you, Cousin. I assume you are now trying to set them right—rather desperately, it would seem—but in view of certain matters of mutual interest, I think it would be beneficial for us to talk soonest. Please call me. You'll find this same message elsewhere."

Rebecca
Anne
Dalton

4 January

"Hi," I say sleepily, opening one eye to Danny. "What's up, Doc?"

He's kneeling on the bed next to me, bouncing. My bones ache. What day of the week is it?

Friday.

"It 'nowing," Danny says.

"Snowing?" I correct.

"Uh-huh."

Shit. We've been lucky with the weather so far. It's been plenty cold, but the roads have stayed clear.

I've made it a rule, ever since Christmas, that we move every day. All part of the quest, I tell Danny when he bitches. But snow is something else, and I feel like garbage. Plus we don't have the right clothes, which means spending money, and what are we going to do about food if we get snowed in?

I get up reluctantly and realize my period has started.

"Stay where you are," I tell him, "I'll be right back."

In the tiny bathroom, I discover I only have two Tampax. That's the bad news. The good news is that I'm not pregnant after all.

Thank God for small favors.

Back in the bedroom, I peer out through the venetian blinds. Thin icy flakes are slanting in descending sheets, and the trunk and rear window of the Tempo are already covered. I can barely make out the far side of the parking lot. For the minute, we're stuck.

The motel, I noticed yesterday, has a state package store attached to it plus some kind of café. At least we won't starve. The posted check-out time is twelve noon, but maybe I can talk them into letting us stay free, at least until the snow stops.

Danny's nose is running, and he starts whining even before his morning cartoons are over. I make us cheese and white bread sandwiches with the crusts trimmed off, but he refuses his. I think maybe he's coming down with something—we've been lucky on that score too—but when I feel his forehead, he doesn't seem to have a fever.

All he wants, it turns out, is to go outside and play in the snow.

"We can't," I say. "It's much too cold, too wet. Plus we don't have the right boots. We don't even have waterproof gloves."

"Me don't care," he wails back. "Me don't need boots. Don't need gubbies."

"Oh no? Your hands would be frozen stiff inside of five minutes."

"No, they won't!"

"Oh yes they would!"

"No, they won't!"

"Take a chill, Phil!"

But his whining gives way, all of a sudden, to real tears. I try teasing him out of it, but he tugs at my sweatpants, screaming now, jabbing at the front door. I push him away angrily. He slams back into me, flailing with his little fists.

"Look," I say, holding his forearms firmly, "I'm not feeling so hot today. I feel lousy, if you want to know the truth. I don't want to go outside."

"Me don't care." Twisting and kicking out. "Me go by my 'elp."

"My-*self*," I say. "You know you can't do that. We've got to stick together. Suppose you ran into a witch? What would happen then?"

"Me don't want a 'itch! Me don't want a quest!"

At least that's what I think he said, because suddenly he isn't just protesting. It's escalated into something else, a total tantrum. I've never had that with him before. He lashes out at me, his face an ugly beet-red, and he scratches, hits, yanks, stomps his feet in frustration, and it takes all my strength to grab him and hold on.

"Danny! Danny Dalton, *stop* it for God's sake! *Stop* it now!"

I lift him off the ground. I pin his arms, clutch him to my shoulder. That does no good. I start to sing to him. No good either. He's beyond consoling. I hold him away from me, shake him. I sit in the one stuffed chair, pull him into me, rock back and forth, rock hard.

"For God's sakes, sweetie! It's me, Becca! *Please* stop it!"

But he can't.

"Take deep breaths," I tell him. "Slow, deep breaths."

Finally he tries. Then he hyperventilates some more, short staccato pants, and squinches his eyes against a new rush of stingers. He coughs, hiccups. He sneezes all over us. I don't have a tissue. I wipe his nose with my sleeve.

"Danny," I say. "Just calm down now. Please. Tell me what's wrong. It's me, Becca, remember?"

And then it all comes out. In a jumble, in sobs.

He hates the quest. Nothing good happens, all we do is go from motel to motel. Every day is the same. The food is bad. He's TV'd out. He hates making poopies in the potties. He misses his own potty at home. He misses his one-eyed bear. He misses the third floor. He doesn't like the coloring books I've gotten him, or the stamp set. We haven't seen any witches. We haven't seen any warlocks except the one. We still don't have a rocket car.

I try to reason with him. I never said the quest wouldn't be boring lots of the time. Quests almost always are.

No good.

This isn't just boredom, I think. And he isn't coming down with something either.

Was it nothing that he called for Georgia in the middle of the night?

"Do you want to go home?" I ask him. "Is that it?" I've got him perched on my knees, facing me, supporting him under the arms. "Look at me, Danny. Is that what you want? Do you want to go home?"

"No," he says, averting his eyes.

"Would you rather be with your mommy and daddy in your own house?"

"No."

"Are you sure?"

But he can't answer. He turns his head away, and I can see his little face squinch up again.

"Look at me, Danny," I insist. "This is important. You have to tell me. Are you sure you wouldn't rather be with your mommy and daddy? And your new sister? At home in your own house?"

His face dissolves into new tears. He shakes his head, chin tucked in as though he's trying to control himself. Then I hear, in his small, stammering voice: "Wanna . . . wanna stay . . . stay with . . . 'arrit."

'arrit. Loud and clear.

It shocks me. I want to say: But that can't be, sweetheart, it's not my name. Instead I pull him back into my shoulder, push his head into the crook of my neck, rock. I pat him on the back, tousle his hair. I understand what he wants. It's things the way they were before, on the third floor, Harriet and Justin. The quest—and Becca, Danny, the cars, the motels—is like a game that's over.

He wants it the way it was before.

It makes me cry too, soundlessly, makes me hug all the tighter, until I realize that that's not doing either of us any good.

"Would you feel better," I say, holding him still, "if you could call me Harriet some of the time?"

"Uh-huh," comes his muffled reply.

"And I called you Justin?"

"Uh-huh."

"Well, I don't see why we can't do that, at least on

special occasions. But only when we're alone together, *never* when there are other people around.
Do you understand?"

"Uh-huh."

"Who are we when other people are around?"

"Becca."

"Becca and . . . ?"

"Danny."

"Right. Well, here's an idea," my voice lightening,
"why don't we make today a special day? Like, why
don't we go out for lunch for a change? In a real
restaurant. Would you like that?"

"Uh-huh."

"You could order whatever you liked. No more of
Becca's crummy sandwiches. You could even have
scrambled eggs and bacon, french fries, would you
like that?"

"Ketchup."

"Ketchup too. Then, if it stops snowing and the
roads are okay, we could find a store and buy real
snow boots. Waterproof mittens. Then we could play
in the snow if you still wanted to."

"Build a 'nowman?"

"Build a snowman, what a great idea! Do you
know how?"

"Uh-huh."

"No kidding. You really do?"

"Uh-huh." Nodding.

"That's *great!* Totally. Well, we've got a lot to do
then. We'd better get organized, beginning with
your teeth, young man. Now go get me your toothbrush, and let's get *cracking!*"

He disentangles himself from my lap. I watch him
head off toward the bathroom as though nothing at

all has happened. Leaving me alone with my
cramps, and my deflated enthusiasm, and the idea
that maybe all I've just done is postpone the inevitable.

We play in the room the rest of the morning. That
is, he colors, I color. I've bought him a pack of Old
Maid cards, but he's still too young for it. I end up
trying to build a castle out of the cards, but he
knocks it down before I can finish the third level.

We're at the motel café early. I figure that will
minimize the risk of anybody recognizing us.

I needn't have worried. Except for a couple of
men in work clothes drinking coffee at the counter,
the place is empty.

"Of course that's the weather," I explain to
Danny. "Otherwise, we'd never have gotten a table
without waiting. You may not know it, but this place
is historic. I even saw it listed in the guidebooks:
'one of the last old-style diners in Ohio.' Who
knows? By the time you grow up, it might not even
be around anymore."

Well, you do what you have to do.

The waitress who serves us catches on. She rec-
ommends, for Danny, their "historic" quarter-
pounder, which comes on a sesame roll with let-
tuce, tomato, onion, pickle and, of course, french
fries, and "from the bar," a shake special, which
combines three flavors of ice cream with a syrup of
his choice and milk straight from the cow.

He takes chocolate syrup in his shake and tops it
all off with a piece of apple pie à la mode. I haven't
seen him eat like this since . . . well, I guess I've
never seen him eat like this. We sit in a booth, side

by side, from which I can watch the front door, also the cars coming into the general store and the motel entrance. I see a couple of Jeeps, pickups with snowplows attached, and out on the main road a big snow remover with a long line of cars inching behind it.

I ask the waitress where we can buy some "heavy-duty" snow gear. She said there's a shopping center a couple of miles away, with a sporting goods store and a discount chain. But will we be able to get through?

"You talking about the snow, honey?" she says. "This is nothing. Around here, we call this a dusting."

Some dusting. At the same time, I have a choice to make. Earlier, the man in the motel office refused to let us stay the afternoon. Check-out time is twelve noon, he said. If we stayed beyond that, I'd have to pay for another day.

But the motel is half-empty, I pointed out to him (a generous estimate), did he really expect to fill it up in the middle of a snowstorm?

Finally, he agreed to let us stay till two. But no later.

Go then? Or stay?

After lunch, Danny votes to stay. We should buy boots and build a snowman. Why do we have to move all the time? He likes it here, and if we stay, we can eat dinner in the café too, can't we?

"Please, Becca, please?"

The truth is, I don't feel like driving around either, looking for another motel, even though the snow has mostly stopped.

We find the mall. The giant discount store has ev-

erything we need. Danny runs around like a wild
man, up and down the aisles. In the toy department,
we have a short war over a plastic Colt .45. (I win,
with the help of a *bo* from *Ninja Turtles*.) Along the
way, I manage to get him into a pair of boots that fit,
and Thinsulate mittens, and even a red-and-blue
hooded snowsuit on a fifty-off sale. The snowsuit is a
size too big—he'll be able to wear it next year, I joke
with myself—but with the pants and sleeves rolled
up, it fits him well enough, and he insists on wearing it out of the store.

The joke about next year makes me weepy. I chalk
it up to my period. I buy buttons for the snowman,
and a pail-and-shovel set designed for sandbox use
but why not snow, and, for myself, boots, gloves, a
new sweats outfit, underpants, tights, Tampax, lip-
stick, shampoo, and, on a whim, a tin drum of popcorn that's been marked down from Christmas.

Not a spree exactly, but still.

Nobody looks at us strangely. As nearly as I can
tell, nobody looks at us at all.

I pay by MasterCard—it's the first time I've used
it except for cars—and to top it off, I buy Danny
three rides, a quarter apiece, on a bucking locomo-
tive near the main entrance.

Back at the motel, we build our snowman. I can't
remember ever having done one before, only ice
sculpture, once, back in Minnesota. It ends up bot-
tom-heavy no matter what we do, a little like an old
woman with full skirts, but thin-torsoed. A notice-
able curve to the spine, I see when we step back,
flushed and sweaty, to inspect our craftsmanship.
Also, the button eyes are slightly crossed.

I fix the eyes, adjust the orange-rind mouth.

"Well, what do you think?" I ask.

"No scarf," he says seriously. "No 'at."

I can do something about the scarf—a pair of pantyhose I was going to chuck anyway—but the hat confounds me, except for his own Pirates cap, which I'm not about to sacrifice.

"Well, maybe it's a woman," I say. "A snow-woman."

"No 'air," he says.

"Well, I don't know, maybe it's a bald snow-woman."

The idea tickles him. He starts to giggle, then laughs contagiously, and I catch it from him, pick him up, toss him hilariously into a snowbank. Then we start a snowball fight, first with balls but then great armfuls of loose snow that, whooping and giggling, we heap on each other from close range. Finally, our faces deliciously wet and cold, we collapse back into the snowbank.

I get his wet clothes off in the motel, pop him in and out of a tub, then make a quick detour to the state liquor store. I ask for Dewar's, a pint bottle. Medicinal, I tell myself with an inner giggle. On account of my cramps. Then I think better of it and buy a fifth.

The woman at the counter doesn't even ask me for proof of age.

I collect a bucket of ice on the way back to the room, fill a plastic glass to the brim with ice and Scotch, and humming, sipping—ahhh, God, when that warmth hits my stomach!—tell Danny to get ready for the big makeover. Then I set him up with TV, pry the lid off the popcorn drum for him, and, with a fresh Scotch within reach, set to work in the shower.

If I shampoo my hair once, I do it six times. I soap, squeeze, twist, rinse, shampoo again. I'm under the steaming water so long that my fingers turn to prunes, my toes too, probably my knees and elbows.

After a bout with the hair dryer, I still haven't gotten rid of all the dye. My hair is now a darkish blond, but still with tints and glints of the unnatural color. It looks a wreck frankly, the worst of both worlds, but it will have to do. Tomorrow, when I make up my mind what we're going to do next, I'll either redye it or shampoo some more. For tonight, I don't give a damn. I'm Harriet Major, and I have a dinner date with a young man named Justin Coffey.

I dress in the new sweats and, still barefoot, go into the room, glass in hand, for fresh ice and another—

The TV is still going.

Danny is sitting on the floor on the far side of the room, his back propped against the wall. The popcorn tin next to him.

Not where I left him.

The man is sitting in the comfortable chair between Danny and the door, filling it to overflowing. Still in his overcoat.

Goddamn, why did we stay over? Why did we build the snowman? Why why why why why why why?

We're caught! We lasted all of two weeks!

"No problem," the man says with a half-wave

when he sees me. "Take your time. We won't have any trouble."

He's holding a plastic glass in one hand. My Scotch!

"Who are you?" I shout at him. "What the hell do you think you're doing here?"

He grins at me. Big, jowly, florid face.

"Oh, you can call me Harry," he says with a laugh. "Or Tom or Dick, no problem. Harry and Harriet. Or would you like Rebecca better, maybe?"

I stare at him. He's big, bulky, about ten times my size. I glance at the door, the phone. He's closer to both. A lot closer to Danny.

Danny is looking up at me.

Scared? Looking for some signal? I can't tell.

"Come on, just cool it," the man says, following my eyes. "The kid's fine. Why don't you pour yourself another drink anyway? We're going to have to wait awhile."

"Wait for what?"

"A call-back."

"What do you mean, a call-back?"

"A telephone call." He gestures at the phone. "We're not going anywhere till it comes."

I start to lose it inside. My stomach has just shriveled up, as though a big fist is grabbing at it.

"Oh?" I get out. "And then where are we going?" No answer. "Who are we waiting for? Who's supposed to call back?"

I'm trying to keep my voice from trembling. He only shrugs and grins at me. Says I led him a merry chase, that I must be some smart cookie. He suggests again that I pour myself a drink.

I don't think he's a cop, although he looks like one.

Somebody's hired hand.

Guess who.

But I can't let myself think about that.

I glance around the room for possible weapons. The Scotch bottle, the ice bucket, a lamp. Danny's plastic *bo?* Our Gap bags, half-filled with stuff?

Or should I fake outrage, start screaming for help?

Or offer him money? How much would it take? I still have over two thousand bucks in cash, my savings left over from working for Georgia, would that do the trick? After all, how much can a guy like him make, overweight and thinning hair, crummy clothes?

But suppose I offered him the money, what would prevent him from simply pocketing it and keeping us there anyway?

And even if he didn't, how could he let us go? If he's waiting for a call-back, doesn't that mean he's already made a call? To announce that he's found us? *So how could he let us go?*

I can't concentrate on it. Why did we stay? Why didn't we just leave? If only we'd left at noon! If only I wasn't saddled with Justin! But if I wasn't saddled with Justin, I wouldn't be here myself, would I? And if I hadn't run away with Robert A. Smith, I wouldn't be here either, would I? And if I hadn't done this, hadn't done that, or gone or been or done or did, if I myself had never . . . *happened!*

It's over, I think. It's going to go fast now. By tomorrow, when I wake up, they'll have given me another shot, a big dosage to welcome me back, and

I'll be all groggy, punchy, dry in the mouth, and everything in between will have been like a dream I dreamt to keep myself from going stark, raving mad.

I *won't!* I *can't!*

I need a drink. I pour myself a Scotch, hold tight to the bottle, sit on the edge of the bed.

The bastards! The goddamn bastards!

The man—Harry—tells me to put the bottle back. Or better yet, give it to him. Carefully, he says.

I do. He tops off his glass.

"Do you have a gun?"

This is Danny, from the floor. For a second, I'd forgotten all about him.

The man laughs.

"Never mind, Danny," I tell him.

"Is he a oarlock?" Danny asks me back, from the floor.

I shake my head, willing him to shut up.

"A what?" the man interrupts.

"Never mind," I answer. Then, thinking better of it, "A warlock."

"What's a warlock?"

"I think you'd better ask my brother," I say.

"Your brother?" The man laughs.

"A man 'itch," Danny answers.

"A what?"

"A male witch," I explain. "A warlock is a male witch."

The man—Harry, if that's his name—thinks that's funny too. He says he's been called a lot of things in his time, but never a male witch.

"Harry the witch," he says. "What is it again? War . . . ?"

"Oarlock," Danny answers.

"Well, what do you know? How come you know so much about things like that?"

Danny holds forth about 'itches, oarlocks, and how they have all kinds of special powers, you have to be very careful how you act around them.

The man listens.

"The reason he knows so much about it," I say, willing Danny into silence, "is that I'm something of one myself."

"Something of what?"

"A witch."

"Oh?" He seems uncertain as to whether I'm fooling around with him or not.

"That's right," I go on. "Actually my mother really is one. You don't know her, do you?"

"Your mother? How would I know your mother?"

"No reason you should," I answer carefully. At least he's answered one of my questions. "She's devoted a lifetime to it. I mean, most people laugh at it, but witchcraft's really a very serious field. I've only picked up a few of the spells, here and there."

"I bet you have," he says, intrigued.

But the phone interrupts us. God*damn!* He lets it ring a second time, and I start forward, but, shaking his head, he waves me off, picks up the receiver.

He listens.

"Yeah, that's right, the both of them," he says. "Yeah, no problem, everything's quiet and peaceful, we're just having a little conversation. . . . Yeah, I won't, no problem."

I hear him give the motel's name and address, followed by road instructions.

Then: "Oh? . . . Yeah, sure, no problem, hold on." Then, smiling at me: "He wants to talk to you."

My body goes stiff.

"Who wants to talk to me?"

"It's Mr. Smith," he answers with a grin. "Be nice now," and he pushes his chair back toward the door, making a passage for me and at the same time blocking my escape.

I take the receiver from him. Goddamn, I've gone stiff all over, stiff like a board, hard as rock. I toss my hair back with a jerk.

"Hello?" I say.

"You've led us some chase, darling." His familiar voice. "But now it's over, thank God. I'm so glad. I hope you are too. I've missed you terribly."

"Where are you, Robert?"

"At the airport."

"The airport? What airport?"

"Columbus, darling. The minute I heard you'd been found, of course I was on the next plane. I'll be with you shortly."

"What do you want?"

"I still need the boy, darling."

"Why? What are you going to do with him?"

"Nothing. No harm will come to him. I need him, that's all." He pauses, just long enough for me to know he's lying. "But I've had a long time to think about us too, dear Becca. I've missed you terribly, even more than I imagined I would."

And even now, I think blindly, you can't resist playing with me.

"In spite of everything," he says, "I don't think it's too late for us. Once this is over, we can pick up where we left off. We might even go away together, let me show you something of the world."

He made the same promise the first day, I remember. Together, we were going to wipe out my past and see the world.

"Why don't you let him go then?" I hear myself ask. "You can have me instead."

"Oh? And how do you propose we go about that? We can't just leave him here, can we? In the middle of Ohio?"

"Let me take him home first."

"Home? Oh no, I'm afraid I couldn't let you do that, darling. But seriously, I've a better idea. Why don't you let Harry take the boy away right now? You wait for me there alone. I won't be long. There'll be just time enough for you to get yourself ready. What do you think? Well?"

But I can't answer. It's not in me to say anything.

"Of course, if you tried to leave yourself, I'd have to hunt you down again. But you already know that, so why bother?"

He's playing with me now, the way he always did, and I'm like a fly struggling feebly in his web. My mouth is clotted, my throat, my brain.

"Well, you decide, darling," he says. "Either you can all wait for me together, or you send them off and wait alone. Either way, I won't be long. Now why don't you put Harry on again, let me explain it to him?"

I hand over the phone obediently. It's over, I think. There's nothing I can say or do or think that will make any difference. Distantly it comes to me: Hasn't he just offered me a last chance? Freedom for Becca? Couldn't I just let them go and then walk out the door myself, get in the car, drive off?

Except I can't. Couldn't.

He knows that too.

I glance at Justin. He hasn't moved. His back is to the wall, his dark eyes focused intensely on me. We're in it together, sweets, I try to tell him. I got you into this, somehow I'll get you out. There's no way I'm going to bug out on you.

The man—Harry—hangs up. He squeezes his bulk out of the chair, stands, stretches. Standing, he seems enormous to me, and his overcoat too small.

"I'm supposed to tell you what he said."

"Yes?"

"Same as he told you. If I take the kid away, though, I better have your car keys. I guess he doesn't want his little birdie flying the coop."

"Did he say that?"

"About your car keys? Yep. That's what the man said." He grins at me. "Also said if you give me any trouble, I can do whatever I want to with you."

The goddamn bastard. He couldn't resist.

I look at Harry, at Justin on the floor, and then, from somewhere deep inside, I feel the anger flowing. I think: *No, it's not over. I'm not going to let it be over. It's not over!*

I study Harry.

"Would you like that?" I ask him, gazing levelly at him.

"Like what?"

"For me to try something? Give you trouble? So that you can do whatever you want to with me?"

He laughs. He even blushes a little. Says nothing.

"Look," I say, dropping the challenge from my

voice, "why don't you at least let me make us another drink. How much time do we have till he gets here?"

"I don't know exactly," he says. "Three-quarters of an hour, maybe an hour. Depends on the traffic."

"Plenty of time," I say, smiling at him.

I watch him hesitate, watch him think on the one hand that he has a job to do, but, on the other . . . ?

Light bulbs in his head.

He stays standing. I walk in front of him, inches away, take the bottle, his glass, cross the room, busy myself with the ice bucket.

I know he's watching me every step. I let him. Not for nothing am I an evil promiscuous bitch. I work him mercilessly. I work him with my eyes, my hands, the swirl of my hair, the twist of my body. My words, my Scotch. He lets on that he's been tracking us since the beginning, and, sitting on the edge of the bed, smoothing the bedspread with my palm, I tell him he had no idea how lonely it got for me, night after night after night. I tell him it's pretty hard to get it off on a three-and-a-half-year-old. He laughs at that. I tell him we have just enough time, that no one need know, Mr. Smith least of all, and what kind of trouble does he want me to make for him?

"What about the kid?" he says hoarsely.

"Don't worry about him," I answer, my eyes on Harry. "He's seen a little bit of everything." Justin is watching me too, and I will him with my mind: *Don't! It's only a game, but I don't want you to look.*

"Come on," I say to Harry finally, "a little witchcraft," and crisscrossing my arms so that when I lift my sweatshirt over my head, my T-shirt with it, my breasts come up before his eyes.

He takes off his overcoat, takes off his jacket. There's a small holster underneath, with a gun in it, and a sweater. He takes them off too. A little unsteady. I will Justin not to look. I have a last-minute panic—God help me if I fail!—and I want to shout at Justin to run for it, just get out the door and take off. But Harry is already on me, so fast I'm unprepared, arms reaching, grabbing, so close I can smell his boozy breath. At the last second, I duck his grasp, let fly with my knee. All my force. I feel the give, hear the crack, his humongous gasp.

He falls into me, grabs at me, misses, grabs bedspread instead. But he doesn't go down. He's reaching, stumbling, bellowing, and I realize Justin has tackled him around the leg and that he's trying to kick Justin free. He loses his balance, though. Down he goes. I'm free. I grab the Dewar's bottle, crack him hard in the face. And again, again when he tries to turn away, a fourth time.

My way! my mind is shouting. *I'm ending it my way!*

Or maybe I'm shouting it out loud. I have this sense of tremendous noise. Justin is screaming too.

I can't shut him up. He doesn't understand. He's Justin again. Danny is dead.

I take the gun from the holster. Then I grab my clothes, my purse, Justin and his snowsuit, and we're out of there.

This time we won't stop for anything. We're both screaming as I drive into the darkness, skidding and

swerving on the slick side roads. Blinding headlights coming the other way.

I blew it, that's all I can think. I should have
waited in the motel with Harry's gun till he walked
in the door. I should have shot him in the stomach
in cold blood.

I didn't. I ran like a scared rabbit. That's my instinct: when in doubt, run, run away, goddamn.
With a head start of what? Fifteen, twenty minutes?
I picture him finding Harry, reviving him, questioning him.

I see the Jaguar in my mind.

He may even have planned it, figuring I'd find a
way to beat Harry, saving the pleasure of hunting us
down himself.

It makes no difference which way we go, north,
south, west. I failed. If I let him find us once, he'll
find again. In my panic, I think my only hope is east.
There's an outside chance he won't expect me to
quit.

I can hardly see to drive. We're going much too
fast for the roads, the headlights, and cars keep
splattering wet stuff onto the windshield that freezes
on contact. Justin is screaming his head off in the
backseat, and no matter how fast I drive, *he'll* be
driving faster.

"*Shut up!*" I roar over my shoulder. "For Christ's
sakes, Justin, take a chill!"

It only makes him scream louder. I can feel him
fighting the car seat, struggling to get free.

I turn on the radio—music, volume up to the top.
I roll down the window and sing at the frigid night.
I careen off the approach road—finally—and onto

the interstate, the white arrow crooking "east," and roar the skidding Tempo into the darkness.

Still I can't drown Justin out. He's totally freaked. I worry that somehow he'll break loose, fly headfirst into the back of the passenger seat. I slow a little, down to seventy, sixty-five, turn off the radio, try to talk to him.

He won't listen.

For the first time, I resent him totally, violently. I don't care if he's only a child, doesn't he realize we're in danger? For God's sake, can't he understand we have to keep going?

No, he can't. Won't.

A few exits down the interstate, I get off. No headlights behind us. We come onto some dark and winding highway where slicks of icy snow stretch across the surface. Few street lights, no traffic. I drive about a mile, then turn off onto another road and stop alongside a snowbank, switch off the headlights.

At least, I think, it's scared my cramps away. The old shock treatment. All I feel now are intermittent dull echoes. But the blackness, stopping in the middle of nowhere, hasn't stopped Justin. I click on the interior light, try to talk to him, but he slams back against his car seat, wrenches at the confining harness. I get out of the car, stumble around through the snow, and pull him free.

I envelop him in my parka for warmth. I squeeze him—no love squeeze. I feel like I have to squeeze some sense into him. Finally, fighting to calm my voice, I subdue him. He sobs and sniffles, and at last I feel his fingers reach into my hair, twisting, pulling, and I hear him sniffing my hair.

Was it the bad man at the motel? I ask him.

He nods against my neck.

Did the man hurt him?

Shakes his head.

Did he think I was going to leave him there?

Nods again.

"But I didn't, did I? Thanks to you, Justin, we made it. All we've got to do now is keep going."

Apparently, though, there's something else. What I expect is: *Me had enough, me want to go home,* but when he manages to get it out, and when I finally understand him, I don't know whether to laugh or cry.

He's hungry. In fact he's "darving."

And I'd promised him we'd have dinner at the café.

And didn't I teach him that, once you make promises, it's for keeps?

I take a deep breath. I have two choices. Either I can stuff him back in his car seat and he can scream his head off while I think through our next move, or I can try to accommodate him.

Another deep breath.

"Yes, sweetie," I tell him, "promises *are* for keeps. You're absolutely right. But sometimes, in very special circumstances, you have to break promises, even though you don't want to."

"Why?"

"Because that *was* a bad man, at the motel. I think he's probably still there, waiting in case we come back. So we can't go to the café."

"Too dangerous?"

"Too dangerous."

"But you took his gun, didn't you?"

"Yes, I did."

"Is he dead?"

"I don't know. I don't think so."

"Was he really a oarlock?"

"No."

"And the one on the telephone?"

I hesitate. Then, holding him tight, I say, "There are no warlocks, sweetie. Not really. That's just pretend. All there are is bad people."

He seems to take it all right, although when I stuff him back into the car seat, he clutches hard at me, and I have to pull myself free. Then we drive off, back onto the interstate, and I promise him we'll find a great place down the road for dinner, at least as good as the café, while all along, inside, I'm trying to figure out how I'm going to tell him what's going to happen next when I don't know myself.

Except I do know, I think. That's the trouble.

A few exits farther, when I spot the crossed fork and spoon on the sign, I get us off again.

"Here it is!" I call out over my shoulder.

"It" turns out to be an IHOP, a brightly lit square in the darkness, free-standing next to two gas stations and a small shopping center. As we drive in and park, I do my "famous restaurant" number again. I tell him how their pancakes are the best anywhere, and how it's called *International* House of Pancakes because the pancake batter is flown in daily, fresh, from many different parts of the world, places like Poland, India, France, even China. The Chinese, I say, are famous for their pancakes. Inside, we sit across from each other in a booth. I can see the entrance, and I keep my purse, with Harry's little gun in it, on the banquette next to me. I let

Justin order all by himself. He chooses pancakes à la mode, with french fries and ketchup, milk—I still insist on milk—and he digs into the food again as though I really have been starving him. I hardly touch mine. Instead, getting it together for what I'm about to say, I drink mug after mug of black coffee.

And now it's time.

"It was very dangerous," he says.

"Well, yes, I guess it was."

" 'arrit very brave."

"Thank you. You were too."

"Y'welcome." Then: "Are you really a 'itch?"

"Me? No, of course not."

"You told him you was."

"I know. The witch's daughter. Well, I had to tell him something, didn't I?"

He grins back at me. Then: "Is your momma a 'itch?"

I hesitate. "No, not really," I say. "She's just a bad person."

"Me thought her is dead."

I shake my head, flustered. This was just something I told him and Georgia. "No," I say, "she's alive." I watch him take in the information. It's the first time, I think, that he's caught me in a lie. "I don't mean bad in every way," I add hurriedly. "Not necessarily. It's just that she did bad things to me."

"To 'arrit?"

"Yes," I nod.

"When?"

"We just never got along. Sometimes that happens. I guess I did bad things to her too."

He struggles with this. Or maybe I'm the one who's struggling. He's too young to understand about bad mommies. I look away, unable to deal with his disapproval.

"Was him a oarlock?" he says.

"Was who a warlock?"

"The man at the motel."

"I told you, Justin. That's just pretend stuff. But he was a bad man."

"Him chase us?"

"Yes, maybe. Or the one on the telephone."

"Him catch'd us?"

"No, we're not going to let anyone catch us."

"You got his gun."

"Yes, I took his gun. But I'm not going to use it."

"Can I see it?"

"No. You know how I feel about guns."

Almost immediately I see his lower lip quiver and I guess what he's thinking about—not Harry's gun, but the plastic Colt .45 he wanted at the discount store. But then he says, "Me brave too."

"I know that, Justin. You're one brave dude. I'm very proud of you."

But now's the time, Becca, like it or not, and like it or not, I know I'm going to hurt him.

"There's something I've got to tell you, sweets," I say, gazing across at him. "I think maybe you know it already. It's over. The quest, the whole thing. All over."

He doesn't react. I repeat it.

"Over, done, finished."

He hears me, but if he understands, he doesn't seem that devastated.

I want to tell him these are genuinely bad people, that it *is* dangerous, that we can't go on in the middle of it. At least not the two of us. I want to tell him that it was all craziness on my part, a bad idea. Instead I say, "Quests are just pretend anyway. Maybe a long time ago people did real quests—knights—but they don't anymore."

"Do too," he says.

"No, Justin. All that was a very long time ago. Knights and ladies and dragons, witches, warlocks, all that stuff, we don't have them anymore."

"Do too," he insists stubbornly.

For God's sake, can't he understand that I'm trying to find an easy way? For both of us?

No, I guess he can't.

"Okay," I say. "But I've made up my mind. We're going home, Justin. That's where we're going tonight."

No response. I can't read his reaction at all.

"Yes, home," I say. "To your mommy and daddy. I'm going to take you there. We've been away a very long time. I think they must miss you very much by now. I think you must miss them too."

He turns his face away, but I see in profile that particular pinched look he gets when he's distressed or in trouble.

" 'arrit come too?" he asks.

"Of course, silly," I say. "Who else do you think is going to take you home?"

"But after?" he asks.

"After what?"

"Will it be just like . . . ? Just like . . . ?"

I take a deep breath. Leave it to him to find the loophole.

"Just like before, you mean?"

"Uh-huh."

"Well," I say, "sometime or other I'm going to

have to decide what I'm going to do with the rest of my life. Like going back to college? And do it. We've talked about that before." But I can see it doesn't help him, and I rush on, lie a little more. "Of course, it wouldn't be forever," I say. "For one thing, college isn't all year. Maybe next summer's not such a bad idea, what do you think? Once you're finished with Group, you'll have plenty of time for adventures. Maybe we could go off together next summer? Just the two of us?"

But he doesn't believe me, I can tell.

"Well?" I plunge on. "What do you think?"

" 'arrit don't love me anymore," he says.

It stuns me.

"But that's ridiculous, Justin! I . . . I *adore* you! You're my best friend!"

"Me don't want to go home yet," comes his answer.

"Look, sweets," I say, reaching across and holding his chin, "let me tell you something about Justin Coffey. Maybe you won't even understand it, but the other night, when you woke up—I think you'd been having a bad dream—you called out, 'Mommy, Mommy.' Remember? You didn't call out 'Becca' or 'Harriet.' You said, 'Mommy.' I think you miss your mommy a lot. And what about your little sister, Zoe? For God's sake, you haven't even seen her yet. If you don't get a move on, she'll be all grown up and you won't even have seen her as a little baby!"

It makes no difference though. Nothing I can do or say will make him believe me. Instead I see the betrayal in his dark eyes. I want to tell him: *Please, Justin, I've got us in a terrible spot, the least I can do is try to get you out of it, please don't do this to me.*

"I do too love you, Justin Coffey," I say. "I swear to God I do."

I let go of his chin. I want to hold him, hug him, but he's turned his head away. He listens in silence while I talk on, making promises I know I'll never keep.

Not another word out of him.

I pay the bill. Cash, MasterCard, what the fuck difference does it make anymore? I take him to the john, then I bundle him back into the car seat. Within fifteen minutes—I can tell by his breathing— he is asleep. I wait a few more minutes, then stop on the shoulder of the interstate and turn off the head-lights.

This stop is for me. I've never had an easy time crying. Sometimes I feel like I'm going to—just now, at the Pancake House—but usually the tears won't come at all and what I get instead is a dry, burning sensation. Now they well out of my eyes, and I let them flow, feel them rolling down my cheeks, taste their salt. I take deep breaths, swivel and arch my neck. After a while, I climb into the backseat, rummage for Justin's snowsuit, manage to get the pants half on him, the jacket draped and wedged around him like a blanket. Then I drive off again. A half hour later, I get off the interstate one last time, to top off the gas tank and buy NoDoz and two Styrofoam containers of black coffee.

5 January

I expect to have to fight to stay awake, but it's not a problem. Maybe I'm too strung out. Every pair of headlights in the rearview, every red taillight up ahead, could be him. Only the trucks, all lights blazing, are my friends. The land grows hillier as I go, and the winding strip of road cuts through dark rock and snowdrifts that loom down suddenly out of the shadows, and I know he could be anywhere, behind or out in front of me, even sitting quietly around the next bend in a dark car parked on the shoulder.

I see no dark cars parked on the shoulders.

I have to plan carefully, down to the last detail, but my mind keeps drifting off, to the familiar rhythm of the "if onlys," starting with *if only* I hadn't let myself get talked into the snowman, and once started—it's an old habit—I can't stop. They mark my life backwards like telephone poles on a train ride. *If only* I hadn't answered Georgia's ad. *If only*, that last day at Looney Tunes, when I came downstairs and there was this distinguished-looking man rising out of the couch in the parlor—really very elegant—I'd had the guts to say, "But I have no Cousin Robert. I've never seen this man before in my life." And if I hadn't slept with too many men, including Uncle Mark, which is what really freaked the Witch out; or if I hadn't gone to St. Jude's Obscure College for Women in frozen Minnesota, or if —this is where it always starts—my father hadn't died.

In fact, as the "care-givers" at Looney Tunes liked to point out, it didn't start there. But I remember the funeral in Bernardsville, the rain, black umbrellas, Uncle Mark holding her elbow. My own dull dread. And thinking: tough shit, Becca, the wrong parent died.

The Witch wore black, with a veil. I wore my high school coat.

And then we were stuck. Beefeater's by the case and the closet for me.

People—the care-givers included—have always thought I exaggerate how bad she was. They can't believe the closet story, that a fifteen-year-old girl would, from time to time, "let" herself be locked in a closet stuffed with old clothes, a steamer trunk that had once belonged to her grandmother, boxes jammed below the shelves as well as on top, or that every time I tried to hide a light bulb there, so much as a flashlight, a box of goddamn Fig Newtons, she found me out. They can't or won't believe that it had been going on for as long as I can remember. *You fat little pig I can't stand to look at you anymore.* Or that I learned, early, not to scream, or fight, certainly not to cry, just to sit, squeezed in the dark, knowing that sooner or later I'd hear her footsteps outside, curses sometimes, knocking into stuff, her clunky key in the keyhole.

I got out as fast as I could. Not the closet, I mean, but Bernardsville. In frozen Minnesota, where the sky gets dark in October, I fell in love. Once I met my Johnny Oakley, I spent more time at the university than at St. Jude's, and I was going to transfer there my sophomore year, until the Witch found out about it. The next thing I knew, if I wanted to go to college at all, it would have to be in New Jersey. Johnny sent me a letter, which I read once and threw out, and a dozen farewell roses, which I buried. Then I went to see Uncle Mark, in the city. I knew they were sleeping together by then, but he was also my father's lawyer, and if he wasn't my real uncle, at least I'd known him since childhood. I called him. He said, "Come on in, Becca," and in I went, to these sensational offices downtown, with the views of the harbor and his name on the door, Lambert Laughin Spain. I showed him the papers I'd stolen from her. Legally, he said, I didn't have a leg to stand on. Yes, the education trust was for my benefit, but didn't I see, it named my mother sole trustee? Empowered to act in her sole discretion?

I took off. Minneapolis by thumb, three days. I guess I wanted to hear it firsthand from Johnny, and I did. Just like his letter said, he couldn't deal with me anymore. We were too young; there was my mother; it was all too complicated. I refused to leave, though. I was abject, I begged, I prostrated myself. I even got a job, waitressing, for two days. But when I found out the real reason—that his new girlfriend was already living on the top floor of the house that had been intended for us—I drew blood. Johnny threatened to call the police, but he must have called the Witch instead. The next thing I knew, I was on a plane home, accompanied by good old Uncle Mark, whom she'd sent out to get me.

Maybe you could say we deserved each other, the Witch and I. As for Mark, afterward he liked to say I seduced him. Maybe I did. I know that plane ride started in tears and ended up with him undressing me, button by button, at the Marriott Hotel at Newark Airport, which led in turn to other venues, including the Witch's bed, where she discovered us one memorable afternoon, Mark with his hands raised in self-defense, I convulsed in giggles. And other vices, other men, the year I finally went crazy and ran away twice, twice retrieved, and became, at home and away, the evil promiscuous bitch of her prediction, which led, eventually, to Looney Tunes, last known address of the congenitally antisocial and mentally unstable, and, last spring, to "Cousin Robert" steering me by the arm out to the gleaming black Jaguar in the driveway.

I never found out how he found me. He wouldn't tell me. I never found out who he really was either. Not a damn thing. I tried for a while, but he was far too careful, too clever. And too charming too, in the beginning. He said, that first day, "The truth would only disappoint you, my dear. It is much too banal. Think of it that I fell out of the sky, an accident of nature. Take advantage of it. Let me invent us."

Harriet Major. Robert A. Smith.

By the time I understood what he wanted of me, it was too late.

I guess with me it always is.

I run out of *if onlys* around four in the morning. I'm blinking my eyes against the uniform darkness, and the beams of my headlights, the blink-blink-blink of the white dashes marking the lanes. I straddle the dashes but even the sounds work against me, the regular seams in the road underneath, the drone of the engine, the steady breathing, when I listen hard for it, of Justin in the backseat. And the soft bluish lights from the dashboard. And the lulling warmth of the heater . . .

I just jerked awake again.

If I try to keep going, I'm going to kill us both.

I pull off at the next exit. I park next to a closed gas station. There's a phone booth outside. I undo my seat belt, lock the doors, check Justin, then stretch sideways in the front seat, pulling my knees up under my parka.

"I do too love you, Justin Coffey," I say.

A little after seven, I wake up and call Georgia.

5 January

"Since when are you calling the shots?"

"Since right now. One-thirty A.M."

"Hey, you're paying me to keep you informed, Mr. Spain. That's all."

"No, you're wrong. It's changed now."

"What's changed?"

"I'm paying you double. Whatever you bill him, you get twice as much from me. And that's retroactive to day one."

"Holy shit. And what am I supposed to do for it?"

"Find the boy. The only difference is, once you find him, you call me first."

"But I can't do that! He's my client. I've got a professional reputation."

"Exactly. And you'd better protect it."

"For Christ's sake, you don't have to threaten me! What do we do about the girl?"

"That's your lookout."

"Yeah, but she's armed now. She put one of my guys in the hospital. I'm not risking their fucking lives. What do we do if she puts up a fight?"

"I said: That's your lookout."

"That's not what my client wants. He wants the girl too, in one piece."

"I said: Find the boy. Don't blow it this time. And call me first. Do I make myself clear?"

Georgia
Levy
Coffey

5 January

I fumble, pick up in a headachy daze. It is barely light outside. I've been dreaming, I can't . . .

"Hullo?" I manage into the mouthpiece.

"Georgia?"

"Yes? Who's this?"

But I *know!* Unless I'm still dreaming?

"It's me, Harriet." The voice is clear as a bell in my ear. "Please listen carefully. I've got Justin with me. I'm bringing him home today. It'll take me a while, and nobody can know. I don't want the police there, anybody. He's in great danger. You've got to guard him with your life."

I'm still babbling after she hangs up, after I know she's hung up. I sit up in bed, babbling, shivering, and Zoe is squalling from the crib. I've no idea what I'm saying. Maybe the police do if it still records after one side hangs up. I'm crying, I discover. I'm crying because it *was* Harriet, and if she says she's bringing Justin home, then, God, I believe her.

Justin is coming home!

I wake up Larry to tell him. Then I call my parents. I wake them up too. I can't imagine Harriet caring about them knowing. They're coming as fast as they can get dressed. I feel the need for people around me, for warmth if nothing else. I can't stop shivering, even with the heat turned up.

It must be just me. My hands are like ice.

I repeat the whole conversation for the police. No matter what she said, I can't keep them from knowing. They have it on tape. Did I have any impressions, listening to her? Any idea where she might have been calling from?

No, none.

All I know is, she's called. She says my boy's coming home!

Now the whole world knows it. I don't know how it happened, but it's driving me crazy. My parents are here. There's been no further word, but the road outside is like outside a church on Sunday, cars bumper to bumper, and I can even see a cop in uniform. Directing traffic? Except it's not Sunday, it's not a church, it's *my* house!

What will Harriet do if she sees all the cars outside?

It's the goddamned media. Somebody—who else but the police?—must have tipped them off. CHRISTMAS KIDNAPPING OVER, now there's a headline. I confront Capriello, confront his boss, the St. George chief of police. (What is *he* doing here, if not to make Section B of the *Times?*) I'm crazed. Harriet insisted *nobody* else be here. She was very specific about it. But she's a fugitive from justice, they tell me, she's committed a serious crime, the police have every obligation to try to catch her. And as for the media, the road is town property; there is no basis for banning them from town property.

I scream at them: "If anything happens to him because of this, it's going to cost St. George millions! I will sue you for the rest of time!"

Then I'm outside, on the front porch. Larry, my father, try to restrain me. I break away from them. Pain tearing at my belly, I still manage to charge the people, men and women, congregated near the foot of the driveway. Cameras, minicams, let them show that on the "Evening News" too: NEGLIGENT MOTHER TURNS SHREW! I tell them Justin's coming home. I beseech them not to get in the way, threaten them with lawsuits if they try to, criminal charges. "This is my son's *life!*" I rage at them. "There can't be anybody here, don't you understand? Goddamn you, you're endangering his *life!*"

It works, some. Back inside the house, I see cars dispersing, driving off through the bare trees. Maybe they've only gone to park around the corner, but I see no police either. If they're there, at least they're hidden from view.

The waiting is driving everybody nuts. The "experts"—that is, Capriello, Larry too—can't understand what's happened. If Harriet's had Justin all this time, then what about the anonymous calls? Was that a crank after all? And what about all the names Larry gave them, the investigation he set in motion?

But Justin is in great danger, didn't she say that?

Suddenly it's noon, hours since she called. She did say it would take a while, but did she mean all day?

I have this terrible flashing premonition that I

won't recognize him. That my own son will be standing in front of me and that I won't know who he is!

Where *did* she call from? The police have no idea. Could it be just another cruel trick? How can I be sure it really was Harriet? Suppose it was just another crank caller, one whose voice sounded approximately the same as hers?

But it *was* Harriet, I'm positive of it!

But suppose something's happened to them? Why aren't they here?

In the kitchen. People talking all around me. I recognize what's going on. It's like mourning, I think, a wake, or sitting shiva. All that's missing are keening women in black.

The phone rings.

It's a little after twelve-thirty. Capriello has already asked me, if she calls again, to try to keep her on the line as long as possible. There's a sudden hush. It's as though the ringing sound has silenced the entire planet.

I pick up, still in the kitchen.

"Hello?"

"It's me again." Her voice is unsteady this time, but it's *her* voice. "I can't do it the way I said."

"Harriet, where *are* you? For God's sake, I'm—"

"I can't explain now. Listen to me, Georgia. Here's what you have to do. I won't repeat it. Do you remember where you took us to lunch that time? The restaurant? It was the week I moved in. You also bought some things for Justin?"

"Of course I do!" I almost blurt out the name.

"How long will it take you to get there?"

"Fifteen, twenty minutes. But—"

"Come to the restaurant as fast as you can. Right now. He'll be there. But you *have* to come alone, Georgia."

She hangs up. I hear the disconnect distinctly.

Almost immediately they're after me: *Where* was she calling from? *Where* does she want me to meet her? *What* restaurant? *Where* is it?

Red-faced Capriello, Larry, even my parents.

I refuse to tell them.

But it's unthinkable that I go by myself! It's far too dangerous! Suppose she isn't alone? Suppose it's a trap of some kind? If not the police, then at least Larry, at least my father!

"For Christ's sake," Larry shouts at me, "he's *my* son, too! I'm going with you!"

I face them all down.

"I'm going to get him." Suddenly I'm very calm. "She insists I come alone, and that's exactly what I'm going to do. No one is coming with me, not you, Larry, not anyone. And I'll tell you this much: If anybody tries to follow me, then I'll stop. I'll just stop. And if anything happens to Justin then, you'll have yourselves to thank for it."

They follow me into the front hall, still arguing. I pull free of them. I have my coat on, and, hands trembling, I'm fumbling in my purse to make sure I have the car keys. Then I'm out the front door, gasping, and down the front steps, and somebody is still shouting at me—"Georgia, for God's sake!"—when I gun the Volvo down the driveway, just missing some people standing in the roadway.

I hit every damn red light. I honk my horn, take chances, try to blast traffic out of my way, but I already know I'm going to be late from the dashboard clock. I have to dodge through local streets all the way to the interstate, then four or five exits west, then another interminable local avenue to the mall. How could I have told her it was fifteen, twenty minutes? More like twenty-five, half an hour, and once, when I think I spot someone following me in the rearview, I swerve onto side streets, thinking I know a shortcut, but I don't, and then there's no one behind me, and I have to U-turn and back the way I came.

It's quarter after one when I reach the mall. The parking lots are jammed. It's the first Saturday after New Year's, probably they're giving the whole mall away. There's no space, at least I can't spot one, and I panic, and then I'm shouting at myself, "For God's sake, what are you worried about a *ticket* for!" I shoot into a handicapped slot nearest the building line, grab my purse, and the hell with the burning sensation in my stomach, I'm running.

I know the place—The Greenhouse. Lots of plantings. Decent enough as mall food goes, right next to one of the department stores. Always a line waiting to get in. There are two entrances—through the mall and directly from the parking lot. I dash in on my side. But the place is almost empty, how can that be? On a Saturday?

And God, no Justin, no Harriet! Where are they? No sign of them!

I see food, dishes, on all the tables, but few people.

I bump among the tables, the potted plants. Then I see a crowd at the mall-side entrance—*God Almighty*—and as I run toward them, I distinctly hear someone say, "Jesus, somebody just snatched a kid."

I clap my hand to my mouth. There's some woman in the middle of the crowd, young, very tall. She's holding on to a stack of something—What are they? Menus? Is she the hostess? But she's talking to some kind of guard. He's black, in uniform, and he's got a walkie-talkie up near his mouth.

What happened? Where's Justin?

Oh my God, suddenly I can't breathe. I feel the whole mall tilting up at me. I think I'm going to faint, suffocate. I push forward blindly. I hear her voice, the tall woman—"But it all happened so *fast!*"—irritating southern accent, and there's something else, something about a shooting on the second level, and somewhere, beyond them in the mall, there's an organ playing Bach, one of those horrible Preludes with the crashing discordant chords.

"WHAT HAPPENED? WHERE IS HE? WHERE'S MY SON?"

I hear myself screaming. Somehow I've got the hostess by the sleeve. I almost knock her down. Her damn menus go flying and her eyes pop, huge. I'm shaking her crazily. "Goddamn it! I'm Justin Coffey's *mother!* Where *is* he?"

But arms grab me from behind. I flail at the woman, screaming. People are trying to pry me loose, and I'm lifted off the ground. I scream again, kick out, drag the hostess with me. *I won't let go, can't let go! He's my son, goddamn it, he's my son!* My mind is roaring inside, and at the same time I can hear somebody shouting, more than one, "Hey, is that the woman? The one on television? The Coffey kid's mother? Hey, was that the Coffey kid just now?"

Yes, I answer hysterically, *yes, goddamn it!* but I start to lose my grip, the mall is lifting dizzily again, I can't stop it, tilting, lights, careening lights and people staring at me with their mouths agog. Gasping for breath, I lose my balance. Arms are pinioning me. Then a terrific rush of blood, and everything scrambles.

I learn about it mostly from my father. He and Larry have come to get me. I've been waiting for them in the mall security office, my head down, weeping inconsolably. I won't talk, can't, can't answer the questions. I cling to his little cap for dear life.

I never did faint. Apparently, or so I'm told now, the Greenhouse hostess did try to tell me what had happened, that some man had carried Justin off, but I've no recollection of it. Apparently I went crazy. I tried to scratch her eyes out, and when the security guard intervened, I clawed him instead.

No recollection there either.

Not that it matters anymore.

I was ten minutes late, no more, maybe less. Nobody is sure. Not that that matters either: I was late.

This is what they say happened: The young woman and the boy—Harriet and Justin—came into the restaurant a little before one o'clock, maybe ten till one. The hostess seated them. She—Harriet—was wearing a navy-blue parka, Justin some sports outfit, orange and black, with a matching cap. Harriet ordered food for both of them. They were served. Then, a few minutes later—at one o'clock or a little after—Harriet got up from the table alone and walked out of the restaurant into the mall. The hostess remembered noticing her leave, thinking it a little peculiar, but she was too busy to pay much attention.

But a few minutes later, the boy—Justin Coffey— came out of the restaurant in tears. He was crying his head off, the hostess said. She talked to him, trying to find out what was wrong, but she couldn't understand what he was saying. He kept pointing, jabbing the air. She thought he was looking for the young woman.

She hesitated, trying to figure out what to do. Then suddenly this man came up to them, out of nowhere. He was tall, well-dressed, maybe fifty, a long leather coat with a fur collar, tweed cap. He took the boy by the arm and told the hostess that it was okay, he was the boy's uncle, and where had the young lady gone who'd been with him?

She didn't know, the hostess answered. She'd left a few minutes before, had gone off into the mall somewhere.

She remembered the man craning his head, as though searching the crowds. Then she realized that the little boy was trying to free himself, pulling away from the man's hand and shouting something, she couldn't hear what. Before she could react—"It all happened so *fast!*"—the man bent down, swooped the boy up into his arms, and simply walked away, walking fast, then breaking into a run, the boy struggling against him. She saw his cap fly off, but by the time she started to run after them herself, shouting for help, it was too late. There were too many people. She found one of the security guards instead. He put out an alarm.

Too late.

They "sealed off" the mall, whatever that meant, but found no trace of them other than Justin's cap, or what they think was Justin's cap.

They've showed me the cap—did I say that already?

It's Pittsburgh Steelers. I've never seen it before. But it's all I have.

There's another, confused part to the story. Just after the man in the leather coat took Justin, there are witnesses who claim they saw Harriet on the upper level. She got into a fight with some people who were blocking her way. She had a small gun in her hand, used it to knock someone down, and she was screaming abusively, and then she ran off, waving the gun at anybody who tried to stop her.

They didn't find Harriet, either. They've found no trace of her.

But they say they've got a pretty good description of the man in the leather coat. They think he had at least one accomplice, in addition to Harriet.

I don't care.

All I can think is, *ten minutes, maybe less*.

And I curse them all, the people in my house who tried to stop me from going, wasting precious minutes, and all the people on the roads, driving to nowhere, and Harriet, for luring me there in order to torture me, and the southern hostess—"But it all happened so *fast!*"—and my own father who's trying to console me. "Georgie, Georgie, there's nothing you could have done."

I know what he's really thinking. He's thinking:

Thank God my daughter *didn't* get here any sooner. *Why? Why?* I cry out to him in answer. *What difference would it make if something bad had happened to me too?*

I look up at him. He looks so small, old, concerned. I guess he feels helpless too. The sight of him brings on my tears again.

And my husband. Now he's got Mission Control going in the mall. There are cops all over the place, crowding into this suffocating room, even a state trooper, the crackling of somebody's walkie-talkie, and Larry's working the room.

I've refused to talk to him. I've nothing to say to him.

It is like a punishment, I keep thinking. Except that I don't know what I've done.

"Come on, Georgie," my father says, bending over me, "let's take you home."

Part Three

6 January

"Good afternoon, Counselor."

"Well, well, well. And on a Sunday too! I was wondering if you'd dropped off the face of the earth. Didn't you get my messages?"

"There was no reason for us to talk before now."

"You might have saved us a lot of trouble if we had, not to say expense. But don't say I didn't warn you, Cousin Robert. Before you even met her, I told you she'd lead you a merry chase."

"Robert Smith is defunct. I think we would both do well to forget about him."

"Do I detect some measure of a threat there?"

"Let's get to the business at hand."

"Look, my friend, as to what happened yesterday, I only did what I had to do. We have too much at stake, you, Leon, and I. In my judgment, you needed help. It was a purely business decision, nothing personal. If anything, you were the one who let the personal get in the way. Come on, we've known each other a long time. Wouldn't you have done the same thing in my shoes?"

"I'd like to get to the business at hand."

"Good. Have you talked to Leon yet?"

"Yes."

"And he's explained the plan to you?"

"Yes. We're meeting tonight."

"And its cost, to each of you, provided we're successful?"

"Yes."

"And is that acceptable to you? Ten percent off the top?"

"Yes."

"You know—I've said this to him too—I could, in good conscience, have demanded more. You of all people will understand that. I trust there are no hard feelings?"

"I understand."

"From your point of view, it's just an added cost of completing the transaction. Well. What do you think of it?"

"Think of what?"

"The plan, of course. Do you think it will work?"

"I don't think it's for me to say. You hold all the cards."

"Come, come. Leon hates it, I hate it, you probably do too, but do you have a better idea?"

"No, I don't."

"Then let's get on with it. We all have our roles to play. You should know that I've put my clients off till Thursday. I told them we're not quite ready."

"Yes."

"Assuming all goes well tomorrow, Thursday should be time sufficient, don't you think?"

"Yes."

"The filings are ready on both sides. We anticipate no complications at Treasury or anywhere else. We

should be able to close in February, March at the outside."

"Good."

"Is that all you have to say? When you think where we were forty-eight hours ago? Forgive me for asking, but for a man who's about to make millions, what's happened to your enthusiasm?"

"I believe that's premature. Before tomorrow."

"Oh, come on. It's an added cost of doing business, that's all. Doesn't everybody have a price? I'm counting on your powers of persuasion, Leon's too, and besides, what alternative does he have?"

"What about Rebecca."

"Rebecca? What about her?"

"Did you find her yesterday?"

"No. The published reports are true. She took off."

"Are they still looking?"

"After you fired them, I called them off. Why bother? She's a fugitive from justice, isn't she? Let the law deal with her. And even if she wanted to, how could she stop us? She doesn't know anything about this, does she?"

"No."

"Not even who you are, does she? Beyond Robert Smith?"

"No."

"I thought so. And Smith is dead. Who else knows who he is? Or was?"

"Only you."

"Ah. Is that what's got you so edgy? Really, I won't even dignify that with a reply. Look, we're so close to the deal now, let's not be at each other's throats. We've got the situation under control, that's the important thing. All right, I'm sorry I offended you.

Maybe I shouldn't have. On the other hand, you should have heard Leon! Look, as far as she's concerned, I doubt we'll ever hear from her again. Have you forgotten how you met her? I know her too, remember? She'll run. She'll run like a rabbit. Don't you agree?"

"For now, yes."

"Exactly."

"I don't like loose ends."

"Who does? But from a practical point of view, I think we can safely forget about her. And that's my advice to you: forget about her. I say it as a friend. You know these . . . well, these relationships . . . are bound to be short-lived, and, from your point of view, she can be replaced at a moment's notice. All you have to do is ask. What the Good Lord taketh away, the good Counselor shall always provide. You understand that, don't you?"

"Yes. I understand everything."

Lawrence Elgin Coffey

6 January

Penzil on the horn, Sunday evening.

"You going in tomorrow?" he wants to know.

"Into the city?" I say. "What the hell for?"

"I don't know. I thought it might do you some good to get out of the house. I understand it's been pretty rough over there."

"You got it."

"Helen says Georgie's been under sedation?"

"I guess so. Her old man prescribed something."

"How is she?"

"That I can't tell you. I'm still kind of persona non grata around here."

"Well, look, Bear, she had a pretty hallucinating experience yesterday, on top of everything. I saw you both on the news. You looked a little green around the gills, but I hardly recognized Georgie. Helen says the best thing is for everybody to stay out of her hair right now."

"I guess so. I've gotten pretty good at that."

"Look, it's all going to blow over once you get Justie back. You and I both know that. The impor-

tant thing is getting the two of you through it. I take
it there's nothing new in the case?"

"Nothing."

"No more phone calls?"

"Nope. Capriello thinks we're going to get hit
with a ransom demand any minute. I hope to fuck
he's wrong."

"What do you mean by that?"

"What'll I do if he's right, plead personal bankruptcy? I don't have the money, Joe."

"Well, that's something we ought to talk about.
Look, Bear, why don't you drive in with me in the
morning? In your impecunious state, I'll even buy
you breakfast. You can come with me to the office,
go to the club, I don't know, even go over to The
Cross. You're still employed, aren't you? I think it's
eating you up, all the waiting and hanging around."

"Oh, I'm okay. But how come you're driving in?
Have they canceled the 7:12?"

"I'm going up to see a client in Connecticut, later
on. I'll need the car."

"What time you leaving?"

"Eight-thirty, nine."

"I don't know. It's pretty tempting. A hell of a
thing, but I feel like I ought to ask somebody for
permission first."

"Come on, big fella, it'll do you good. Get yourself
all suited up for a business day. I'll pick you up at
nine. Be ready."

7 January

I'm waiting on the front porch when Joe drives up in the morning. Briefcase in hand, which is some kind of joke. It's a gray day, but not as cold as it should be for January. We talk about that—the greenhouse effect, the warming of the planet, real estate in Canada. We talk tennis too—he hasn't played in a long time either, and if we don't get busy, Spain and Furth, Spain's partner, are going to run the Bear and the Runt off the courts in the spring. Joe must have it in mind to talk about any topic so long as it's not Justie or The Cross, which is okay with me, and I don't even notice at first that we've shot by the cutoff road to the Holland Tunnel and gone through the Turnpike toll booths instead.

"Hey, babe, you just blew it, didn't you?" I say.

"I didn't blow it."

"No? Then where the hell are we going?"

"Lincoln Tunnel. Midtown."

"Midtown? Since when do you work in midtown?"

He tells me to let him concentrate on his driving. True, it's Monday morning on the Turnpike, take-no-prisoners time. From the traffic, every swinging semi in America must be headed for the Big Apple.

He says something about taking me to breakfast in style.

"Come on, Joe," I say, "don't give me this breakfast shit. What the hell's going on? Why are we going to midtown?"

He doesn't answer for a minute. I don't get it. My stomach does a little roll-over. I say it again: "What the fuck's going on, Joe?"

"Okay," he says, his eyes on the road. "The truth is, I'm taking you to a meeting. That's all I can tell you, Bear, but, believe me, it's for your own good."

I laugh out loud.

"A meeting? What kind of meeting? Who with? Hey, Runt, this is your friend, remember? What the fuck's going on?"

But I can't get it out of him. I can't believe it, but it's no joke, the guy's dead serious. I end up swearing at him. If we're going to a meeting, then the whole thing was a fucking setup, wasn't it, starting with his phone call last night? *It'd do you good to get out of the house,* what a crock! And how can he pull this on me, for Christ's sake, he's my best friend! But all I can get out of him, the only thing, is: "Trust me, Bear. Just keep your cool. It's for your own good, I promise you."

It has to do with Justie, I can smell it. But why all the hush-hush, is it the fucking Mafia? The smart money behind the banks? Ever since I started naming names, I've been afraid of something like this happening, but where in hell does Penzil fit in?

I've broken out into a sweat, for Christ's sake.

We drive in silence the rest of the way. No more small talk. A half hour later, we're parked in front of a small hotel a few blocks south of Grand Central. Penzil has one of these NYPD Captain's Association cards which he sticks in his windshield—claims he's never once gotten a ticket when he's used it—and we go in past a reception desk to the elevators.

Eleventh floor. He doesn't even have to ask. He leads me down a corridor to the door of a suite. The last thing he says before he knocks is, "You're in for a surprise, Bear, but it's okay. Just listen to what they've got to say and keep your wits about you."

"Listen to what who's—" I start, but a uniformed waiter has already got the door open, and behind the waiter, in the living room . . .

Well, what do you know?

I must have gone into shock for a second, when it simply doesn't register. But now, sweet Jesus, it *registers!*

Leon Gamble is standing next to a breakfast table, the Great White himself. And sitting behind him, coffee cup in hand, is none other than my rabbi.

Francis Hale Holbrook.

I haven't talked to him since New Year's Eve, when he called to find out what was going on.

As for the Great White, I haven't talked to him since he called to tell me they were keeping my contract in force.

But the two of them *together!*

Penzil has gone, and once there's a fresh silver pot of coffee on the table, the Great White dismisses the waiter and sits down himself.

I'm sitting down too. Have we shaken hands? Holbrook and Gamble, Gamble and Holbrook. It stones me.

Apparently they've had breakfast together. The tablecloth is clear except for coffee cups, but I can still smell food.

The Great White and the Rabbi.

"Larry," Gamble starts in without preamble, "it looks like we've all gotten ourselves into the quicksand together. It's been one hell of a mess, hasn't it, compounded of mistakes and misunderstandings you wouldn't believe. Well, there's no taking back the past. Done is done. But it's our intention, Frank's and mine, to straighten it out with you right here and now—this morning—and make you whole."

I stare at Holbrook—what quicksand? what do you have to do with the quicksand?—but he has nothing to say.

"Once I learned of your special relationship with Frank," the Great White is saying, "and I gather it goes back a lot of years, I invited him to join us. It seemed like the right thing to do. And he wanted to be here as an interested party."

An interested party? To what? But what do I know? I'm still locked on the single fact: *that they know each other!* Well, they're allowed to, aren't they? Wall Street's like a small town. And this meeting—all the hocus-pocus with Joe, the anonymous hotel suite in midtown—that's much more Holbrook's style, not Gamble's.

You want paranoia, Christ Almighty, how much have I told him? My mind spins with it. New Year's Eve, I think that's the last time I talked to him. It seems like years ago. He called to wish me well, polite as always. But did I tell him about Richter? I remember him cautioning me: *Don't do anything you'll regret later.* Karnishak came later, after the phone calls. I gave all my stuff to Karnishak first, and then Richter.

But there's Penzil too! For God's sake, I've told Joe *everything!*

I've missed half of what Gamble's been saying. I've been looking right at him but not hearing. I've got ocean waves in my ears, like listening to a conch shell. If I told Joe everything, don't I have to assume they know it too?

"Wait a minute, Leon," I interrupt him, fighting off panic. "I don't get it. I mean, what are you talking about? What quicksand? You're not by any chance talking about Justin, are you? My son? Because if you are, how in the hell are you going to make me whole?"

"Larry, we're well aware of what you've been going through," he says sympathetically. "The whole business with your son, on top of our misunderstandings at The Cross. Your whole life coming apart, all at once, do you think I don't understand? I know you've been running around like a lunatic, making all sorts of wild charges against the company and people we do business with. Some of them are serious. You know what my first reaction was? I said, 'We're going to sue his fucking ass off—for slander, libel, you name it.' But the more I thought about it . . . well, you *were* going through hell, weren't you? I even thought: In Larry Coffey's shoes, I might be doing the same thing. So we've done nothing on that score, so far. And then of course there's the matter of your contract. We felt the least we could do, under the circumstances, was extend it indefinitely."

If the charges are so wild, though, slanderous, libelous, then what on God's green earth are we doing in a secret meeting, uptown, in the middle of the morning? And what does Frank Holbrook have to do with it?

"But it wasn't enough, Larry," Gamble is saying. "Look, I know we went too far with you too fast. I admit it freely. Last fall—you know it as well as I do

—a kind of mass hysteria set in on the Street. A lot of us went looking for radical solutions, and we at The Cross decided to clean house. It was high time anyway, but in a few special cases such as yours—inevitably—we threw the baby out with the bath water. What's more, I think we even knew it at the time. But no two ways about it, it was corporate panic, corporate stupidity at its worst. *Mea culpa*, and you had every right to be pissed."

He's glossing over stuff, I realize, but I can't focus on it.

"I'm sorry, Leon," I said, "but I still don't get it. If you're saying you fucked me over, I agree. But—"

"As much as that was a business decision," he goes on, "and a bad one, there's also been the personal side since. Look, I'm sorry about it, what can I tell you? The story of your missing kid, it's horrendous. Absolutely horrendous. That business the other day, at that mall out in New Jersey? You came within an inch of getting him back, didn't you?"

I can't answer. I'm watching his white head shake in sympathy. The Great Sympathizer. Everything so far, I bet, has been for softening up. You start with shock treatment—Holbrook being here—and then the Great White makes nice-nice. *Mea culpa.*

While Holbrook keeps quiet?

Gamble's eyebrows go up, come down, stay down. He leans forward in his chair, elbows on the table, his eyes boring in on mine.

Crunch time, I think, and watch out for your ass.

"I'm not going to screw around with you, Larry," he says. "By a fluke—really, it's a tremendous coincidence—we've learned something about the case. About your son's case. We're absolutely unable and unwilling to go into any of the details," leaning further forward, "but I think we can deliver him back to you, safe and sound. In fact, we're ready to commit ourselves to it."

He says it slowly, emphatically. Or maybe that's me, listening. Can you put a voice in slow motion? I glance quickly at Holbrook. He doesn't seem even to be listening. Then back at the Great White's intense stare.

"Is it just a fluke?" I say.

"Is what a fluke?"

"You just said you found out something about the case 'by a fluke.' A 'tremendous coincidence.' Well? Is it one?"

He returns me stare for stare, just like that morning in his office.

"That's what I said," he answers levelly.

The son of a bitch is lying through his teeth.

And then—so help me—I can't hold it back anymore.

"Come on, Leon," I accuse him, "how big of a goddamn jerk do you take me for? Was it a *fluke* that you strung me out at The Cross, or were you afraid of canning me because of what I know? Do you think I don't know who's looking at you? And was it a *fluke* my son got snatched at the same time? Was it a *fluke* I get anonymous phone calls in the middle of the night telling me to keep my mouth shut if I want him back? While all the time I'm making these supposedly 'wild' charges? And now you're telling me that by another *fluke*—this 'tremendous coincidence'—you just happen to know something about the case? Come on, Leon, tell me you just *stumbled* onto it, like dogshit. I'm ready to believe anything today."

He doesn't so much as blink.

"Are you making an accusation?" he asks.

"I don't have to," I retort. "You guys are accusing yourselves." I see him glance at Holbrook. No reaction. "Come on, Leon," I say, "this big hush-hush meeting, and all your sympathy and commiseration and your *mea* fucking *culpa* and we're here to make you whole out of the kindness of our hearts? Come on, I know you too well for that."

The Great White pushes off abruptly on his palms, stands up. He says he wants a word in private with Frank, and with a nod and jerk of his head he leads Holbrook to the windows at the other end of the suite.

I watch them, head to head. Faces pale. Gamble's doing most of the talking. I realize my palms are sweating and that I'm twisting my hair between my fingers. Georgie always criticizes the habit, says it's making me bald. Well, then I'll be bald. But I stop anyway.

They come back. Holbrook has his head down. I can't read him. Gamble's eyes are on me. He leans forward across the table again, and his white hair gleams in the light. A deep breath, exhales, then he says, "What you just suggested, Larry, is pure paranoia. I'm not even going to dignify it with a response. But we've agreed to tell you this much, although if you ever say we said it, we'll deny it out of hand, just the way we'll deny this meeting ever took place. We've no interest in damaging innocent people. But it so happens we know something about the girl—Harriet—the one who worked for you, except that's not her real name. She comes from a family—well, that some of us happen to know. An old Wall Street connection, if you insist, but it's one that goes back before your time. It also happens that she's, let us say, a little mentally off. In fact, sometime last year she disappeared from an institution. She's been missing ever since, and it seems she landed—this was sheer coincidence—in your household. And that's all I'm going to say about it. The situation is highly delicate, but if you let us handle it our way, I think we can keep it from blowing up in our collective faces. The only important thing, as far as you're concerned, is that your boy is okay and that we can get him back for you."

He sits back, studying me, his brows in a straight line across. I can't absorb it all. Harriet a nut case? And not her name? I catch a glimpse of her in my mind, the little prick teaser.

"Then why are we sitting here?" I manage to say. "If you can get him back, why haven't you done it?"

"Because there's something we want in exchange, Larry."

But it's not the Great White who said that. It's Holbrook.

And now—here it comes—it's Holbrook's turn.

They must have worked it all out ahead of time. They must have decided: If they leave it to the Great White to tell me what they want in exchange for Justie, there's a risk I'll tell him to go fuck himself. But Francis Hale Holbrook has been my friend, my rabbi, for over ten years. In spite of everything, they must have figured his presence would convince me that the magic could be mine one more time.

Or maybe, convince me that there's no other magic, no other way.

It works too, I guess.

Not that I'm blind to the play, but I'm listening. Listening hard. Holbrook starts out with the stick: what they want from me. Very simple. I'm too fucking stunned to say anything. And now comes the carrot: what they're willing to do for me in exchange.

If I agree to it, Justie will be returned to me, alive and well, within twenty-four hours.

The abduction case will be considered closed. No charges will be brought by me or my family. If the authorities persist in criminal proceedings against the young woman or any third party, we may obviously be obliged to participate, but there's reason to think the authorities will let the matter drop.

I will be rehired by Shaw Cross on an independent basis—the same arrangement already proposed by the Great White with, however, full company benefits and a minimum guarantee of $200,000 a year, net of all expenses, for a minimum term of five years. If I decide to take another job or start another business while the agreement is in effect, Shaw Cross will make up the difference, if any, between my new earnings and $200,000.

There's more to it—fine-print stuff—but that's the gist of it. Simple, like I said. All I have to do is sell my soul to the devil and I'll get my son back, plus a million bucks over five years to ease the pain.

"We invite your comments," Holbrook says finally.

I take a deep breath. Keep it short, keep it cool, I tell myself. Hold your fucking temper.

"In other words, if I decide to sit on my duff for five years, I'll still get my two hundred grand?"

"That's right," Holbrook answers. He smiles at me. "But knowing you, Larry, I can't imagine that happening."

"Maybe, maybe not. If I do what you want me to do, I'm not going to be able to get a job as a janitor. Not on Wall Street anyway."

They say nothing. It's true enough, and they know it: if I do what they want me to do, I'll be a fucking pariah. So long, Big Bear.

"Gee, Frank, I don't know. Two hundred grand is quite a come-down from where I am now. And five years? With a family to support?"

I say it half as a joke—a pretty last-ditch one, I admit.

"I'd have thought all you cared about was Justin's welfare," Holbrook reproaches me.

"That may be so," I answer, "but if that's what you thought, then why are you offering me the money too? Out of the goodness of your hearts? Come on, Frank, Leon said you weren't going to screw around with me."

All of a sudden, I can feel the tension level in the room—theirs as well as mine. Gamble's anyway. As for me, I've got Georgie in my mind, screaming: *You've got a chance to get Justie back and you're arguing about money?*

But Georgie doesn't understand. It's a bribe. Call it want you want, guys, it's still a bribe, and that gives me leverage.

"We're not screwing around with you," Holbrook says. "I found the offer eminently fair. I can't speak for Shaw Cross, of course, but—"

"I can," Gamble interrupts tersely. "If we can agree on everything else, I've got give on the numbers. Let's hear what else you've got."

I look at him, eye to eye.

"What's going to happen when they come after me?" I say.

"When who comes after you?"

"The Justice Department, anybody. Do you think they're going to take this lying down? They've got other stuff on you. What happens if they put me under oath, what am I supposed to say then?"

"You just tell them the truth."

"The truth? What's the truth?"

"That you don't actually know squat. Not a goddamn thing. That you spoke out under personal duress and extreme frustration."

"And that's why you've just offered me two hundred grand a year for five years? Because I don't know a goddamn thing? What the hell do you take me for?"

Eye to eye, throat for throat.

Keep your cool, Bear.

"I think the point's well taken, Leon," Holbrook says mildly, glancing from me to Gamble. "Again, I can't speak for Shaw Cross, but it seems to me any legal expenses Larry incurs ought to be fully reimbursable. I also think you personally, as well as Shaw Cross, ought to pledge to participate vigorously in Larry's defense, if it ever comes to that."

"Done," Gamble says. "But I still say it's pretty fucking remote. Without Coffey . . ." I see Gamble glance down at his watch. "What else you got, other than the money?" he says to me. "Anything else?"

"I want to think it over," I answer.

"Think what over?"

"Think the whole deal over. What you've just offered me."

"Thanks, but no thanks. There's no time for that. Either we walk out of here with a deal, right now, or there's no deal."

That's an old tactic too: You lock everybody in a room and nobody leaves till you reach an agreement.

But does he mean it? What happens if I walk now?

Better put: What happens to Justie?

"Just one other thing," I say. "I want my son released first. Before anything else happens."

It's my last card, I realize, but it seems to take them by surprise. I see them glance at each other. It's as though they don't know how to answer.

Holbrook shakes his head.

"That can't be, Larry," he says. "The whole deal hangs on your fulfilling your part of the bargain immediately."

"How come?" I ask, my last shot. "Where's my leverage, your way? Look at it from my point of view, Frank. Once I do it, I'm out in the cold. How do I know you'll deliver Justin? Suppose you don't, or you guys get run over by a truck, where does that leave me? Whereas from your point of view, once I've got Justin back, you'll still have my money, won't you? To keep me honest?"

I've been looking at Holbrook. I don't even see the Great White take the gloves off.

"I think I've had enough of this," he says. He stands up abruptly, bumping the table and rattling the cups. He glowers down at me, one part contempt, one part pissed. "I think we've spent enough time here, and frankly, Coffey, I'm tired of wet-nursing you. You do what we tell you to do, and I'm ready to write in three hundred grand a year and eight years. That's firm and it's also final. Two million four."

Suddenly I don't care anymore. "Discounted, it's more like a million six, Leon," I point out to him.

"Discount it however you fucking want!" He's shouting now. "But that's what's on the table. Take it, don't take it, I don't give a shit. But if you don't take it, you've got zero. You want to play hardball? Go ahead, bring your charges, shout your goddamn head off! We'll fight you every inch of the way. Maybe it'll even turn out the only one who did anything illegal at Shaw Cross, if anyone did, was Larry Coffey. Want to try that one on for size? And as far as your kid's concerned, you'll be on your own, buddy boy. Strictly on your own. This meeting'll never have happened. We'll both deny it till the fucking cows come home."

If it's a bluff, it's still vintage Great White, and right out on the table. I'd give my left nut to call him out on it—just this once—but there's no way.

"Let's stop right there," Holbrook says. He stays Gamble with his hand. Then, to me: "You know, Larry, there comes a time in any negotiation when certain things have to be taken on faith. I doubt I'm—"

"*Faith!* For—"

"Please," he goes on. "You're right, you know. You're absolutely right. Doing it our way, you'll have no leverage left. Except this." Now his eyes are locked on mine. "Whatever else you may think of me now, I'm a man of my word. Once I make a commitment, I stick to it. Believe me when I say that if we could do it your way, we would. Everybody wants this sorry affair behind us. The best I can do is give you my solemn word: What we say will happen will happen."

And this is vintage Holbrook.

"What are you doing in the middle of this, Frank?" I blurt out. "What's in it for you?"

For just a hair of a second, I see strain in his face. I mean, he looks old, distracted, as though his mind is totally elsewhere. But then he focuses in again, and he's smiling at me faintly.

"I'm just protecting my investments," he says.

"Your investments?"

"In you, for one thing." The old ironic, New England voice. "In Shaw Cross for another."

In Shaw Cross?

The Cross, I know, is the largest privately held firm left on the Street. But doesn't the family still own the lion's share? And Gamble, they say, has a piece.

Holbrook too?

Since when?

What was it he once said: networks within networks?

I feel the lump in my throat. I can't help it. Jesus Christ, he's been my rabbi for thirteen years!

"And what if I still refuse?" I manage to get out.

"Don't, Larry," he says. "By any criterion, you've done very well this morning. Now just let's play it out."

* * *

The same afternoon, downtown, I meet by appointment with one Joseph A. Richter, attorney at the Department of Justice, in his office. I'm accompanied by Joseph Penzil, Esq., of Lambert Laughin Spain.

I'm there to recant.

Everything.

Everything I might have told or intimated to Richter about Shaw Cross & Company and its customers was a fabrication, a fantasy. Everything I might have told or intimated to Special Agent Karnishak of the FBI on the same subject was a fabrication, a fantasy. Shaw Cross & Company, to the best of my knowledge, has never been party to any dirty-money or money-laundering schemes. To the best of my knowledge, none of the customers I've dealt with at Shaw Cross has engaged in any illegal activities or activities contrary to federal banking regulations. The same goes for any individuals I might have named to him or Agent Karnishak. No officer or director or other employee of any of the lending institutions I've done business with at Shaw Cross have ever suggested to me, in direct statement or by innuendo, that the funds invested with Shaw Cross were derived from illegal sources or activities.

It was all pure invention on my part.

At the end, I apologize to Richter, and to the Department of Justice, the FBI as well, for any inconvenience I might inadvertently have caused them.

Richter's clearly taken by surprise. He takes notes at first—I, myself, am working from notes Penzil and I put together over lunch—but partway through, he tilts his chair back on its rear legs and just listens, hands linked behind his head.

I look up, done. His pale and freckled skin has gone ruddy. Suddenly he catapults forward on his chair and slams his fist so hard on his yellow pad that the pencil he's been holding snaps in two.

"Inconvenient?" he explodes at me. *"Inadvertent?* Goddamn it, Coffey, is all this your idea of a joke? Do you really think you can make a mockery of this whole organization and then just say, 'Gosh, I'm sorry but I take it all back' and walk out the fucking door?"

He has a lot more to say. About wasting the department's time and the taxpayers' money. About the willful obstruction of one criminal investigation (his) and giving false information in another (Justin's kidnapping). As far as his—Richter's—investigation into certain Wall Street practices is concerned, it's ongoing and nothing I can say will stop it. Furthermore, if it turns out I'm lying now, and if I go on lying in the face of other evidence, then the department will come after me personally with every resource at their disposal.

"You better believe it, friend," Richter says. "Every fucking resource. So make up your mind right now, because I'll be goddamned if I'm letting you off the hook. Which version is the truth? What you've told Karnishak and me or the bullshit you're giving me today? And which one are you going to testify to under oath?"

Penzil warned me. He knows Richter from the Street, says he's got a short fuse. He's kept mostly quiet to this point, but now, leaning forward, he asks Richter if we can have a few minutes alone.

"Be my guest," Richter says. He stands, leaves.

Penzil pulls two pads from his briefcase.

"We may be bugged," he writes, pushing one pad in front of me. "Keep talking but write the important stuff down."

We communicate through a mix of speech and writing. Penzil says the important thing is that I keep my cool. Richter's bluffing, he says. What I told them—him and Karnishak—will lead them nowhere by itself. What Penzil suspects is that, prematurely, Richter has blown up their conversations with me into a full-scale scandal, at least inside the Justice Department, and now he's going to have to eat it.

"Don't worry about him," Penzil half-says, half-writes. "Keep to your story. If it comes to it, maybe you said some things you shouldn't have, to him and Karnishak, but you were distraught, crazed, not yourself. There was your situation at Shaw Cross, your wife had just had a baby, then your kid was snatched right out of your house. More than any sane man could tolerate. You were angry, despondent, even paranoid. Drinking too much. Maybe you made some accusations that had no substance, but it was a crazy time for you. Okay, and now you regret it. That's why you're here, to make a clean breast. Now who, I ask you—even in a court of law —is going to hold that against you? Do you see what I mean?"

It's not in me to argue. I'm thinking of Georgie and Justie, neither of whom is ever likely to understand what I'm doing. I'm thinking of Penzil, the fuck who sold me out, but here I am agreeing to whatever he says.

Then Penzil calls Richter back into his office.

"Well?" Richter says to me. "What have you decided?"

"What we'd like to do, Joe," Penzil answers, "is give you a sworn statement."

This catches Richter short.

"A sworn statement? Great! When can I have it, Counselor?"

"What's wrong with right here and now?" Penzil says.

"Right here and now? Nothing. Nothing at all."

"Can you lend us a secretary who takes shorthand?"

"Shit, no. I've already wasted enough taxpayers' money on you bastards. I'll give you a keyboard, that's all. You can type the damn thing out yourselves."

We end up squeezed into a little cubicle, which is the best Richter says he can find for us. Penzil does the typing, on an ancient IBM. The statement pretty much summarizes what I told Richter before—"I, the undersigned, Lawrence Elgin Coffey," recant fully, of my own free will and in the absence of coercion from any third party—and it ends with the same blanket apology that drove Richter up the wall. We make two copies of it on a department photocopier, one for each of us, and I sign, Penzil witnesses.

Richter makes a show of keeping us waiting. We wait in the corridor outside his office. Finally he meets us in his doorway, in his shirtsleeves, takes the copy of the statement. He glances at it.

"They really got to you, didn't they?" he says to me. "Well, let me tell you something, Coffey. This won't be the last you'll hear from us, you can make book on that. We've got long memories around here. Memories like fucking elephants."

This morning, I guess, I could have hung Penzil up by the thumbs, but by the time we leave Richter, the fight's pretty much gone out of me. All I can think of is holing up somewhere with a bottle. Instead, we do it together. Joe's idea. Come on, the Runt says, we better talk this through. We start in the city and work our way to Hoboken and points west.

I kept saying stuff like: "This has been the worst day of my life. I've been betrayed by the people closest to me—Frank Holbrook, for Christ's sake!—and I've sold out. I've sold my fucking soul down the river, and all for a lousy two million four. Discounted to a million six."

All with your help, Joe.

"And then there's you," I say, "you son of a bitch. I told you *everything!* You *betrayed* me!"

Not so, Penzil insists. What about Justie, he says? I've got to remember Justie. I didn't do it for the money, I did it to save my son.

Every time I think of Justie, though, I think of Georgie. I need to tell her, but I can't tell her anything. Not only did I swear myself to secrecy in the hotel suite, but if I tell her Justie's coming home, she won't believe me unless I also tell her I've cut a deal. I'm not ready for that.

I'm supposed to meet with Karnishak tomorrow morning. What am I going to say to Karnishak?

"Why do you have to tell anybody anything?" Penzil says. "Why can't you just let it all happen?"

"Yeah, it'll all be over in twenty-four hours. That's their time limit on delivering Justie, right?"

My best fucking friend.

I can't believe he sold me out. For Christ's sake, he knows everything, I told him everything!

He keeps saying he only got the call from Gamble yesterday. Gamble only recruited him because he knew we were friends, that's all.

"Besides," he tells me, "when you look at it objectively, Bear, aren't you a damn sight better off now than you were twenty-four hours ago?"

But there's a missing link, somewhere out there in the fog. Why did he only get the call yesterday? Was it because of what happened at the mall? And why him? Maybe he's a genius, but he got a late start in the law, and he's still only an associate at Lambert Laughin Spain, and guys like Gamble and Holbrook deal with partners, not associates.

And then it hits me—*dunnnh*—right between the eyeballs. Because who else could have tipped Gamble off? Who else could have said: Hey, I've got this associate working for me who also happens to be Larry Coffey's best friend?

I can see the bastard across the net, old hawk face ready to pound a volley at my feet.

"Where does Spain fit in, Joe? Come on, it's too big a coincidence! Mark's got to be in it up to his neck—I can smell it—and why the hell won't you tell me? You owe me, you son of a bitch. You *owe* me!"

I work him on it. I pound at him. "Who's protecting who, Joe? I mean there's *got* to be more to it! Wall Street companies are always being investigated, and maybe I knew stuff about them, maybe

Richter has a file yea thick, but to nail them? For Christ's sake, kidnapping's a *felony!* And all this shit they laid on me about the girl, Harriet? Whatever her real name is? Maybe she *is* a nut case, what do I know, but there's got to be something else! What the hell were they so scared of?"

"I think you're confusing two separate things," Penzil says.

"I think I'm confusing a lot of things! You're damned right I am! But they were *scared* this morning, Joe! I had them by the balls! You *owe* me, Joe! You've got to tell me."

Back and forth, and he keeps saying he doesn't know, that he's only the go-between, the messenger, and I don't believe him. I bring up the man in the leather coat too, the tweed cap, the one who grabbed Justie at the mall. Who was he? How do I know it wasn't one of them?

"That's crazy," Penzil says. "Guys on Wall Street aren't into kidnapping, for Christ's sake! It was Harriet, whatever her name is, who snatched Justie. All they're doing is getting him back for you."

"Yeah, out of the goodness of their fucking hearts."

Finally, though, he stumbles. Has *he* had too much to drink? Else I've worn him down. Else they told him it doesn't matter anymore, what I know or don't.

"What you're missing, Bear," he tells me, "is that your alma mater—Shaw Cross & Company—is in the process of being sold."

The news hits me like a load of concrete.

"The Cross is on the block? You've got to be kidding!"

"More than on the block. It's practically a done deal."

I can't believe it. I think of MacFarlane, all the stuff he told me. But they weren't dealing with an investigation, they were selling the company!

"It's been one of the best-kept secrets I've ever run into," Penzil is saying. "I never even heard a rumor about it before yesterday, when Gamble himself let it out."

My mouth is open wide enough to catch a pigeon.

"I can't believe it," I say. "I can't fucking believe it. Who're they selling to?"

"That he wouldn't tell me," Penzil answers. "I understand it's foreign money. But don't you see, Bear? A company like The Cross, they've got millions riding on it, probably hundreds of millions. It's a very major deal. That's why they couldn't afford to have you rocking the boat."

Say no more, ole buddy. I get it, even in my cups. I get it all. So they were peddling the company. As far back as October probably, they were peddling the company. The last thing they wanted was an investigation. Not because of an investigation itself, but because even the rumor of one might make a buyer look closer. At what, for instance, went into the balance sheet and income statements. Would make them want to talk, for instance, to people like . . . Lawrence Elgin Coffey.

Unless Lawrence Elgin Coffey has already discredited himself, in public? Which I just did, in Joe Richter's office?

Who'd believe me now?

Jesus Christ.

That's why they didn't can me, in October. They

were afraid I'd start squawking. That's why they strung me out, and why, when the going got rough, they panicked and stole Justie.

And Spain. It figures. Mark Spain is the missing link, the deal-maker behind the scenes. Otherwise it's just too big a coincidence.

Forty-love, set and match.

"Who was it who brought them together, Runt? The sellers and the buyers? It was Spain, wasn't it? Your boss? Isn't that what got you into it, because Spain's your boss?"

But all he'll say is that, at Gamble's urgent request, he drove up to New Canaan late yesterday. Gamble asked him what he thought it would take to get me to go to Richter.

Justin's return, he told Gamble. And money in my pocket.

Jesus Christ.

I think that's when I take a swing at him. We're in a john somewhere. I've got my head over the sink, dumping water on my face, and when I look up, I see him in the mirror. My best fucking friend.

I miss anyway. Probably I'd have missed him sober. The Runt was some kind of regimental boxing champ in the Marines.

"I let them off cheap, the bastards!" I shout at him. "They gave me three hundred grand for eight years, and they're making millions! I had them by the fucking balls!"

There's more to it. I think I end up bawling. I don't think I've been this drunk since Hanover, New Hampshire, class of '77. The Runt keeps telling me I've done just fine. He has his arm around my shoulders. People like us, he says, we're not in their

league. He says I went up against the heavyweights
—Holbrook and Gamble. The only way to look at it
is that now I'm getting Justie back, and a sweet deal
on top.

Oh, yeah. Oh, yeah.

8 January

That's about the last thing I remember, that and that
on the worst day of my life, when I sold my soul
down the river, we still somehow ended up friends.
Big Bear and the Runt.

I must have passed out in his car. I guess he must
have loaded me into the house.

It's four in the morning now. I just woke up, on
the couch in the den. My head is pounding and I've
still got all my clothes on.

Remember Justie. That's about all I can tell myself.

Twenty-four hours—less now.

That's all that matters.

Hey, I can't re-recant anyway, can I?

8 January

"Good morning, Mr. Chairman! How does it feel to be an almost very rich man?"

"Almost is for horseshoes and grenades. You know, somebody could have called me before now."

"Called you about what?"

"Yesterday afternoon, for Christ's sake! I didn't sleep a fucking wink. I'm a nervous wreck!"

"You mean nobody's called you?"

"That's what I said."

"Oh my God. I—oh for crying out loud, I know what happened."

"What's so fucking funny about it?"

"Never mind. Jesus, I'm sorry though. It was an oversight—a simple oversight—on my part. Not that I found out myself till after midnight. But the important thing is that it went like clockwork. Hats off, my friend, to you and your partner. However you did it, you set him up perfectly."

"All it took was money."

"I told you so. How much?"

"Plenty."

"Look, whatever it cost you, it was a drop in the

bucket. I understand Mr. Richter's been baying at the moon, but let him. As far as I'm concerned, I see no reason why we can't start Thursday. Do you? With signing scheduled for Friday?"

"No. No problem. But who's keeping up our side of the bargain?"

"It's all being taken care of."

"And there'll be no loose ends at that end?"

"Practically speaking, not a one. How's your partner doing?"

"Him? It beats me. The minute we finished up yesterday, he was gone. After all we've been through. No postmortems, nothing. Just send me the check when it's over. I don't mean he actually said that, but that's what it was like. Maybe I'll hear from him today, but somehow I doubt it."

"Probably you're better off that way."

"Yeah, I guess so. At the end of the day, he's pretty fucking weird, if you know what I mean. You never know what he's really thinking."

"That's his reputation."

"Yeah, the cold fish of Wall Street."

"Maybe the best way to look at it is that, from your point of view, he's served his purpose."

"Amen to that."

Georgia Levy Coffey

8 January

My husband came home last night after midnight, dead drunk. According to Helen Penzil, it was Joe who brought him home.

He's spent the whole morning closeted in Mission Control. I've heard them shouting at each other. Then, just a little while ago, Joe called for him, and he came rushing out to take it, and when I accosted him after he hung up, his moon face all sweaty and red-eyed, all he'd say, in a loud whisper, was, "It's all fixed, Georgie. Our little boy's coming home, but —this is crucial—you don't know a goddamn thing about it."

Great! It's all fixed, is it?

"*What's* all fixed?" I shouted at him, but he was already gone, back in the den, the door shut behind him.

I can't stand it anymore. I just walked in on them. Karnishak of the FBI, Conforti, the local lawyer, Capriello in blue serge and the too-tight collar. My husband.

The room reeks of men.

"I have to talk to you privately," I say to Larry.

"Georgia, honey, we're in the midst, can't you see? Honey, I'm sorry, but—"

"Just a minute, please."

This is Karnishak. He's standing, holding some papers in one hand. His normally bland face is furrowed, serious.

"Mrs. Coffey," he says, "Larry's given us a statement he made yesterday to a colleague of mine at the Justice Department. I'd like to hear what you know about it."

"She doesn't know anything about it! I haven't had a chance—"

"Please, Larry," Karnishak interrupts, not taking his eyes off me. "I want to hear about it from Mrs. Coffey herself."

He's holding the papers out to me. I don't take them.

"I'm sorry," I say. "I don't know anything about a statement."

"Larry's recanted, Mrs. Coffey. Everything. Everything he told us about Shaw Cross and other people, he now says he was lying."

"I didn't say lying!"

"A fabrication," Karnishak persists, and now I can hear the angry irritation in his voice. "An invention. Now he's saying he made it all up, under pressure. I needn't tell you how serious this can be, if it turns out he's lying now."

"Jack, that sounds pretty coercive to me." This is Conforti speaking. "I don't think she has any obligation to say anything at all."

The FBI agent shrugs, tightens his lips. "She can say whatever she wants," he says tersely.

I'm aware of Larry in the background, but I can't bear to look at him. *It's all fixed*, he said. Is this what he meant?

"I don't know what you're talking about," I tell Karnishak. "I've hardly seen Larry the last few days. I don't know what he's been doing."

"But you're aware of the charges he made before?"

"What charges?"

"Against Shaw Cross and the others. I remember going over the names with you myself."

"Yes," I answer.

"And you took them seriously, didn't you?"

"Yes, of course I did."

"Thank you," Karnishak says. "That's very helpful. We'll be out of your hair in a little while."

Just a few anxious moments—God, what has he done now?—and then, from my bedroom window, I watch their cars roll down the driveway, and here comes Larry, climbing the stairs.

"I made a deal, honey," he says.

I stare at him, sweaty, puffy face, eyes small and bloodshot. I don't know how I'm supposed to react. It's almost funny—*another* deal? (complete with fingers twiddling at his hair?)—but somehow it isn't.

"Our little family's going to be back together again."

Am I supposed to believe him?

He's all full of it, though, full of himself. I'm sworn to secrecy, he says. The police, Karnishak, can never know. No one can know. It's Gamble, he says, Holbrook too. Yes, what Karnishak said was true: He did recant, everything, but only in exchange for Justin. That was the deal. Mark Spain's involved in it too, he says, even the Runt, his old buddy. It all has to do with The Cross, but not in the way we thought. The company's being sold.

"*What* has to do with Shaw Cross? I don't understand. Are you saying *they* kidnapped Justin?"

"No, for Christ's sake! Harriet kidnapped Justie, except Harriet Major's not her real name."

"Oh? What's her real name?"

"I don't know. They wouldn't tell me. It's a complicated story. She comes from some old Wall Street family, I think that's why they're trying to cover it all up. I know that sounds lame—it does to me too now, probably we'll never know the whole truth—but what difference does it make? All that matters is that they're getting Justie back for us."

"*Who's* getting Justin back for us?"

"Gamble and Holbrook. It's all fixed. They're in it together. It turns out Holbrook owns a piece of The Cross."

Suddenly I can't take it anymore. All his goddamned Mission Control, the cloak-and-dagger stuff, the *deals*. While his son—*my* son—is caught in the middle!

"Where is he then?" I snap at him.

"Where's who?"

"Justin, for God's sake! Where's our son? You just said we're getting him back."

"I said it's complicated. They need twenty-four hours, but it's going to happen."

"How do you know it's going to happen?"

"Georgie, for Christ's sake, I've got a head like Vesuvius! You don't know what I've been through!

They've had me in the fucking wringer all day, and it's not over, I could be in big—''

"I don't give a *damn* about your head!'' I shout at him, fists clenched. "How do you *know* it's going to happen?''

"Because they gave me their word!''

"Who gave you their word?''

"Gamble, Holbrook! The Runt too! It's all part of the deal.''

Suddenly it explodes out of me. He's so . . . so goddamn *dumb!* I'm screaming at him, I don't even know what—"If anything happens to Justin!''—and he's screaming back. He's like some hulking ruined teddy bear, ten times my size, but I could smash him, flatten him.

"For Christ's sake, Georgie, don't you realize she's *crazy?* Harriet, whatever her name is? The woman you *hired?* That she was institutionalized?''

"You *fucked* her, you bastard! She's the same woman you wanted to fuck!''

"Goddamn it, I never—''

"Don't you *goddamn* me! You've lied so much, you don't know what's true anymore, and what's a bald-faced lie!''

"Georgie, I *swear*—''

And now, so help me—hound-dog eyes—he's reaching for me.

"Don't you realize,'' I say, backing off, "I don't give a good goddamn whether you fucked her or not?'' Then, my voice hoarse, "I want you out of here now, Larry. Out of my house.''

This stops him. He stares at me for a second, mouth wide open.

"But Georgie, that's nuts! Good God Almighty,

Justie's coming home! *That's* what this is all about, I swear it! He's coming home!"

"Out," I say, pointing. "I want you out."

"This is my house too, remember? And he's *my* son."

"For God's sake," I hurl at him, "go make another *deal!*"

I'm heaving painfully, deep gulps of air.

He turns tail. Doesn't leave the house, though. I can hear him downstairs, his voice. The phone? For what it's worth, I'm no longer tempted to listen in.

This is what life's become for us, I think. The downstairs is his, the second floor mine. The kitchen: neutral territory.

Later, his footsteps on the stairs again.

He's standing in the doorway. I glance up. He's got on the shaggy coat, the one with the alpaca lining, and a stupid-looking ragg cap on his head.

"Remember, Georgie," he says, "whatever happens, you don't know anything about this. Everything I told you. That's vital."

I say nothing.

"I'm going now. I'm going to find out what's happened."

No answer from me.

"Fuck you, Georgie," he says.

Nice.

It's almost dusk. A minute later, I can hear the grinding of gravel outside.

It's pitch-dark now. Over by the chaise longue is an abandoned turkey sandwich and a mug of milk, no longer warm, but I'm lying on the bed, in my bathrobe, reading Adrienne Rich, or trying to. It's not Rich's fault that I can't concentrate. Zoe, changed and fed, sleeps in the portable crib next to the bed. Meowie, Justin's calico, is curled in a ball at my feet.

The phone's rung several times, but I can't bring myself to talk to anyone in other than monosyllables. Once it was Larry, but just to ask if I've heard anything. Heard anything about what? About Justin. No, I said, at which he hung up.

I ought to call someone, to find out what this is all about, but whom? To find out what? Confirmation that my husband is a total asshole?

I'm very calm, strangely. I sent my parents home yesterday and, over my mother's better judgment, let the baby nurse go, who was useless anyway. For once there are no sounds. It's as though the whole earth is uninhabited, except for this one room. Else fogged in. Else muffled in snow. Except there's no snow, of course. There never is anymore. People in St. George like to reminisce about the last blizzard, a couple of years before we moved in, and who got stuck where that night, but—

The front bell just rang.

Or did it?

But Meowie must have heard it too! She just trampolined off the bed in a brown blur.

It can't be Larry; he has the master code.

I glance at the alarm panel on the far wall. The red light is on, thank God, the system still armed.

I hold my breath, strain for porch sounds, footsteps, anything.

Nothing.

Is that a car engine? No. It's more of a whine, high-pitched, and too far off.

It's stopped anyway, gone.

I wait for a second ring.

Nothing.

Could I have imagined it?

Finally I make my way out to the top of the stairs.

The stairwell is dark, the front hall too. The only source of light is behind me in the bedroom.

I go down gingerly, bare feet, avoiding the creaky spots. I'm conscious of my heart thumping. Even the front hall mirror is black, no reflection. All I see is a corresponding dot of red light, the downstairs alarm panel.

Suddenly I remember Zoe, upstairs, alone.

Should I call someone first? But whom, the police?

All I have to do is press the panic button and they'll come. But what if I've invented the whole thing, what would I say?

I open the inner door. It has a faint creak at the hinges. I hear nothing else. The porch light is on outside, but through the lace panels that cover the front door glass, I can see only a hazy light, shadows from the columns. I'm prepared for there to be nothing out there—some prankster? kids ringing doorbells and running away?

On tiptoe, I pull aside the panels, making a narrow break between them.

I just barely have the presence of mind to reach back and disarm the system before I yank the door open.

Justin is standing on the front porch.

My son is standing on the front porch, all alone, just standing there.

* * *

"Oh, my darling! Oh, my darling boy!"

I'm on my knees in the front hall. I'm holding his face in my hands. I'm flooding. Whatever else has happened, he's alive, he's home. My little boy. Justin. Thank you, God.

I pick him up in my arms, talking to him, murmuring. He's wearing high-top sneakers I've never seen before, and some grubby sweats outfit that seems too big for him. He's all skin and bones inside, a featherweight. Could these be the same clothes as the description from the mall? But didn't they change him? Didn't they feed him?

I realize now that I'm crying. Big tears, no sound. He hasn't said anything, not a word. I carry him into the kitchen. He seems bewildered. Is it the lights? Sudden lights after darkness?

"You're home, darling," I babble at him. "It's Mommy. It's your own mommy. You're home, Justin. This is your own house. You're home at last. Can I fix you something to eat? A turkey sandwich? Your grandma was here this weekend, she roasted a whole turkey for us."

Finally—such a small voice—he says he's thirsty.

I sit him down on the butcher-block counter, his legs dangling over the side. Then I panic—suppose he falls?—and put him instead on one of the kitchen stools. I hug him again, pull his head into my breast, but now I'm afraid of squeezing him too hard. He doesn't react, though, just lets it happen. My tears—I can't stop them. Oh God, he's so *skin-and-bones!*

I pour him a glass of milk, set it before him. Averting my head, I dry my eyes. I'm aware of the trembling in my lips, my aching throat.

For God's sake, what's happening to me? He's *home!* My son is *home!*

He doesn't touch the milk.

"What's wrong, darling? What is it? I thought you said you were thirsty."

"Don't want milk."

"Okay, what can I get you?"

"Jutesy," he says.

The familiar word, the same old Justin word. I find a bottle of apple juice in the refrigerator. Hands shaking, I pour him a large glass, set it in front of him.

He doesn't touch it.

"Please, Justin, I—"

"Box," he says.

"A box?"

"Jutesy in a box."

God, he wants it in a box. I fling open the tall cupboard, rummage in the shelves, find one of his little three-packs. It's apple and cranberry mixed. Please God, let that be all right. I tear at the cardboard, have trouble getting the cellophane off the damn straw, finally punch it into the hole.

At last he sips.

"Who brought you here, Justin darling? Please tell Momma. Who was it who brought you home just now?"

No answer.

"It wasn't Harriet, was it? It couldn't have been Harriet."

He shakes his head.

"Then who, Justin?"

"The oarlock."

"Who? The what?"

"Oarlock," he repeats.

Oh my God.

"What's an oarlock?"

"A man 'itch."

"You mean a male witch? A warlock?"

He nods, sipping.

"But who is he? What's his name? Do you know his name?"

He shakes his head.

"But where were you? Where have you been all this time?"

"Rocket car," he says. "The dungeon."

"The dungeon?"

"Uh-huh."

"What dungeon?"

My God, I think, but that *is* Harriet! Harriet and all that medieval claptrap she filled his head with! God*damn* her, god*damn* her!

I try to question him further, get nowhere. He's emptied the juice box. I tear free another, set it up for him, but he doesn't touch it.

"Are you sure you don't want something to eat, darling? A turkey sandwich? I don't know what else there is. Would you like some soup?"

He shakes his head.

It flusters me. I can't help it. I want to tell him I've been worried sick, scared to death, but how can I tell him things like that? I want to ask him what's wrong, but dare I? Instead, I punch out the pediatrician's number on the wall phone.

I give the answering service my name, number, say I want to talk to Braden urgently. The operator says Dr. Braden's not on call tonight, it's Dr. Felici.

I know Felici, a woman about my age who's second fiddle in the practice, but I want Ray Braden!

"Who's the patient, please?"

"Just tell him it's Justin Coffey, my son. He'll understand. It's an emergency."

"How old is the patient, please?"

"What difference does it make how old he is? Just tell him it's Justin Coffey! It's an emergency, he knows the whole story! And I don't want Felici, I want Dr. Braden!"

I hang up. I ask Justin if he doesn't want a quick shower? He shakes his head. Or a tub bath, at least a change into fresh clothes? Pajamas? No. And when I hug him again, and even though I'm babbling again, telling him all over again how thrilled I am that he's home, so thankful—and I feel again the great swell of emotion in me, the ache in my throat —it's not that he resists, but somehow it's worse than if he did. Totally without affect. He's like a noodle, a bag of bones.

Then I think of Zoe. God, how long have I left her alone?

"Please come with me, Justin. Come upstairs now. There's someone upstairs I'm very anxious for you to meet."

But why is my voice suddenly so formal?

I hold out my arms to him. Instead, he slips off the stool. I take his hand in mine.

Together, we go up to the second floor, but he breaks away from me on the landing. One minute he's holding my hand, the next he's headed up the stairs toward the third floor.

"Justin, where are you going?"

No answer.

I don't understand. Or rather I do, in a wounding flash, but can't face it. I want to shout at him—*Justin, for God's sake, it's Mommy, you're home, don't you understand?* Instead, I switch on the third-floor landing light from below and climb after him. But I stop short of the top step. I haven't been up there myself since it happened.

I see the light go on in Harriet's room, then off. Then he emerges. I watch him cross to his room, light on, off. Then back onto the landing, his dark eyes on me.

"Her not here," he says.

"Who's not here?"

" 'arrit."

"No, of course she's not, darling," fighting for calm in my voice. "You were the last one to see her. Was she with you these last few days?"

No answer and, worse, no expression on his face. And the questions come pouring out of me.

"Who brought you home, darling? Tell Momma. You *have* to tell Momma. Where have you been? Was Harriet with you the whole time? Were you alone or were there men too? Where did they take you? Did anybody hurt you? What happened at the mall, Saturday? Do you remember that? The restaurant? The Greenhouse? We were there before, remember? Your momma came to get you, but the man had already taken you away. Who was he, Justin? You've got to tell Momma."

But he is so distant, so uncommunicative, that I flood with despair.

Why is he so bewildered? Disoriented?

Is it me? Or did they do something to him?

9 January

I pass a terrible night. I don't know where to find Larry. By the time he comes home, I'm still awake. I've put Justin in my bed with all his clothes on. I beg Larry not to disturb him, but he insists on picking him up, the blankets with him, and he's shouting something like "Hey, Tiger, it's Daddy! Oh my God, Justie! Welcome home!," parading Justin around the room in his arms. And Justin does come half-awake, at least his eyes open, but it's as though he doesn't know where he is, and then his head nods forward again onto Larry's shoulder.

Larry turns to me. "God, Georgie, what's wrong with him?" Alarm in his voice.

"Wrong? What do you mean, what's wrong? Can't you see he's exhausted?"

I take Justin from him. While I lay him back down on the bed, tucking him in, Larry talks exuberantly at me. Apparently he's had a "hallucinating" night, went a little haywire, something about Penzil, Leon Gamble, that he'd thought they were reneging. But then—what is it? some phone call?—he found out that Justie was already home, and he thinks he made it from the Lincoln Tunnel inside of twenty minutes.

It's not in me to care. Clearly he wants to talk about it, find out what happened, celebrate, sing and dance for all I know, but I plead exhaustion too. I tell him I've an early appointment with Braden in the morning. He wants to know why. Just a precaution, I say. Just to make sure Justin's okay physically. Good idea, he says. Finally he's gone, and I lie down next to Justin, sheltering him, half-cuddling him. But the tears come again, I'm helpless to stop them, and then I'm wide awake. Up again. Standing in the dark, watching over my children. In the end, I'm able to doze fitfully on the chaise longue, but if I get up once to hover over them, it's a dozen times, and every time I drop off to sleep, I jerk awake within minutes, tormented by nightmares I can't begin to describe.

We're off to Braden's office, by special dispensation, at seven forty-five. At the last second, I realize I've nobody to leave Zoe with. Larry is still asleep. I decide to take her with us. I lock her carrier into the backseat, but this leaves no car seat for Justin. (Of course not! Didn't Harriet take his?) But I can't put a normal seat belt across him, he's still too little. In the end, I stick him next to me, without a seat belt, and creep through St. George, one hand poised to grab him.

Ray Braden is big, paunchy, bald, gruff, fortyish. He has six children of his own, two Mercedeses, and a mammoth practice. Normally his waiting room is jammed, but we're there ahead of the nurses, and the doctor greets us alone, in a rugby shirt and jeans.

"Hey there, Chief," he booms at Justin. "Welcome home. What do you think of this kid sister of yours? Isn't she a doll?"

No answer from Justin. He endures the examination with the same docile stoicism as last night, and when the needle punctures his arm for blood, he doesn't cry out, doesn't so much as wince.

I wince for him.

"Hey, you a Pittsburgh Steelers fan?" Braden asks.

I explain, embarrassed, that that's what Justin was wearing when he came home, and I haven't been able to get it off his back.

"But even a Steeler has to get his uniform cleaned between games, doesn't he?" No answer. "I'll tell you what I'm going to do, Chief. I'm putting you on the D.L. for two weeks, do you know what the D.L. is?"

Justin shakes his head.

"It's the Disabled List, for guys who get hurt on the field. Two weeks for you. I want you eating, sleeping, drinking your milk, taking it easy. Then I'll check you out again, and chances are we'll have you back in action in time for the Super Bowl, okay?"

We escort Justin out to the playroom and stand in the doorway. I'm holding Zoe in my arms.

"He seems basically none the worse for wear, Georgia," Braden says to me. "A little tired. We'll see what the blood workup gives, but I don't expect to find anything."

I stare at him, confused.

"For God's sake," I manage, "it's not as though he's been sent home from school with a *cold!* He's been gone for three weeks! God knows what he's been through, I can't get him to talk to me about it, but just look at him! Are you telling me that's *normal?*"

"I'm only an amateur psychologist," Braden says, "but I'd say give him time. Keep him quiet, rest and relaxation, fatten him up as much as you can. Is he taking vitamins?"

"Vitamins?" I blurt out. "Well, yes. At least he was."

"Give him vitamins. And while I'm prescribing, Momma, I'd say that if anybody ought to be on the D.L., it's you. Two weeks of R&R for you too, then bring him in again and let me take another look."

Larry's up by the time we get home. I barely have time to tell him what Braden said when, a few minutes later, Joe Penzil arrives.

I don't understand. Isn't he one of *them?*

"I asked Joe to come over," Larry explains. "In a little while, this place is going to be crawling with police, the media too, probably. We're going to need all the help we can get." He feels compelled to explain everything now, how he was half-crazed when he left me yesterday, because the twenty-four hours were up and he'd thought they were reneging on him, and how he went on a rampage in New York, he'd even assaulted Leon Gamble. "But it's all over now," he says. "I don't give a shit, Georgie. We've got our kid back, that's all that counts."

At this, he picks Justin up in his arms, tousles his hair, tries to get a rise out of him. But my son, I notice, reacts to his father with no more emotion than he's shown toward me.

"They're going to want to know what happened, Georgie," Joe Penzil says to me. "The police in particular."

I turn to him. He fixes me with his dark-eyed stare. I've known him for years, have always looked on him as Larry's friend, of course, but mine too. Now that's all gone.

"Then maybe you'd better explain to me first what did happen," I say acidly to him.

"As far as you're concerned," he replies, "it's exactly what you experienced. Nothing more."

"Meaning what?"

"You tell us. Tell us what happened here last night."

He questions me on the details. By this time, we've moved into the living room. I realize that Joe's rehearsing me, and I resent it. Nonetheless I give him the details: the doorbell ringing, the cat jumping, my finding Justin on the front porch.

"And you've no idea how he got there, do you?" he asks. "Or who put him there?"

"No, I don't."

"You don't know who it was. All you know is somebody brought him back, and the rest is a mystery."

"As far as I'm concerned, yes. But what about Larry's latest deal?"

"What deal?"

I glance at Larry, then back.

"Don't take me for a total idiot, Joe," I say. "Larry told me he made a deal with Gamble and Holbrook. He said it was all fixed. He said Mark Spain was involved, and so were you."

"There was never any deal," he says.

"Not for public consumption anyway," Larry adds.

"Not for *any* consumption," Joe corrects. "I've told you, Bear, and let's all get this absolutely straight: If anyone ever claims there was, it will be categorically denied."

I stare at the two of them, from one to the other. I

suppose I ought to be appalled—maybe I am—but somehow I'm not all that surprised. The one thing that's clear to me, without knowing the details, is that Larry has let himself be manipulated. I also know what he'd say: *I did it all for Justie, all for our little family.*

"Look, Georgie—" Larry begins.

"There's no need for anyone to explain further."

"Maybe there is," Joe Penzil says. "Just so you know, the fact is that your baby-sitter did take Justin. From what I've been given to understand, she's a very screwed-up young woman. She's now a fugitive from justice. Maybe the police will find her, maybe they won't. But we—that is, certain parties— were able to arrange to get Justin back from her and deliver him to you."

"And that's that?" I say.

"What do you mean?"

"I mean it was you—one of your 'certain parties' —who took him at the mall Saturday, wasn't it? Where I'd gone to collect him? How do you explain that? I was there, remember?"

"Georgie, it's complicated. But whatever else you may think of us, we're not ax murderers. Beyond that . . ."

"Except that it gave you time to get whatever it is you wanted to get out of Larry, didn't it? Isn't that the truth? Else why didn't you bring Justin back here Saturday?"

"Georgie," my husband intervenes, "the important thing—the *only* important thing—is that we've got him back. The rest of it is all bullshit."

I start to snap at him, but Joe interrupts me.

"He's right, Georgie. Finally, cutting through everything, he's right. And believe me, it's best for everybody concerned—and that includes Larry and you—that this be the end of it."

Yes, I think bitterly. And meanwhile, my son's a wreck.

From where I've been sitting, in the living room, I've kept an eye on him. He's in front of the big-screen TV in the next room. Cartoons. If he's been trying to listen in on us, I've seen no sign of it.

How are they going to shut *him* up, I wonder, if ever he decides to tell what happened to him?

I guess Joe Penzil must have followed my gaze.

"The police may want to talk to Justin," he says. "Almost certainly they will. I don't think you should allow it for the time being."

"After all he's been through?" Larry says. "You're damn right."

So there's my answer.

"Are you agreed, Georgie?" Penzil says, his eyes on mine.

In other words, am I going to cooperate or become a problem for them? For a fleeting second, I wonder what they'd do.

"Yes, sure," I say, looking at Justin again, the back of his head.

"Who's your pediatrician?"

"Braden," I answer.

"Ray Braden? I know him pretty well. With your permission, I'd like to give him a call now."

Everybody wants to do things for me. I let them, except where Justin and Zoe are concerned. With two exceptions, I won't let them out of my sight for more than five minutes.

The first is for Capriello. He wants to talk to me alone. Conforti, the lawyer, advises me that I'm under no obligation to, but I decide to get it over with and, no, I don't feel the need for counsel. Why should I?

"I've already gotten Larry's version, Mrs. Coffey," Capriello says mildly in my living room. "Now I'd like to get yours."

I tell him. I doubt it takes me more than sixty seconds. He questions me further on a few details—how long did it take me to get downstairs once the bell rang? Was I sure I heard nothing, no footsteps, no car motor?—but he doesn't even ask me to speculate on who it might have been.

He takes a few notes as I talk.

"What does Justin have to say about it?" he asks.

"Nothing."

"Nothing at all? About who brought him here? Or where he's been kept all this time?"

"I haven't been able to get him to talk about it."

He studies me, beady eyes in the ruddy, glistening face. I'd be hard put to have to describe him—beyond "small-town Italian cop in his fifties"—but why is it I have the impression he'd be just as happy to have the case go away now? Is it because of what he knows? Or what he doesn't know?

"I'd like to talk to Justin myself," he says.

"I'm sorry, I can't allow that. Not today."

"No, of course not today. But as soon as possible."

"We'll have to see, Lieutenant. My son's welfare is uppermost in my mind."

"As well it should be, Mrs. Coffey. But like it or

not, we've got a case to wrap up. A situation like this, we really need the family's cooperation.''

He mentions something about a court order. He hopes that won't prove necessary. I, in turn, mention Ray Braden. By this time, I know that Braden has already ordained that Justin be left alone by the police.

He shrugs it off, as though that's a detail, or maybe a detail he won't have to deal with personally.

"The important thing," he concludes, "is that you've got him back, safe and sound. Rest assured, though, we're not going to quit on Harriet Major. She's beaten us so far, but that's not gonna last forever. Someday she'll have to answer for what she did.''

Capriello, it occurs to me, has simply been saying what he has to say. All along.

But so, I realize, have I.

The house has filled with people, downstairs, and it's all I can do to keep them away from Justin. Outside, the media have resumed their state of siege. The telephone rings off the hook. Even Helga Harris calls and, later, Selma Brodkey in Helga's behalf. "She really wants it, Georgia. She wants it exclusive, but she'll settle for non. Look, sweetie, she did you a favor once, don't you think you owe her?''

Somehow I don't feel as though I owe anyone, not today. I put Selma off. Maybe that's mean-spirited of me: even though I can't share in it, the spirit of the day is clearly one of congratulations, that and a sense of relief that it's all over. Only my father, when I talk to him in his office, asks how Justin is, really, but when I expose some of my anxiety to him, he offers the same prescription as everybody else: "Just give him time, Georgie. He'll snap out of it, and meanwhile I think your doctor's absolutely right. Keep him quiet, fatten him up, love him."

Quite.

In the afternoon, my husband accosts me in the upstairs hall. He's wearing a forest-green shetland over matching corduroys, and an air of weary triumph. The inevitable tasseled loafers. Brown for home, black for business.

"If it's okay with you, honey," he says, "I'd like to spend a little time alone with Justie."

"Why?" I ask him.

"Don't worry, honey, I'm not going to pump him. I'd just like to spend a little quality time with my son. Maybe we'll go for a walk."

"Are you crazy?" I say. "With that mob outside?"

"Yeah, you're right. I forgot." Ducking his head, the sheepish grin. "Look, honey, it's all going to go away. Things'll get back to normal. I'll just take him down to the den, then."

I follow them downstairs, carrying Zoe in her Kanga-rocka-roo. They go into the den, Zoe and I into the kitchen where Helen Penzil now presides, just as Joe, I've noticed, has taken over the comings and goings of officialdom.

I tell Helen my story—Justin's mysterious appearance—which has now become the official version. I wonder, in passing, if she knows anything more, but if she does, she's keeping it to herself. She asks how Justin is. I hear myself say he's just tired, that Ray Braden wants him to rest. We chat on. Once, on some pretext, I walk out past the den. The door is ajar. Apparently they're watching TV together. I can hear the sound and spot Justin, small in the Stickley chair.

So much, I think, for quality time.

I retreat to the kitchen. I play with Zoe while Helen talks at me, but I can't concentrate. I find myself growing tenser by the minute. *Give him time, I keep telling myself, for God's sake, he's hasn't even been back twenty-four hours.*

Finally, I go out into the front hall again.

The door to the den is wide open.

I see Larry talking on the phone, but no Justin.

My God, where is he?

I must have shouted it aloud. Larry's standing at his desk, his hand cupped over the mouthpiece.

"What is it, honey?"

"Where's Justin?"

He shrugs with his shoulders. "I don't know. I got this call I had to take. I guess he got tired of—"

"Oh my God!" I scream at him. "You dumb son of a bitch!"

I stumble as I swerve around, almost fall. I rush through the downstairs, calling out his name. He couldn't have gone into the basement; the door's held shut by a hook above his reach. But the front door! People have been coming in and out all day!

I clamber up the stairs on the run. I call out to him, but there's no answer, only voices from down below. Where did he go? My God, someone could have *taken* him again! Right out the front door!

Then it hits me, where he is. I feel myself start to cry. I don't even stop to look on the second floor. I keep going.

He's standing in her room, gazing out the window. He has Meowie, his cat, draped over one shoulder like some kind of regimental sash.

I stop a few paces behind him, forcing myself to catch my breath. Surely he knows I'm there, but he doesn't acknowledge me. Only the cat watches me.

From his vantage point, the view is bleak, wintry, a gray and sunless sky, the trees bare and brown-gray. The great oaks of St. George, the mulberrys, beeches, down to the spreading split-leaf maples. Our lawns look barren, muddy.

"What are you doing, Justin?" I ask him softly.

He doesn't answer, doesn't budge.

"You're looking for her, aren't you? Harriet?"

I see him nod slowly.

"I don't think she's coming back, darling."

"Yes her is," he says.

"I don't really think so."

"Yes her is."

"She is," I correct automatically. "But I don't think so, Justin. Chances are she's a long way from here by now." He shakes his head. "That's what I think I'd do in her shoes, don't you? Tell me honestly, if you were Harriet, wouldn't you get as far away from here as you could?"

He shakes his head again. God, does he really not understand? Even at three and a half?

"Her promise," he says, his eyes still on the view.

"What did she promise, darling?" I ask him.

"Her promise to come get me. Wherever I is. All I got to do . . . is be brave."

His voice has broken now. Even without seeing his face, I can feel the anguish inside him.

"You *are* brave, Justin. I think you're very brave."

He turns. Meowie wriggles from his grasp and

jumps free. Great globules of tears are welling in his sad, little face. I hold out my arms, and this time he comes toward me, and I think my heart is about to break in two.

I pick him up. Finally, at long last, I'm able to hug him close. His arms are around my neck, I feel his hands in my hair. We grip each other tightly. We're both crying now, and somehow there's no need for words.

I sit down on the bed, her bed, and hug him. We rock together. At some point Larry appears in the doorway. "Are you all right?" he wants to know, but I tell him to go away. I can't make Justin stop crying, even though we are there a long time, till it's almost dark outside and there is nothing more to see.

He and I may be the only ones in the world who realize that it's not over.

8 February

"Well, I've had one hell of time tracking you down," says the Runt on the horn. "For Christ's sake, what are you doing in a *hotel?*"

"Oh, it's not so bad," I say. "Room service, porn movies, minibar, free shampoo."

"No shit, Bear, what's going on?"

"In a nutshell, she threw me out."

"Who threw you out? Georgie?"

"No, my mother."

"Jesus. Since when? What happened?"

"It's only been a few days," I say, though actually it's been more than that.

"And you didn't tell anybody?"

"I guess I've been kind of licking my wounds. Actually, it's not so bad."

"*Not so bad?* Jesus. Look, old man, what are you doing for lunch today? I can still clear my decks. I've got something I want to tell you anyway. Good news. Why don't you come down and break bread with me?"

I start to say no—not that I'm that booked up

these days—but then I say to myself: Come on, big guy, maybe it'll do you some good. When the shit hit the fan with Georgie, I went to a hotel over the club so I wouldn't have to explain, but I guess I can't stay holed up forever, watching daytime talk shows.

"Hey," the Runt says, "let me get off. I can still wangle us a table at Windows. Meet me there—what?—twelve-thirty? One?"

I smile at that, thinking how Georgie would react. She's very big on class, class differences between people, and it's true, nobody at The Cross would be caught dead eating lunch at Windows on the World. Whereas, to the Runt, it's still top of the line.

But who am I to talk? I haven't been downtown since the night I tried to strangle the Great White. The twenty-four hours had run out when they were supposed to deliver Justie, and Georgie blew her cork at me, and when they wouldn't let me upstairs in the building at The Cross, I went a little ape. I hung around outside in the freezing dark, me and the homeless, until the car showed up that takes him home—he didn't leave the goddamned office till after eight!—and when I saw him walk across the sidewalk in his white socks and one of those black Russian fur hats, I barged in after him. We were on the FDR, almost up to the Triboro, when the call came through on his car phone.

Well, at least I scared the shit out of him.

I ride the E train down to the World Trade. That's part of the new Coffey: subways, no cabs. Low-class stuff. It's been a long time, except for the PATH train from Hoboken, but ever since Georgie told me I'd better get a lawyer, I've started economizing. Sometimes, I admit, I think why don't I tell her to go fuck

herself and spend every last shekel I get my hands
on and we'll all go down the tubes together? But
then there are the kids, and who's going to put them
through Dartmouth in the twenty-first century?

At the World Trade, I ride the elevators up to the
top and fight my way through the guys from Keo-
kuk, the wives from Chattanooga, the Japs from
wherever the Japs come from, until I can find out
where Mr. Penzil's table is. And there we are, the
Bear and the Runt, side by side on our side of the
net, with a great view of New Jersey.

Dewar's for me. Bass Ale for the Runt.

"It's all on me," the Runt says. "In fact, we've got
something to celebrate. But first I want to hear what
the hell's going on."

Actually, I have trouble telling him. Same as with
that therapist I went to. I start at the end: "She
threw me out," because that's the truth, even
though, there too, it wasn't Georgie in one of her
crazy tantrums. She was very cool and collected
about it. Cold, I guess. Like she had it all figured
out.

"She just said she doesn't want me around anymore. Said it's bad for her, bad for the kids too."

"Bad for the kids? Hey—"

"That's what she said. Look, she's all in a stew
about Justie. He hasn't come around yet. He still
won't talk about what happened, not a word, and
the little preschool he went to asked Georgie not to
bring him anymore."

"How come?"

"I don't know. Something about him being too
disruptive for the other kids. He's run away from
her a couple of times too, outside the house. A regu-

lar disappearing act. Not that he's gotten very far, but it makes her nuts."

"Is he still mooning around after Harriet?"

"Yeah." I can't help grinning. "Not that I can blame him for that. She was really something."

"Were you shacking with her, Bear?"

"Me? No. The truth is that I tried—not one of my finest hours—but she turned me down."

He laughs at that.

"Then I still don't get it," he says. "What in hell is she talking about? What's so bad for her, having you around?"

I know what she said, but I've trouble repeating it. Maybe it's that it's Joe, maybe that I'm just not used to talking about stuff like this. And the context was different too. It wasn't even a shouting match so much as me trying to get her to explain.

"Among other things, she said, 'Maybe I just don't like what you do for a living.' "

"What? You got to be kidding!"

"No, that's pretty much a direct quote, but—"

"Jesus Christ. How long have you been married, anyway?"

"Something like eight years."

"And she suddenly wakes up to the fact that she doesn't like what you do for a living?"

"Yes and no. She admits she never paid any attention, before Justie. Now she says she's lost her respect for me, and she doesn't think she can spend the rest of her life living with a man she has no respect for."

"Boy, I've got a lot of trouble with that," Joe says. "Just who does she think's been paying her bills all this time?"

Actually I said pretty much the same thing to her.
I was pissed off enough to run them down for her:
the house, the help, all her antiques and her jewels
and her gardeners and her trainers and her shrinks
and her Madison Avenue hairdressers, not to say the
charge-card bills that show up every month in
scented envelopes. Justie aside, if I hadn't made my
deal with Gamble and Holbrook, who did she think
was going to pay for them?

No, I wasn't pissed off so much as shook.
Shocked. I wanted to beat up on her, I guess, for
beating up on me. Wanted to make her cry, except
(though this is something I can't tell anybody) I was
the one who ended up bawling.

But that was later.

She admitted I was right about the money. She'd
been living off the same money, high on the hog.
Only now it made her feel dirty. She said she wasn't
going to do it anymore.

But that's not it either, exactly.

"What's her recommendation?" Joe says sarcasti-
cally. "Are you supposed to go out in the fields and
plant corn? Join the Peace Corps? What does she
want, a fucking university professor?"

He makes me smile, the Runt. I guess that's one
thing Georgie can't understand very well, the kinds
of bottom-line loyalties that tie men together.

"It's more than the money," I tell him. "It's pretty
complicated stuff. It's the people too."

"What people?"

"You know, the people I used to work with. Gamble, Schwartzenberg, people like that. Gerry Mulcahy. Frank Holbrook. She can't believe I'd still talk
to Frank Holbrook after what he did to me."

"What exactly does she think he did to you?"

"Look, Joe, let's not fuck around with each other. They used me, they really did. Frank, Gamble. And whatever you say, your boss was in the middle of it."

"I—"

But I cut him off. "Let's not go into it. I know what you're going to say: There's stuff it's better I don't know, and maybe you're right. The party line is that Harriet ran off with my kid and they got him back, but they sure put my tits in the wringer along the way."

"If what you're saying is that they exploited a situation for their own ends, sure, I'll go along with that."

"They held him for three days, Runt."

"That's right."

"And you helped them."

"Only at the last minute. I swear it, Bear, I—"

"You don't have to swear to anything. Look, I may be naïve, but I'm not a Boy Scout either. I still remember the phone calls in the middle of the night, some son of a bitch telling me I better keep my mouth shut if I want my kid back. That wasn't Harriet. Maybe it was some buddy of hers, but I doubt it."

"What exactly are you saying?"

"I'm not saying anything. They wanted me out of the way? They got me out of the way. Fine. I did what I had to do, for me and my family, and I'm living with it. I'm just trying to explain it from Georgie's point of view."

"Which is what? I still don't get it."

I wasn't going to mention it—let Georgie fight her

own battles—but if I'm letting it hang out, then I'm going to let it hang out.

"I'll tell you this much, Runt. If she knew who I was having lunch with right now, she'd blow her fucking cork."

We're interrupted right then: food. He motions to my drink, but I cover my glass: another sign of the new Coffey. He orders another ale. Then, cutlery raised, he says, "Sorry, Big Bear, you better run that one by me again."

I try, though it's awkward as hell. What she actually said, in a cold and pretty much holier-than-thou way, was, "The fact that you still call Joe Penzil your best friend, after what he did to you, strikes me as either beyond belief or beneath contempt."

I guess I soften it a little, telling Joe.

He thinks about it. Finally he says at least it explains one thing: ever since the day Justie came home, Georgie has cut Helen dead. Apparently Helen's been upset about it, and he, asshole that he is, has been advising her to cool it.

"Look," he says, "as far as that goes, we can handle it. Georgie doesn't want to be friends? Okay, so we won't be friends. Life'll go on. But what really sticks in my craw is what she's doing to you. On the one hand, she's telling you to get out, get lost, out of her life. She doesn't like what you do to put bread on the table, she doesn't like the people you associate with, your friends suck. The idea that you have lunch with Joe Penzil is 'beneath contempt.' So what the fuck are you supposed to do, join a *monastery*?"

I laugh again, but he's all wound up. She must've seen too many movies, he says. What does she think, that we're all a bunch of Gordon Gekkos? He's had it up to here with people who don't know squat bashing Wall Street. Maybe it's a dirty system, some of the time, but what's not dirty most of the time? Who's kidding whom? And what gives Georgie Coffey the right to stand in judgment on us poor slobs who sweat for a living?

He says: "You know, when you first started talking, I was thinking you guys ought to see a marriage counselor. But maybe that's wrong. Maybe you ought to get out while the going's good."

"Funny you should mention it, but I've already been to see somebody."

"What do you mean, a shrink?"

"Yeah. Nobody knows about it, not even Georgie, so I'd appreciate—"

"Sure, I understand. But *you*, Bear? Going to a *shrink*? I can't believe it."

"Neither can I, I guess. She's a lot more into that stuff than I am."

"Well, how many times have you gone?"

"Just once. I don't know if I'll go back."

"What did he say?"

"Not a hell of a lot. The one thing he was very big on was what do *I* want. I mean, not what's good for Georgie or the kids, but me."

"Yeah, and what did you say?"

"I said I didn't know," I answer, and then I realize I've got my fingers working at my hair, just what she's always bitched about. I stop. "I told him I'm a little confused right now. That's true too. I'm kind of on overload—all the shit that went on at The Cross, the Justie thing, now this with Georgie. Sometimes I think I want to just chuck it all. Just say fuck it, and so long, everybody. But the thing is, I *like* what I do. Or what I did. Maybe I shut my eyes to a lot of stuff, okay. You do what you have to do. And it wasn't the money either. So you buy a better car once or twice, but how often can you do that? As far as that goes, I made it; she spent it. But I *liked* it. Liked the action. And all the people she's always dumped on—I don't mean Gamble, people like that, but my customers— I *liked* them. I don't mean I *loved* them necessarily, as individuals, but I liked them. And taking care of them, schmoozing them? Making them a buck, and The Cross, me too? And the trainees I was bringing along, all the kids in the Aquarium?"

"You're good at it too," Joe says.

"I don't know. Maybe yes, maybe no. I—"

"Come on, Bear, don't say that. You're goddamn good at it. You're the goddamn best!"

"Well, okay. At least I was."

"Why *was?* Are you telling me you're all washed up?"

"Well, I'm almost thirty-six. And right now, I'm pretty tarnished goods. Who's going to hire me?"

"And I say that's so much bullshit. The business is going to turn around, you know that as well as I do, and the minute it does, a guy like you'll be in a position to name your fucking ticket. And meanwhile, the deal you made, who's going to starve? Answer me that, Bear. Whatever happens between you and Georgie, who's going to starve?"

He's staring at me, eyebrows furrowed in a kind of straight line across his brow. Georgie, before she declared him Public Enemy Number One, or Two, always talked about how intense he was. I guess that's the word for it.

"Thank you, Runt," I say, meaning it. "When the day comes, maybe I'd better take you on as my agent."

"You got it, babe," says Penzil. "Whenever you're ready."

I walk him back to his building. We were about the last ones out of the restaurant, and down in the street, it's all cold wind and shadows, but still we keep on talking on the sidewalk. He tells me the gossip about The Cross. Apparently the deal is going through—that much has been in the papers—and Gamble, though it hasn't been announced yet, is staying on as CEO under the new ownership. According to Penzil, the Brits made him some humongous offer.

Well, good for the Great White. I wonder if he's told them yet about my gray accounts.

Look, I may be obtuse some of the time, but I'm not a total asshole. In a sense, Georgie's not wrong. They did, as the Runt said, "exploit" my situation, and he helped them, and maybe, although he denies it, he let drop stuff he shouldn't have about what I was up to. The shrink seemed surprised—though you never know with those guys—that I don't feel any great resentment toward him. Maybe a twinge, sure, but you've got to keep moving forward. What was it Satchel Paige said? Don't look back, they may be gaining on you?

The trouble with shrinks, and I said this to the guy, is that they get you chewing over the past so much that you practically have to stop living.

Anyway, I feel pretty much the same way about Penzil's news. He waits till we're down in the street to tell me. He's making partner at Lambert Laughin Spain, almost a year ahead of schedule.

"Jesus, Runt," I tell him, "that's great. It's fucking fabulous."

"Well, at least it means I'll get my name on the stationery."

"That and a piece of the pie," I say.

"Some pie," he grumbles. "The only lawyers making a buck this year are the bankruptcy guys."

"Come on, Runt," I needle him. "The Penzil family's not about to starve either."

"True," he says. Then, looking up at me, "I've got you to thank for it too, Bear."

"Me? How do you mean?"

He's got this sly crinkle around his eyes.

"I sure as shit shouldn't tell you this, old buddy, but that whole business with Leon and Frank? The Sunday I got called up to see Leon? The truth is that I didn't want to touch it, not with a ten-foot pole. I told him, 'Look, Larry Coffey's my friend, I'm not doing anything that's going to hurt him.' It took some tall convincing for me to believe that your best interests were at stake. Along the way, though, I managed to score some points for myself."

"You mean you cut a deal of your own?"

"More or less."

"On the spot? With Mark?"

"That's right. No hard feelings, I hope?"

Maybe a twinge, nothing more. Okay, maybe I'm a little pissed, but he's still my friend.

"No hard feelings, Runt," I answer. "You do what you have to do," and if Georgie can't accept that, well, I guess that's baseball.

* * *

I call Georgie.

It's the same night, and I've just done something a little crazy—thanks, in part, to the Runt. The shrink too, maybe. I mean, while the Runt and I stood on the sidewalk this afternoon, shooting the shit, I said that, even with his partnership and me with my eight-year cushion, we were still a pair of bongo players compared to Gamble, Holbrook, and Spain. And he said sure we were, by comparison, but they were all guys in their fifties. Mark Spain was even talking about retirement. Just give us another ten years, he said, and we'd be the high rollers while they were off in the Caribbean playing shuffleboard.

I guess I believed him. Wanted to, anyway. Enough to do something a little crazy.

Not that I tell Georgie.

I say, "Look, I'd like to see you tomorrow."

She answers, "Well, you're going to, aren't you? Aren't you coming for Justin?"

In fact, I've half-forgotten. When you're living the way I do, the days kind of meld together.

"Sure," I say, recovering, "but I mean without the kids. I'd like us to spend a little bit of time together. Either before or after Justie."

She's evasive.

"That's hard for me. I *do* have the children. Isn't it something we can talk about on the phone?"

"I'd rather not," I say. "Can't you get somebody to deal with them for a little while? It won't take long."

She's noncommittal, says she'll try but she can't promise. In any case, it'd be after, not before.

"Either way," I say, "but it's kind of important to me."

"I'll try," she repeats.

9 February

It's funny. Even before I actually left, Saturdays somehow became mine with Justie. I don't remember our talking about it, Georgie and me, it just sort of happened—a kind of grim preview, I guess, of the divorced daddies we used to joke about, weekends, when we still lived in the city. As far as I'm concerned right now, it could be any day of the week, or more than one, but Saturdays it is. I try to do special things with him—not so easy with a three-and-a-half-year-old kid who doesn't seem to much care where he is and whose mother is scared to death I'm somehow going to lose him. We've been to the flicks. Once I got a pair of tickets to a day game at the Garden (she bitched about that), but it didn't interest him and we left early. Last week I drove him in to the new Central Park Zoo and we froze our nuts off. This week, though, I've got nothing planned.

Saturday morning. I take the PATH to Hoboken, which (part of the New Economics) is where I now park the car. I head west. I'm all revved up, and I keep running it through my head, all the things I'm going to say to her, but when I get to St. George, even though I know exactly where I'm going, it all seems foreign to me, and so, weirdly, does the house.

I don't get it. After how many years, and I've been gone less than two weeks?

And then I do get it, at the last second, rolling up under the porte-cochère. It's that I feel like a fumbling high school kid. Because of Georgie. Because of what I've got in my pocket.

And there she is at the door. With Justie, all ready in what looks like a new snow jacket and a wool cap that half hides his face.

"Lynne's coming out later," Georgie says, holding onto Justie's shoulders. A bad omen, I think—Lynne Snyder's an old feminist buddy of Georgie's, and no great fan of mine—but what the hell. "She's taking the three o'clock bus, and she'll take care of the children. So, say anytime after four?"

She hands me the keys to the Volvo, which has Justie's seat in back, and I'm about to drive off when she calls after us from the front porch: "You forgot to tell me where you're going!"

Another Saturday ritual.

I roll down the window.

"I don't know," I say. "We're going out to lunch, and then we'll play it by ear."

She frowns.

"Please be careful," she says.

Much as I hate to say it, it's torture. We go to one of those big highway diners which, outside the Spaniards and the Portuguese in Newark, are about the only honest restaurants in north Jersey. I order Justie what he says he wants: a cheese omelet and french fries, but he only pokes at the food. Ditto ice cream for dessert. We're finished at twelve forty-five, even though I try to stretch it out. I buy a cou-

ple of bucks in quarters—there are arcade machines
in the entranceway—and I pick him up to play, but
he's gunned down in a hurry the first couple of
times, Game Over, and he loses interest. Too young,
I guess.

I've bought a *Star-Ledger* and combed the movie
entries, but I can't find anything that's likely to appeal to a three-and-a-half-year-old. Or, for that matter, a thirty-five-and-a-half-year-old either.

"Well, we're sort of stuck, Justie, old man," I tell
him, but he doesn't seem to care, one way or the
other. It's not that he's sullen exactly, but there's
little eye contact, and he makes it pretty clear that,
as far as he's concerned, we're only marking time.

We're back in the Volvo, Justie behind, me in
front. Fuck it, I say to myself, what do weekend fa-
thers do in New Jersey? With kids who'd rather be
someplace else? I think of a mall. Then I think if
Georgie ever found out I took him to a mall, any
mall, she'd shoot me in cold blood.

In the end, we drive around, more or less. There's
a great tropical fish store on Route 46 in Clifton
that's almost like an aquarium, and I take him there
to look at the fish. It's jammed on Saturday and
steamy, but I pick him up in my arms and walk him
around, eyeball to eyeball with some pretty weird
species in Day-Glo colors, some of which cost in the
hundreds of dollars. We manage to kill the better
part of an hour that way. Then I find a couple of
free-standing toy stores where we work the aisles.
The only thing that catches his attention, in one of
them, is a low-slung remote-controlled car that
looks like something out of *Buck Rogers*. I show him
how it works, in the aisle, but he has trouble

manipulating the controls. Still, he says he wants it. I buy it for him. Batteries not included. I remember Georgie saying something about battery-operated toys, at his age. I think she's against them. Too bad. I buy the batteries too.

I offer to stop in St. George for ice cream, even though it's February. He doesn't want any. Neither do I. Popcorn? No. A bag of mixed nuts? No. A soda? No. Doesn't he have to go to the bathroom? Nyet.

We're home at four on the dot, actually three fifty-five on the dashboard clock.

I suggest to Georgie that we go out. We could just go into town, have a drink at one of the saloons.

"Neutral turf," I say jokingly.

But she doesn't want to. She says it's because she doesn't want to leave Lynne alone with the children. She says if I want a drink, I should just help myself.

It's all wrong, I can feel it in my gut. The whole damn place feels alien to me, even though I paid for it. Lynne has gone upstairs with Zoe and Justie—that's a plus, but it also leaves us standing together like two strangers.

We end up in the kitchen. She's got something in the oven—smells like chicken roasting, or turkey.

"Please," I say, "let's at least sit down a minute."

We sit on stools. I reach into my jacket pocket, just to make sure it's still there. It is.

"Look, honey," I start, then try to censor the "honey." "Georgie," I begin again, "I've thought a lot about everything you said, believe me. For the first time in years, I've had a little time to think, take stock. A kind of personal inventory. Who was it who did that? Buckminster Fuller, wasn't it?"

When I was at Dartmouth, Buckminster Fuller was still a kind of legend. The wise guys called him Bucky.

"Maybe in that sense," I say, "what happened to us isn't all bad."

My voice sounds hollow though, a little preachy, and she's not much help. She's listening all right, but the expression on her face is like she's expecting me to trip over my own feet any second. Then, excusing herself, she has to baste at the oven, with one of those plastic tubes with the rubber bulb.

I watch her bending over, ass up. Still looks pretty damned good, for the mother of two.

She sits down again.

"Look, honey," I start again, "I may not be the most introspective guy in the world, but a lot of what you had to say sounds right to me. I mean, your criticisms of me. On the one hand, I am what I am. On the other, that doesn't mean I'm incapable of changing. Maybe it took—"

"For God's sake, Larry," she breaks in, "you don't have to apologize for yourself. Not to me."

"Well, maybe I do. The thing is, I heard you, Georgie, I really did. You blew the whistle. For a long time, I'd just been going along, doing stuff like I always had. I mean, without stepping back and taking a hard look. But then the Justie thing happened, and it hit me just as hard as it did you. I found myself in a kind of trap, but I kept thinking: The *only* thing that matters is getting him back. So maybe I did some stuff I shouldn't have, wouldn't have otherwise, but at least I did it with good intentions.''

I've wandered off from my prepared script. I was leading up to going to the shrink, but now I don't even remember what I'm supposed to say next. The worst part is that she's just sitting there, looking up at me, and I'm not getting any signals one way or the other. I feel like saying, *Oh, fuck it, honey, I still love you*, something like that, taking her into my arms, but something's telling me that would really blow it.

Now I realize I'm futzing at my hair, and that she notices it.

I stop.

I go on. I remind her of that TV flick we saw once —*The Day After the War*, something like that. What it would be like after the bombs have fallen. I thought it was pretty powerful, Georgie didn't. Anyway, I tell her, we've had our bombs fall, but when it's all over, we're still intact, our little family. Maybe she's worried about Justie right now, but he'll straighten out. And Zoe's cute as a button. And she and I are still young, we've got our resources. Yeah, it's true, I'm out of a job right now, a real one anyway, but things are going to turn around for me, and, for once, I'm going to take the time to figure out what it really is I want to do.

I think: plus we've got eight years' worth of cushion, that's not nothing, but I stop myself short of saying it.

She interrupts me anyway. All of a sudden she's on her feet, hand raised like a stop sign, and listening at the back stairs that go up to the second floor.

Listening to what?

"I'm sorry," she says with a sigh, coming back to the counter. "I thought I heard Zoe crying. Please go on."

Go on? But I feel like I'm almost done!

Damn! Her saying nothing has thrown me totally. I feel like I'm slogging along in mud up to my knees, and thinking that thought, damn if I don't catch my hand on its way up to my scalp again.

Okay, Georgie, I'll slog along.

"All I want to say is that I want us to start over again. The war *is* over, it's the day after. It's like it's a whole new . . . well, a whole new season. It's like—I know this is going to sound funny to you, Georgie, but I feel like I want to ask you to marry me."

When I rehearsed it, I thought she'd laugh at this, but all I get is a faint smile. Kind of a sad smile. But nothing more, no signals, and suddenly I think: What are you doing, you dumb bastard, can't you see it written on her face? But I can't stop now, even with my stomach starting to twist up.

"I guess that's what I'm doing, Georgie," I say, standing. "I'm asking you to marry me. All over again." At the same time I'm fumbling in my blazer pocket. "At the same time," I say, "I did something a little crazy." I fish out the oblong box, gift-wrapped by the store in silver paper with a silver rose attached to it. "I bought you something. I picked it out by myself, and if you don't like it, you can always exchange it. I thought it would go with a lot of your clothes."

I hand her the package. She holds it in silence, head bent over it so all I can see is her curly hair.

"Go on, Georgie," I say, "open it. It's for you."

It's the first time I ever bought her jewelry by myself. A few times I've been with her, but she's always done the choosing. And this is big time, Fifth Avenue, ten grand plus tax on the Gold Card.

So much for the New Economics.

She opens it. There's one of those black velvet cases inside the silver paper. She opens the case. Somehow it seems smaller to me now. It's a diamond choker, set in gold. The saleswoman who helped me looked a little like Georgie, and when she tried it on in the store, I thought it looked great.

Now I think it's all wrong. She doesn't even have to say it. Shit, I wish to hell I'd never taken the box out, wish to hell I'd never bought it. I wish to hell . . .

"I'm sorry, Larry," she says, lifting her face. "It's . . . it's very beautiful." For a second I think she's about to cry. Her mouth screws up, her chin, her eyes go small. I see her swallow. ". . . very sweet, Larry . . ." Shakes her head slowly. "But I can't accept it."

"Why not?" I say.

She hasn't even taken it out of the case. Now she's handing it back to me.

I don't take it.

"Tell me," I say. "Why not?"

"I don't think you want to know," she says, shaking her head again.

"Oh, come on, Georgie, for Christ's sake!"

But her eyes lower. Now she's staring down at the damned thing as though she doesn't know what it is.

"I think we shouldn't be talking at all, right now," she says dully. "I don't think we should."

"But we've got to!" I protest. "Georgie, for Christ's sake, this is *us!*"

She shakes her head slowly, side to side, sighs, like she's talking to some moron who doesn't have a clue. And that's what she says—not that I'm a moron, but: "You don't understand, do you, Larry. You really don't."

"Don't understand what? If I don't understand, then you better tell me!"

"You've just done it all over again," she says.

"Done what? For Christ's—"

"*You've* gone off, and *you've* done your great self-examination, and *you've* decided, 'Oh, maybe there are a few things wrong, but there's nothing I can't fix.' It's very typical of you. You've even done the same thing with Justin. 'Oh,' you say, 'I know you're worried about him right now, but he'll straighten out.' You really believe that."

"Of course I believe it!" I say. "Don't—"

"Why?"

She's looking up at me again, eyes questioning.

"Why what?"

"Why do you believe he'll straighten out?"

"Why? Because . . . because he's our kid! Because he's a good kid, for Christ's sake! Okay, so he's had a bad experience, but he'll snap out of it. He's not going to stay this way for the rest of his life."

"How can you be so sure of that?"

"Georgie, what are you talking about?"

"I'll tell you why you're so sure of it," she goes on. "It's because it's what you've decided. It's *your* decision, therefore that's how it's going to be."

"Just a minute, just—"

"And where am *I* in all this? How do *I* fit into your great new scheme of things?" At least, for better or worse, we're getting onto familiar ground. I can hear the shrillness coming into her voice, and suddenly her fists are clenched tight. "You don't have to tell me, I already know. I'm just supposed to go along with everything *you've* decided. Because I'm the good little wifey. Because that's what good little wifeys do. Well—"

Finally, it gets to me. "But that's not fair, Georgie! What do you think I wanted to see you about? I came here to discuss it!"

"Discuss what?"

"Us! Everything!"

"You did no such thing!" she cries out. "You don't have a *clue* as to who I am! You came here to announce what was going to happen because *you* had it all worked out."

"That's not true! I've even been to a shrink myself!"

I wasn't going to mention it, but at least it surprises her.

"You what?" she says.

"That's right. I went to see somebody."

"Why?"

"Because . . . because everything was screwed up. You and Justie, me too. I felt like I'd lost control of things."

"And did the shrink help you get control?"

"Georgie, you don't have to be sarcastic."

"I'm not being sarcastic. Not at all. But did he—I assume it was a man—did he help you get control?"

"No, not in one meeting."

"But what did he say?"

"Not a hell of a lot. You know how they are. He thought I ought to figure out what I want."

"Oh? And have you?"

Suddenly, I see the trap. I see it, like a hole I've just dug. And I resent it, resent what I know she's going to say even before she's said it.

"Well?" she says. "Have you figured it out?"

But I can't answer. Not that that matters.

"Well," she goes on, "I guess you have, else why would you be here?" She laughs her shrill, sarcastic laugh. "Now let me see if I've got this straight. You go one time to a shrink, one visit. Maybe it's something you've always mocked, but what the hell, things have gotten out of hand, you feel you've lost control. So you go. God knows what you tell him, but the shrink says you ought to figure out what it is you want. The next thing that happens, well, here you are, aren't you? And you've got it all worked out, it's all been decided. The New Universe according to Larry Coffey, with a little help from Buckminster Fuller. Buckminster Fuller, for God's sake! Well? But that's it, isn't it? You *have* figured it out, haven't you? Oh, there've been a few mistakes here and there, but nothing you can't fix. Justin's going to snap out of it, I'm going to snap out of it—that's what you've figured out—and now it's all there in a neat package, like one of your—what did you call them?—your 'Big Bears'?—and all you've got to do is *sell* it. And all I've got to do is *buy* it! Well? Isn't that it?"

It's like an onslaught, her sarcasm. I can feel her rage building like lava, and there's not a goddamn thing I can do or say to stop it, even if I wanted to.

"Well, Mister," she shouts at me, "I'm not *buy-*

ing!" Her face has gone white. "It's because of you that *my* life's a wreck, as well as my son's, and we're not taking my marching orders from you anymore! Proposing marriage, for God's sake! With this stupid . . . this stupid goddamn *trinket!"*

She's been holding on to the case the whole time. Suddenly she flings it across the counter at me. The damn choker doesn't even fall out.

"Who the fuck do you think you are?" she shrieks at me. "Peter *Minuit?"*

For a second, I don't even get it. Then I do. Cute. New York, from the Indians. Twenty-four dollars in trinkets. And I see red. I see purple, orange, pink, all the fucking shades in between. I see Lynne Snyder, standing at the top of the back steps, listening in.

"And who do you think you are," I shout up at her, "her fucking cheering section?"

But Georgie's still sitting on the kitchen stool. I think she's crying—or trying to. Or trying not to, what do I know? But I can't look at her anymore.

As for me, I guess I've already shed my tears.

"Please go, Larry," she's saying, her voice low and trembly. "Let's not do this anymore. Please just go."

That's exactly what I do.

Out the door, into my car, off. Quick, surgical, no more questions. I'm thinking: Baby, you just did it to me for the last time.

Somehow, I've even got the fucking velvet case back in my pocket. Must have picked it up.

I stop at a shopping strip. I'm still shaking inside. Booze is cheaper in New Jersey than New York. I buy the 1.75-liter Dewar's. On second thought, I buy a second. So much for the new Coffey.

Big Bear, I say to myself, just cool out. Whatever happens, you gave it your best shot, you really did. The thing is, old man, and don't you forget it: Whatever you did, whatever you said, you could have crawled through a bed of nails on your fucking kneecaps, she was going to shoot you down. The fix was in.

I roar off toward the tunnels. Fuck Hoboken! I'll park in the hotel garage, twenty-five bucks a day or whatever they charge, stick it on the tab.

Anybody out there want a diamond-and-gold choker, ten thousand bucks plus tax?

Part Four

Georgia
Levy
Coffey

5 April

Friday night, my diary open on my lap, some movie I'm not watching on Lifetime. The packers didn't finish till after six. They're still not finished. Then, when I finally put Zoe down, Justin woke up again, and I had to lie down with him, stroking his hair, telling him a story, telling him everything's going to be all right. When I'm not at all sure it is.

Finally, after three months, he's driven me off the edge.

I took him into the city, Wednesday afternoon, to show him the new apartment. I thought it important that he see for himself, let the reality of change sink in before it actually happens. There were still workmen there, dropcloths all over the place, ladders, the reek of fresh paint. I showed him his new room —it has a lovely view of the river—and then I was looking over some fabric samples with the decorator. The next thing I knew, he was gone. Somehow he walked out of the apartment, rode the elevator down eleven floors by himself, and out into the street. Nobody stopped him, nobody saw him.

I went nuts. The Patz boy, the Patz boy! This was New York City, not St. George, and Justin doesn't know the Village at all. I ended up waiting, with my father, in a dreary police station on Tenth Street. The cops came and went; we sat. It was after dark and drizzling by the time they found him, all the way over in Tompkins Square Park, that charming showplace of the East Village where they've had all the trouble with the pushers and the squatters.

He was sitting on a bench, by himself.

He was hungry.

He'd gone looking for his goddamned beloved Harriet.

It was my father who got that out of him. I could hardly talk to him. He told his grandfather that he was looking for " 'arrit."

But isn't that why we're moving? So he'll stop looking? So there'll be no third floor, no room, no memory triggers? Because everything else I tried— getting rid of all her stuff, every trace, and moving him downstairs to the second floor—failed totally? I even had a gate installed at the bottom of the stairs going up—what a joke! It took him all of ten seconds to figure out how to climb it, and then I'd find him staring out her windows again, staring out at . . . nothing!

His "mute resistance." That's what they called it at Group. They said his "mute resistance"—refusal to talk, sing, whatever it was they were doing—was too "disruptive" for the other children.

His therapist called that "attention-getting" on Justin's part.

I'll say.

And all it takes is a moment's inattention on mine.

"But what am I supposed to do?" I asked her hysterically. This was yesterday, after the New York experience. "Am I supposed to tether him to me?"

"I'm afraid, for the moment, there's not a lot else you can do," she answered sympathetically.

"But should I cancel New York? I mean, I've got the movers coming tomorrow morning, but maybe it's all a terrible mistake!"

"I don't think so," she said. "I think you've got to give him time. And me time."

Time.

That's what everybody says.

But time for what?

The little light in the alarm panel on the bedroom wall just went from red to green!

I jump at first, but now I'm fuming. Goddamn him! Who else in the world but Larry has the code? And didn't we agree, through the lawyers, that he could come anytime he wanted this weekend for his stuff but that he had to call me ahead of time?

I don't need this now. Don't need it, don't need it!

What does he want from me? Does he want to hear it all over again—that we're a walking cliché? One of those "great" suburban marriages that, at the first crisis, turn out to be hollow at the core? Or that it was my fault as well as his? Or nobody's fault? Or Harriet Major's fault? Or whatever "spin" he wants to put on it this time?

Or is it the money? He knows—over my lawyer's dead body—that I don't want alimony. I even hit my father up for the loan to get us to New York because I refused to ask Larry. But I damn well do want child support.

I turn off the TV, throw on my robe. From the top of the stairs, I can't hear a sound.

Very un-Larry.

Unless this is his idea of a joke?

I call out his name softly. No response.

Unless . . . good God, could he have given someone else the code?

Should I check the children first?

I start down, flicking on the front hall sconces from above. Damn, why didn't I change the locks?

Still no sound. From the curve in the stairs, all I can see is cartons, stacks of them. The most depressing of sights. They take up almost the whole downstairs.

Then, *her* voice—and simultaneously I spot her between two of the stacks, gazing up at me.

I don't move. I can't believe it.

Goddamn it, she wrecked my life, and now she's standing in my house!

She looks awful too. Tired, hair all scraggly, and she's wearing some dirty misshapen parka, hands jammed in the center pouch.

"How did you get in here?" I say. Instinctively, I pull the ends of my bathrobe together.

"Easy. My code's still in the system. You programmed in the digits of my birthday, remember? I knew you'd forget to take it out."

She's right, I did forget.

"What are you doing here, Harriet?" I say, struggling to keep the shrillness out of my voice. "Why have you come?"

"But what's all this stuff?" she says. "God, you're not moving, are you?"

"I think you'd better go."

"I don't believe it! You're moving? Out of this house?"

"It'd be best if you just left. Right now."

"I want to see Justin," she says. "To make sure he's all right."

I stiffen on the stairs. No, not in a million years.

"He's not here," I answer quickly.

"Not here? But where is he?"

"Not that it's any of your business, but he's at his grandparents', in New York."

Still she makes no move to leave.

"There's no need for you to be afraid, Georgia," she says. "Not of me. I don't mean you any harm."

She's smiling up at me now. The eyes, at least, haven't changed. Innocent, long-lashed, blue-gray eyes.

"I'm not afraid," I reply. "Why should I be afraid? I just want you out of my house. If you go right now, I promise I won't call the police."

For some reason this makes her laugh. But then she says she can't go, not until she's talked to me.

"But what makes you think I want to talk to you, Harriet?" I say. "It's over, done. I have nothing to say to you."

"No, it's not over," she says. "Not for me, anyway. Not as long as you hate me."

The remark makes me jump inside.

(How does she know? How does she know that every time Justin runs away from me, I hate her all over again?)

I bite my tongue. I have to think practically. For God's sake, I have two children upstairs, and I'm alone in the house. Is she dangerous? How do I know she's not? How do I know anything until I find out what she's come for?

"I don't hate you," I say. I come the rest of the way down the stairs. "Where have you been all this time?"

"Oh, here and there."

Great answer, I think. For three months, she's been here and there.

On closer inspection, she doesn't look so much tired as strung out. It reminds me of college, the way people used to look at exams when they'd been up the whole night before on NoDoz and coffee. There's a wet, musty smell about her too. It's been raining off and on all week.

I hesitate. I want her gone, out of my life, but how am I going to get rid of her? And she was institutionalized, wasn't she? (Who was it who told us that? Joe Penzil?)

"Let's go into the kitchen," I say. She starts down the back hall, but the back hall is almost totally blocked. "It's easier through the dining room," I tell her, and I follow her through the doorway. The dining room is completely done. My round oak table top is resting on its side, packed and strapped in quilting, and the base with the lion's claw feet stands weirdly alone. The art-glass Handel chandelier is gone; the built-in glass oak cabinets, as old as the house itself, have been emptied out.

The kitchen is about half-dismantled. The cabinets are done there too. The plumbers are coming in the morning to unhook my Viking range, which I had to sell in the tag sale because there's no room for it in the city. Larry's lawyer agreed that I could hold the tag sale and keep the proceeds, as long as I kept a record.

"I still can't believe it," Harriet says, gazing around. "You loved this house, and it's so . . . so perfect! How could you bear to move?"

I see no reason to answer. She goes automatically to the closed side of the butcher-block counter, her back to the range. I stay on the open side. We sit on facing stools, about equidistant from the wall phone.

She seems to be waiting for me.

"All right," I say in a measured voice, "tell me why I shouldn't hate you. Tell me why you stole my son, and why you didn't bring him home, that day you called."

She doesn't seem able to answer at first. She sits rigidly, chin jutting, hands still jammed into the pouch of the ratty parka, and under the strong recessed floods of the kitchen, I see how worn she looks. Her skin has an unnatural pallor, almost gray. Could she have been locked up somewhere?

"My real name's Rebecca," she says finally. "Rebecca Dalton. People mostly call me Becca. I lied to you about practically everything."

"I know that," I say. "But it's not important anymore."

"Yes it is. To me anyway. I lied to you in the beginning because you'd never have hired me if you knew the truth. Later on, it was because I was forced to. Robert A. Smith forced me to, the man I told you was my stepfather. It was because of him that I took Justin away."

"It doesn't matter anymore," I say to her. "None of it matters."

"Oh, yes it does."

"We know Robert A. Smith was a fake name."

"So did I," she says. "But finally, just the other day, I found out who he really was."

Just the other day? When you were here and there?

She waits for me to answer, or ask, I don't know which. Don't I want to know? But I'm thinking: The last thing in the world I want tonight is to relive it. Any of it. Not with my son asleep upstairs, who I just said was at his grandparents'.

"Holbrook," she says. "Francis Hale Holbrook."

She's eyeing me, as though watching my reaction.

"You knew him, didn't you?" she asks.

"No. I never met him. Larry knows him."

"Yes. And that's what it was all about, Georgia, don't you see? He wanted something out of Larry. That's why I was permitted to come to work for you in the first place. And that's why I ran away with Justin."

Maybe I'm supposed to be shocked. Maybe once I would have been. Maybe the news that Frank Holbrook had been behind it all—my husband's old "mentor," the CIA type who, Larry always said, pulled all the strings—would have sent me climbing the walls.

If she's telling the truth.

But no more. It's over. My husband betrayed us, and my son's an emotional mess, and I'm dealing with both as best I can.

For the rest, I no longer care.

I say as much.

"I'm sorry, Georgia," she insists, "but you're going to have to listen whether you want to or not. It's too important. You don't know what they did to me."

Now, underneath her level tone, I hear the menace and, in her eyes, see that old, steady, grim expression from when I'd catch her unawares. And suddenly, seeing that brings it all back in a rush—the references I never checked, the double-dealing with Larry, the weirdness of those weekends when she would insist on leaving no matter what was going on.

To go to him? Robert A. Smith? Frank Holbrook? So she said.

And Justin on the slide! Of all the terrible things that happened, this is what my brain singles out. Why, when I've long since forgotten it? That first week, my son all alone at the top of the slide, so small . . . Her . . . her *recklessness*. Her goddamn *recklessness*!

Oh God, why didn't I fire her, that same day? When it was in me to fire her?

And now she's back! How do I know she's *not* crazy?

"I'd like a drink," she says evenly.

Rattled, I point to the refrigerator, tell her to help herself.

No, she explains. Hard liquor.

"Another lie," she says, laughing. "I know, the whole time I was here, I always refused a drink."

I'd forgotten that.

"You could try the den," I say. "Though I've no idea what you'll find."

I see her glance at the wall phone.

"Okay," she says. But then, half-smiling, "I think you'd better come along with me."

In a daze—is this really happening?—I follow her back through the dining room to the front hall, the den. All Larry's stuff, untouched. From the doorway, I watch her find the Scotch and a glass tumbler. She fills the tumbler to the brim, no ice, holds the glass with both hands, sips.

"Where's Larry?" she asks.

"He's not here."

"I know," she says. "At least his car hasn't been."

I do a double-take at the remark.

"What do you mean, 'his car hasn't been here'?" I ask her. She doesn't answer. "Just how long have you been hanging around?"

"The last couple of nights," she says casually. "I guess I was working up my courage."

"Working up your *courage*?" I repeat. The admission—its casualness—enrages me. "What were you doing, hiding in the bushes? Spying on us? Waiting for *him?* Well, if it's him you want, you've got a goddamn long wait! I'll be glad to tell you where you can find him!"

I see her recoil.

"Please, Georgia," she stammers out. "You've got it all wrong! It was a setup. I was supposed to seduce Larry, but I couldn't do it. I swear, I never—"

This, above all, I don't need to hear.

"What makes you think I give a damn whether you slept with him or not?"

I want her gone now, out. I don't care if she's crazy or dangerous or a fugitive from justice or whatever the hell she is. Out!

But I hear a cry above our heads, then, seconds later, a full-fledged wail. A rush of panic inside. Thank God, it's only Zoe. But how can I let Harriet upstairs? And she's *not* going to leave of her own free will, what am I supposed to do?

In my own house, damn it! This is going on in my own house!

I fight to control myself.

"It's just the baby," I say. "She must be hungry. I'm going to run up and get her. I'll bring her down to the kitchen. Just wait for me there." I force a smile. "Please don't worry," I say. "I'm not going to call anybody. I promise."

For a second, I think she's going to follow me anyway—what will I do then?—but she doesn't. Upstairs in the nursery I pick Zoe up, all red-faced and soaked, and with my free hand throw the traveling diaper bag, which has everything I need, into the Kanga-rocka-roo. Back in the hallway, listening. Not a sound, either from downstairs or Justin's room. His door is wide open, though. I put the carrier down, pull his door closed but not all the way shut. He still has trouble with doorknobs.

I'm *not* going to let her intimidate me!

Then down the back stairs, with Zoe, to the kitchen. Where Harriet is waiting for us, her glass already half-empty.

It's a long and, I judge, largely self-serving story. Zoe, changed and fed, sleeps through it on the kitchen counter. I listen, distracted. It's the kind of story, I think, Dickens might have invented on an otherwise dreary day—complete with the punishing mother (still alive, it turns out; I'd always thought she was dead), the callow boyfriend, the seducer-uncle who wasn't her uncle, the running away and the being brought back, followed by the mental in-

stitution and finally the hapless young beauty in
thrall to the aging monster.

Smith. Holbrook.

It's not that I disbelieve it entirely (although the
idea that she would run off from the institution with
a man she claims she'd never seen before stretches
my imagination). More likely, I think, it's a mixture
of truth and fantasy. Is that maybe who Harriet is: a
mixture of truth and fantasy? Either way, though,
my mind keeps wandering off. How am I going to
get rid of her? And why is she telling me all this,
three months later? What does she really want from
me? Is it sympathy, for God's sake? Absolution?

There are times, while she talks, when I even find
myself lulled by the voice. Not the content—she de-
scribes what Holbrook did to her in horrific detail—
but the soft, soothing tone. In spite of myself, it
takes me back to the Harriet of my pregnancy, the
back rubs, the dreamy afternoons when her voice
descended on my relaxing body, raising the hairs on
my back, my neck, in little prickles. I have to jerk
myself back to reality—to my kitchen, to this be-
draggled creature, her glass now empty, hands
stuffed in the parka pouch, who, if she is to be believed, was stampeded by Holbrook into taking my
son away because she was terrified about what he
might do to him, and at the same time so panicked
that she could tell neither me nor my husband nor
the police nor anybody on the planet what was happening.

She has a reason, it seems, for everything.

I'm even treated to an account of how great my
child was on the road, motel-hopping, such a brave
little trouper, and the story, horrendous if true, of

what happened when Holbrook caught up with them. And then her phone call to me, the next morning, and finally the scene at the mall.

"I wanted to bring him home, Georgia," she says. "I really meant to. I'd even asked him—Holbrook—I'd begged him—to let me take Justin home. But after I called you, I realized they'd be watching the house. It was too dangerous. That's when I thought of the mall. When I called you the second time, we were already there."

I've hardly said a word up to now. But like it or not, she's brought me back to the reality of that awful Saturday.

"Then why weren't you with him, at The Greenhouse?" I snap at her.

"But I *was!* I waited till the last minute, at least what I thought was the last minute. You were late yourself, weren't you?"

"Late? All of ten minutes! Why couldn't you have waited with him?"

"But I did! I even put a note in his pocket, telling you he was in danger. And I did wait. I didn't want to be around when you actually got there, but I watched the whole thing from the second level! I saw it all happen, Georgia!"

Her voice has risen. I guess mine has too. Suddenly we are both shouting at each other. She's telling me something about the police, that she thought I'd bring the police with me, and I can't help it, it's all becoming vivid again—running through the restaurant, my heart pounding, and the crashing sound of the organ, and the goddamned hostess with the southern accent: "But it all happened so *fast!*"

"I saw it all!" Harriet is saying. "I saw him pick

Justin up! I couldn't hear it, but I could *see* Justin calling my name. It drove me wild. But it wasn't Holbrook, Georgia. It wasn't Holbrook! It was Mark Spain!''

She rushes on, something about a pistol, running after them, too late, but I'm just staring at her. Did I miss something? What did Mark Spain have to do with it? How does she know Mark Spain?

She notices my confusion.

"What's the matter?" she says, stopping abruptly. "Don't you believe me?"

I shake my head. It's not that.

"How do you know Mark Spain?" I ask her.

"Georgia, haven't you been listening? Haven't you heard a word I've said? Who did you think I was talking about before? My uncle Mark?"

I did hear it. It just hadn't registered. Something about the uncle who wasn't really her uncle, some old friend of her father's.

But Mark Spain? Why should this Uncle Mark of hers be Mark Spain?

"He was my mother's lover, for God's sake! And mine too, at the same time! A regular slimeball. But don't you *see*, Georgia? They were in it together! They were in it together the whole time! It used to drive me crazy how Robert—Holbrook—had found me in the first place. He'd never tell me. All he'd say was that he'd had a letter, introducing him as my cousin Robert, although he never had to use it. But a letter from *whom? Who'd* sent him? He'd never ever tell me. Well, but I know now! It was my uncle Mark, Mark Spain. Mark Spain wrote that letter! He *sold* me to Holbrook. He—but Georgia, what's the matter? You don't know him, do you? Do you know Mark Spain?''

I nod. For the minute, I can't get the words out. Yes, I know Mark Spain! The bastard! Yes, he's Joe Penzil's boss, and Joe Penzil, oh yes, is, or was, my husband's best friend. I knew it too, knew Spain was somehow mixed up in the deal they got Larry to agree to, just before Justin came home. At least that's what Larry always said. But he'd also said— or was it Joe Penzil?—that it was all Harriet's doing, something about an old Wall Street family, and Harriet was—what? mentally unstable?—and somehow they'd managed to get Justin back from her? Never clear how? But it was complicated, wasn't it? Oh yes, it was complicated.

But suppose everything she's been telling me is *true?* Her whole, rambling story? Because how else explain the missing whatever it was—seventy-two hours?—between the scene at the mall, the way she's just described it, and the night I found Justin on my front porch?

"Don't you understand, Georgia?" she goes on. "All along I thought it was just Holbrook—Robert A. Smith, I thought then—and it *was* him. But not at the mall. That was Mark. I *saw* him! He picked Justin up in his arms and ran with him, and I saw Justin calling my name! My God! They must have been working together the whole time. It freaked me totally. I knew it was Larry they were after, but they'd used me, and now they were going to use Justin. I failed, Georgia, don't you see? I tried to save him—I . . . I *love* him—but I *failed!*"

I've never seen her like this before. It's in her

voice, the emotion wrenching loose, and tears flood her eyes.

"I'm sorry," she stammers. "Every time I think about it, I see Justin. Even though I know he got home okay. But at the mall that day, I couldn't hear him—there was too much noise—but I could . . . I could *see* him. Oh my God, Georgia . . ."

I believe her. Finally I think I do believe her. And, momentarily at least, I share her revulsion, her outrage.

But there's some kind of failure in me too.

"What happened next?" I ask, staring back at her. "After the mall?"

She shrugs, looks away.

"I did what I always do," she says, her voice still choked. "I ran away."

"And you've been running away ever since?"

"Just about," she manages. "At least till now."

She pauses, still looking away, and her hands are stuffed in the pouch of the parka, and now I see her jaw jut out fiercely. Finally her head turns, and her eyes come back to mine.

"I went to see him the other day," she says.

"Went to see whom?"

"Mark."

"Mark Spain? For God's sake, what for?"

"I knew where he lived," she goes on, "so I went there. I had to—well, I had to find out what had happened. He was—what should I say?—pretty surprised to see me. After all this time. It wasn't a very pleasant conversation, but I got it out of him. Who Smith really was, and what their connection was. Did you know I was only one of many girls he kept in that house?"

I nod, remembering, but she doesn't seem to notice.

"I don't think I was the only one Mark found for him either. Anyway, he—Mark—said I was crazy to have come back. Said that if nobody had found me in three months, nobody was going to, and if I was still worried about that, it was sheer paranoia. He laughed at me, Georgia. He actually *laughed* at me! Well, as I say, it wasn't a very pleasant conversation."

Her voice trails off. She's dry-eyed again, tense, expectant. It's as though she's waiting for me to comment. Instead, I glance at the wall clock. She's been here almost two hours, and I'm thinking: Maybe what they did to you was as horrible as you say, but I can't help that. At the end of the day, whatever your reasons, even if they were good ones, you were responsible for my son, and you took him away from me. That's my reality check. It happened, and now it's over. All that's left for me to do is pick up the pieces, which is exactly what I'm trying to do. Larry's gone, and these men—Mark Spain, Holbrook, Gamble, whoever else was involved—are no longer a threat to me or my children. So don't ask me for help or compassion or whatever it is you want from me. Maybe that's a failure on my part, maybe it's even cruel, but I don't have room for you right now. All I really care about, you see, are my children and me.

Maybe I'd even have said these things to her.

I'll never know.

Because now what I was afraid of, and have half-forgotten, has just happened.

* * *

"*Mom-mee? Mom-mee?*"

The cry drives right through my heart.

I glance wildly behind me, at the back stairs, then back at Harriet. She's half-risen off her stool, her mouth agape.

"Stay right where you are!" I hiss at her in a half-whisper. Then, to the stairs, my "normal" voice: "It's okay, darling, I'll be right there!" An afterthought: "I've been on the phone!"

I'm on my feet, mind racing. God Almighty, what am I going to *do?*

She says something like: "But I thought you said he was at his grandparents'?"

"Shut up!" I command her in a harsh whisper. "Do you think you're the only one capable of lying?"

"*Mom-mee?*" it comes again. "Me need you *now!*"

"I'm coming, Justin, I'll be right there!" Then I whirl on her. "If you try to come upstairs, if you so much as let him see you or hear your voice, I'll kill you. I *swear* it!"

"But please, Georgia! For God's sake! How can you say that? You've *got* to let me see him! It's why I *came!* You don't understand, I haven't told you everything. He's the only person I care about in the whole world. Or who cares about me!"

I can't shut her up. I'm about to scream, strangle her, and at the same time I can hear him crying. At the top of the stairs now!

"Just a minute, Justin!" I cry out. My mind is a whirlwind, confused, shrieking. Because suddenly I'm thinking: Give him time, that's what everybody says, isn't it? Give him time. But I have no time, there is no time! If anything, he's worse. And I'm thinking: It's the last thing in the world *I* want, the very last twisting thing in the nightmare I'm living, but maybe I've got to do it, maybe for him, his sake, save him, stop it, at long last, *let* him have his god-damn beloved Harriet! *Let* him see her! Go on, for God's sake, *let* him, what do you have to lose?

But there's this other voice in me too that's laughing, crazy, sobbing laughter, how could you do that, Georgia, how on earth, she's crazy, she's wrecked your life, she's *ka-ray-zee!*

I turn to her, hand raised, willing myself to stop shaking.

"Shut up!" I hiss at her again. Then, my voice low: "Maybe I will," I say. "I'm not promising you anything. You're to stay right here. I'll call down to you. But if I let you see him, it's for one thing, one thing only. You've come to say good-bye. That's all. It's good-bye, and it's forever. I want you to promise me."

She nods. She's crying again.

"That's what I came for," she's saying.

I'm aware of her face, a white blur. I grab Zoe, her carrier, then I'm on my way up the back stairs.

He's waiting for me at the top. I can see his silhouette against the dim light.

"Mom-mee?" he says again, his arms stretching forward. He's still half-asleep, drenched in sleep.

I swoop him up in my free arm. He clings to me. I'm panting, struggling for air, I can't help it. I manage to ask him if he has to pee. He nods drowsily, buries his head in my neck. I carry him and Zoe into the big bathroom at the end of the hall, put Zoe on the floor, then, both hands free, support him at the toilet while he fumbles for his penis.

He pees, then reaches forward to flush as I've taught him to. Then I take him and Zoe into his room and close the door behind us.

I realize I'm crying too, silent tears. *The last thing in the world I want.* I can't stop, can't control myself.

I get him back into bed but not to sleep. I can feel his tension on top of mine. I can't get either one of us to relax.

"Justin, it's the middle of the night," I say. "You've *got* to go back to sleep."

"Jutesy," he says.

I have a juice box waiting for him on his night table. With trembling hands I get it open, the straw inserted. I prop him while he drinks.

He sinks back into his pillows. Even in the near-darkness, I can tell that his eyes are on me.

"Is her here?" he says.

"Is who here, Justin?" I answer, fighting my voice.

"'arrit."

"Harriet? What makes you think that?"

"Me hear her. Her promise."

Oh my God.

"What did she promise?"

"Her come back. Her promise."

"Justin, you must have been dreaming!"

"No. Me hear her! Yes I *did!*"

He starts to wail. My God. It's not full-fledged, but at any second he's going to let go, and then he'll wake Zoe up, and then I think I'll be the one to go crazy—raving, full-fledged mayhem.

Please, Justin, I beg him in my mind, *please!*

But it's no use.

I take a deep breath. Here goes nothing.

"You're right, darling," I tell him as softly as I can. "You're absolutely right. You did hear her voice. In fact, she's downstairs right now. She came to say good-bye to you. In a minute, I'm going to ask her to come up. She's going for good, and she only has a few minutes, but before she goes, she wants especially to say good-bye to you."

"Her promise," he says again.

"You're right," I answer crazily. "She promised."

I stand, Zoe's carrier in my hand. From the top of the stairs, I can see Harriet looking up.

I motion to her. I think: Georgia, you're going to regret this the rest of your life.

But it's too late for that, isn't it?

I talk to her hastily at the top of the stairs, my voice low. "I've told him you're going away for good. That you only have a few minutes, but you want to say good-bye to him." She nods, wordless. "I swear to you, Harriet, anything more—any promises, any anything—and I'll get you if it's the last thing I do."

She nods again, and then she's gone inside his door.

It's more than a few minutes. It seems forever. I stand in the hall of my own house, my almost ex-house, holding my sleeping daughter's carrier in my hand. I can't bring myself to put it down, can't bring myself to pick Zoe out of it. I listen, half-listen. I can hear Harriet's voice like a murmur, but few of the words, and if he says anything, I miss it altogether. Otherwise it is very still, night-still, except, possibly, for the sound of Georgia Levy Coffey trying to swallow.

I hate her for it now, hate her from the bottom of my heart. For what she's done to us, her power over us. Now I'm an exile in my own house, locked out. How do I know what she's telling him?

You're doing it for *him*, I keep telling myself. For three months he's been like a caged animal trying to get out, and you've been stuffing him back in, telling him it's all right. When you know in your heart that it isn't.

That's why I'm standing in the hall, biting my lip raw.

I'm praying now. I think maybe, just maybe, it's like the end of something and before something else has begun. An interval, a time warp, like the gorge between death and birth if you believe in reincarnation. I know I'm not a praying person, but dear God, please let it be true. Please let it be the end of something, and the beginning of something else. Please let my son, Justin, be a normal, loving child again.

Oh my God.

Whatever God is doing at the moment, though, the little prayer calms me.

I stand guard.

"Georgia." It's Harriet, emerging from his doorway. She has her finger to her lips. "He's asleep," she says.

I brush past her. In the dim light from the hall, I see his little head burrowed into the pillow. His eyes are closed, his breathing slow, even. I'm aware that my own heart is pulsing as I lean over him, but there's no telling. No telling what she said to him; no telling what he now believes.

* * *

She's not in the hall when I come out. In a daze, I put Zoe down in the nursery.

When I come down the stairs again, she's back in the kitchen. I notice she's refilled her glass. Does she think, it occurs to me crazily—does she think she can make herself at home now?

Move back in?

It's almost midnight on the wall clock. I'm too strung out to go on. I tell her so, but she makes no move to leave.

"Why did you lie before?" she asks me. "Why didn't you want me to know he was here?"

"Because I didn't think it would be good for him to see you."

"But why not, Georgia? I *love* Justin. Even though he didn't think so."

"What do you mean, he didn't think so?"

"It was about the last thing he said to me. I mean, our last night on the road. It was when I told him I was taking him home. He said it meant I didn't love him. It made me wild. I promised him I'd come back, by summer at the latest, maybe before. I did promise. And now I have. But I did exactly what you wanted me to do. I told him I'm going away for good. I said good-bye." She hesitates. "He's okay, isn't he? I mean, he seems okay. He is, isn't he?"

I don't know what I feel toward her now. The resentment is gone. But I'm not going to let myself be sucked into a discussion of his well-being.

"Yes," I say, "he's okay. But I have to ask you to leave now, Harriet. Please. You've gotten what you came for."

The words sound so cold—I don't mean them that

way—but they only make her laugh. She looks at me, protrudes her lower lip, shakes her head.

"You don't have a clue, do you?" she says.

"A clue as to what?"

She doesn't answer, laughs again, a little snorting sound. Then: "The thing is, I'm finished with lying. With running away too. It never did me any good."

"I guess that's fine," I say, "but—"

She cuts me off.

"He's a great kid, Georgia, don't you *see*? He's special. You're just his mother, I don't know if you get what he's really like. He's so smart. He's thinking in there all the time. And he never forgets anything. He's also brave," she says, "very gutsy. He's strong inside. He's going to be somebody. No, that's wrong, he already *is* somebody."

But why does she feel compelled to defend him to *me*? Have I said that he's an emotional wreck, that I don't think I can deal with him anymore? Have I said anything like that?

"But there's one thing you don't get," she says.

"Oh? What's that?"

"The one he really loves, most of all, is you."

Her eyes are measuring me, as though gauging my reaction.

"We were very close," she goes on. "We did everything together, Georgia. I know it's strange, but a lot of the time on the road, when they were hunting us, it was fun. We had a lot of fun. We built a snowman together. I'd never done that. I guess he was a little in love with me. I mean, really in love, like he will be when he's older. But even so, do you know who it was that he cried out for in the middle of the night? I mean, when he was having a bad dream?

Or when he woke up scared, not knowing where he was? It wasn't me, Georgia, even though I was right there. It was you. It was his mommy. It was his mommy he wanted."

A strange validation, I think. But what am I supposed to feel? Gratitude? Resentment? Both?

"You know something, Georgia," she says, and now her blue-gray eyes are locked on mine, "and this'll sound really weird to you, but in spite of everything that was going on, those were the happiest days of my life? From the minute I rang your bell? I mean, when I was living here, working with Justin, and you were pregnant?"

Nostalgia in her tone, bittersweet. Defiance, too. It's almost as though she's saying: Take me back, Georgia, take her in. And yes, I know that's impossible, doesn't she? And yet, at the same time . . .

"It was a happy time for me too," I hear myself answer, my voice suddenly gentle. "In spite of everything."

Do I mean it? Yes, weirdly, I think I do. At midnight, in my kitchen, there's this peculiar, momentary kinship. I know it makes no sense, how can it make any sense? But if it makes no sense, then why am I on the verge of tears?

"But it's over, Harriet," I say. "Or is it Becca? Rebecca? I'm afraid I'll always think of you as Harriet."

"Harriet's better," she says with a half-smile.

"But it *is* over, you know," I repeat. "There's no way for us to bring it back. No way, even if we wanted to."

She nods.

"No, there isn't," she says. "Is that why you're moving?"

The question startles me. I've never thought of it like that.

"In a way," I say. "Yes, I guess it is."

"Where are you going?"

I shake my head—my reflex is not to tell her—but then I say, "New York. Back to the city."

She nods again. She seems satisfied by that. At least she falls silent. Her drink, I notice, is half-empty again, but she makes no move to finish it. She simply sits there, hands in her pouch, rocking a little. Her eyes are on me, the light and shadow of her cheekbones sharp in the kitchen light. Perfect bone structure, I notice in passing. A gorgeous face, even as tired as she looks now. And I think—for the last time, I hope—what a strange creature she is, and how, in the space of one exhausting evening, she's managed to run me up and down a whole emotional gauntlet.

I want her to go now, but it's clear she won't until she's ready to. As though in response, she looks away, half-rises. But then subsides again. Thinks. Says slowly, reflectively:

"I guess the only important thing, to me, is that you understand that I'm not crazy. I'm not, you know. Sometimes I may do crazy things, but there's always a reason. I'd like to think that, whatever happens to me, you and Justin will know I'm not crazy."

"I don't think you're crazy. But what do you mean, 'whatever happens to me'? That sounds awfully melodramatic."

She shrugs.

"Maybe all I'm saying is that I don't want you to hate me anymore."

Upstairs, a little while ago, I could have torn her to shreds. Now it's gone. I just want her to leave.

"I don't hate you, Harriet," I say. "Believe me."

She takes a deep breath, sighs.

"I'm going in a minute," she says. "Out of your hair, out of your life. But what if you were me, Georgia?" she says. "What would you do now? Try to put yourself in my shoes. Imagine that you're twenty-two again and you feel like you've already lived through hell and you're still not out of it. What would you do?"

Georgia, the oracle?

But she's serious about it. She leans forward over the counter, eyes intently watching me.

I don't want to disappoint her, but suddenly I have the uneasy feeling I'm going to, whatever I say.

"It's hardly for me to tell you that," I answer.

"Still, I want to hear it." She smiles wryly. "You said you were my friend, remember? On TV?"

I've forgotten about that. She must have seen it after all.

I take a deep breath of my own.

"I think if I were you," I say, "I'd try to put it all behind me. Everything. Close out the past. I'd go as far away as I could, get away from here, all the bad things that happened. I'd try to free myself from it. And that, by the way, includes Justin and me."

Pretty self-serving, I think. But it also happens to be true.

"Yes," she says, nodding. "And then?"

"Then?"

"Well, suppose I did do that? Then what?"

"Well," I say, hesitant. "Then I guess I'd see about inventing my life."

She's gone now.

Why, though, instead of relief, do I have the nagging feeling that I've let her down?

And what if I did? Why is that important?

Strange young woman. What's going to become of her now? Technically I think she's still a fugitive, but what would the police do with her if they found her?

I reminded her that, once she left, it would be for good. We even shook hands on it, awkwardly, and I, in turn, was reminded how she'd never liked to be touched.

This was in the front hall, among the stacks of cartons. She commented on the house again, my beautiful house. She said she couldn't believe I was moving, couldn't imagine anyone else living here. But the last thing she said to me was, "God, Georgia, how can you be so strong?"

Justin first, now me. Both so strong. I don't remember what I said, but the more I think of it, the more I'll take that on my tombstone:

HERE LIETH GEORGIA, HOW COULD SHE BE SO STRONG?

I'm lying on my side now, on the edge of my son's bed, in near-total darkness. There's just a slit of light from the hallway, the door ajar in case Zoe wakes up in the nursery. Somewhere below my feet, on the floor, is another box of juice I brought up from the kitchen.

I'm stroking Justin's hair lightly. He doesn't seem to feel it. He's facing me, one arm flung up over the side of his face, and all I can hear is the faint wheeze of air entering and leaving his nostrils.

It's the only sound, other than my own occasional voice.

"We're going to make it, my darling," I whisper to him. "She's gone now. It's all over. Together, we're going to invent our own lives."

I've no idea what time it is. No matter. I think it's in me to lie here, stroking his hair, until he wakes up in the morning.

WALL STREET EXECUTIVE SLAIN
Headed Own Firm

Pound Ridge, NY, April 8 (AP)—Francis Hale Holbrook, 57, prominent Wall Street figure and Chairman, CEO, of Holbrook & Company, investment bankers, was shot and killed last night at his Pound Ridge, New York, estate. The victim was apparently alone at the time. His body was discovered early this morning by his caretaker couple, Mr. and Mrs. Derek Murphy, when they arrived for work. Police investigators say Mr. Holbrook was murdered in his living room sometime after 10:30 P.M., when he telephoned the Murphys, having just returned from a weekend's absence. There is no evidence that a struggle took place, and no indication of breaking and entering. According to one official source, robbery could not have been the perpetrator's motive.

The victim's wife, Margaret Frame Holbrook, who was at their home in Palm Beach, Florida, at the time of the crime, could not be reached for comment. Mr. Holbrook's two children, Francis Hale Jr. and Dorothea, are away at school. A spokesperson for Holbrook & Company said: "This is shocking, an atrocious crime. Frank Holbrook was a dynamic and brilliant leader, and greatly admired as a human being. We can't believe what's happened. The loss to us is incalculable."